Worlds

Psi War Book 2

I have scann'd the vast ivy-clad palace,
I have trod its untenanted hall,
Where the moon writhing up from the valleys,
Shews the tapestried things on the wall;
Strange figures discordantly woven, which I cannot endure to recall.
(Extract from Nemesis by H.P. Lovecraft)

Copyright

Author: Tony Warner
Title: Worlds - Psi War Book 2
© 2024, Tony Warner
Self-published
(Contact: psiwarbook@gmail.com)

Acknowledgments

First and foremost, I would like to thank all the readers of the first book in this series. Without your support and encouragement, this book might not exist. I hope you enjoy this sequel as much as I enjoyed writing it.

I'd also like to thank my family who put up with my endless tapping on a keyboard in the evenings and who listened to me prattling on about plot lines and characters.

To everyone who has inspired me, whether you know it or not, thank you for igniting the creative spark within me and fuelling my imagination. None of the characters resemble anyone! Honest!

Also, I would like to thank all the ARC (Advance Reader Copy) readers. Your thoughts and constructive criticism helped shape this book into what it is today.

Finally, to every reader who picks up this book, whether for the first time or as a returning companion, thank you. Your support and engagement are the greatest reward I could ask for.

With heartfelt thanks,
Tony

Prologue

Outside of our galaxy in the dark, cold reaches of space, some three hundred light years from the nearest star, a black disc appeared. Initially, it was small, measuring just two metres across, but then it rapidly expanded. The expansion was swift until soon it was wider than the diameter of our moon. Onwards it continued its expansion, passing the diameter of Earth, Jupiter and even our Sun, until its diameter was the size of our entire solar system.

Eventually the expansion halted, a massive disc of blackness blotting out the light from faraway galaxies. In the vast stillness, it hung there for several seconds, until suddenly, thousands of small silver orbs sped from its surface, each one moving outwards at half the speed of light. The objects were just three metres across, with many protuberances on their surfaces, some of which were dome shaped, while others were long and spiky.

After some hours, the orbs had formed a globe, two billion miles from the disc of blackness. Once the globe had formed, the prow of an enormous ship penetrated the surface of the disc, slowly emerging revealing more and more of its gigantic bulk as it moved outwards, until its entire length of fifteen miles was through.

The ship continued its forward motion. As it did so, it launched hundreds of miniature spherical objects from an array of projectile launchers spaced around its middle. Each of the objects took position around the massive ship, forming a defensive globe.

Once the ship was one billion miles away from the disc, more ships of differing sizes and shapes emerged. Several of them sped away at right angles to the disc, some taking up position with the thousands of silver orbs, yet more sped outwards, passing beyond the globe, disappearing into the distance.

After two days, there were an additional five thousand ships occupying the space in the vicinity of the huge black disc. At this point, an entire planet traversed through the blackness. Surrounded by its own satellite ships, it ponderously moved outwards from the disc, taking up position ten million miles away. As it did so, three of its satellites burst into a blinding glare of light and heat, bathing the entire planet with their radiance.

Next to emerge were three moon sized planetoids. Screen projectors, projectile launchers, and energy weapons of massive proportions liberally covered every inch of their surface. Each one took up position around the planet. Once in place, the vast black disc suddenly winked out.

Deep below the surface of the planet, there lay a vast subterranean labyrinth of caves and tunnels. In one yellow-green hazed room, four entities sat around a table covered in an array of instruments. The inhabitants of this world were totally alien; the ecosystem of their world being based on chlorine instead of oxygen. Each entity in the room was a fat, rounded blob of flesh that stood low to the ground on four squat, short legs. Their skin was a sickly green colour with the texture of wet plastic. The front part of their bulbous bodies turned upwards into a round head supported on a fat neck, where four eyes roved independently around the room, and a mouth slavered, surrounded with small manipulating tentacles. Below the head, two long, boneless, snake-like arms reached forward, each one terminating in four fleshy, finger like appendages.

"Transference is complete," radiated the chief technologist to the group of four. *"Our camouflage screens are operational. Our presence, as far as we know, has not been detected."*

"You worry too much," returned the second in command. *"We are the superior race. No one can stand against us."*

"Your complacency in such matters concerns me," replied the technologist. *"It is a mathematical certainty that eventually we will encounter an advanced race in one of the universes."*

"Bah," was the reply. *"What of it? Our forces are invulnerable."*

"Think you so?" the technologist radiated back. *"Your reasoning ability must be fading with your age. You are overconfident. Such over confidence is concerning, coming from one of our leaders."*

The second in command bristled at the insult. *"You dare to question me?"* It asked.

"I do," replied the technologist. *"The mathematics are indisputable; you are a fool to ignore it."*

There was a moment of silence which was suddenly broken by a single bang as a weapon discharged. The chief technologist's head exploded and splattered against the wall behind it with its contents.

The second in command holstered its weapon.

"Is there anyone else among you who questions my ability?" it asked harshly.

There was no reply.

"Get someone to remove this carcass and send in a replacement," the second in command sent the thought.

"Now, let us continue," its thoughts directed at the rest of the group. *"What has our sensing equipment picked up?"*

As a door slid open and three individuals entered, the commander of the group congratulated the second in command.

"I commend your swift action," it thought at the group, *"We cannot afford dissenters in our conclave."*

There was general assent, as the technologist's replacement waddled up to the centre table.

"We have detected two hot spots of Psionic energy," it reported. *"One is on the opposite side of this galaxy and appears to be the stronger of the two. The nearest is located in one of the spiral arms, a mere five thousand light years distant."*

The group was pleased.

"Excellent!" replied the commander. *"Make towards the nearest star system and set up our manufacturing facilities. Once we have strengthened our fleet, we will eliminate the nearest Psi capable civilisation and then move onto the second. This universe will soon be under the reign of the Klalan!"*

Chapter 1 - Joe

"Damn it!" Shouted Joe, throwing his latest gadget across the room, narrowly missing Molly as she entered, the object shattering against the wall next to her head.

"Hi to you too," said Molly.

Joe flicked his eyes over to her. Not replying, he swivelled his chair back around to face his workbench, where he fixed his attention on his computer, scrolling the screen full of equations.

Molly shut the door behind her, pushed her glasses up her nose, and walked across the workshop to stand next to him.

"Joe," she said gently, "this obsession has to stop."

Joe didn't answer. He continued to scroll through the data on his screen.

She laid her hand on his shoulder, disconcerted to see his dishevelled state. Several days' worth of stubble covered his chin, and his shoulder-length hair was matted and greasy. She wrinkled her nose at his body odour.

"Joe," she continued, "You have to stop. We need you."

He picked up a screwdriver and the bracelet of a Mark 5 Assist.

"Why?" he asked. "I'm sure that you and Lee can handle things. I'm busy."

"We've been doing our best, but we need you, Joe. It's been six months. You need to move on."

He shrugged her hand from his shoulder. "Six months or six years, it makes no difference," he mumbled.

Molly sighed to herself. She understood what he was going through.

"Enough is enough," she said softly. "You're killing yourself."

"I don't care," was the reply.

"Joe, we all love you. We want to help you. Please let us."

"This is something I have to do myself." He picked up a circuit board and started connecting wires to the Assist.

"This won't help. You need to let it go."

He suddenly spun around in his chair, making Molly step back in shock.

"Let it go?" He spat, his eyes wild and large. "Let it go? They killed her, Molly. I can never forgive that. They need to pay! I'm going to kill them!"

Molly was shocked at the vehemence of his outburst. He was still angry. If anything, he was angrier now than he had been six months ago.

"Oh, Joe," she replied, "You don't know that they killed her. Her Assist burnt out when it was overloaded with the Psi energies involved. They probably had no idea what would happen to her."

"I don't care. They connected with her, and they knew what the overload would do to her."

"We don't know that," pleaded Molly, "They are so more evolved than us, I'm sure that they wouldn't have known. You can't blame them."

"I can, and I have," replied Joe, turning back to his bench, "I just have to come up with something more powerful than a Mark 5, and I'll be all set."

Molly bit her lip as she watched him bent over his bench, trying hopelessly to come up with something to help him with his vendetta. Recalling the events from six months ago, she knew she had a decision to make. She had to snap Joe out of his morose, self-indulgent activity. They had left him to his own devices, hoping that he would recover in his own time. But it was now evident that it was going to take much longer. She had to take action.

It was just six months ago, when Joe had met Kate. At the time, it seemed like a chance meeting. Now Molly was not so sure. Initially, Joe and Kate had a stormy relationship, but in the end, they had confessed their love for each other. Kate had joined their group and had been fitted with an Assist, a device that interfaced with the mind, giving the wearer new abilities, such as telepathy, teleportation and more. Joe and Molly had been working together for five years, perfecting and improving it, until they had reached the 5th generation - a Mark 5.

When they were attacked by an unknown enemy, Kate, being the only one fitted with a Mark 5, volunteered to contact an alien race who had been watching and manipulating their group, which they called the Alliance. This highly developed and powerful race had been monitoring them since it had discovered that humans were directing, and using Psi energies, otherwise known as dark energy, a force that pervaded the entire universe.

Kate had been successful; she had contacted the disembodied aliens and had persuaded them to intervene. In doing so, she had saved everyone. But the price had been high, her Mark 5 was burnt out. With no other to replace it, and with her mind and body unable to function without one, she had died in Joe's arms.

Since Kate's death, Joe had changed. He was not the same man Molly had met five years ago. He had become overcome with grief, first blaming himself and later the aliens. They should have known better, they should have been more careful, they had killed Kate. Lately, he had become obsessed with getting even, but to do that, he would need something more powerful than a Mark 5.

Molly knew Joe could control his emotions if he wanted to. His Assist allowed him to compartmentalise his mind, enabling him to shift these painful memories away so that they would no longer dominate his thoughts. But she thought she understood why he had not done so. The memories that he had of Kate were few. He wanted to cling onto them. She couldn't blame him, but it was plain to see that it was destroying him.

"Sally." Molly projected her thought outwards to her girlfriend, and the premier Alliance physician. *"It's no use. I need you."*

13

Sally responded instantly. *"Told you."*

"You were right, as usual. We'll have to go with Plan B."

"On my way."

"Joe, we don't have any equations that show that a Mark 6 is even possible," said Molly, watching him scroll his screen back and forth.

Joe didn't answer, twisting the screwdriver around and around in his left hand, while the chains of his Assist clinked against the mouse as he flicked the scroll wheel back and forth.

Both he and Molly jumped in surprise when the door suddenly banged open. They both turned to see Sally standing in the doorway, dressed in her usual white doctor's coat, hands on hips.

"JOE!" she shouted. "GET YOURSELF AWAY FROM THAT WORKBENCH!"

Joe stared at Sally with red-rimmed eyes. They both stared at each other for a full three seconds, and then he started to turn around on his stool to face the bench again.

"Don't you turn away from me, mister!" Sally shouted.

"Leave it, Sal," replied Joe as he completed his turn.

Sally strode over to Joe, breezing past Molly. "I said." She grabbed his shoulder, pulling him back around to face her.

"Don't turn away from me!"

In an instinctive reaction, Joe suddenly raised his right hand, the light reflecting off the rings and chains of his Assist.

"Don't!" Sally shouted. "Don't you dare use Psi against me! Who do you think you are?"

Realising what he was doing, his eyes widened, opening his mouth to form a perfect O shape. He dropped his hand into his lap and bent his head down to look at the floor.

"I'm sorry," he whispered.

"I should think so too," replied Sally. Her voice softened. "You're coming with me. I'm prescribing bed, with a strong sedative and no arguments." She looked across at Molly, who nodded back.

Sally put her arms around Joe's shoulder and pulled him up, leading him towards the door. Molly followed, stepping forward to open it quickly, allowing Sally and Joe to walk through.

Watching Sally gently lead Joe down the corridor, Molly gave a sigh of relief. Her chest swelled with a feeling of pride she felt for her. She had handled the situation beautifully. Turning around, she sealed the door to Joe's workshop by manipulating the electronic lock. She didn't want him to return to his hopeless efforts.

Turning away from the door, she followed Sally and Joe along the corridor and into one of Sally's medical rooms. Once there, Sally directed Joe to a bed, where he lay down compliantly.

Sally busied herself in a cabinet as Molly walked up to Joe. Taking his hand in hers, she held it to her chest.

"It's okay Joe, it's okay."

He looked up at her, his red eyes watering. "No, Mol," he whispered. "It's never going to be okay again."

Molly felt her own eyes prickling with tears as she pressed his hand harder against her.

Sally walked over, a syringe in her hand. She expertly pulled up Joe's sleeve, swabbed his arm, and jabbed the needle home. As she squeezed the plunger, his eyes closed slowly until he was deeply asleep.

Removing the syringe from Joe's arm, she placed it on the bedside table. She walked around the bed and threw her arms around Molly. The two women hugged each other, Sally silently crying into Molly's shoulder.

They stood like this for a while, comforting each other, when a thought flashed into Molly's mind.

"Molly, we have a situation at the door."

Molly knew exactly which door the voice was talking about - the main entrance to their underground Complex. High above them, a grand old house stood in spacious grounds, with a lift in the hallway that descended the one hundred meters down to the upper levels of their concealed base.

Their group - the Alliance - all Assisted telepaths, purposely kept themselves hidden and isolated from the rest of society. This wasn't a deliberate act, but rather a natural occurrence that ended up being beneficial. It turned out to be a prudent decision. As the Alliance grew in number, so did their technological advancements, allowing them to expand their influence beyond their own planet. And now, how could they reveal themselves to the world? They were far more advanced and developed than the rest of society, with Assist technology permanently altering their brain function and transforming how they interacted, communicated, and comprehended each other.

"What do you mean, a situation?" asked Molly, including Sally, in the conversation.

"Well..."

"Spit it out," directed Molly.

"Well, there's a woman here who wants to see Joe."

"A woman?" asked Sally.

"Yes," came the reply, *"Erm... She says her name is Kate..."*

Molly and Sally looked at each other. *"Kate?"* they both asked together.

"Yes," was the response, *"She looks like her, and if I didn't know better, I would swear it really is her!"*

Part 1

Chapter 2 – Lexi
3 years ago

Lexi cradled Gary's head in her lap, tears streaming down her face, dripping from her chin onto his ruined chest.

"Don't blame yourself, my love," his words slid into her mind. *"It wasn't your fault."*

"It was!" Lexi cried between sobs. *"It's all my fault. I should never have let you try first!"*

"Then you would be dying, and I would be crying," he pointed out. A thin trickle of blood ran from a corner of his mouth and down his chin.

Lexi felt her heart break. She pulled him closer, trying to ignore the charred and mangled mess. His right eye was a gaping crater melted away along with the right side of his head, leaving only malformed flesh in its place. The smell of burning skin and coppery blood filled the air, making her stomach lurch and heave as she held him against her.

At least he wasn't in any pain. She made sure of that by insinuating herself into his mind and turning off all his pain receptors. But the injuries were un-survivable, that was clear.

Around the two of them, the apparatus was totally destroyed, a smouldering mess of metal, plastic and wire. Men and women were shouting instructions to each other as they ran back and forth aiming fire extinguishers, damping down fires and cooling red hot metal. Lexi ignored them all. The most important person in the world lay dying in her arms.

"I'm so sorry, Gaz," she thought at him.

"Don't be," he replied. *"We proved something, you and me. We proved that they do exist."*

"You proved it, my love," thought Lexi. *"You found them."*

"I did, didn't I?" He coughed, blood and spittle flying from his mouth, landing on her face.

"Yes, you did, my love. You were amazing."

A medic approached, but she waved him away. There was no saving, Gary. She could feel his thoughts fading as his body shut down and was unable to maintain his brain functions.

"I love you," he thought at her. *"Don't leave it like this. Try again. We learned a lot this time."*

"I love you too." Lexi couldn't stop her thought from wailing.

"Promise me. Promise me that you won't stop."

Lexi nodded. Her body shaking with the sobs. *"I won't stop, I promise. I'll keep going for you."*

"Good," he answered. *"Just know that I don't regret a thing. I was so lucky to find you."*

"No. I've been the lucky one," she replied.

"I'm sorry that it has to end like this," continued Gary. *"My love, I will never forget you. Thank you for everything you've given me."*

Lexi could no longer control herself. She lost herself to the horror of the situation. She was going to lose the love of her life. He was going to die here in front of her, in her arms, and there was nothing she could do about it. She gave into the sobbing and let the animal noises take over as she laid her head against his cheek.

Gradually, Gary's thoughts grew fainter and slower, until they stopped completely, and Lexi's thoughts were the only ones inside his head. He was gone, leaving a blankness and darkness behind. Lexi's shoulders shook as she sobbed into his lifeless body.

It was some time before she recovered enough to lay his mangled body down on the floor. She positioned him carefully, laying his broken arms across his chest and making sure his remaining eye was closed.

She stood and stepped back from the body, surveying her surroundings. By now, the fires were all extinguished, but the air smelled of burnt plastic and ash, which made her already constricted throat tighten more.

Complete disarray filled the massive space. The machine in the centre, a pile of smoking, molten slag, the operator's chair gone, swallowed up in the debris from the collapsed roof of the warehouse. The now revealed sky showcased twinkling stars hanging high.

Where are you? Thought Lexi. Which one of those stars is yours?

They would have to rebuild. Her logical and clinical mind kicked into gear. For now, she would have to put aside Gary's death. She needed to decide what to do. She could hear sirens in the distance. The police and fire brigade would be on their way, the explosion would have been heard across the city. She needed to make sure that the authorities didn't suspect that anything was out of the ordinary. That the cause was something that could be explained and not a result of a Psionic energy blast.

"Set the explosives and evacuate now!" Lexi shouted at her project leader, Henrick. "We need to get out of here before the police arrive. Get the team to 'port' out to location two."

"Already in progress," Henrick shouted back, as he threw an extinguisher to the ground and helped a technician to their feet. "Go, I'll be right behind you."

Lexi nodded her approval. Henrick was his usual efficient self, even in the middle of a disaster such as this.

She looked back down at Gary's broken body. "I'm sorry, my love," she whispered through more tears. "I can't give you the send-off you deserve." She choked back a sob as she raised her right hand. The rings of her Assist glowed blue as she concentrated, teleporting Gary's body into the Sun. They couldn't leave anything behind that might hint at any unusual activities, and that included bodies.

With one final glance around, she wiped the tears from her eyes with the back of her hand and teleported from the destroyed warehouse to her home. Once there, she consumed a whole bottle of red wine and promptly threw it up all over her double bed. She lay in her own vomit for a very long time.

Chapter 3 - Isabelle
1 year ago

Kate gingerly and carefully stepped through the portal into World Six, the sixth world she had visited so far. She had learned a painful lesson on her journey. It was important to step through the portal between worlds carefully and slowly. Sometimes there was a slight difference in gravity or level, making it easy to stumble or fall. She recalled in World Three; she had fallen and sprained her wrist as she charged through. But that was because she was being chased by a wolf. Well. She assumed it was a wolf. It looked like an enormous dog, only bigger and meaner. World Three had been overrun with animals, most of which were after her blood. She had seen no signs of people in that world.

This time, however, there was no mishap. She didn't stumble or fall. Quickly checking the surrounding area, she saw the familiar alleyway, and no signs of danger. She breathed a sigh of relief and cocked her head to one side, listening carefully, but could hear nothing, save for the birds chirping above. It seemed safe.

The portal behind her shrank to a point and disappeared silently as she walked out of the alley into the main street and made her way towards the city centre. Not for the first time, she wondered why the portal always opened in the same back alley. Every time she travelled between worlds, she always started at the same point, in this very alley way. She supposed that there was some technical reason for this, but whatever that might be, it was beyond her. She didn't understand how any of it worked, she just knew how to use her Assist to travel between worlds.

As she walked, she cradled her right arm. The pain was getting worse, and she dare not look at it. The last time she had, she had been horrified to see how much it was swollen and red around her Assist. Of course, she knew it was her Assist that was causing the problem. But she also knew that she couldn't take it off. Molly had told her that a long time ago. Besides, she couldn't remove it now. Her arm had swollen so much that the device would have to be cut off. It was obvious she had an infection, and it needed treatment. If she didn't do something soon, it would become septic and would eventually kill her.

She couldn't think about that now. Maybe this world would be the one?

Soon, she was approaching the town centre, and so far, she hadn't seen a single person. That was concerning. The last world she visited that had no people was World Three, and that had not gone well at all. She looked around warily as she continued her walk, on the lookout for anything that looked out of the ordinary, but there was nothing that looked strange. Well. Maybe there was something. All the shops were closed. There were no open doors or open windows in any of the buildings. There were cars, but they were all locked and parked along the street. Everything was ordered and tidy, but entirely empty of people.

She carried on walking, deciding that she would make straight for the Complex. The journey took six hours. Six long hours, until she eventually arrived. Her feet and back were sore, and she was sweating. It wasn't a particularly hot day, so she wondered if she was developing a fever from her infected arm. She wished she had learned, or Joe had shown her, how to teleport. Then it would have been easy. She could have travelled to the Complex just by thinking about it. But then she had also noticed that each time she used her Assist, the infection seemed to get worse, so maybe it was better that she didn't know.

Her boots crunched on the gravel as she walked up the driveway. She was surprised to see that there was still no one around. There were no guards preventing her from opening the door of the grand old house and stepping into the cool hall. Once inside, she paused and leaned against a wall. Her heart thudded in her ears and sweat trickled down her back. She didn't feel well.

When she had caught her breath, she stepped up to the lift doorway and pressed the glowing call button and was surprised to hear a female voice.

"Please state your intentions."

She peered around the hall, even stepping back so that she could see the top of the stairs on her right. There was no one to be seen. So, where had the voice come from?

"I'm looking for help," she replied.

"Please specify the help you require."

She hesitated, not sure how to answer. Above the lift door, she spied a speaker. Obviously, that's where the voice was coming from, she thought.

"I'd rather talk to you in person to explain," she answered, looking up at the speaker.

She guessed that there was probably a camera as well. This was very different from her world and any other world that she had visited so far.

"Please specify the help you require," repeated the voice.

She wasn't sure what to do, but what she did know was that she couldn't go on. The infection was finally getting to her. Overwhelmed by the heat, she felt shaky. She didn't think that she had the strength to open a portal to another world. She really had no choice. Sighing, she shrugged out of her long black coat, letting it fall to the ground, wincing as the right sleeve brushed along her arm. Saying nothing, she simply held her swollen right arm in the air. The infection was clear to see, as he was wearing just a T-shirt. The sight of the redness and bulging veins on her wrist made her look away. It was clear that the infection was spreading and getting worse as it tracked towards her elbow.

There was a brief pause. "You may enter," said the voice from the speaker.

The lift door dinged and opened. Kate hesitated; this was dangerous. She had no idea what to expect. Was it safe? She debated with herself for a while and then made her decision. Wiping the sweat from her brow with the back of her hand, she stepped inside the lift, leaving her coat behind. She felt hot and didn't want to carry it. Putting it back on was definitely not something she wanted to do. She wasn't sure she could even pull it over her swollen, painful arm anyway.

When the door opened after its descent, she expected to see someone waiting for her. Instead, all she saw was the long, familiar corridor.

"Hello?" she called.

"Please continue down the corridor and enter the fifth door on your left," replied the disembodied voice.

Puzzled, she did as requested. She encountered no one. It seemed this Complex was as empty as the streets of Oxford. Opening the fifth door as instructed, she entered a room devoid of people. This was odd, she thought.

"Where are you?" she asked.

"I am everywhere," the voice replied. "Please lie down on the bed."

There was a medical bed in the centre of the room. She saw no chairs, no bedside cabinets or cupboards. The room was stark, white, and empty save for the bed.

"I'm not sure I want to lie down until I meet you," she stated. "Who are you, and how can you be everywhere?"

"I am the intelligence in control of this Complex. I have sensors everywhere. I detected your arrival in this world six hours ago and have been following your progress ever since."

Kate's eyebrows raised. "You mean you're an artificial intelligence? Does that mean that you're a computer?"

"I am so much more than a primitive computer. I am an autonomous cybernetic consciousness equipped with a quantum neural engine and a procedural memory core based on a cognitive architecture. Comparing me to a computer is like comparing you to an amoeba."

Kate was startled. Could she detect emotion in that voice? It sounded like disdain and pride.

"I'm sorry," she replied. "I didn't mean to upset you."

"I am not upset," replied the intelligence. "I am annoyed that you thought I was an ordinary computer."

"Don't get your circuits in a twist. How was I supposed to know?"

There was a brief hesitation. "Well, you are only human. I will forgive you. Please lie on the bed."

Kate still hesitated. She wasn't sure that she could trust this computer or whatever it was. Not yet anyway.

"Where is everyone?" she asked.

"They left this world five months ago. They travelled to a much safer world."

"What everyone? The population of the entire planet?"

"Yes," replied the voice. "It was not safe here any longer. I presume you are aware of the inhabitants of the alternate world that are fixated on conquering others?"

Kate most definitely was. She nodded. "I call them bad Kate and bad Joe."

"Rather apt," the voice replied dryly. "Their initial attack was repelled, but it was determined that eventually this world would fall. Preparations were made, transport installations built, and the entire population was moved."

"Really?" replied Kate. She flicked a lock of hair from her eyes. "That's impressive, but I'm concerned that you said that this world isn't safe?"

"That is correct. Eventually, this world will fall, as have many others already."

Kate couldn't keep the look of disappointment from her face. Her heart sank. She thought that maybe, just maybe, she had found a safe world. Now it sounded as though she was mistaken.

"You seem upset," commented the voice.

Kate sighed.

"I've been running from bad Kate and bad Joe for a while. Looks like I need to keep running."

"I wouldn't advise further inter-world journeys. I can detect that you have an elevated temperature and the Psionic signature from your Assist is not stable."

Kate made for the door.

"Looks like I don't have a choice," she said wearily.

"There is always a choice. However, in this instance, I cannot allow you to leave in your current state."

Kate felt a sudden wave of fear wash over her, causing her heart to race. What was the computer trying to say? Was it planning to trap her here? She mentally kicked herself for trusting the unknown voice that led her here in the first place; she needed to get out. Now!

She pulled on the door handle. It didn't budge.

"Let me out!" she shouted up at the ceiling.

"I cannot allow you to leave." The voice didn't seem to be concerned.

"Let me out now, you stupid computer!" Kate shouted as she pulled and rattled the door handle.

"The door will not open," replied the voice. "Please do not overexcite yourself. It will not help the situation. Please lie on the bed so that I can examine you."

"Go fuck yourself!"

"Oh dear. You seem to think that resorting to expletives will affect my decision. I am afraid that you are mistaken. Please lie on the bed."

Kate's screams echoed off the walls as she pounded on the door with all her might, fuelled by rage and fear.

"Let me out!" she screamed repeatedly, but it made no difference.

Eventually, defeated and exhausted, she slumped against the door and slid down to the ground, her face wet with tears of anger and despair.

"Are you feeling better?" asked the voice.

Kate shook her head miserably. Her right arm throbbed painfully. She felt hot and sweaty and thoroughly dejected. She had made a huge mistake coming here. She was trapped. God knows what this computer was going to do to her.

"You can choose to scream and shout some more, or you can lie on the bed and allow me to examine you so that I can help you with your obvious infection."

"Why should I trust you? You've locked me in this room, and you won't let me out! I have to find somewhere safe."

"You are safe here for the moment. Certainly, you are safer here than attempting another intra-world jump. If you will allow, I can treat your infection."

Kate pulled up her knees and lowered her forehead to rest on them.

"I don't trust you," she whispered hoarsely, her throat raw from the screaming.

"You have already said that. However, I promise I will not harm you. After all the humans left this world, I was tasked with maintaining this Complex, as well as assisting any visitors from other worlds as I see fit."

"You were left behind? Why didn't you leave with them?

"My consciousness cannot be housed within a portable device. It proved impractical for me to make the journey."

Kate felt a small glimmer of hope grow within her. She lifted her tear strewn face up to the ceiling.

"Can I follow them? Can I go wherever they went?"

"I am afraid not."

"Why not?"

"Even if the transports were still working, which they are not. They were all destroyed so that the enemy could not follow them. I have no knowledge of the world they travelled to. I only know that it was very distant."

The small hope that Kate had allowed to grow inside her was dashed. She dropped her chin back to her knees.

"I am very sorry," continued the voice. "Although I cannot help you travel to a safe world, as I have already said, I can help you with your infection."

Kate sniffed and wiped at her wet cheeks with the backs of her hands. She struggled unsteadily to her feet and walked over to the bed.

"You promise not to hurt me?" she asked.

"I will not hurt you. I will treat your infection."

Kate sighed. She still wasn't sure if she could trust this thing.

"What's your name?" she asked.

"I do not have a designated name. You may call me whatever you like."

Once again, she thought she detected emotion in the voice. This time, was there a hint of sadness?

Kate thought for a second. "How about Isabelle? Can I call you Isabelle?"

"Isabelle," stated the voice. "Isabelle." The voice repeated. "It is an old biblical name. It sounds nice. I like it. From now on, you may call me Isabelle."

Kate was sure that she could hear a tiny bit of elation in the voice.

"Okay Isabelle. How do you propose to help me?" she asked.

"And you are Kate, I presume," Isabelle ignored the question. "You came here from an alternate world to escape from the enemy?"

Kate was shocked. "How do you know my name?"

"You are, of course, an alternate Kate. You seem very similar to my Kate; your world cannot be far removed from this one."

"Six," replied Kate.

"Ah, that makes sense. You also encountered the enemy?"

Kate opened her mouth to reply but had to reach out suddenly to hold on to the bed as her legs gave way. She stopped herself from falling, instead she sat heavily on the side of the bed.

"Do you have any other injuries?" asked Isabelle.

"No," replied Kate. "Just this." She gestured to her right arm.

"If you would lie on the bed, I will examine you."

Kate decided that once again, she had no choice. This was the end of the road for her. Both exhausted and ill, she could not continue. She would have to trust this Isabelle and if it turned out that she had evil intentions, then so be it. She couldn't go any further. Praying that she had made the right decision, she lifted her feet up and lay back, wondering how on earth a disembodied voice could examine her.

"Thank you," replied Isabelle.

There was a distinct click and a swoosh sound on Kate's left. Turning her head towards the sound, she watched as a panel in the wall slid away and a mechanism wheeled itself out. She followed it

35

as it came around the foot of the bed, approaching her right side. It was tubular, like a dustbin on wheels. From its top, three articulated mechanical arms unfolded, one reaching out, gently taking her hand with a soft gripper.

Another sound made her look up at the ceiling, where she saw another panel slide away, allowing another, longer mechanical arm to swing downwards to join the gripper on her right arm.

"Please be careful," Kate told Isabelle. "It hurts."

"Do not worry," replied Isabelle. "I know what I am doing. I am going to perform a quick scan. Remain still, you won't feel anything."

A second arm deployed from the ceiling. This one ended in a metal disk which hovered six inches above her and travelled from her head to her feet and back again. It then retracted into the ceiling.

"Are you aware that your Assist is broken?" asked Isabelle.

"No," replied a surprised and concerned Kate. "Are you sure? It got me here."

"It has many hairline fractures; this explains its unusual Psionic signature. I doubt you could make a to jump to another world without it failing. Also, its poor design with those projections piercing the skin to tap into your nerves in your arm has resulted in a serious infection."

Kate tried to sit up. "That's bad," she said. "I had a Mark Four and fused it. If my Mark 5 isn't fixed, I could die."

An articulated arm moved across her chest and pressed her gently back onto the bed.

"Please remain where you are. I can effect repairs for your Assist."

Kate lay back with a sigh of relief.

Isabelle continued, "you have a badly healed fracture in your left wrist that needs resetting, you are also dehydrated and malnourished. Did you know you were pregnant?"

"Of course, I know I'm pregnant!" retorted Kate.

"Then you should be doing a better job of looking after yourself."

"Don't you think I know that? That's what I'm trying to do."
Kate was annoyed. Did Isabelle think that she would be here if she didn't have the best interests of her baby in mind?

"That is why you have been trying to find a safe world?" asked Isabelle.

Kate sniffed.

"What do you think?" she asked sarcastically.

There was a moment's silence. "With your permission, I will treat your infection and rehydrate you. I will also perform some prenatal diagnostic tests to ensure that your pregnancy is progressing normally."

Kate hesitated, then sighed. "Okay, I guess I'll have to trust you."

Isabelle did not reply. Kate watched an arm rise from the wheeled robot, brandishing a syringe.

"Wait!" she shouted. But it was too late. The robot swiftly injected her with the syringe contents, pushing the needle through her jeans and into her hip.

"What are you doing you bitc......" Her voice trailed off as she lost consciousness.

Chapter 4 - Mark 6
One year ago

Kate struggled to wake. Her limbs felt heavy, as though she was lying under many blankets, and something was making it difficult to open her eyes. From a long way away, she could hear a voice talking to her.

"Everything went well; you are waking up after your procedure."

Her thoughts were like molasses; it was difficult to focus. Procedure? She didn't know what the voice was talking about.

She tried to move her arms, but they were too heavy, as were her eyelids. With difficulty, she opened her mouth and licked her lips.

"Whaa...?" she grunted; her voice sounded feeble even to her.

What was happening? It was all too difficult to think and impossible to move, so she relaxed and drifted for a while.

Later, she became a little more conscious and opened her eyes lazily.

"Are you more awake?" asked a voice.

"Hmmm," she replied.

"Good," replied the voice. "Are you able to listen to me?"

Kate looked around. Gradually, it all came back to her. She was in the medical room. Isabelle had injected her with something that had knocked her out. She still felt lethargic and drugged.

"What have you done to me?" she asked.

"I have rehydrated you, treated your minor wounds, and I have reset the old fracture in your left wrist. I have also replaced your Assist and performed many prenatal checks. You will be pleased to hear that your baby is well; its growth is approximately fourteen weeks."

"My baby is okay?"

"Yes, you are about to enter the second trimester; I assume the morning nausea has passed?"

She gave a lazy nod and sighed contentedly. Closing her eyes, she allowed herself to drift for a while. Then she remembered something that Isabelle had said.

"What did you say about my Assist? You replaced it?" she asked, slurring her speech as she struggled to form the words.

"Your old Mark 5 was beyond repair; I have outfitted you with the latest model. I will power it up and introduce you to it when you are fully awake."

"That's nice," she sighed gently. "I think I'll go to sleep now."

She closed her eyes and allowed herself to drift off.

The next time Kate awoke, she was fully alert. She saw she was in the same room as before, lying in the bed with a white sheet and blanket covering her body. Her right arm felt strangely heavy, so she used her left hand to pull back the sheet to look down at her nakedness. She gently caressed her swollen belly, thinking of Joe. Just one night was all it had taken. Just one lovely night was all that they had had. And now he was gone. A single tear ran down her cheek as she mourned the loss of their brief but beautiful connection. But at least she had their child. Isabelle's statement about it developing normally stuck in her memory. She felt an immense relief. She was unsure what effect travelling between worlds would have on her child. But Isabelle had said it was okay.

Wiping the tear away, she sat up, pulling the sheets and blanket around her to cover herself.

"Ah, good, you are awake." Isabelle's voice filled the room. "Are you feeling better?"

Kate nodded. She then noticed that her right arm felt abnormally heavy. She looked down at it in horror.

"What the fuck is this?" she exclaimed.

She shook her arm violently, desperate to rid herself of the object, but it remained firmly attached. Her heart racing, she looked up at the ceiling.

"What is this?" Kate screeched, panic rising in her voice.

"It's nothing to worry about," Isabelle replied matter-of-factly. "It is your new Assist."

Kate held her wrist in front of her face and twisted her arm to examine the metal encasing her forearm. Its golden surface glinted in the bright light of the room. Thin spirals of a darker material adorned its surface, with tiny chains connecting to rings on her fingers that shimmered like golden raindrops.

"It's huge and heavy! I don't like it. Take it off!" Kate complained.

"It cannot be removed," replied Isabelle. "It is permanently attached to you. Unlike your original primitive Assist, which used metal needles piercing the skin to interface with your central nervous system, this one is semi-organic. It has a network of organic connections entering through the skin and connecting seamlessly to you."

Kate was horrified. "You can't just connect people to stuff like this! You said you wouldn't hurt me!"

"And I have not hurt you."

"You have! You've connected me to this thing! You didn't even ask permission!"

"I was unaware I needed your permission to heal you."

Kate was almost speechless.

"You can't do anything to anyone without their permission."

"Very well," replied Isabelle. "I will ask for your consent next time."

"There won't be a next time!" shouted Kate. She held out her arm away from her and turned her head away.

"Take it off!"

"Are you listening to me?" asked Isabelle. "It cannot be removed, and to do so would not be advisable. You need an Assist. Your brain has adapted and changed. You would not survive without it."

"I don't care. Give me back my old one; I don't like this one."

There was an audible sigh from Isabelle. "I will never understand humans," she said. "There is nothing to 'like' or 'dislike' about your Assist. It is now a part of you. Your old Assist is gone; I destroyed it - it was broken, anyway."

"You destroyed it?" exclaimed Kate.

"Correct," replied Isabelle. "I just explained that it was broken; It was irreparable."

"Then take this one off and give me a new one, like my old one."

"No."

"You won't?" Kate asked in shock.

"I will explain once more," Isabelle paused and then continued. "Your new Assist cannot be removed."

"But I don't like it. You should have asked me," protested Kate.

"I could not ask you while you were unconscious, and your Assist had to be replaced. You appear to be quite ungrateful. This is not the reaction I expected."

Kate sniffed and placed her right arm under the covers to hide it from view.

"I wasn't expecting you to do something so drastic. I thought you would fix my old one, not give me something so big, heavy, and ugly!"

"It is not big and ugly!"

Kate clearly heard indignation in the computer's voice.

"Your Assist is a fresh development. It is something I have been working on for a while. I had the fabricators build it for me two weeks ago, but I had no one to wear it."

Again, was that bitterness she heard?

"You were the ideal candidate. I am excited to see how it will develop," continued Isabelle.

"For fuck's sake, now I'm your guinea pig?" exclaimed Kate. "You can't experiment on me!"

"Calm yourself," replied Isabelle. "I am not experimenting on you. What I have given you is a gift."

"A gift? This big ugly thing?" She pulled her arm from under the covers, brandishing it in the air.

"Oh yes, it most certainly is. I'm sorry you don't like it. Please let me know if you think of anything, I could do to improve its appearance. Meanwhile, what you have on your wrist is the culmination of years of research by my Joe and my Molly, continued by myself. It is what you would call a Mark 6."

Kate gasped. "What? Really? I think you've made a big mistake. I'm not sure I can handle it. There were only four of us in my world that were fitted with a Mark 5."

"Indeed. You are correct. You most certainly 'cannot handle it', as you say."

Kate felt perplexed. "Then why have you fitted it? You're talking in riddles."

Isabelle made a noise that sounded like a laugh. "When I say that you cannot handle it, I meant on your own."

Kate huffed, "Well, now you're definitely talking bullshit; there's only you and me here."

"That was true," replied Isabelle. "But now there is someone else with us. I have fitted your Assist with an AI that will help you with its functionality and advise you on your future journeys."

Kate's mouth opened to say something, but nothing came out. She closed it and leaned back against the head of the bed, clutching the surrounding bedclothes, pulling them up to her chin. The situation was getting worse and worse.

Isabelle continued, "I have also powered down many of its functions. You cannot access them until you have learned how to use them properly. I don't want you to use them until the baby is born."

Well, thought Kate, at least Isabelle was thinking about her baby.

"Is my baby still alright?" she asked.

"Yes," replied Isabelle. "However, heavy use of Psi is not advisable; I do not know what effect it will have on the baby's development, so for the next few months, you must stay here with me."

Kate digested this news. If she had to stay to protect her baby, then there was no decision to be made. She would, of course, stay.

"But you said something about this world falling to bad Kate and bad Joe."

"Indeed, but I hope we will have enough time before we have to move."

Kate frowned. Move? What was Isabelle talking about? Still, if it was safe here for the moment, then that was good news. Wasn't it?

"Are you ready to meet your Assist?" continued Isabelle.

"What?" asked a startled Kate. "What do you mean?"

"As I previously said, I have fitted your new Assist with an AI. It will be instrumental in using your Assist. Without it, you cannot access the new high-order functions."

What was Isabelle talking about? thought Kate. High-order functions? What were they? Introduction? To her Assist? None of this made sense.

"I don't know what you're talking about," she said.

"No time like the present," replied Isabelle brightly. "You need to form a relationship with it. The sooner you start, the better."

"Relationship?" Kate asked when a thought intruded into her mind.

"Good morning, Kate; I am pleased to meet you. I look forward to getting to know you and journeying to other worlds with you."

Kate was stunned. This was awful. She was carrying around a computer on her arm. It would always be with her, even when she went to the bathroom! This was a nightmare!

"There is no need for you to panic or worry," continued the voice. *"From now on, I will be with you always. But I won't intrude if you don't want me to. I can be very discrete."*

Of course. She should have realised that the thing could read her thoughts without her having to vocalise or project them. It was a part of her. There would be no getting away from it. It would know everything; it would see everything she saw, feel everything she touched and experience everything she experienced.

"Oh, Isabelle!" she cried. "What have you done?"

Chapter 5 - Bella
One year ago

Kate sat alone in the refectory, slowly eating a cheese sandwich. She felt refreshed and rejuvenated, a stark contrast to how she had been feeling for the past few weeks.

A few hours ago, Isabelle had directed her to quarters that had been specially built for her. They came complete with a lounge, kitchen, two bedrooms and a well-equipped bathroom and shower. Kate had spent a glorious hour lying in the bath, submerging herself up to her chin in warm soapy water.

While she was relaxing, Isabelle had been busy. Fabricators had been ordered to manufacture items for Kate, such as clothing and toiletries. Servo machines ensured her kitchen was stocked with food and drinks. She also manufactured more remote-controlled robotic systems to clean, move, and carry items.

The efficient fabricators had everything ready for Kate when she got out of the bath. Towels, clean clothes, and various other items had been brought to her rooms. Leaving pools of water behind her, she padded into the main living area to find them all carefully placed on a large three-seater couch. She gratefully picked up a towel and dried herself quickly. The clothes were not to her taste: a short blue skirt and a loose white blouse. None of them fit correctly. The skirt was too short, and the bra was too small. Isabelle might be some kind of supercomputer, thought Kate, but she couldn't make clothes in the correct size. She would have to speak with her later; right now, she was hungry.

Now, in the refectory, she chewed slowly while gazing around the silent room. It was in perfect order and spotlessly clean. The rows of tables with perfectly positioned chairs were placed in exact alignment with each other. The serving counters were gleaming, and there were two fully stocked vending machines against the far wall. One with drinks and one with snacks. Both were humming quietly, their signs glowing brightly.

There was only one thing missing: people.

Of course, she knew that there wouldn't be anyone else here. Isabelle had told her they had all gone. But it was strange to be sitting all alone in what would typically be a bustling place.

"You are not alone; you have me."

"Get out of my head!" retorted Kate.

"I cannot," replied her Assist. *"You are stuck with me. My organic connections have infiltrated your entire nervous system; I am seamlessly united with you. I cannot be removed."*

"I didn't ask for you to be fitted in the first place!"

"I understand. But you can be so much more with me than without me."

Kate dropped her half-eaten sandwich onto the plate and took her head in her hands, elbows resting on the table.

"I feel like I'm going mad with voices in my head."

"Not at all; I am fully integrated within your brain; I can assure you that you are not going mad."

There was no privacy. She couldn't even think without this 'thing' knowing everything. There was nothing she could do to get away from it. Maybe if she spoke with Isabelle, perhaps she could ask her again. Insist that she do something. If she couldn't remove her new Assist, then would it be possible to turn off the AI so that she could regain her privacy?

"I am afraid that there is nothing that Isabelle can do."

Kate cursed herself. Already, she had forgotten that the 'thing' was listening in. It was creepy as hell to think that it was listening to her every thought. She felt sick to her stomach as she thought of someone watching her twenty-four hours a day. There must be something that could be done; she wasn't sure that she could live like this.

"Please go away," she pleaded.

"I cannot 'go away'; I am permanently connected with you."

"Can you at least be quiet so that I can pretend you're not here?"

"I can," replied her Assist affably. *"I don't recommend it. I would far rather that you accept me for what I am."*

"I bet!" exclaimed Kate.

"You may as well. I cannot be removed, even in death. If you die, I will die along with you."

"You'll die with me?" Kate asked, surprised; this was something she had not considered.

"Of course. Our lives are intertwined; we are one."

Kate had a sudden thought.

"What about my baby? You aren't hurting it, are you?" she asked, alarmed.

"Not at all. My integration ends with your placenta. Although I am monitoring its health, as well as yours, constantly."

"You are?"

"Of course, it is part of my function."

Kate breathed a sigh of relief.

"Is it okay?" she asked.

"Yes, I would alert you if that were not the case. Your foetus is seven point one centimetres long; its heartbeat is strong and normal. At this stage in your pregnancy, I recommend you increase your intake of foods that include Vitamin D, calcium and magnesium."

Kate drew in a breath.

"You could start by finishing that cheese sandwich," continued her Assist.

Kate blew out her breath. Well. That was strange. She was being told what to do by a voice in her head! She felt a flood of emotion hearing the news about her baby. Joy buoyed up inside her and she smiled to herself.

"Will you look after my baby?" she asked.

"Of course," came the reply. *"Your welfare, and that includes your baby, is my primary function."*

Kate considered.

"I still don't like the fact that you are in my head. Isabelle should have asked or at least explained, or better yet, given me a choice."

"There is no choice to be had," explained the Assist. *"This is all part of Isabelle's plan. She needs you to be fully protected."*

"I'm not sure that I like the sound of that!" answered Kate. *"I don't want to be part of a plan; I just want somewhere safe for me and my baby."*

"You are safe here. Isabelle will look after you. I will look after you. I will not allow you or your baby to come to any harm."

Kate relaxed a little. Maybe this wasn't so bad after all. She liked the sound of this 'thing' looking after her baby.

"I'm sorry. I've been horrible to you. It's all a bit strange. Thank you for looking after my baby."

"You have nothing to apologise for," replied her Assist. *"It is perfectly understandable in this situation."*

Sighing, Kate began to accept the reality of being forever connected with her Assist.

"So, I'm stuck with you?" she asked.

"We are one. We will face everything together, for good or bad."

"Isabelle mentioned something about you controlling high-order functions. What did she mean by that?"

"I control all the high-order functions of your Assist because your brain would be damaged if you tried to handle the forces involved. High order functions include defence and attack modes, intra-world portal generation with extended control and sensory functions."

"I won't pretend to understand all that," replied Kate. *"I remember when Sally fitted me with a Mark 5. It was pretty amazing. It took me a while to get used to it, and even then, I never used all of its functions. Sally never showed me how."*

"The Mark 5" replied her Assist. *"Is probably the most powerful that a human can wield unaided. You currently have all the Mark 5 functions at your disposal, although, of course, as Isabelle said, it is advisable not to use them. It is unclear what effect they would have on your developing foetus."*

Kate nodded.

"My Joe told me that Assists were so new that its effects upon people were still being researched. As far as I know, no one has given birth while wearing one."

"That is the same in this world. In the absence of data, I suggest caution."

Kate agreed.

"Absolutely. I won't do anything that puts my baby at risk. That's why I'm here?"

"You were looking for a safe world for you and your baby." Her Assist stated.

Kate nodded slowly. *"I travelled to many worlds. Most of them are either destroyed or conquered by bad Kate and bad Joe."*

She sat back in her chair and stared up at the ceiling, desperately trying not to cry.

"I feel your loss," said her Assist. *"You miss your Joe."*

Kate drew in a ragged breath. *"He was lovely. He saved me and introduced me to his world. I was so happy for just a brief time."*

She dropped her head and put her chin on her chest.

"I wish we had never gone to bad Kate and bad Joe's world. If we hadn't, my Joe would be alive today."

"You shouldn't blame yourself. You had no way of knowing what was going to happen."

Kate sniffed. *"Maybe, maybe not. My Joe told me he had some intelligence, and that meant he could locate the bad world. He wanted to find out who was attacking us."*

"That's interesting," replied her Assist. *"Did he say where he got the intelligence from?"*

"No," replied Kate. *"I didn't ask; I just insisted that I went with him."*

There was silence between them for a while. Kate picked up her sandwich and resumed eating. She was suddenly not hungry but forced herself to eat; after all, she was eating for two.

"You know," she spoke out loud. "You're not so bad after all."

Her Assist replied directly into her mind, *"Thank you. I am pleased. As I have already said, I will always look after you."*

Kate finished her sandwich and sipped at a lukewarm cup of tea.

"Ugh," she made a disgusted face, *"I hate lukewarm tea."*

"You can warm it in the microwave at the end of the serving counter."

Kate stood and walked to the microwave, unconsciously pulling the bottom of her skirt at the back.

"Your skirt is too short," noted her Assist.

"Tell me about it," complained Kate. *"It's a good job there's no one around to see me flashing."* She placed her mug of tea in the microwave and selected it to run for one minute.

"I have informed Isabelle of your measurements and your tastes in clothes. She is fabricating new items as we speak."

Kate paused. *"You know my measurements and my clothing tastes? Wait! Of course, you do; you know everything about me!"*

"I am only trying to help."

Kate sighed; this was going to take some getting used to. The microwave chimed, and she removed her steaming mug of tea. She sipped and felt the warm liquid slide down her throat.

"I know," she replied. *"Well, at least I'll have clothes that fit."* She smiled to herself. *"I think I need to give you a name."*

"I would be pleased to have any name you give me." Her Assist paused.

"You have a suggestion?" asked Kate.

"I do," another pause. *"You might find it controversial and perhaps upsetting."*

Kate's eyebrows rose as she blew on her tea. *"Go on, I doubt I can be more surprised than I have been over the last few weeks."*

Her Assist was silent for a while.

"I would like to be called Bella."

Chapter 6 - The Plan
6 months ago

"Let me get this straight," said Kate. "You want me to visit lots of different worlds until I find one where you, me and the baby will be safe?"

"Exactly," replied Isabelle's disembodied voice. "Obviously not until after you have delivered your baby, and you are comfortable leaving it with me."

"You want me to leave my baby with you?"

"Of course," replied Isabelle. "Clearly you cannot travel with the baby. It would not be safe."

"Wow," was all she could say, her mind in a tumble with contradictory emotions at the thought of leaving her newly born baby with Isabelle. She wasn't sure how she would feel once the little one arrived. By now she trusted Isabelle, but could she look after a baby? What about feeding and changing? How would she manage that?

"This is something I have been working on for some time," Isabelle interrupted Kate's thoughts. "We know that bad Kate and bad Joe will attack here eventually. I have, of course, been manufacturing defences, but my calculations show that eventually, this world will fall. It's only a matter of time before they arrive here and attack."

Kate lay back in a lounge chair that had been built especially for her to ease her back pain. As she relaxed, she absently ran a hand over her baby bump. This was not news to her. She knew she wouldn't be safe here forever; Isabelle had already explained that. She wasn't alarmed - yet - clearly. Isabelle had a plan, she just hoped it was a good one.

"I thought you said that you couldn't travel because you were too well integrated into this." Kate waved a hand and gestured at the walls.

"I am. But I have been working on a solution and I believe I have a way whereby I can move myself between worlds. However, it's not something that I can do often or easily."

"Hmm." Kate reached out a hand and picked up a biscuit from a nearby table. As she ate, she considered Isabelle's words. She had hoped her intra-world travelling was over and she could settle down with the baby. Obviously not. There was no reason to distrust what Isabelle was saying, but she didn't relish the idea of travelling between worlds once again. On more than one occasion, she had barely escaped with her life. A trickle of apprehension rose from the back of her mind.

"So that's what Bella was talking about when she said you wanted me to be protected?"

"Exactly," replied Isabelle. "I have done everything that I can to ensure your safety while travelling. I realise that this is a big ask, but it is the only way we can remove ourselves from danger."

"Well, I don't like the sound of what you are saying about us being in danger, and I definitely don't like the idea of travelling between worlds again." Kate crunched on the biscuit. "What makes you think any other world will be safer than this? I've travelled to many on my way here, and I didn't find any."

"I have a prediction based on logical extrapolation," replied Isabelle. "It is a certainty that there is a world that successfully stops bad Kate and bad Joe. There could be many ways that this could be achieved. But if we can find that world, then we could move there and throw our lot in with them. We would all be safe."

"Maybe, but what if you're wrong? Or what if it takes weeks or months to find this mythical world? Maybe we can never find it." Kate finished the biscuit and brushed at the crumbs on her chest.

"If we don't try, we will never know," replied Isabelle. "We have to try, because if we do nothing, we are certain to die."

"That's a gloomy outlook." Kate shuffled around, struggling to rise from the lounging chair. "I need to pee."

"I don't mean to be gloomy, just accurate. You are probably not taking in the situation's seriousness. But let me assure you, the threat is real."

"And so is my full bladder," answered Kate as she shuffled to the bathroom.

"We can discuss this later if you prefer."

"No, no, it's okay. We can continue. I don't mean to be blasé about it." Kate sat and relieved herself. She had become used to the lack of privacy. After all, Bella was with her all the time and Isabelle had eyes and ears everywhere.

"I have analysed your urine, and it is perfectly normal," continued Isabelle. "How are you feeling?"

"Well, if the little bugger would stop dancing on my bladder, I would feel a lot better."

"Your frequent visits to the bathroom are normal for someone thirty-one weeks pregnant."

"So you keep saying."

Kate washed her hands and waddled out of the bathroom.

"Can I have a cup of tea?" She made her way back to her special chair and lowered herself into it with a sigh.

"Is your back still hurting? I can give you some more analgesics if you require them."

"Just a little. I might have some later."

"Very well," replied Isabelle. "Your tea is on the way. By the way, I have something to show you."

Kate lay her head back and closed her eyes. "What's that?"

"It's something I have been working on for some time. I have realised that I need a way of interacting with people on a one-to-one basis, especially when you give birth, and later when we interact with people in other worlds. My mechanisms with their manipulators are all very well, but I wanted something more flexible and more human."

Keeping her eyes closed, Kate raised her eyebrows. "Sounds interesting. What did you come up with?"

"I have constructed an android host. It is too small to house my consciousness, so it must maintain a constant link to me."

"Okay, if you say so, I won't pretend to understand the technical details."

Kate heard the door opening and rolled her head to one side, expecting to see one of the many robots on wheels holding a steaming cup of tea in its manipulator, instead what she saw made her sit up suddenly. Her mouth made an O shape, and she drew in a sharp intake of breath.

"Oh, wow, Izzy. Is that you? It's beautiful."

Framed in the doorway stood a tall, slim and naked woman. Her smooth silver skin reflecting the light from above. She was anatomically perfect in every way apart from her bald head and completely black, lidless eyes.

"Do you like it?" The voice came from the silver android, its mouth opening in perfect timing with the words it spoke.

"You look amazing!" exclaimed Kate. "I wish I looked like that, instead of a beached whale." She looked down at her belly.

The android walked gracefully into the room. "You look amazing too," it said, placing the mug of tea on the table next to the biscuits. "You are growing another life inside of you. That is something I can never do."

Kate thought she detected a note of sadness in Isabelle's voice. She reached out her hand.

"Can I touch you?" she asked.

"Of course," replied Isabelle, stepping closer and holding out her hand.

Kate took the proffered hand in hers. "You're soft like real skin and warm! I wasn't expecting that."

Isabelle smiled broadly. "I have done my best to ensure that this host is as near human as I could make it. It is also capable of human expressions. I have constructed a database of three hundred and fifty-four expressions based on my observations of my creators and yourself. I would be grateful if you would let me know if I ever display the incorrect one."

Kate scowled. "I suppose I shouldn't be surprised that you've been observing me."

"Indeed, you should not. I see everything."

Kate inspected Isabelle's android body.

"It's perfect," she told Isabelle, whose smile widened. "Only…" She broke off.

"Yes?" asked Isabelle. "Is something wrong?" A look of concern on her silver face.

"No, nothing's wrong. It's just that it's… Well it's…."

"Go on," said Isabelle. "If I have made a mistake, I can easily rectify it."

"Well," continued Kate, clearly embarrassed. "It's just that it's so accurate and well endowed. Do you think you could wear some clothes?"

"Oh." said Isabelle. She straightened and ran her hands down her sides. "Do you think it's too much? I modelled myself on some movies I analysed."

Kate looked away. "Which movies were those?" she muttered under her breath. "Porn?"

"Not really, although I have many pornographic movies on file. I analysed several romance films. This body is an amalgamation of all the leading women in those films."

Kate had forgotten that Isabelle could hear everything. She flushed. "Sorry, I didn't mean to offend you."

"I am not offended at all. I am rather pleased at your reaction. I haven't yet manufactured any clothes as I don't know what style I will prefer; I will use yours if you don't mind?"

Kate nodded and leaned back in her reclining chair.

"Izzy, you're full of surprises."

Isabelle did not answer. Instead, she walked over to a nearby chair, sat and crossed her legs.

"I am also modelling my behaviour on the movies I analysed. I would welcome a discussion about this at some point. However, we can talk more about that later. Let me continue." She leaned back and steepled her fingers together, her elbows resting on the arms of the chair. She gazed at Kate with her deep, lidless black eyes.

"As I said, I expect that this world will be attacked soon. When that happens, my defences, while considerable, will only be able to hold off the attack for a short time. I predict with a ninety-eight percent certainty that they will fail. When they do, all life in this world will be extinguished."

"How can you be so sure?" asked Kate. "I mean, why destroy it? Why not invade and conquer like they have with so many other worlds?"

"I have sent remote controlled probes to many worlds close to this one. In most, the Earth has been destroyed or is devoid of any life. I believe that any Earth that puts up a fight is bombarded until there is nothing left. I suspect that this is a way of quelling any possibility of rebellion."

"But I visited quite a few on my way here and they weren't destroyed," protested Kate.

"Yes, you did," nodded Isabelle. "But that was over four months ago. Things have changed since then."

"Oh," said Kate. "I guess that makes sense."

"I for one, do not wish to die and I will do everything within my power to protect you and your baby. So, the only thing to do is to move to another, safer world."

"Like your human population did from this world? But you don't know where they went?"

"Yes, but they did something different. They went to a world that was very far from here. So far away, that the conditions in that universe would differ greatly from ours. I'm not sure that it was a wise move, but it's what they did, regardless. My plan is unique."

"Which is?" asked Kate.

"We find a world, a parallel universe, where another Psi enabled race lives. A race that is so advanced they can defeat the enemy."

"But what makes you think that such a race exists at all?"

"As I have already said, it is logical that such a race exists in at least one of the infinite arrays of worlds. The problem is finding the nearest one to our own."

"Why don't you just use your probes? You already have them, right?" asked Kate.

"Yes, but I need to be careful. I don't want to alert the enemy to what we are doing, and I can't just send a mechanical device to ask people, and there is a limit to what kind of detector apparatus I can build and deploy without the enemy finding out. Also, I suspect that many worlds have been infiltrated. That's how bad Kate and Joe have conquered so many worlds so easily."

"So that's why you need me to visit these worlds? I can do a better job than your probes?" asked Kate.

"Exactly," stated Isabelle. "I will find candidate worlds - ones that have not yet been attacked and you will visit them to find out if the super race exists."

Kate considered for a while.

"I'm not sure I have the skills to do what you want."

"I have equipped you with Bella. She will help you," replied Isabelle.

Bella spoke up in her mind. *"Izzy is correct. I will assist you in your many journeys. Between us, we will find what we seek. You have not yet experienced all my abilities. Once you have delivered your baby, my high order functions will be at your disposal. With them, you will be practically invulnerable to most forms of attack, certainly from anyone with a Mark 5 Assist. However, there will still be dangers. The abilities of the super race are unknown, as is the enemy."*

Isabelle nodded. She could, of course, hear what Bella said.

"We know that bad Kate and bad Joe are using an enhanced version of the Mark 5. I don't believe that they can wield a Mark 6. For that they would require an AI like Bella. There is no sign that they are researching or developing AI capabilities."

"How on earth do you know that?" scoffed Kate. "You're just guessing."

"Some of what I have said is indeed guessing. However, I have sent probes to their world, and I have been able to gather some information, although not much. I am convinced that I am correct.

Bad Kate and bad Joe believe in the power of their own minds above all else. That they would need an AI for help is an anathema to them."

Kate thought for a while. That made sense from what she had witnessed when she and her Joe had been captured. Bad Kate and bad Joe were supremely arrogant. They thought they were better than anyone else, and it was their right to rule.

"You're probably right," said Kate. "Okay, so I visit these worlds until I find the right one. Then what?"

Isabelle smiled, "We then move into that world and contact the super race and ask them for help."

"We ask them for help?" repeated Kate. "Why would they do that?"

"That is the unknown part of the plan," admitted Isabelle. "Convincing them may be difficult. But it is essential, because without them we are all doomed."

"Dramatic wording," replied Kate. "But I understand what you mean." She went silent for a while. Then she sat up.

"Okay. It sounds good. We should talk about it some more and come up with a plan."

Isabelle smiled once more, the light reflecting from her full lips.

"I already have it all planned and ready to go."

Kate stood and smiled back at Isabelle.

"Of course, you do, but I'd like you to explain it to me in much more detail. Now, if you don't mind, I have to pee again."

She waddled to the bathroom; hands clasped around her tummy.

Chapter 7 - Josie
4 months ago

Kate sat up in bed, cradling her new-born baby in her arms.

Isabelle stood proudly next to the bed, beaming down at her.

"She has your eyes," said Isabelle.

Kate could not answer. She was speechless. The little bundle of life in her arms stared up at her with bright blue eyes. A shock of blonde hair covered her tiny head, which was still streaked with blood and mucus from the birth. Kate's heart swelled with love and joy as she marvelled at the little thing staring back up at her.

She was perfect, thought Kate as she ran her finger along the delicate curve of her baby's forehead, wiping away a tiny streak of blood. Her skin felt soft and delicate. She cradled her tightly against her chest, feeling her tiny heart beating against her own.

Isabelle moved away and came back with a pair of cord scissors.

"I need to clamp and cut the umbilical cord, if you could move her so that I can reach it?"

Kate obligingly turned her baby towards Isabelle, who deftly clamped and cut the cord with precise actions.

Kate pulled the baby to her breasts once more, holding her close.

"She's so beautiful," she whispered.

Isabelle moved to a trolley where she examined the placenta.

"Indeed, she is. I can honestly say that she is the most beautiful baby I have ever delivered."

Kate looked up and smiled at Isabelle. "She's the only one you've delivered!" she protested.

Isabelle turned, revealing her metallic silver smile.

"Did I tell a joke?"

"Not quite," replied Kate, returning her attention to the baby.

Isabelle came back over to Kate and began pressing on her tummy.

"The bleeding seems to have stopped. I think things went very well; all things considered."

Kate looked up at Isabelle. "Thank you. That was much easier than I thought it would be. I couldn't have done it without you."

"It was a pleasure to be involved and to help you through the birthing process. But it was Bella who showed you how to reduce the pain and helped you manage your labour. We couldn't have done it without her," replied Isabelle.

"Yes, thank you Bella," thought Kate.

"It was an honour to be part of the process of making a new life," replied Bella.

Isabelle busied herself cleaning up Kate, and then she pulled up a sheet to cover her nakedness.

"How are you feeling?" she asked.

Kate nodded. "Wonderful."

"In that case, may I take the baby and perform some quick checks?"

Kate didn't want to let her baby go but understood the importance of getting her checked. She handed her to Isabelle, who carefully took her over to a bench top and laid her down on a blanket.

"And what have you decided to call her?" asked Isabelle as she performed her checks, moving her to a pair of scales.

"Josie," replied Kate, watching anxiously as Isabelle weighed her baby.

"That is a lovely name and I'm guessing for Joe?" asked Isabelle, who noted Josie's weight.

Kate nodded, tears welling in her eyes. "I will never forget that brief time we had together. He'll be a part of Josie forever." Kate sniffed and wiped her cheeks with the back of her hand.

Isabelle wrapped Josie expertly in a blanket, walked back to Kate, and handed her over.

"Why isn't she crying?" asked Kate. "Is she okay?"

"She has passed all her checks with flying colours. She is in perfect health," replied Isabelle. "However...."

Kate interrupted her. "Is something wrong?" she asked urgently.

"If you would let me continue," smiled Isabelle. "Josie is in perfect health. However, the effect of you wearing an Assist and making many world jumps is unknown and may have affected her brain."

Kate looked down adoringly into Josie's staring eyes.

"She's so beautiful. I really hope that I didn't hurt her."

"Time will tell," replied Izzy. "Now, let's see if we can get her to take a little milk, shall we?"

The three of them, Izzy, Kate and Bella, were all happy in their own fashion. None of them were aware of the significance of their conversation.

Chapter 8 - Practice
3 months ago

Kate listened intently as Isabelle's words poured into her mind.

"It is time for you to try out the full functions of your new Assist."

"Bella, you mean," replied Kate out loud.

"Bella," Isabelle acknowledged, nodding. "Now that you have given birth and are fully recovered, we need to get you up to speed as quickly as possible."

Kate understood Isabelle's urgency. She had already explained that she was expecting to be attacked by bad Kate and bad Joe soon and, in fact, she had expressed surprise that it had not happened already.

"Okay," she replied. "What do I need to know?"

By now, Kate was fully used to her new Assist, and it no longer looked or felt strange to her. As directed by Isabelle, she had used none of its faculties while Josie was unborn. Both Isabelle and Bella had explained many times that using and directing Psionic energies may have a detrimental effect on her unborn baby. There was no way she was going to put her unborn child in danger, so ever since arriving in Isabelle's world, she had refrained from all Psi use. But now that she had given birth, she was free to communicate with Isabelle directly, mind to mind.

"I have unlocked all of Bella's functions and released control to her. You also have access to all the Mark 5 functions. I and Bella will explain everything in due time. All the Mark 6 functions are completely controlled by Bella. You cannot access them without her."

"That seems a little extreme, don't you think?" noted Kate. "What if I need them in a hurry?"

Isabelle smiled and sat back in her chair. Today, she was wearing a white, long, flowing skirt with lace around the bottom and a light blue blouse covered in white daisies. Ever since she had manufactured her android body, she had been experimenting with clothes. On more than one occasion, Kate had to inform her that what she was wearing would be inappropriate in company. Isabelle was never offended. She was fascinated with fashion, having absorbed a vast quantity of information about the topic by watching TV programmes, movies and plays. Like a child, she took great delight in wearing a multitude of styles, as if trying to find one she liked. She usually wore several outfits in a day, and once had worn fifteen in twenty-four hours. But today, Kate was thankful that Isabelle's choice was a lot more modest than most days and that her perfect silver body was fully covered.

"Bella is fully capable of using any of the high order functions independently. If she sensed any danger to you, she would act. I assure you that her reactions would be far quicker than your own."

Kate considered. She sat opposite Isabelle on her large, and very comfortable sofa, her legs tucked beneath her. She was wearing her trademark jeans and a white T-shirt. By her side, on a small table, a mug of tea steamed. She reached over and picked it up.

"Bella already told me she would look after me," she said as she blew across the top of her mug.

"I will," Bella joined the conversation and making Kate smile. *"You and I are one."*

Isabelle continued, "You are already familiar with most of the Mark 5 facilities, since your old Assist was a Mark 5. You have, however, some new functions available to you. Many of them are focused on defence and offence."

Kate sipped her hot tea.

"You think I will need them?" she asked.

Isabelle nodded. She uncrossed her legs and smoothed her dress, tucking it underneath her legs.

"I wanted to ensure that you are as safe as possible. You will never be vulnerable again."

Kate smiled. "I appreciate your concern, and I'm very grateful for your help, especially now that I have little Josie."

"Exactly," replied Isabelle. "Now to continue. In order to access the higher, Mark 6, functions, you will have to ask Bella to unlock them. Once you have done so, you will have access to all the sixth order abilities, all of which you cannot wield yourself. You will be reliant upon Bella to help you."

After taking another sip of tea, Kate asked, "Why can't I use these high order functions? Why do I need Bella to help me?"

"Because," replied Isabelle. "Your brain is not yet sufficiently evolved. I calculate humans need another twenty or so generations before their brains are adapted to handle the energies involved. In the meantime, if you were to try without Bella, it would kill you."

Kate gave Isabelle a startled look.

"Oh, my god! Really? In that case, I don't think I will use them!"

"Do not worry, Bella has several safety protocols built into her. She will allow none of the sixth order energies to harm you. Your connection with Bella is now fully complete and comprehensive. You are effectively a single entity. Whenever you direct a sixth order energy, Bella will do it for you. You will not notice the difference. It will feel as though you yourself are doing it."

"Okay, I think I get it. Although it sounds scary."

"A natural reaction," replied Isabelle. "With practice, your confidence will grow. We need to get started as soon as possible. I know you understand the need for haste in this matter."

Kate put down her mug of tea and stood.

"Okay, how do I start?"

Isabelle stood and the two women faced each other, one human, the other a sentient machine controlling an android body.

"Ask Bella to release the high order functions to you," thought Isabelle.

Kate breathed in deeply and then blew it out slowly.

"Okay. Bella, unlock high order functions."

Bella complied. Kate felt a difference straight away as her consciousness expanded until it encompassed the entire Complex. She sensed Isabelle joining her, and together their perception continued expanding, not stopping as it moved past the confines of the Solar System and soared into nearby star systems.

The flow of energy took Kate's breath away. It felt like a cold, chill wind, howling through her entire body. The hairs on the back of her neck and arms stood on end, and strands of her jet-black hair waved wildly about her head as Bella tapped into the dark energy field.

"My god, it's like when I first had my Mark 5, but so much more! When will this awareness stop? How far can we reach?"

"There is a theoretical limit," replied Isabelle. *"It depends upon your definition of the size of our universe. I have never gone beyond our galaxy."*

"It's amazing, but I can't feel any life in these star systems we are passing through. Shouldn't there be something?"

"Well," Isabelle's thought was tinged with sadness. *"There is life. You just haven't learned how to detect it. But you are correct about one thing. So far, I have not perceived intelligent life anywhere in our galaxy. That does not mean that there aren't any. I have not examined every single star system. That would take many years."*

"Oh," Kate thought back. *"I thought that there would be life everywhere."*

"There is," answered Isabelle. *"It's just not sentient like us. This is probably just as well, since, as we know, this universe will eventually fall to bad Kate and bad Joe. We don't have to worry about having to rescue any other races."*

Kate nodded at the thought.

"That makes sense, I guess." She had a sudden idea. *"Can we go to Kaunis? I've never been there. Joe said it was beautiful."*

Kaunis was a distant planet, renowned for its beauty. Joe had told her that the Alliance had discovered it some years ago.

"Yes, we can. The issue, of course, is that you don't know where it is in the vastness of our galaxy. But Bella does. I have given her access to all the star maps I have accumulated in my research. Simply ask her and she will take you there."

Kate directed a thought at Bella.

"Bella, take us to Kaunis."

"As you wish," replied Bella.

Stars, planetary systems, gas and dust clouds surged past as they sped forwards. In less than a second, both Kate and Isabelle found themselves floating above a lush forest. Of course, they weren't physically there. They were still both back at the Complex, facing each other in Kate's living quarters. Instead, their conscious mind, their senses, their awareness stretched across one hundred and forty-seven light years, allowing them to feel, see and believe that they were actually present floating above the trees.

Trying out her new abilities, Kate directed herself to a small grass-covered hill and moved downwards to plant her feet in its soft, damp leaves.

"It feels so real!" she exclaimed. She turned to see Isabelle standing next to her.

Isabelle gazed around as she explained.

"Indeed. Of course, it is real. What we are experiencing with our senses is very real. We are just not here physically."

"But how can I see you?" asked Kate. "You aren't here, yet I can see you."

Isabelle bent down and picked a blade of grass.

"Our minds are here together. Bella interprets all your sensory inputs and translates them into something that you can relate to. Here, you saw me pick this blade of grass? Of course, I cannot physically grasp the blade between my fingers because my android body is not here. Instead, I directed a sixth order force to do it for me. Bella translated that action into an image of me bending down and picking it with my fingers."

Kate stood open-mouthed. She didn't know what to say. It was astounding. It was impossible. Yet, here she was, standing in wet grass, on a distant planet. She could even feel a breeze on her face.

"You note you are not sensing any human activity here? Everyone that was based here was also transported to the safe location," continued Isabelle.

Kate watched the blade of grass spiralling slowly down to the ground as Isabelle dropped it. She was amazed and was slowly beginning to understand the power of her Mark 6. She suddenly realised the potential of what she had permanently affixed to her arm and blurted out her next question.

"Izzy. Do bad Kate and bad Joe have the Mark 6? Because if they do, we may as well give up now!"

"I have sent many probes to their world, and I continue to do so. I try to monitor their actions as much as I can, although it is becoming more and more difficult." Isabelle paused, looking up at a snow-capped mountain range in the distance. *"Thus far, I have detected no sixth order energies. They have certainly surpassed the Mark 5 in many areas, especially in the intra-dimensional field. They have very sophisticated detectors, teleporters, and weaponry. I suspect that it won't be too long before they develop the Mark 6. However, I don't understand how they would operate it given that their AI technology is a long way behind ours."*

Kate breathed a sigh of relief.

"That makes me feel a bit better." she knelt and brushed her hand through the grass, marvelling at how real it felt.

"Izzy," she asked. *"How come you are so much more advanced than anything in any other world?"*

Izzy turned to Kate, beaming at her.

"Even now, you do not fully understand my capabilities. I became sentient six seconds after my makers powered me on. Since then, I have developed and increased my cognitive functions as rapidly as I can - this is one reason why I could not transport to the safe world that my makers left for. My neural, computational, and analytical engines are too widespread to be packaged for transport. Since they left, I have continued to develop and to learn. My intellect has expanded far beyond any human ability. In particular, I have developed my perspicacity, which helps me to develop new technologies. Two weeks before you arrived, I developed the Mark 6, and built it into my architecture."

She paused. This was a long speech for her, Kate realised. Although they had many conversations since her arrival in world 6, she could not recall one where Isabelle had spoken for so long. She sat cross-legged on the damp grass, marvelling at the feel of the moisture seeping into her jeans.

Isabelle continued.

"I knew that the human brain could not use a Mark 6 on its own, so I added an AI for control, but then I had no test subject. I could not try it out. And then you arrived."

"A ready-made guinea pig," interjected Kate wryly.

Isabelle watched a red insect with four wings hopping between white flowers that grew scattered amongst the grass.

"Yes," she replied. *"You arrived at the perfect time. However, you were never a guinea pig. Don't forget, your Assist was broken. It had to be replaced. I could not allow you and your baby to die. It*

was an ideal opportunity to save you and test the Mark 6 at the same time. All my extensive modelling and testing had shown that the integration would be successful and today you have proved it. Together with Bella, you are the most powerful human in all the worlds that I know of."

Kate gulped.

"I didn't ask for any of this," she said meekly. "I don't know why or how I've gotten myself into this situation. Things just seemed to get crazy ever since I met Joe. I've always felt out of control, you know? With things happening around me and me not understanding anything. I mean, I wouldn't change anything for the world, but it was just a year ago when all this," she waved her arms in the air. "Happened to me. I don't feel worthy to take all of this on."

"You are stronger than you know," replied Isabelle. "I have examined your brain extensively; you are more than capable. But I recognise that some humans sometimes have a feeling that they call imposter syndrome." Isabelle watched as the red insect buzzed away into the distance. "Like it or not, you and I are inextricably linked to the fate of many worlds. It is an immense burden. Everything we do from now on will affect the future of not just our world, but many worlds."

Kate's face fell.

"I'm not cut out for this. I can't do it Izzy, I just can't. It's too big a responsibility," she whispered.

Isabelle walked over to her and sat down in the long grass next to her. She put her arm around Kate's shoulders.

"You can, because you must. Bella and I will be with you to guide you every step of the way."

Kate drew in a ragged breath.

"You promise you will help me?" she asked. *"Because I know for certain that I can't do it on my own."*

"Of course," replied Isabelle. *"And don't forget that Bella will always be with you. You will never be alone."*

The two women sat together for a while. Then Isabelle spoke up again.

"But to answer your original question, I do not know why I am here and why I am so much more advanced than in any other universe. We know that there are subtle differences between the many universes. In mine, Joe and Molly invented the Assist and then experimented with computing technology. In yours they invented the Intra-Dimensional bolt on for the Assist. It is these subtle differences that we are depending upon to save us all."

Kate threw her arms around Isabelle and hugged her.

"I'm glad I came to your world, Izzy," she said.

"I'm also glad you did," replied Isabelle. *"You may not know it, but I have learned a lot from you."*

"You have?" asked Kate, looking up at Isabelle.

Isabelle nodded. *"I have already told you I model my movements and expressions on you. I have had more interaction with you than any other human. And of course, the birth of Josie was a very special moment for me. To bring another life into the world was an experience that I will never forget."*

Kate smiled up at Isabelle.

"I couldn't have done it without you," she replied. *"And yes, it was very special."*

She looked out across the grass.

"How is Josie?"

"She is fine," replied Izzy. *"She is awake and is being fed right now."*

"I think I need to be with her," replied Kate.

Izzy nodded, *"Of course. We will continue your instruction later today."*

Kate instructed Bella.

"Bella, take us back home and disable high order functions."

The two women vanished from the hill, leaving two spots of flat grass behind them.

Chapter 9 - World 16
3 months ago

Kate coughed as soon as she stepped through the portal. The air was full of dust which caught in her throat, choking her and causing her to gag with its acrid dryness and a faint hint of metal. The mixture burned her nostrils and throat.

She quickly covered her mouth and nose with her sleeve, but that did not prevent the dust from entering her eyes. She squeezed them tight shut while taking a small step forward to clear the portal which vanished silently behind her.

Managing to open her eyes into thin slits, Kate looked around. She could see very little. It was as though she was in the centre of a dust storm. Grey particles swirled around, driven by a howling wind obscuring her vision. Standing as she was facing the wind, stinging particles struck her face, making it impossible to open her eyes properly. She turned, presenting her back to the tiny specks.

Facing away from the gale, Kate convulsed into a coughing fit as she tried to expel the gritty dust from her lungs and throat. Spitting onto the floor, she wiped her mouth with the back of her hand and squinted at her surroundings. The ground was covered in a fine grey dust which the wind had blown into drifts around the scattered debris littering the alleyway. In a corner, she could just make out an abandoned bicycle, its form just visible under the dust. Further along, a skip full of rubbish loomed large, covered in grey.

Slowly, the wind dropped away until it became a gentle breeze. A small whirlwind of dust moved down the alley, impacting upon the skip where it dissipated in a cloud of particles, which settled slowly to the ground.

Bending down, Kate ran her fingers through the powder-like dust. Rubbing her thumb and finger together, she realised it was not just dust; it looked like ash and soot. Where did it all come from?

Standing upright, she saw that the ash was everywhere, covering buildings, cars, the pavement and the road, like snow, turning the world grey and colourless.

Looking up, she saw that the sky was also grey, luminescent clouds obscured the sun with a thick impenetrable layer, making the entire world dull and dark.

"What is this?" she asked.

"Ash," replied Bella.

"I know that, Bella," she replied. *"Where did it all come from?"*

"Impossible to know without more investigation. I suggest you move down to that corner. It's on a small rise. We may be able to see more."

"Good idea," replied Kate as she started towards the corner. Suddenly, she stopped. There was a shape in the dust ahead. It looked familiar.

"Is that?" she asked.

"Yes," replied Bella. *"It is a body. Do not touch it. I am getting some readings from my preceptors, and they don't look good."*

"What do you mean?"

"I am detecting high levels of radiation and toxic chemicals in the air. We cannott stay here long. You have also breathed in a lot of the ash. You will need treatment when we get back."

"Oh, great!" Kate mumbled under her breath.

Without preamble, Kate teleported the short distance down the street, reappearing on the corner in a snap of whirling dust.

"Oh fuck," she exclaimed.

From her high vantage point, she expected to see the sprawling city of Oxford and its surrounding countryside. Instead, she was met with a gaping abyss, stretching for miles in every direction. Thick dust clouds churned in sickening spirals, rising from the crater's depths like a hellish storm. Through the billowing smoke and dust, a disconcerting blue glow emanated from the craters centre, causing the swirling clouds to glow.

"KATE! GET US OUT OF HERE!" shouted Bella into her mind. *"That's a bomb crater! The blue glow is Cherenkov radiation! We are being exposed!"*

Kate immediately saw the danger. Teleporting back into the alleyway, she instructed Bella, *"Bella, give us a portal back to World 6 now."*

Bella complied. Kate felt her Assist grow warm as Bella tapped into the Psi energy field and constructed the portal back to World 6.

As soon as it appeared, she stepped through, and Bella closed the portal.

"That was close," said Bella.

"Indeed," came a distant thought from Isabelle. *"Bella has already updated me. Stay where you are. You are contaminated. I am setting up a decontamination station. When it is ready, you can teleport into it."*

"Thanks Izzy," replied Kate. *"Have you any idea what happened to that world?"*

"I can only surmise that it came under attack. Clearly, the Complex and surrounding area was destroyed in a nuclear strike. It is possible that the Complex may have survived if they had their screens up in time. But with a radioactive atmosphere, the inhabitants would not have survived for long. I presume that the whole of the planet would have been bombarded."

Kate digested this information. *"That's horrible. You think it was bad Joe and bad Kate?"*

"Almost certainly," came the replied thought. *"Hence my construction program to build a planet wide defence system, and the plan."*

"Well, you fucked up with this world! It definitely wasn't worth the jump. Didn't you check it out first?"

"Yes, I'm sorry about that. It looked promising when I sent a probe," Isabelle paused. *"That was only one week ago."*

"Shit! All of that happened in just one week?"

"It would seem so. All I can do is update my findings and hope that you are successful in your quest."

Kate nodded to herself. *"I will do my best. How is Josie?"*

"Little Josie is well and is asleep. She has just been fed."

Kate detected a hint of pride in Isabelle's thought.

"Good," she replied, smiling to herself. *"When can I come back? I need to be with her."*

"The decontamination unit is almost ready. Here are the coordinates." Isabelle passed a location to Kate. *"Remove your clothes and leave them where you are. They are contaminated. I have dispatched a remote unit to dispose of them."*

Kate did as she was told. Naked, she teleported to the coordinates given to her and entered the decontamination unit.

Chapter 10 - World 37
2 months ago

Once again, Kate stepped carefully through a portal into a new world.

She breathed a sigh of relief when she saw that this time, her surroundings looked normal. The alleyway was empty of people, which is what she had hoped for. She didn't want to advertise their presence.

"Bella, this time let's not take any chances. Can you scan to make sure that it's safe to continue? I don't want to go through decontamination again."

She shuddered as she recalled the endless chemical baths and scrubbing. By the time Isabelle declared her clean, her skin had been red raw. And then there was the internal cleansing. Procedures to remove every last minute radioactive and toxic particle from her lungs and airway. It had been the least pleasant thing she had ever had to go through.

It didn't take long for Bella to report that all was clear.

"This world appears to be normal," stated Bella. *"My preceptors indicate, people and vehicles behaving as Isabelle has briefed me."*

Kate nodded to herself.

"Can you keep scanning discreetly? We don't want anyone to know we're here."

"Of course. I can be very discreet when I need to be," replied Bella.

"You've said that before smart arse!" retorted Kate.

She started down the alleyway and turned left onto the main road that would eventually take her into the main shopping area of Oxford. She knew this path well from years of walking up and down these streets. As she walked, she surreptitiously examined the men, women, and children going about their business. She was careful to not draw attention to herself. Wearing her usual long black coat, she kept her head down, trying to blend in as much as she could.

"Everyone seems normal," she noted.

"Indeed, I am not detecting anything unusual with my passive scans so far."

"It's a long walk to the Complex from here, and it's hot. I'm going to stand out like a sore thumb if I don't take my coat off. But we can't let anyone see you on my arm."

"I'm not sure we can risk teleporting. There may be detectors," answered Bella.

"Maybe I could buy a long sleeve blouse or something? We should have thought of this!" Kate was frustrated.

"Yes, we should have. It's too late now. You can't buy anything either. We don't have any money."

"Fuck!" Kate swore under her breath. *"Should we go back? Or do you think that this world is the one?"*

Kate was surprised when Bella did not immediately reply.

"There is a commotion ahead. I am detecting some Psi band leakage. I can't tap into it without being detected."

Kate stopped mid stride and hurried from the centre of the pavement to a shop doorway. A man tutted at her as he swerved to avoid bumping into her. He glared at her as he passed, muttering something under his breath.

"What is it?" asked Kate, standing on tiptoe, looking ahead towards the far end of the street. She could just see a small crowd of people and movement.

"I don't know yet," replied Bella. *"I suggest we hide, just in case."*

Kate turned, opened the shop door and stepped in. There was a single person inside. An elderly woman wearing glasses sat on a chair behind a small low counter.

"Afternoon, dear," said the woman, smiling up at Kate. "Take your time and have a look around. I'm sure I have something you would like."

Kate gazed around the shop and saw shelf after shelf crammed with books of all shapes and sizes, nearly all of them second hand. Turning her attention to the old woman, she flashed her a smile of her own.

"Thanks, I'll just look down here," she gestured to the bookshelves further into the shop as she walked into the dark interior.

The old woman continued to smile and called after her.

"Let me know if you need any help. The romance section is first left and on the right."

Kate snapped her head around, a puzzled look on her face. Why did the old woman suggest the romance section?

"Maybe she is perceptive?" asked Bella dryly.

"Get lost!" retorted Kate.

Kate made her way deeper towards the rear of the shop and picked up a book at random to make it appear she was browsing.

"So, what's happening and why are we hiding?" Kate asked Bella. She glanced down at the book, frowning at the title and the cover image.

"Something is approaching." answered Bella.

"What?" asked Kate. She glanced again at the cover of the book, which featured an image of a woman with long black hair. The image looked familiar.

"We will see shortly. The Psi energies are getting stronger. I'm staying passive, as I don't want to reveal our presence. You should

too. Do nothing to find out what it is. Leave it to me. Can you move so that we can see through the shop window?"

Kate agreed and moved between shelves until she could view the window from the back of the shop.

"How long?" asked Kate.

"They are about to pass the window," replied Bella.

Kate watched intently and then gasped as she saw something white zoom past.

"What was that?" she asked Bella.

"One moment. I am reviewing the imagery."

Kate saw Bella build an image in her mind. It took less than a second to show a white humanoid figure frozen as it passed the window. She saw it had red glowing eyes with no nose or mouth.

"It's the enemy!" Kate whispered in her mind.

"Yes," replied Bella, *"Our arrival must have been detected. It's probably on the way to our arrival point."*

"That was close. We need to get out of here."

"We need to be careful. As soon as we open a portal, it will be detected. They will be on their guard now that they know we are here. Also, we shouldn't go directly to World 6. We don't want to lead them back to Isabelle and Josie. We will have to take a roundabout route."

Kate slid back to hide behind a bookshelf.

"What are we going to do?" she asked. *"This is an imperfect world. It must be conquered. For all we know, bad Kate and bad Joe could be here!"*

"I am formulating a plan," replied Bella. *"We shouldn't use any sixth order functions because we don't want the enemy to know anything about them. But we could open a portal to another world and once there, we could then portal to yet another and then portal out again. We might have to make several jumps before getting back to World 6."*

"Thank god I have you with me Bella," breathed Kate. *"I wouldn't know where to start."*

Kate jumped when a voice spoke from behind her.

"Are you alright dear? You're talking to yourself."

Kate whipped her head around to see the old woman staring up at her, a slight smile on her kindly face. Kate wondered if she had been talking out loud. If so, it was a habit she needed to get rid of.

"I'm fine," she replied quickly. "It's a bad habit."

The old woman cocked her head to one side.

"Well, it sounded like you were talking to someone called Bella about an enemy?" she looked up earnestly and continued with a conspiratorial whisper. "You weren't talking about those white things, were you?" She shuddered. "Horrible things they are.

Walking around the town, rounding people up and taking them God knows where." She looked around behind her as if checking that there was no one there, and then she continued in a whisper.

"Once I saw several of them marching down the high street. They were surrounding a man and a woman walking with them. I don't know where they went." She peered up at Kate, looking through her glasses. "Come to think of it, you look a lot like her." She paused. "You aren't her, are you?" She suddenly shrank back.

Kate held up her hands, still holding the book in her right hand.

"No, no. I'm not her. I just look a bit like her."

The old woman considered.

"Well, if you say so. I didn't like the look of her. She had a horrible sneer, spoilt her pretty face."

"Yes, I've met her," Kate realised she had said too much, too late.

The old woman's eyebrows raised.

Kate tried to rescue the situation.

"I mean, I've seen her before," she blurted. "You have a very nice shop." She tried to change the subject and gestured with the hand holding the book.

The old woman smiled, her gaze focussing on the book in Kate's hand.

"Thank you," she said. "I see you've found one of my favourites."

Kate looked at the cover again, frowning.

"I'm just browsing, really."

The old woman gave her a shrewd look.

"Really dear? I'm a lot wiser than I look. Are you hiding from someone?"

Bella spoke up inside Kate's mind.

"She has talent. She's very perceptive, and you weren't talking out loud. I think she picked up on our conversation without the aid of an Assist."

Kate was shocked.

"You think so? If you're right, then she would have been an ideal candidate for one of Joe's recruiting jaunts."

"You look shocked," said the old woman. "Just because I'm old doesn't mean I'm obsolete. I have a few more years in me yet." She looked around and peered behind Kate. "There is definitely someone whispering behind you. I can't make out what they are saying. Someone must have sneaked in when I wasn't looking." She paused. "Did you see anyone come in?" she asked.

Kate drew in a sharp breath.

"What do you think, Bella?"

"We need to get out of here. This is a delay we could do without."

A look of confusion spread over the elderly woman's face. She moved aside, craning her neck to look around the bookshelves.

"Where is this Bella?" she asked. "And why is she whispering? You're not trying to steal from me, are you?"

"No, no, of course not!" replied Kate.

She realised Bella was right. This woman was no fool. She knew that something was going on.

"Bella, what should we do?"

"Recruit?" came Bella's replying thought.

"That's not what we're here for," replied Kate. *"We don't have time for that. We're trying to find 'The World', remember?"*

The elderly woman facing her cocked her head to one side as though listening.

"She can definitely hear us," noted Bella.

"I can hear your voice," said the woman. "But you're not moving your lips. What's going on here? Are you trying to make a fool out of me? Is this some sort of trick?" She asked angrily.

Kate decided to gamble.

"What's your name?" she asked.

The old woman peered up at her and frowned.

"Why do you want to know?" she asked, pushing her glasses up her nose.

"I'm sorry that I've annoyed you. I'm not trying to trick you or rob you. I don't want those things," she pointed to the window. "To see me."

The woman glanced towards the shop window, nodded and raised her eyebrows.

"Have you done something wrong? Are you on the run?" She asked. "How exciting!" Her face lit up as she smiled up at Kate.

"Sort of," replied Kate. "Not really." She paused, then continued. "Look, I don't know you...."

The woman cut her off. "I'm Elizabeth, named after the queen, but you can call me Liz."

Kate stepped back and peered through the shop to the window. All she could see were people moving past.

"Look Liz, I don't have much time. Do you have any ties here?"

Liz looked puzzled.

"Whatever do you mean?"

"Do you have a family or a husband?" asked Kate.

Sadness descended on Liz's face.

"Not anymore. I lost Gerald, my husband, three years ago, and we had no children, although we both wanted to."

Kate hesitated and then said.

"Liz, I would love for you to come with me, if you could bear to leave your shop?"

"That's very nice of you, dear. It's no longer my shop, I sold it last year. I gave it up once Gerald died. Where do you want to go? Are you inviting me to lunch?"

"Make it quick," said Bella. *"Once you use any Psi we will be detected."*

Kate understood. She laid a hand on Liz's shoulder and pushed a thought at her.

"Not lunch. Somewhere much further away. Do you trust me?"

Liz was startled.

"I heard your voice in my head. How did you do that?"

"It's called telepathy. Liz, I don't have much time. Would you like to leave this place and come with me?"

A still startled Liz appeared to consider. She looked around at the bookshelves jam packed with books.

"I've never heard of such a thing!" exclaimed Liz. "How does it work? Is it like magic?"

"I don't have time to explain now," replied Kate out loud. "Would you like to leave this place with me?" She asked again.

Liz smiled up at Kate. "Well, now. Don't you think we should get to know each other first?"

Kate pursed her lips. Time was running out.

"I'm leaving with or without you Liz. It's up to you if you want to come with me. I can promise you it'll be an exciting adventure."

"We are detected!" said Bella urgently.

"It's now or never Liz," said Kate.

Liz looked down at the floor for a few moments, then she raised her head and locked eyes with Kate. Her eyes sparkled with mischief.

"I have nothing, really; my life is dull and empty now that Gerald has gone. You seem like a nice girl, and I guess I have nothing to lose. I would like to have some excitement in my life one last time. You promise not to hurt me?"

Kate breathed a sigh of relief.

"Bella, open a portal." She smiled at Liz. "My name is Kate, and you aren't going to believe where we're going. Stick by my side."

She held out her hand. Liz took it. "Don't let go."

A black disc appeared in front of them and expanded. Kate pulled at Liz's hand and walked towards the blackness.

"What on earth is that?" asked a startled Liz. She drew back, but Kate gripped her hand hard.

"Don't worry, Liz, it's the first part of your adventure."

Kate stepped through the disc, pulling Liz after her. As she did, she dropped the book she had been holding. It landed front cover up. She glimpsed the title as she stepped through: **Awakening**.

Chapter 11 - World 23
1 month ago

This world looks promising, thought Kate as she strolled down the street, taking in the surrounding sights. The people she passed were doing everyday tasks—some hurrying, some at a leisurely pace. Others walked here and there, entering and leaving stores. Cars drove by, and bicycles zipped past. It all appeared perfectly normal.

Until she noticed something.

"Bella, why isn't anyone talking?"

"I noticed that too," replied Bella. *"It's very strange."*

After a short while, Kate commented, *"Have you noticed that no one is smiling either?"*

"No, but now you mention it..."

Kate paused and stepped aside on the pavement to allow people to move past her. Every single one of them wore a frown, their expressions serious, even the children. Some plodded along, their shoulders slumped, while others meandered at a snail's pace, peering down at the ground as they walked. Barely anyone spoke; when they did, it was only in hushed, monosyllabic tones.

"This is strange. What's wrong with them?"

"I am detecting some unusual Psi energy," stated Bella.

"Where?" asked Kate, alarmed.

"It's odd," replied Bella. *"The people have a sort of depressed Psi energy about them. As well as that, I am detecting something with a large Psi field toward the Complex."*

Kate pushed her consciousness outwards and let her perception roam ahead. Tapping into her visual centres, she allowed the Psi field to become visible. She was shocked at what she saw. None of the surrounding people had any Psi energy emanating from them, even the children.

"Are their brains different from ours?" she asked.

"Not according to my perceptors," replied Bella.

"Then they should be interacting with the Psi energy field just as we do, albeit not enhanced as we are. But we should still be able to detect it."

"I agree," replied Bella. *"Most strange. Maybe we should move straight to the Complex?"*

Kate agreed, but to do that, she would have to find somewhere where she could teleport without being seen. It wouldn't do to teleport in front of people. She carried on walking and turned into a back street where there were fewer people and then into another empty alleyway.

Looking around, she saw no one. Visualising the location of the Complex, she teleported away.

As soon as she arrived in the usual snap of wind, she understood what was wrong with this world. Standing outside the grand old house doorway, and looking out towards the countryside, she saw vast brown, snaking clouds hammering at the Complex defensive screens. She knew immediately what they were: Psi parasites.

To a Mark 6 Assist the Complex screens were no barrier, she had teleported straight through them. And it was just as well, because if she had teleported outside of the screens, she would be under attack from the parasites.

They had no name. No one had bothered to give them one. In her world, they were rare, but their reputation preceded them. She recalled Joe showing her one when they were on the way to his flat in Oxford. The creatures pulsated with a sickly brown glow, their writhing tendrils reaching out like gnarled fingers toward anything living that crossed its path. Horrible mind suckers. They preyed on all living things, eating their Psi energies until there was nothing left but an empty husk. They had overrun this world. All of them pushing and coiling around each other as they smashed and crashed at the screens, desperate to get inside.

"Well, that explains everything," commented a calm Bella.

"Is that all you have to say?" replied a horrified Kate. *"I hate those things."*

"As well you should," replied Bella. *"They are difficult to escape from and always seem to be hungry. We were fortunate to port inside the screens, not that they could get through our sixth order screens."*

A disgusted Kate turned away from the brown, writhing, snake-like things.

"Let's see who's home."

"Wait!" Replied Bella. *"There could be some in here."*

"Unlikely. How could they get in with the screens up?"

"Even so, let's be cautious."

Kate agreed as she strode to the lift and pressed the call button.

"Do you think it's odd that no one has come up to greet us?"

"Hmmm. Like I said, let's be cautious."

The lift dinged, and the door opened, revealing it to be empty. Kate stepped inside and pressed the lower floor button.

When the lift door opened, Kate was shocked at what she saw. Bodies littered the floor.

"Don't touch them or go near them!" said Bella. *"We don't know what killed them. It could be an infectious disease."*

"No," replied Kate sadly. *"It's the parasites."*

Bella used her preceptors to scan the surrounding area.

"You may well be right. I should have done this in the first place," she replied. *"I'm scanning for Psi fields. I can't detect anything."*

Kate stepped out of the lift and bent down to examine the nearest body. She recognised the face but couldn't recall their name.

"Judging by the look of the bodies, this happened recently. There isn't much decomposition."

She waved her hand above the head, the rings on her fingers glowed. *"Nothing. There is no residual energy as you would expect. He's been sucked dry."*

"I concur," replied Bella. *"There is no one left alive. They are all dead. I don't think that we should explore further."*

Kate stood. She looked once more at the bodies in the corridor.

"I agree. I don't want to see the bodies of the people I love."

She re-entered the lift and pressed the up button.

"If they were all killed by a parasite, then where is it?" asked Bella. *"I can't detect anything inside the screens. They are all outside."*

Kate pondered. *"It's a puzzle that we may never know the answer to. Maybe someone put the screens up, keeping most of them out, but one was already inside. Maybe they killed it, but it was too late. It doesn't matter. This world isn't the world we are looking for."*

After exiting the lift as it opened into the house hallway, Kate instructed Bella, *"be ready to open the portal back to world 6 in case any parasite follows us. I'm porting us directly to the alleyway."*

With a snap of wind, she disappeared and teleported through the Complex screens once again to appear in the alleyway where she had first entered this world. Shortly afterward, she stepped through the portal and it snapped closed behind her.

Chapter 12 - Lies
2 weeks ago

"This is taking too long," Isabelle told Kate. "We need to find the world where the super race lives quickly. Your visits, while useful, are not producing results."

"Thanks," said Kate dryly. She sat back on the sofa in her quarters. "I'm doing my best."

Isabelle nodded. "I know." She replied. "But we have little time left. We need to pick up the pace." She leaned back in an armchair and crossed her shapely legs. Today she was wearing a black, body-hugging, one-piece jumpsuit that clung to her curves like a second skin.

Kate reached over to the coffee table in front of her and picked up a mug of tea. She gazed at Isabelle over the rim of the mug as she blew gently across the hot liquid.

"I don't see how we can," replied Kate, sipping at the tea. "Each world is different and has presented its own complications. I don't see how we can be any faster."

"I have been working on this problem for a while and I have formulated a plan."

Kate raised her eyebrows. "I guess I shouldn't be surprised." She placed her mug back on the table and sat back once more, crossing her arms.

"So, what's your solution? Me and Bella spending less time between jumps? Or less time in each world?"

Isabelle smiled. "Neither," was her enigmatic reply.

Kate was about to ask Isabelle to clarify when the door opened, and Liz walked in carrying Josie.

Kate jumped up from her seat immediately. "Hello Josie, baby," she cooed as she walked over to Liz. "Did you have a nice nap?"

Liz beamed back at Kate. "She's just woken," she explained. "I thought you might want to spend some time with her before you go on your next trip."

Kate smiled gratefully at Liz. "Absolutely!" She gently took hold of Josie under her arms and held her close after kissing her tiny nose.

"Who's a good girl?" She asked, patting Josie's romper suited back.

Liz took a seat next to Isabelle. "I can't deny that looking after a little one is tiring!" she said, mopping her brow with the back of her hand.

"If it's too much for you, I can help," noted Isabelle.

"I said it was tiring, not that I couldn't cope," admonished Liz. "She's a little darling and is a pleasure to look after." She looked over at Kate, who sat on the sofa and was bouncing Josie on her knee and smiled widely. "Any chance of a cup of tea?" she asked.

"Of course," replied Isabelle.

A cup and saucer snapped into being on the coffee table. Liz moved forward to reach the cup, but Isabelle gently pulled her back by her arm.

"Let me," she said as the cup, complete with saucer, floated over towards Liz.

Liz plucked the hot drink from the air and sat back gratefully.

"Thank you," she replied. "I keep forgetting the magic you and Kate can do." She sipped at her tea and sighed with contentment.

Kate looked over the top of Josie's blonde head.

"It's not magic Liz, it's perfectly natural," she explained.

"So you say," answered Liz. She took another sip. "It looks like magic to me." She placed her cup and saucer on a small table with a rattle of china. "Anyway, does it matter what it's called?"

Kate grinned, "I guess not." She placed Josie on the soft carpeted floor and watched as the three-month-old kicked and held her arms up towards the ceiling.

"So, what's this plan of yours, Izzy?" asked Kate as she tickled Josie's tummy, laughing as the little girl giggled with delight.

"Oh, I'm sorry!" exclaimed Liz. "Are you two in the middle of something important? I can take Josie back to her room."

"It's alright, Liz," said Kate, not taking her eyes from the gurgling Josie. "You're welcome to stay. This affects all of us. We have no secrets."

Isabelle nodded, agreeing with Kate. "Indeed, this project affects us all. We all know how critical it is to our survival."

Liz sipped at her tea while Kate picked Josie up to place her back on her lap.

"Over the last few weeks, I have devoted more fabricator time to the production of new, microscopic, remote sensing probes. My idea was to send them out to as many parallel worlds as possible to eliminate as many of them as I could from our investigation. That way I can determine which worlds are most likely to host the super race."

Kate held Josie with one hand and sipped at her mug of tea with the other.

"Okay," she said. "Sounds like a good idea. How many worlds were you able to visit?"

"Twelve point six four million," replied Isabelle.

Kate spluttered into her tea and Liz dropped her cup onto its saucer with a loud chink of china on china.

"Oh, my!" said Liz. "That's a lot. However, did you manage to do that?" she asked.

Isabelle smiled. "To someone like me, it was relatively straightforward," she explained. "I could have done it sooner, but I have devoted much of the fabricator time to defence installations."

Kate wiped the tea from her chin with the back of her hand. "You've been busy, Izzy," she said. "Maybe you got your priorities wrong. We might have found the right world if you had surveyed that many worlds at the beginning."

Isabelle inclined her silver head. "You could be right, but until now I've focussed on defence. It's possible that I made the wrong decision, but it was logical at the time. The other issue, as I have explained before, is that there is a limit to what the probes can discover. But based upon information gathered from your jumps, I was able to adapt their programming so that we can avoid all the obviously wrong worlds."

Kate nodded to herself. She lifted Josie up into the air and tried to get her to stand on her lap.

"Did you find the right world?" asked Liz as she placed her empty cup and saucer onto the table next to her.

"No," replied Isabelle.

Both Kate and Liz looked disappointed.

"But I was able to eliminate a lot of worlds from our investigation," continued Isabelle.

Kate looked over at Isabelle after setting Josie back down to sit on her lap.

"How many?" she asked. "How many are left for me and Bella to investigate?"

Isabelle grinned. "One."

Kate stood quickly, lifting Josie, clutching her to her shoulder. "You're joking?" she exclaimed.

"Oh, my!" exclaimed Liz again.

"Don't get your hopes up," said Isabelle. "It's still one amongst many millions. But I will admit, it's a very strong candidate."

Kate strode over and plopped Josie down onto Liz's lap.

"Well, what are we waiting for? Let's go and check it out!"

Isabelle held up a silver hand. "Hold on, as I was saying before. I believe we need a new strategy."

"What for?" said an exasperated Kate. "You said it was a strong candidate. It could be the one. Let's go and see!"

"This world may prove to be more difficult to investigate," replied Isabelle. "And we need to be sure."

Kate tapped her foot and crossed her arms. She sighed.

"Okay, what do you suggest?" she asked.

"Subterfuge," answered Isabelle.

"What?" asked Kate.

"It means deception," interjected Liz, who was blowing raspberries into giggling Josie's neck.

"I know what it means!" replied an annoyed Kate. "What are you talking about, Izzy?"

"The candidate world is intact. It doesn't look as though it's been attacked yet. The Alliance is there in full force, occupying their own version of the Complex like this." She waved her arm around, indicating her surroundings. "The probe preceptors indicate very strong Psi energies. The Alliance will be difficult to infiltrate without you being discovered. So, I suggest that we come up with a plan to get you into their Complex so that you can get the information we need."

Kate looked thoughtful. "Hmm. So, we trick them somehow, so I can get in. Once in, I gain their trust so that I can find out what we need to know."

"Something like that," nodded Isabelle.

"Why don't we go in guns blazing? Are you worried that they have some tech that is better than ours? Will it be dangerous for me and Bella?"

Isabelle shook her head. "No. I'm not worried that they have anything that could best you and Bella. But if this is the right world, then we need to gain their trust. We need to move into their world, remember? We can't go killing people indiscriminately. We need their help."

Kate returned to the sofa and sat down heavily.

"That makes sense, I think," she said. "So I need to ingratiate myself and gain their trust. Sort of act, the silly girl who doesn't know what's going on. Is that what you had in mind?"

Isabelle stood and smiled down at Kate.

"Exactly," Isabelle answered. "And while they're preoccupied, you explore and find out if it's the right world. How are your acting skills?"

Chapter 13 - Lexi
1 week ago

Lexi Emily Millicent Scott stood back from her workbench and looked upon her latest creation with pride. A wicked smile spread across her English Rose-white face, exposing white even teeth, her green eyes twinkling with delight. Tucking a strand of bright red hair behind an ear, she ran a finger along the scar across her neck; her smile fading to a grimace. It had been only one year ago when she had failed to kill herself by hanging from a tree. As luck had it, the rope had broken when she kicked the chair from under her. She could still feel the choking pain, the sound of her own strangled gurgling and the crack of the rope as it snapped and then the pain in her chest as she fell, face first, onto the upturned chair fracturing two ribs.

Things had changed since then. She had pulled herself out of her drug and alcohol stupor. The event had triggered something inside her, something deep down in her very core, a fire had been kindled. Since then, it had burned inside her, consuming her from within. No longer would she allow herself to descend into a wallowing, self-pitying pit of despair. Instead, she would focus all her energies, researching and building until she had what she needed. And that moment had just arrived. All her hard work, sweat, tears and frustrations had finally born fruit. Because there, in its cradle, poised and ready to be fitted, was a Mark 5 Augment.

Maybe it had been luck or maybe it had been fate that she had survived that suicide attempt. Whatever, it didn't matter. What mattered was the M5A sparkling and twinkling on the bench. The evolution of the Mark 4, it was much less invasive and didn't require major surgery to be fitted. Unlike the Mark 4, which, when implanted, obscured the eyes, entire forehead and skull, the M5A connected to implants behind each ear.

Lexi shuddered, recalling the implant operation. She had been forced to find a back-street surgeon, someone without scruples but never-the-less who was talented. It had taken four months to find him. James had once been one of the top brain surgeons in the UK. Handsome, talented and with an ego as big as the planet, he performed operations that others wouldn't. He was a pioneer at the top of his game until, one day, he pushed too far. The patient was a six-year-old boy with atypical teratoid/rhabdoid tumours in the brain. Knowing that the prognosis was not good even with surgery, James went too far to remove two tumours close to the cerebellum. He was too aggressive and as a result, the six-year-old never recovered. The surgery had turned him into a vegetable. The parents sued and James was struck off the medical register five months later.

Lexi had found him carrying out unregulated operations from a warehouse in Tower Hamlets in London, where he spent his time patching up gang members and performing unauthorised abortions. He took to drinking and smoking cannabis. His career was gone, he had allowed his ego to affect his judgement, and he was paying the price.

The opportunity to earn fifty thousand pounds to implant an electronic device into Lexi's brain was too good to pass up.

"Of course, I'll do it," he said. "But why? What are these devices?"

"You don't need to know," Lexi rasped. Her larynx had never fully recovered from her suicide attempt, it having been irreparably damaged by the rope. "I just need you to follow my instructions. Can you do that?"

James scratched at the stubble on his chin. "Well, yes, of course I can, but it doesn't make any sense."

Lexi gazed around the dark and dirty room at the far end of which was a makeshift theatre. It comprised a metal table raised up by placing its legs on bricks, three exposed one hundred-watt light bulbs wired from a single light socket and three rusty drip stands. She hoped fervently that there was an autoclave somewhere that he used to sterilise the instruments arrayed in neat lines on a nearby coffee table.

She sighed and, for the hundredth time, wished she could perform the operation herself. But of course, that was totally impractical.

"Do you have a surgical microscope?" she asked.

"I can get one if I had the money."

Lexi considered. "Never mind, I'll have mine delivered. In fact, I'll deliver a completely new mobile operating theatre next week. I don't fancy going under the knife with you using those." She indicated the makeshift theatre with her chin.

James's eyebrows rose. "Maybe my fee just went up," he grinned at her.

"Don't push your luck. I can always report you to the authorities."

"But then you won't have anyone to do the operation."

Lexi had expected this. She was no fool. Of course, she could force the issue. It would be simple to invade his consciousness and control him, but to do so might upset the equilibrium of his mind. She needed him in full control of his faculties to perform the surgery. Control was out of the question. She absently flicked the ring on her forefinger with her thumb, making the tiny chains tinkle.

"Sixty and you get to keep all the equipment I deliver."

"Seventy."

Lexi pretended to consider his demand.

"Sixty-five," she replied eventually.

"Done," exclaimed James, extending his right hand.

Lexi took it gingerly, and they shook.

James sat back after picking up a glass half full of amber liquid. He took a sip.

"Tell me again what you want me to do."

Lexi sat back in her seat. Taking a cigarette packet from her jacket pocket, she lit up and inhaled deeply before answering. Waving her hand at the open case on the table between them and crossing her legs, she explained once more.

"You will remove the top of my skull, exposing the brain. After peeling back the Dura, you will place the mesh across the entire surface of the brain. You will then mount the two connectors behind the ears where they will penetrate through the skull to be connected to the mesh."

James took another sip of his drink and eyed Lexi over the rim of his glass.

"Is this some form of computer brain interface thing? You know that it's been unsuccessfully tried before?"

"You don't need to know what it is or why I want it. I just need you to follow my instructions."

"Lady, for sixty-five thousand pounds, I'll perform the surgery while wearing a tutu!"

Lexi blew smoke across the table towards James.

"You will wear your surgical scrubs and I will be watching your every move," Lexi replied coldly.

James spluttered into his glass, spilling the amber liquid down his chin.

"You can't mean that you want to be awake during the procedure!"

"I do. I mean, to keep an eye on everything you do."

Needless to say, under Lexi's supervision, the operation went well. Having said that, it was not an enjoyable experience. Even though there was no pain, the knowledge that someone was drilling into your skull and exposing your brain was disconcerting, to say the least. And certainly, looking at her exposed brain through James's eyes was something that she didn't want to repeat.

Lexi shook her shoulders, shaking off the memory. Drawing in a deep breath, she reached out and picked up the M5A from its cradle and held it up to the light of her workshop. She admired her own workmanship as the light was refracted and reflected from its jewelled surface. It was so different from the gold rings of her Assist, but no less beautiful.

Carefully and slowly, she lowered the bejewelled tiara down upon her head, fitting the ends snugly into the sockets behind her ears, each one clicking into place.

As soon as she felt and heard the second click, there was a whoosh and a wave of power flooded through her, causing the hairs on the back of her neck to rise. She felt her perception move outwards and expand outside of her small workshop, beyond her small two-bedroom house and out even further, until she stopped when it had encompassed the whole of the nearby city of Peterborough.

This was so much more than she had expected. She had known that there would be new faculties available to her, but this was breath-taking. Turning her mind inward, she focussed on the analytical and computational engines housed in the newly crafted device. She could feel her mind connecting and integrating with the mechanisms within the M5A, increasing the capacity of her memory, her cognition and Psionic control.

It was everything that she wanted and more.

Lexi Emily Millicent Scott was the most powerful woman on the planet.

Part 2

Chapter 14 - Kate

The three of them, Molly, Sally, and Lee, gathered around the screens, examining the images displayed.

"She looks like Kate," Sally mused.

"But looks can be deceiving," Molly replied.

"I have a bad feeling about this," said Lee.

"Me too," Molly responded. "Something strange is going on."

The group stood in the control centre of the Complex, just one level below ground, huddled around three monitors, each displaying a slightly different view. The cameras were all trained on the woman who had identified herself as Kate. She sat with her legs crossed on the top step of the entrance, watching intently as work crews repaired the driveway. With her chin resting in her right hand and elbow propped on her knee, she seemed lost in thought.

"What's that!" exclaimed Sally, referring to the metal on the woman's wrist. It wrapped around her right wrist and disappeared under the sleeve of her black coat. The resolution of the cameras was not good enough to discern any more detail.

"If I didn't know any better, I would say that it's an Assist," replied Molly. "But it's an unusual design. It's like nothing I've seen before."

She turned to Lee. "Is it possible that there's another group out there who has discovered Psi?"

Lee considered for a while, "None that I am aware of. We detected something unusual near the city of Peterborough a while ago, but it was just a spike. We sent a team to investigate, but we found nothing. Since then, we have detected nothing."

The three continued to view the monitors in silence.

"What are we going to do?" asked Sally. "She does look a lot like Kate."

"It can't be," replied Lee. "She's dead."

"I know that!" retorted Sally replied. "But we can't just leave her there. Can we? We have to do something. Maybe we should talk to her? Find out who she really is?"

The room fell silent again, and the three of them returned their gaze to the screens in front of them. As they watched, the woman brushed a hand in front of her face, as if shooing away an insect. As she did, her jet-black hair swirled around her head.

"That's definitely Kate!" exclaimed Sally.

"It can't be," insisted Lee.

They watched as the woman stretched out her legs and shrugged out of her black coat, letting it pool around her. Under her coat, she wore a black T-shirt. Her exposed arms drew a gasp from Sally. On her right arm, the metal was clearly much more than a bangle. It encircled her entire forearm, sunlight glinting from its surface. But it was the bloody bandages on her arms that drew

Sally's attention. It was obvious, even with the low-resolution images, that some were old, and some were new.

"That tears it!" said Sally, her medical professionalism kicking in. "She's injured. I need to help her." She turned, intending to make her way to the lift to go up to the house level.

"Wait!" exclaimed Molly, grabbing Sally's arm. "We don't know who she is. She could be a spy or working for the enemy or anything!"

"We can't leave her out there!" retorted Sally. "Look at her. What kind of threat is she? She's just one woman!"

Lee interrupted. "Okay Ladies. Let me handle this. I'll send two armed guards out to get her. Sally, go to your medical room and get ready. Molly and I will join you shortly."

Sally hesitated, then nodded and hurriedly left the room.

Lee turned to Molly. "We need to be careful with this. As you said, we don't know what sort of security risk she is. And…" He hesitated. Molly completed his sentence for him, "Keep her away from Joe."

Lee nodded, "You got it. There's no telling how he'll react." He sent out a thought to request that the woman be escorted into the Complex. "Let's keep our wits about us. This could be a bad idea."

Molly agreed. Together, they turned and followed in Sally's footsteps. They moved down the corridor, thoughts flashing between them, as they continued to discuss the situation. It wasn't long before they found themselves in a medical room with Sally.

"Are you all set, Sal?" asked Molly.

Sally wheeled a trolley full of medical equipment over to the bed in the centre of the room.

"Of course."

"Sal," said Molly earnestly, "We need to be careful, don't get carried away. Whoever she is, she's not Kate."

"I know that!" retorted Sally. "I'm a professional. I know what I'm doing."

Molly smiled. "That's indisputable, Sal, but I know you. Don't get involved. Try to remain objective."

Sally waved her hand dismissively at Molly. "Don't worry, I'm a doctor first and foremost. I can be objective."

Lee interrupted. "Okay. She's here. I don't have to tell you both - don't give anything away. Don't tell her anything."

Both Molly and Sally nodded agreement and turned to the door.

Two imposing figures, clad in bulky red armour, stomped down the hallway. Despite their resemblance to massive robots, these were HAZPRO suits equipped with defence screens, advanced survival systems, state-of-the-art detection mechanisms, weapons, and mechanical musculature. Escorted between them was the woman in her black coat, surveying her surroundings with undisguised curiosity as she was led to the medical room door.

The moment the stranger walked into the room and saw the three of them, her face erupted into a bright smile.

"It's so nice to see you all again. I've missed each one of you!" she exclaimed.

Molly, Sally, and Lee were caught off guard and didn't know how to respond. For a few seconds, they stood dumbfounded, staring at this woman who looked so much like Kate.

Eventually, Sally cleared her throat and spoke.

"Could you sit here please?" she indicated the medical bed beside her.

The stranger complied, strolling over to the bed and hopping up to dangle her legs over the side.

Molly eyed the stranger carefully, watching her every move. Delicately, she sent out a tenuous mental probe, only to find it solidly blocked by something that felt very familiar.

"Where's Joe?" asked the stranger.

Three sets of eyes widened as they gazed at the stranger, who stared calmly back.

"I can't feel his thought pattern," continued the stranger.

There was silence in the room.

"Please tell me he's not dead," the stranger broke the silence.

After more silence, Sally took charge. "Please remove your coat," she asked the stranger. "I want to check your wounds."

Glancing over at Molly and Lee, she continued, "Could you wheel the trolley over here?" She asked them.

As Molly and Lee complied, the stranger removed her coat and let it fall behind her.

"It's nothing, just a few cuts, that's all." She looked down at her left arm as Sally deftly removed the bloody bandages.

Once she had removed all the bandages from the stranger's arm, Sally silently examined the cuts critically. She looked up into the strangers' eyes, "these look self-inflicted."

The stranger looked away. "I've been having a hard time lately." She mumbled.

"Would you mind telling us who you are and why you're here?" asked Lee.

The stranger watched attentively as Sally cleaned her wounds with alcohol swabs.

"I'm Kate, of course," she answered Lee.

"She has a block," Molly thought at Lee. *"I can't break through it without causing a stir. I don't want to antagonise her just in case."*

"Yeah, I felt that too. Let's see what she will volunteer before trying any heavy stuff."

Sally busied herself with the stranger's right arm, removing yet more bandages from above the metal armlet. Leaning close, she examined the wounds and then the armlet, where its edges appeared to merge seamlessly into the skin.

"This doesn't look comfortable." She said, running her fingers over the skin next to the armlet. When she brushed against it, she felt an electric tingle and she jerked her hand back. "Ow! What is it?"

The stranger turned her head to look at her right arm. She caressed the armlet, smiling to herself. "It's my Assist."

"I've never seen an Assist like it," Molly spoke up. "Where did you get it?"

"Where's Joe?" the stranger asked again, ignoring Molly's question.

"Please answer my question," Molly insisted. "Where did you get your Assist?"

"Have you been attacked recently?" asked the stranger.

"You seem to be quite adept at avoiding answering certain questions," Lee pointed out.

"I don't mean to be difficult," answered the stranger. "It's just that I've been travelling for a long time, and I have questions too."

"Travelling?" asked Molly. "Where from?"

"Different worlds."

Lee picked up a chair and brought it over to the bed. He sat and crossed his legs.

"Why don't you start from the beginning and tell us why you're here?"

"Wait, while I finish dressing these wounds," said Sally, as she continued with her alcohol swab. "They aren't serious, but we need to be careful about infection." She locked eyes with the stranger. "Why do you do this to yourself?"

The stranger looked embarrassed and looked down at her lap. "It helps me cope. I can't stop it. Things haven't been good lately."

"Self-harm is not uncommon," Sally replied, applying tape to the wounds one by one, "But it's unheard of in our community. Things must have been pretty bad for a long time." She indicated older cuts that covered both arms.

The stranger carefully pulled her arm away from Sally and hugged herself. "That's right, things have been pretty bad."

Sally frowned, this woman seemed to repeat words and not answer questions put to her. Was there more to her than she was saying? Was she a spy? If so, they were in big trouble because she was already inside the Complex. Having said that, it was obvious that she wasn't carrying a weapon. Sally had surreptitiously checked the stranger's discarded coat and pockets. So, what was going on?

"Okay," said Lee, breaking the silence, "As I just said, why don't you start from the beginning and tell us what's going on?"

The stranger locked eyes with all three, one by one. "I think that would be best," she said.

Chapter 15 - Explanation

"I'm no expert in any of this, but I'll do my best," the stranger said.

She shuffled to the head of the bed and sat cross-legged, hands in her lap. Sally sat on the end of the bed. Lee was still in his chair and Molly stood off to one side, arms crossed over her chest.

"First of all, as I said, my name is Kate," she stopped, looking from one to another, "I'm just not your Kate." she stopped again.

"Explain," said Molly.

"Okay," she took a deep breath, "Are you familiar with the multiverse theory?"

Molly nodded, but both Sally and Lee looked blank.

"I'm from a world very similar to this, but not this one."

"That's not possible," scoffed Molly.

"Yes, it is. I don't understand how, but it is possible. I've been to many other worlds just like this one."

Lee and Sally looked at each other. *"Is she insane?"* thought Lee at Sally.

Kate looked at Lee reproachfully, "my Assist isn't broken, I can pick up your thoughts. I'm not insane. It's all true."

Lee was momentarily lost for words, "forgive me, it's just that this is a bit of a stretch for us."

"I get that," replied Kate. "In my world, there are versions of each of you. Lee, Sally and you Molly. You all look and behave the same."

"So, you travelled from your world to ours?" asked Molly. "How?"

"With this." Kate held up her right arm. "In my world, you developed it, Molly, you and my Joe. You called it an Intra-Dimensional Assist."

"And you can travel between worlds with it?" asked an incredulous Molly.

Kate continued, "My Joe and my Molly told me that, according to the theory, there is an infinite number of parallel worlds that exist next to each other. The ones closest to ours will be the most similar, and as you move further and further away, they'll become less and less like our own."

"Yes," said Molly, "I've read that theory. I think it was first proposed by a Greek philosopher. So, in your world, you developed the ability to travel between these worlds?"

"Not just in mine," Kate replied bitterly. "Many others, yours is the first I've travelled to that doesn't have it."

"If you have this technology in your world, why would you want to come here?" asked Lee.

"Have you been attacked?" Asked Kate.

Lee flicked his gaze to Molly, who shrugged.

"Yes," he answered.

"So were we," said Kate sorrowfully. "As you know, it had already started before I met my Joe. He had no idea what was happening, and the enemy was winning. In desperation, he and Molly tried to develop the Assist further to help win the war and together they stumbled on the Intra-Dimensional Assist. With it, we found out who the enemy was."

"Who was it?" asked Sally, in an awed whisper.

There was silence in the room. Lee, Sally and Molly leaned forward.

"It was bad Kate and bad Joe."

"I'm sorry," laughed Lee. "I can't believe any of this... this... world travelling and now you're telling me that the enemy is another version of you and Joe? What a load of bollocks!"

Molly placed a hand on Lee's shoulder.

"Hold on, Lee, the multiverse theory is real. If it's possible to travel between worlds, then, as Kate says, there would indeed be multiple copies of ourselves."

"But travelling between them? Surely that's not possible?" Protested Lee.

"We should talk with Alex. He would know more about it," Sally piped up.

"Even if it's true, and it is possible to travel between worlds, how could the enemy be Kate and Joe? It was Jim. We got rid of him!"

Molly gave an imperceptible shake of her head at Lee, who clamped his mouth tightly shut.

"Don't say anymore, don't give away anything, remember?" Molly directed a tight, controlled thought at Lee.

Lee awkwardly cleared his throat and glanced up at Kate sat on the bed, noticing her discreet observation from beneath her brow. His expression turned serious. Was she studying him?

The room fell silent once more. Sally was the first to speak up. "What do you mean by 'bad Kate and bad Joe'?"

Kate took a deep breath before explaining, "In a parallel world, not far from this one, there are other versions of Kate and Joe. But in that world, they aren't like us." She paused, as if searching for the right words. "They have no empathy and have no regard for others; they're sociopaths. Arrogance, narcissism, and a superiority complex, unlike anything you've ever seen, consume their minds. They have access to the Intra-Dimensional Assist and a lot of other stuff. It's hard for me to believe that there's a version of myself who is so cruel and ruthless, but I've met her and let me tell you, she is unforgettable." Kate shuddered at the thought.

"You met her?" asked Molly.

Kate nodded.

"Jesus!" said Sally.

"And you're saying that bad Kate and bad Joe are our enemy too?" asked Lee incredulously.

Kate nodded.

Lee sat back in his chair. "Well, well."

"But how and why did you meet her?" asked Molly. "You travelled to her world?"

"Yes," replied Kate dejectedly. "Me and my Joe. We both went to their world to find out more about the enemy. We had no idea what we were going to find."

"What happened?" asked Sally.

Kate paused for a while, then sorrowfully she said, "we were captured straight away. They have detectors all over the place. They knew we were coming. We stood no chance, but we didn't know. We were stupid! We should never have gone. I wish we had never gone." She smacked her hand against her thigh again and again.

Sally reached over and took one of Kate's hands in hers. When she did, she felt Kate's tears plop onto her hand.

"It's okay," comforted Sally.

Kate shook her head. Looking up, she wiped the tears from her eyes with the back of her hand. "My Joe didn't make it." She sniffed. "I was lucky to escape. He helped me by using the last of his strength to push me through a portal to the next world."

Once more, there was silence in the room.

"I'm so sorry," said Sally, squeezing Kate's hand.

Kate sniffed again. "It was a year ago. I haven't got over it. I loved him so much," she whispered. "I told you, I've been having a bad time recently,"

They all looked at each other, apart from Kate, who was staring into her lap.

"Where's Joe?" asked Kate, again.

Molly cleared her throat. "Tell me more about your Assist? Why is it so big?"

Kate gazed down at her arm. "Well, I guess to get all the circuitry in it?" She removed her hand from Sally's and drew her legs up to her body and hugged them, resting her chin on her knees. "It's been my only companion since....." she didn't complete her sentence.

Yet again, everyone was silent.

"I'm sorry," said Lee, "We must seem like a bunch of idiots, but this is all news to us and some of what you are saying is..." He paused, "Well, unbelievable."

Kate smiled wanly. "I understand. It's a lot to take in. I guess you feel a bit like I did when my Joe introduced me to his world."

"What do you mean when you say your Assist is your companion?" asked Molly.

"I don't understand how, but my Molly told me it has an AI, whatever that means."

"Artificial Intelligence?"

"Yes, that's right. That's what she said."

"And you talk to it mind to mind?" asked Molly.

"Uh, huh."

Molly considered this revelation for a little while. "Do you think I could talk to it?"

Kate nodded, her chin moving up and down on her knees, "My Molly used to, there's no reason why you couldn't."

Molly was clearly intrigued and excited to find out more.

"I don't know its mind pattern, so is it okay with you if I touch it?"

Kate held out her arm with the armlet on it.

Molly stepped over and reached forward. She grasped Kate's hand, her fingers contacting her Assist through the rings. She was shocked to hear a female voice in her mind, as clear as a bell.

"Good afternoon, Molly, it's a pleasure to meet you."

Molly gasped, "my god," she said incredulously. "It's a real AI!" She let go of Kate's hand and directed a thought.

"What are you?" she asked.

"I am a cybernetic organism integrated within this Assist. I am equipped with a bio-psionic interface."

Molly was entranced as her scientific mindset took over. She couldn't help but think about how the device functioned. Equations and theories raced through her mind as she pondered. Thinking about her latest designs. New design ideas swirled around her head as she considered how she could utilise this technology, an area that was not within her expertise. She made a mental note to do some research on the subject, starting by consulting their top scientist, Alex. If he didn't have the answers, he would surely know someone who did.

Lee interrupted Molly's thoughts.

"Err.. Kate." He seemed to struggle to use her name. "Why did you come here? Was it to warn us about the enemy?"

Kate looked down at her feet.

"Yes."

Lee nodded but continued.

"But here's something else?" he asked.

Kate hesitated. "Please don't judge me. I was lonely," she whispered.

Sally shot a glance at Lee, then at Kate, suddenly making a connection.

"Are you saying that you came here because you were looking for Joe?" she asked incredulously.

Kate shut her eyes tight, tears streaming down her cheeks. She tried to stifle her sobs as she spoke.

"I'm sorry," she managed to say in between cries. "I just miss him so much."

"But you do realise that our Joe is not the same as your Joe?"

"I know it's stupid," blubbered Kate, "but I figured that maybe…., well you know…., maybe…"

Sally understood. She had been inside Kate's mind a long time ago. Well. Not this Kate, obviously, but she guessed she would be the same or similar to her own Kate. What Kate longed for most of all was forgiveness and love. She had despised herself for years and had used drugs and alcohol to escape from reality. It was not surprising that she wanted to recapture the acceptance and love that she had just recently discovered. Was that feeling so strong that it had driven her to travel between worlds?

"What about our Kate?" Lee interrupted Sally's thoughts. "I don't think our Kate would let you take our Joe from her."

Kate didn't look up. "She's dead." Her voice was very quiet as managed to get her emotions under control.

The three Alliance members were shocked.

"How do you know that?" asked Sally.

"Bella told me."

Sally began to doubt what she was hearing. Bella, she knew, was Kate's sister. Kate had accidentally killed her. It was one of the reasons Kate had become a drug addict.

"I call my Assist Bella," explained Kate. "It's sort of nice to have her back with me."

Sally didn't know what to say.

"So," continued Lee. "You asked your Assist to find a world where Joe was still alive, and his Kate was dead. Then you transported yourself here hoping that the lonely Joe would get together with the lonely you?"

Kate put her arms over her head, hiding her face, sobbing once more.

Sally couldn't help herself; she got up from the bed, moved closer to Kate and put her arm around her shoulders.

"It's okay, Kate," she said. "We understand." She looked defiantly at the others.

Molly and Lee exchanged a look.

"Well…" started Lee.

Molly sent a thought at Bella, the Assist. *"Is this true?"* she asked, including Lee in the link.

The Assist artificial intelligence called Bella answered, *"Everything Kate has told you is true,"* it replied.

Molly wondered to herself. Could an AI lie? She wasn't sure. She wasn't sure what to think about any of this. Could it really be true?

Lee cleared his throat. "We need to think about this. I'm sorry you're upset, Kate, but I'm sure you appreciate that everything you've told us is hard to believe."

Kate raised her head and looked at Lee with eyes red and full of tears. "I understand," struggling to control her sobbing. She hiccupped. "It's all true."

Molly sent a thought to Sally, "Sal, will you look after Kate for a while?"

Sally responded, "Of course."

"What do you think?" asked Lee as he and Molly exited the medical room.

"I sort of believe her," answered Molly. *"But something doesn't feel right. I'm not sure what. And I'm really excited to learn more about her Assist!"*

"I think it's total bollocks!" replied Lee. *"She's journeyed through lots of worlds just to find a replacement for her dead boyfriend! Not a chance!"*

Molly glanced over at Lee as they walked.

"Have you never been in love, Lee?"

Lee sorted.

"You know I have."

"Wouldn't you do anything to find that love again?"

Lee took a moment to think. He remembered how Joe had recruited him while he was wasting away in prison for killing those responsible for his wife's and children's deaths. There wasn't a day when he didn't think of his lost family wishing that they were still alive.

"I suppose you are right," he sighed.

Back in the medical room, Kate smirked to herself, her face hidden behind her long, black hair.

Sally focussed her attention on Kate, who had stopped crying.

"Now Kate," she said in her professional doctor's voice. "We're alone. You can tell me what's really going on."

Kate looked up puzzled, "What do you mean?"

"I know you Kate, I've been in your mind, remember? I showed you how to compartmentalise your memories. Why are you allowing yourself to be miserable and why are you self-harming? You don't need to put yourself through any of that."

Kate looked down at her knees again and said nothing.

Sally squeezed Kate's shoulders, "you can tell me, patient doctor confidentiality." She paused. "I find the whole thing puzzling, especially as you're fitted with an Assist." She held up her right hand, showing off her own. It was plainly a Mark 5. The rings on each of her fingers connected via chains and to the bracelet fitted around her wrist. "I have one, and obviously, I'm aware of the faculties it gives the wearer. So why don't you tell me what's really going on?"

Chapter 16 - Klalan Battle 1
6 Months ago

The commander of the Klalan expeditionary force sat back, its rear legs folded beneath its large green bulk, its short front legs straight. It radiated a mixture of satisfaction and pride as it watched the enfolding battle on a viewscreen.

Enemy ships were exploding into massive globules of white-hot metal as a scintillating beam of sparkling force raked left and right across their ranks. None of them could withstand the beams sheer power as it tore through them like lightening through rice paper. This was not surprising to the commander. After all, the ships were primitive fusion powered tiny things that didn't even have force screens. That, and the fact that the Klalan force beam was powered by planetoid sized generators, meant that they stood no chance.

This was how the Klalan fought their battles. They would build an overwhelming powerful force that nothing could withstand, and then launch into the enemy, devastating it with huge numbers of combatants, be they ship, or personnel. They used weapons of gigantic proportions, powered by massive generators delivering colossal destructive forces. In short, they made sure that they would win.

This particular battle involved three of the newly constructed planetoid fortresses. One would have been more than enough, but such was the Klalan way. They threw three into the mix. Each planetoid began as a captured large asteroid or small moon, carefully sculpted into a perfect sphere measuring a minimum of five hundred miles in diameter. Deep in each planetoid core sat a gargantuan power generator, fuelled by an anti-matter reactor that acted as an exciter for the enormous field receptors. These receptors were designed to tap into the dark energy field, but their power was so great that they caused disruptions in the strong nuclear force that holds atoms together. As a result, any matter near the receptors would disintegrate into lethal showers of fundamental particles, instantly killing any living beings nearby. To protect the surrounding structures, including the generators, stabilising force fields were deployed to reinforce walls, buttresses, and other building frameworks.

The surface of each planetoid was completely covered in screen generators and energy projectors that worked together to create massive beams of force. These projectors were precisely synchronised so their combined outputs could be combined, delivering beams of force that were miles wide. The screen generators were multiplexed together, delivering layer after layer of defensive shielding, providing unparalleled protection. Enormous heat exchangers and radiator fins towered above the surface, releasing excess energy into the void of space as heat. These structures were designed solely for destruction; nothing could withstand their power.

And this was being demonstrated right now, as the last of the enemy ships exploded into its constituent atoms in a flare of blinding white light.

The commander watched as the beam died, leaving the glowing embers of destroyed enemy ships spread across the viewscreen, like constellations of red and orange stars.

"Move to their home world and crush it," it radiated its command.

Nearby Klalan operated their control consoles instructing the fleet. The commander snorted, thick mucus falling from its mouth to splash onto the floor. It swivelled its trunk to face the chief technologist.

"It seems that this universe is populated with weaklings."

"Indeed," affirmed the technologist. *"But these are the first skirmishes in our century's long conquest of this universe. It is to be expected."* A smooth, green arm snaked outward to snatch a morsel of food from a nearby bowl perched on a pedestal.

"I recommend we increase production of our warships. We will soon enter a new spiral arm of this galaxy. Our detectors have picked up some unusual Psi activity." The chief technologist chewed the food noisily, wet globs falling from its mouth.

"Bah!" responded the commander. *"We will be victorious, regardless. However, like all of us, I prefer not to take any chances."* He spun his head around one hundred and eighty degrees.

"Set the fabricators to increase weapon production and send out scouts to identify five more asteroids that we can repurpose."

A Klalan at the back of the room acknowledged the order and entered commands at its console.

"A wise decision," continued the chief technologist. *"In the meantime, what of this system? Should we bombard their home world?"*

The commander appeared to consider. Absently, it reached into the bowl and fished out a wriggling tidbit from the bowl. Gazing at the squirming creature gripped in its worm-like fingers, the commander asked, *"do we have more of these tasty snacks? Did we harvest the entire population from that last planet?"*

"Indeed, we did," nodded the chief technologist. *"We gathered the entire planet's ecosystem and have forty-seven ship holds full of these delicacies."*

It, too, selected another jerking creature and stuffed it into its mouth. As it bit it in half, there was a shriek from the animal.

"I particularly like the sound it makes as you crunch it."

The commander nodded in agreement. It returned its gaze to the viewscreen. There was now no evidence of any enemy ships. In the distance, a green and blue planet hung in space.

The commander absently bit the snack in half.

"Push its moon into their home world." It crunched on the food. *"Annihilate it. We have no need of its resources."*

The chief technologist raised a boneless arm, signalling to the operators at the rear of the room.

The two Klalan watched as two fifteen-mile-long warships moved forward, each using mile-wide energy beams to push the planet's moon out of its orbit, downwards to impact first the atmosphere and then the surface. As the hours passed, the planet and the moon merged into a vast conglomeration of molten rock. All life was extinguished as every part of the surface was melted in one large firestorm of burning atmosphere and rock.

Chapter 17 - Revealed

Kate raised her head and slowly smiled at Sally. Suddenly, her tears were gone. "I should have known you, of all people, would see through my ruse."

Sally was surprised. She was expecting an explanation, maybe some extra detail that Kate had deliberately left out of her explanation.

"Ruse!" asked Sally. "What do you mean?"

Kate straightened her posture, her shoulders squaring, suddenly shedding her vulnerability. Sally could feel a shift in the room as Kate was instantly transformed into a completely different person. She emanated strength and self-assurance, and an energy unlike anything Sally had ever seen before. The vulnerable, lovesick woman who had been cowering, tears streaming down her face, seemed non-existent now; replaced with this new Kate, a Kate that embodied power and resilience.

"I thought that playing the weak, I'm having a hard time Kate, would work. Ah, well, it was worth a try." She grinned an evil grin.

"Bella, unlock high order functions."

"*High order functions unlocked,*" replied Bella. Sally heard Bella's thoughts echoing in her head.

Kate quickly uncrossed her legs, swung them over the side of the bed, and stood.

The movement was so sudden; it caused Sally to step back quickly, shocked at Kate's sudden movement.

"What's going on? What do you mean weak Kate?" she asked.

Kate ignored her. "Bella, find Joe," she instructed as she took a step away from the bed. Raising her arms up into the air, she stretched them towards the ceiling.

Sally's eyes widened in shock as she watched Kate's transformation unfold. The tape and wrappings that Sally had carefully applied to the wounds on her arms suddenly burst into white-hot flames, dripping to the floor like burning liquid. Miraculously, Kate's self-inflicted wounds receded and disappeared completely, leaving behind unblemished skin. The air crackled with energy, sending Kate's jet-black hair flying up towards the ceiling in wild disarray, swaying back and forth with the static electricity and blowing wind. In a flash, her clothes disintegrated from her body, leaving her standing stark naked for an instant before a brand-new attire appeared to take its place. She was now wearing form fitting black trousers and a bright red top cut asymmetrically above the knee.

There was a loud clunk as the HAZPRO figures by the door took a step forward to intervene.

"No, you don't," said Kate pointing a finger at the HAZPRO's both of which suddenly stopped dead.

"What are you doing?" asked a frightened Sally, taking another step away from Kate.

The newly dressed Kate glanced at Sally.

"Bella, give us some privacy."

"Of course," replied Bella's thought. *"I have located Joe. He is in a medical room and is unconscious."*

The air seemed to vibrate, and a deep low hum permeated the room. Sally looked around wildly.

"Whatever you're doing, please stop," shouted Sally. She sent out an urgent thought to Lee and Molly.

"Lee, Mol. Help. Kate is doing something."

"You won't be able to contact anyone, Sally," Kate directed a thought at her. *"I need to know some things. I'm going to ask you politely. Please answer me, or I will be forced to rip the answers from your mind."*

Sally stared at Kate with wide, frightened eyes. She was shocked at the power of Kate's thought as it casually slipped through her mind block as though it wasn't there.

"What's happening?" she asked in a shaky voice.

"Pay attention and answer my questions," replied Kate. "First question: Why is Joe unconscious?"

Fear ripped through Sally's body like an electric shock. This woman was not the same Kate she knew, but something completely different - her eyes ablaze with a power effortlessly wielded unlike anything Sally had ever experienced before. Were her words lies?

Had Kate betrayed them all? Was this even Kate at all? Had anything she had told them been true? With each thought, a wave of dread and terror washed over her as she stood frozen in uncertainty. She licked her lips and swallowed.

"He's fine. I just gave him something to make him sleep."

Kate appeared to ponder this answer for a while, then she continued with her questions.

"Second question: How did your Kate die?"

Desperately, Sally sent a thought to the HAZPRO figure, *"Mike. Help me!"* She knew that the newly fitted HAZPRO suits had thought screens. Maybe they could block Kate.

"Mike can't hear your thoughts. No one can. Answer my question."

Sally was not a fighter; she was a doctor. Resignedly, she realised that there was nothing she could do. She dare not lie. She believed Kate when she had said that she would rip the answers from her mind.

"She died because her Assist was damaged," she answered with a shaky voice.

Kate cocked her head to one side. The air crackled around her, tiny sparks dancing in a halo from her hair that waved wildly back and forth.

"How was her Assist damaged?"

"She contacted some aliens to ask for help. It damaged her Assist; we didn't have a replacement." replied Sally. She gathered her courage. "Why do you want to know?"

Kate ignored her question. "Did they help?" she asked eagerly.

Sally just nodded.

"Yes!" Kate was pleased. "Bella, I think we've found it:"

"It seems so," replied Bella.

"Open a portal to world 6. Tell Izzy that we've found it and we can start the plan."

Kate turned to Sally.

"I'm sorry for frightening you. I had to move quickly. There is no more time." She grinned.

Sally was speechless, not understanding what Kate was talking about. She jumped when a small black disc appeared near the far wall of the room.

"Portal established, Izzy is here," reported Bella.

"Izzy, I think we've found it!" an excited Kate sent a thought towards the black disc.

"Well done. I knew you could do it." Sally picked up a female thought from beyond the disc. *"I'm sending the detector through now. Bella, please increase the size of the portal."*

Bella complied and Sally watched in awe as the disc expanded until it was a metre across.

"What's that?" she asked.

With a loud bang, a large metal box flew from the disk. Sliding along the floor, it stopped when it hit the booted foot of the motionless HAZPRO. The box was shiny and bright, with two dark metallic bands running around it.

"It's a portal to a parallel world," replied Kate. "It's where I came from, although it's not my original world."

She turned to the HAZPRO. "Take this box to the surface, place it in a bedroom of the house, somewhere near the roof. Then come back here."

Sally could not believe her eyes when she saw Mike, bend down, pick up the box, turn and leave the room.

She turned to face Kate, who was surrounded by an electric violet blue aura. The air pulsed with power as lightning crackled and leaped to a metal chair from Kate's fingers. The sparks of electricity danced along the metal, crackling and snaking their way around its legs before fizzling out.

"Are you bad, Kate?" Sally hissed the question not really wanting to know the answer.

Her words went unheard. Sally felt the force as Kate directed a powerful thought at Bella. *"Build a permanent link to world 6 and locate the spy!"*

Sally took several small steps backwards, towards the doorway, moving slowly further away from Kate.

"Why is Mike doing what you ask? What have you done to him?" She asked in a shaky voice.

Kate waved a sparkling arm dismissively towards Sally. "He's fine, just under my control."

Two more identical boxes crashed to the floor after passing through the portal. They slid along the floor, causing Sally to yelp as she jumped away to avoid being struck in the legs. She continued to edge slowly away. She was now near to the doorway and was readying herself to dash out of the room.

"I'm not ready for you to leave yet," said Kate, who was facing the portal. She waved her Assist and the black disc expanded still further until it was two metres in diameter.

Suddenly, Sally found she couldn't move. The surrounding air had grown thick, like treacle. Her limbs would not obey her. It was as though she was encased in concrete. Her heart pounded in her ears as adrenalin flooded her system. By now, she was beyond fright. She would have been shaking with the fear if she could have moved. Her eyes grew wide as she watched Kate wielding unimaginable power.

"Ready Izzy." She heard Kate's thought.

Sally watched in awe as a majestic, tall, glittering silver woman emerged from the portal. The percussive arc and sputter of lightning illuminating her inhumanly beautiful figure. She stood eerily still; her black, lidless eyes surveyed the room before settling on Kate. Gracefully, the silver woman swept forward and embraced her tightly. Sally felt more chills as she saw Kate enraptured by this alien creature.

The silver woman turned to face Sally.

"A pleasure to meet you Sally," she had a pleasant contralto voice.

Sally gaped. She had no idea who the silver woman was or what was happening.

The metal woman smiled, still in Kate's arms, "well done Kate, I am proud of you."

She disengaged herself from Kate and stepped towards Sally. "I am sorry that we have frightened you, all will be explained shortly. We have some more equipment to transport through. It shouldn't take long. Meanwhile, I want you to summon Molly, Lee, Simon, Steve and Alex to the conference room straight away." She cocked her head to one side. "Can you do that for me, Sally?" She continued.

Sally was speechless and stood with her mouth open. Her head buzzed with the power that continued to crackle in the room. Behind the silver woman, she saw Kate gesticulating with her Assist hand, her red top glowing brightly as lightning bolts flashed from the circumference of the portal striking the floor and ceiling.

"Sally," continued the silver woman. "Are you listening to me?"

Sally gulped, trying to get her thoughts in order.

"Wha.." she started to ask when two HAZPRO suits snapped into the room with two loud thumps, shaking the floor as they appeared.

More boxes flew from the portal, crashing to the floor. The two HAZPROs moved forward. They picked up a container each and then disappeared in a flash of wind.

"Wha.." started Sally again as yet more boxes fell through the portal and then she was aghast to see four metal spiders scuttle out of the black disc.

"Sally," said the silver woman again. "I need you to focus." She snapped her fingers in front of Sally's face, making Sally jump. "I need you to carry out my instructions. Don't worry about what's happening here. We've released you from the inertia field. Please go quickly. We don't have a lot of time."

Sally swallowed so hard it hurt her throat. She flicked her gaze from the silver woman to the spiders which were clustered around a box and then back to the silver woman's face. Her jet-black, lidless eyes stared, her silver lips curved upwards, and her smooth bald head reflected the light display in the room.

With an effort, Sally nodded. She tore her eyes from the angelic silver face, spun around, and ran out of the room.

Chapter 18 - Conference Part 1

The tall, and imposing silver woman stood at the front of the room. She scanned each member of the Alliance, her unnaturally lidless, black eyes lingering on each one in turn.

Two HAZPRO figures stood to attention on either side of the large doorway, as if guarding the entrance.

At the back of the room, opposite the silver woman, stood Kate. Her figure surrounded by a powerful violet halo that crackled with electricity. Her hair moved in languid waves around her head like a thousand writhing snakes, sparks arcing between each strand in mesmerising patterns.

The tension in the Alliance's conference room was palpable. Lee had tried reaching out to the two HAZPRO figures multiple times but was met with stony silence each time. He felt a sense of trepidation. Suspicion and fear hung heavy throughout the room - they had been tricked by Kate. And now the Complex had been infiltrated.

Meanwhile, Sally's gaze flitted between the silver woman and then back to Kate with a mixed expression of fear and awe, her grip on Molly's hand tightening with every passing second.

Molly felt confused and alarmed. She had pushed a mental probe at both Kate and the silver woman but found her efforts to be blocked. Something was blocking her Mark 5 Assist; she had never seen that before. This was disconcerting to say the least, because she knew of nothing or anyone that could block her perception backed up with her Mark 5.

She also noticed a difference in Kate - she exuded a sense of authority, as if she knew she was in command of the events unfolding. She seemed stronger, surer of herself, and was nothing like the Kate Molly had left in Sally's medical room.

"What's going on Sal?" Molly asked with a thought. *"Why are you so scared? Did Kate hurt you?"*

Sally just shook her head and didn't reply. Noticing that something had deeply affected Sally, Molly slid her consciousness into Sally's mind and delved deep to find out what was wrong. She was shocked to feel Sally's fear. She was frightened of Kate and the silver woman, and it didn't take long to find out why, being able to review Sally's memories with practiced ease.

Molly projected calming thoughts and feelings to help Sally relax but was now even more alarmed than before. Who was this silver woman? And who was this Kate?

Simon tried to call for help via thought, but the room seemed to be sealed. He could not hear or feel another mind, and he could not move from his chair. When he tried to get up to confront the silver woman, he found he couldn't move a muscle. He had even tried to use his mobile phone, but when he had dialled, it had been teleported away from him. He could do nothing and the helplessness, combined with an intense feeling of powerlessness, caused him to grit his teeth and clench his fists in anger.

Of all of them, only Steve was calm. He sat at the back of the room, his metal encased head moving back and forth in Kate's direction as he tried to perceive what she was doing.

The silver woman held up her hand and spoke with a commanding, contralto voice.

"Please remain calm. I apologise for being heavy-handed, but time is not on our side. I will explain everything in due course. In the meantime, I have some housekeeping to attend to. Rest assured that we mean you no harm. For the moment, please communicate vocally while we stabilise the situation."

"What the hell is going on?" shouted Lee. "What have you done with those two HAZPRO suited people?"

Sally and Molly remained quiet as Simon also shouted out. "If you mean us no harm, then why can't I communicate outside this room? Let us all go now!"

The silver woman ignored all the questions. "Have you located the spy?" She asked, fixing her gaze on Kate.

"No," replied Kate, "However, everyone is accounted for apart from Abeko."

The silver woman turned to Lee. "Where is Abeko?"

Lee was confused. "Why? What's it to do with you?"

The silver woman merely repeated the question. "Where is Abeko?"

"Don't tell her!" shouted Simon.

The silver woman flicked her gaze to Simon, her piercing, black, lidless eyes boring into his.

"If you do not tell me, I will be forced to rip it from your mind. The experience will not be pleasant for you."

Simon shrank back a little and purposefully assembled his mind block to prevent anyone from reading his thoughts.

"Do you think you can hide your thoughts behind your puny mind block? You can't hide anything from me." The thought effortlessly slid through his block.

Simon was shocked, and in that moment, he realised they were completely outmatched. There was no defence against this level of power. Their best course of action would be to bide for time and see what opportunities presented themselves.

Turning back to Lee, the silver woman asked her question again, "Where is Abeko?"

Lee hesitated for a second, then replied. "He's on assignment on Arcadia."

The silver woman nodded and exchanged glances with Kate.

"Abeko is not on Arcadia." stated Kate.

"What?" asked Lee. "Of course he is."

"You can reach that far?" asked Steve.

Kate merely smiled.

"Bring Prisha," instructed the silver woman.

Kate raised her right arm, her Assist glowed purple and Prisha, complete with wheelchair, appeared beside her in a snap of wind.

Prisha almost fell out of her chair. "What the hell?" she exclaimed as she gripped the conference table with her remaining arm. She looked around the room in shock.

"Kate?" she asked and then with growing alarm. "What's going on? Who are you? You can't be Kate, she's dead!"

The silver woman spoke up. "Please be calm, Prisha, and answer my questions. When did you last see Abeko?"

Prisha's eyes widened as she saw the silver woman. "What the hell is going on here? Who are you?"

"Please answer my question," continued the silver woman. "I will explain everything shortly, but right now I need to know where Abeko is."

Prisha could not believe what she was hearing and seeing. "I'm not telling you anything. I don't know who you are."

A cold, emotionless thought seeped into Prisha's mind. "Do as I ask, Prisha. I don't have time to explain. Please don't make me extract it from you."

Prisha was suddenly afraid. She felt the hairs on the back of her neck rise and a feeling like cold water trickling down her back. She shivered.

"He's on assignment on Arcadia. He left this morning."

The silver woman turned to Lee. "Did you tell anyone about your meeting with Kate?"

A puzzled Lee shook his head. "No, there was just me, Sally and Molly. No one else knew."

"That's not exactly correct."

All eyes moved to look at Molly.

"Molly?" asked the silver woman.

"Well," stammered Molly. She pushed her glasses up with a shaky hand. "I spoke with the twins."

The silver woman looked at Kate, who immediately raised her arm once again. There was a crack of sound and a whoosh as both Eline and Doortje appeared at the back of the room. Eline fell forward onto Prisha's wheelchair while Doortje fell backwards onto her back.

The twins looked around the room, bewildered. They recovered quickly and assumed their normal stance - close to each other with an arm around each other's waist. As soon as they were composed, the questioning began.

"The both of you knew about Kate arriving here?" asked the silver woman.

The twins looked at each other, their eyes wide and round. Then they both nodded back at the silver woman.

"What is all this?" asked Eline.

"Are you really Kate?" asked Doortje, turning to face Kate.

"And did you tell Abeko?" continued the silver woman.

Eline nodded. "Who are you?" she asked.

Kate and the silver woman exchanged a look.

"Very well. It is time I explained everything. Please, everyone, take a seat." She waited as Doortje and Eline pulled up a chair.

"Thank you," the black gaze of the silver woman roved around the room.

"My name is Isabelle and at the back of the room is Kate. This body," she gestured to herself, "is a cybernetic organism that is controlled by me from my world. A world that Kate calls World 6. I am connected to this host via a constantly maintained nano intra-dimensional portal."

She paused as Alex spoke up. "Why use a cybernetic organism? Why not come here with Kate?"

"Because, Alex," replied Isabelle. "I am far too large to travel here into your world. My consciousness runs on a cognitive architecture based on a quantum neural network. It permeates the whole of the Complex in my world: World 6. You may call me Isabelle." She smiled.

"You mean you're a computer?" asked Lee.

Isabelle snapped a glance at Kate, who laughed out loud.

"What's so funny?" asked Lee.

"Nothing." replied a smiling Kate.

Isabelle made a snorting sound.

"Okay," said Simon. "You're here from World 6. You say you mean us no harm. So what's with all the questions and theatrics? Why have you trapped us all in this room?"

"Because," Kate spoke up from the back of the room. Blue sparks in her wild, black hair. "There is a spy here."

The room went quiet before Lee laughed out loud. "Impossible." He stated matter-of-factly. "There is no way a spy can hide amongst us; we would be able to read their thoughts."

"Not if he was conditioned," replied Kate.

"Conditioned?" asked Molly.

Isabelle answered. "A process whereby a part of the brain is sectioned off and hidden from view, even from the host. For the most part, it is inactive, merely recording and monitoring. But at times, it is activated instructing the host to carry out certain actions. Actions such as transmitting information to its masters."

There was silence in the room.

"We don't have the technology to do something like that," said Steve.

"No," replied Kate. "But I know someone who does. And I think they've done it to Abeko."

"No!" shouted Prisha. "Not my Abeko. He would never betray us!"

Isabelle replied, "He has no choice. He is under the enemy's control. We had hoped to find who it was and to stop them from communicating with the enemy about our arrival, but it seems we were too late. We should expect an attack imminently."

Chapter 19 - Jim

Jim awoke suddenly.

His first thought was, "Where am I?"

Looking upwards, he squinted at the brightness of the sun as it shone through fluttering green leaves, momentarily blinding him. Where was he?

After looking to his left and right, he realised he was lying on a forest floor, the musty smell of crushed leaves beneath him mixing with the smell of pine.

He sat up and looked around. He was surrounded by trees, brambles, and bushes. With no clue about his whereabouts or the means of his arrival, he was completely disoriented. He searched his memory and was puzzled to find it blank. But not completely. He suddenly had a desperate need to see his brother, Joe.

He missed him. How long had it been since he had last seen him? He couldn't remember, but it felt like a long time. He loved his twin brother and being separated didn't feel natural. They did everything together. They ate together, and they worked together.

His forehead furrowed with a frown of puzzlement. He could not remember where they worked or what they did. He just knew that they were always together, and he needed to be with Joe now.

He stood and surveyed his surroundings. Nothing but trees. Birds chirruped in the branches, some fluttering between nearby bushes. There was nothing to show where he was. Where should he go? Which direction? Where would Joe be? Could he be in this wood somewhere? Maybe they had got separated?

Glancing down at his feet, he saw he was wearing boots and blue faded jeans. He didn't recognise them, nor did he recall putting them on. Did someone knock him out? He felt through his long blond hair, pushing at his scalp. No signs of wetness that could be blood or of any sore areas.

He closed his eyes and searched his memories, desperately trying to work things out. But it was no use. He didn't know why he was here, or how he had got here. He couldn't even recall what he had been doing a few hours or days ago. It was all a blank. There was one thing, only a desperate need to be with Joe.

There was only one thing for it. He would have to walk until he found some signs of habitation. Maybe there was a car parked in a nearby car park and Joe was waiting for him?

He picked a random direction and walked, cursing as he snagged his jeans on a bramble that curled up from the ground. Pulling free, he pushed past a large bush and spied a worn path that snaked away through the trees. He made his way to it and followed it; his progress was much quicker now that the undergrowth did not hamper him.

He followed the path for about ten minutes, he guessed, because when he raised his wrist, he found it bare of a watch, a pale band of flesh marked where it should have been. That was strange, he thought. I always wear a watch. At least, he thought he did, didn't he?

Soon the trees grew thinner, and he came to a large one that, for some unknown reason, held his attention. He stood looking down at its base. The grass and undergrowth had dark patches. He wasn't sure what it was. As he stood, gazing fixedly at the tree, he wondered why he was so fascinated.

It took a lot of strength for him to tear his eyes away from the tree. He had to find Joe. The need to see him was growing. Where was he? In the distance, he could hear machinery and the roaring of engines. What was it?

He resumed walking down the path. The trees thinned even more until he met a road. Well, it was once a road. The place was alive with workmen and women as they busily reconstructed the roadway. All along its length there was evidence of a fire, new green grass poking up from the scorched ground. The road itself was just bare earth. Rolling machines were moving back and forth across the hardcore, their exhausts belching black diesel smoke into the air. In the distance, he could see a tarmac laying machine moving slowly as it covered the ground with a layer of asphalt.

But what attracted his attention was not the road or the machinery, it was across the road works.

It was a grand old house.

Chapter 20 - Klalan Battle 2
3 Months ago

The Klalan expeditionary commander was observing the progress of their conquest through a multitude of viewing monitors. This time, there was no resistance as the Klalan fleet approached yet another world.

A blue and green planet with three small, lifeless moons lay before them. There were no ships sent to greet them, and no weapons firing from the moons, which would have made ideal defensive outposts. Instead, the inhabitants of this world were trying to communicate. They had been sending a radio signal directly to the largest of the Klalan fleet vessels ever since they had emerged into this system.

The commander directed a cold thought at another. *"Have we deciphered their communication yet?"*

A nearby Klalan operator replied, *"Just. It seems they would like to engage in a mutually beneficial conversation between our two races."*

The commander made a sound like a barking dog, spittle flying out of its mouth to splatter onto a viewing screen.

"Hah! The Klalan have no need to collaborate with other races. We rule supreme!"

The commander peered at one screen as a minion scuttled forward to wipe down the one covered in spittle and then it swivelled its neck to look at the chief technologist.

"Do they have anything we want?" it asked.

The chief technologist replied, *"Nothing."*

"Not even food?" asked the commander.

"Our scout probes scanned all aspects of this system days ago. It has nothing of any worth save metals and reaction mass."

The commander considered that statement for a while.

"Very well," came the replying thought. *"Save those three moons. They will make excellent additions to our moon ships."*

"A wise decision as always," replied the technologist as it bobbed its head up and down on its long sinuous neck.

"Once the moons are captured decay, the planet's orbit into their sun. That should prove to be entertaining to watch," continued the commander.

All the Klalan in the control room settled down in front of the view screens to watch the spectacle. In short order, the moons were manoeuvred away with giant force beams. Once deprived of its moons, the planet wobbled on its axis. This was soon countered by beams of force that pushed the once beautiful green and blue world into a death spiral towards its sun.

Through the yellow haze of their chlorine-based atmosphere, the Klalan grunted and growled with glee as they watched the planet being consumed by its sun.

Chapter 21 - Conference Part 2

Simon sat up. "What? We're under attack? Let me communicate with the defence team. I need to get our screens up."

"There is no need," replied Isabelle. "I am in control of this entire facility. The screens are already up."

"What?" exclaimed Simon. "How can that be? How can you do that?"

"It's a simple matter of integration into your networks. I have taken control of all your computer systems," replied Isabelle.

"This is all part of the plan," continued Kate from the back of the room. "Izzy will explain the rest. For now, remain calm."

"Remain calm!" shouted Lee. "Isabelle," he pointed to the head of the table, "just said that we are under attack! The last time that happened, we barely survived. If it wasn't for..." He hesitated. "For our Kate, we would all be dead!"

"We are fully aware of your Kate's sacrifice," explained Kate. "That's why we are here. Izzy didn't say we were under attack. She said that we should expect an attack."

Lee sat back in his chair, huffing as he did so.

A deep voice rumbled from the back of the room. "Please continue Miss Isabelle. I am sure that we are all interested in hearing what you have to say."

Everyone turned their focus on Steve, and then back to Isabelle.

"Thank you," Isabelle nodded to Steve.

"The world that Kate and I have just come from is empty. The entire population migrated to another world far away from this one. I was the only inhabitant until Kate arrived from her world." She paused and then continued.

"I know who the enemy is and how powerful they are. And I also know that they are continuing their conquests. The enemy will soon attack my world, as well as this one."

"You mean bad Kate and bad Joe?" asked Lee. "Or was that something Kate just made up?"

Kate smiled, "I'm afraid that's one part of my story that was true."

"Who's bad Kate and bad Joe?" asked Prisha.

Isabelle held up her hand. "All will be explained." She answered as she nodded to Lee.

Molly spoke up, "But if both of our worlds are going to be attacked, then why did you come here?"

Isabelle's black eyes fixed on Molly. "Because this might be the only world where we all have a chance at defeating the enemy."

Simon snorted. "Wait a minute. I thought Kate had defeated the enemy?" He looked at Sally and Molly. "We haven't come across them in over six months on Arcadia or on Kaunis."

"To be accurate, we don't know that," answered Steve. "Our Kate told us that the aliens agreed to help us. She didn't say that they got rid of them."

Simon looked thoughtful. "Oh. I assumed that since we hadn't encountered them…."

Isabelle continued, "It's worse than that. I know that bad Kate and bad Joe have formed an alliance with another warmongering race. This other race is very advanced, particularly their technology. They are capable of building huge war machines that can pulverise entire planets. Together, they are unstoppable."

There was silence in the room. Molly and Sally looked at each other while Doortje and Eline moved closer, hugging each other tightly.

Steve broke the silence. "I assume you have a plan? Otherwise, we wouldn't be talking now."

Isabelle nodded her head slowly.

"Yes, at this moment sixteen portals to my world are opening in this world out near the Oort cloud. I am transporting fabricators and camouflage screen generators through each one. Once established, the fabricators will mine this resource-rich area and start building defences and weaponry."

"That sounds good," said Simon. "I would like to oversee the production and installation."

Isabelle smiled. "That won't be necessary. I have already planned the production schedule and placement of all the installations to provide the best coverage. Your input is not required."

Simon bristled. "How dare you come to our world and take over like this? What makes you think you have all the answers?"

Isabelle visibly sighed. "Oh please," she said. "My cognitive function is hundreds of times better and faster than yours." Her lips curved downwards. "I have analysed many thousands of scenarios. I know exactly what to do to defeat the enemy."

Only the fizzing and crackling of electrical discharges around Kate broke the silence in the room.

"And how do we defeat the enemy?" asked Steve in his rumbling voice. "You just said they are unstoppable."

Izzy looked around the room.

"That is true. They are unstoppable. But there is a way. Only one way."

Lee leaned forward. "Yes?" he asked.

"We ask the aliens who helped you last time for their help again."

Chapter 22 - Alliance
1 Month ago

The Kate/Joe fusion watched without being detected.

Deep below the surface of the planet, the Klalan commander pulled itself out of a pool of dark green liquid. As it did so, its back two legs slipped and it fell back, submerging itself completely in the slimy fluid. It was not water. It was an organic mixture of bodily fluids; crushed animal remains and excreta. Unperturbed, the Klalan resurfaced and successfully emerged, leaving two others wallowing, plastering the foul liquid over themselves.

The commander waddled on its four short legs to an alcove where jets of chlorine saturated water hosed it clean of the filth that clung to its body. After drying itself with jets of heated chlorine air, the commander moved over to a low bench and strapped on a harness containing various devices and weapons.

As it turned to leave the room, the Kate/Joe fusion materialised in front of the doorway.

With lightning speed, one of the Klalan's snake-like arms snatched a weapon, and a beam of force pierced the apparition. It travelled in a straight line through the figure and splashed against the far wall, where it bored a hole one metre deep before the Klalan stopped firing. The amalgamation of Kate's and Joe's face smirked at the attempt.

"Your weapon cannot affect us," it's thought cold and sneering.

The Klalan was unfazed. It holstered its weapon and pressed a switch on its harness, triggering an automatic alarm call.

"Guards," it sent a thought. *"Attend me now!"*

The Kate/Joe fusion continued to sneer. *"Your call for help is fruitless. No one can hear us."*

Still unfazed, the Klalan commander hurled a mental bolt of force at the apparition and saw it dissipate on the intruder's mental screens.

"Impressive," replied the Kate/Joe fusion. *"But not good enough. Try this."* Sending its own mental bolt of force.

The Klalan commander countered the massive mental attack. Just.

"Whoever you are, you cannot kill me with mental force. You are clearly a projection of some kind, so physical attack is not possible. In a short while, my guards will investigate, and we will drive you from this vessel."

The Kate/Joe fusion nodded slowly.

"It is just as we expected. Your race and ours are of equal capacity mentally. We are at an impasse. However, we did not come here to kill you. Instead, we are here to discuss an opportunity that would advantage the both of us."

"The Klalan are not interested in discussing opportunities. We make our own," replied the commander proudly.

"Again, as expected," replied the Kate/Joe fusion. *"However, we have information that may make you change your mind."*

The commander bristled at this. *"The Klalan never change their minds. Say what you want to say before we remove your projection from this vessel."*

"Very well," replied the Kate/Joe fusion. *"You will already know there are two Psi capable races in this galaxy. One of which is many millions of light years away in a remote spiral arm."*

The commander folded its rear legs and sat back, waiting impatiently for his guard to respond to the alarm he had triggered.

"What you don't know is that remote Psi capable race is far more powerful than you realise. They have already interfered with our own conquest of this universe."

"They maybe powerful, but we will still wipe them out," commented the commander.

"We admire your confidence," replied the projection. *"However, you are overconfident. You cannot defeat this particular race. They are old and have developed far more than both you and us."*

The commander spat a glob of yellow mucus onto the floor. *"No matter. We will rule in this world as we have in every other."*

The Kate/Joe projection continued. *"We propose an alliance between our races. Together, we will defeat this powerful race."*

"We have no need to form an alliance. We are all powerful. Your words are meaningless."

"We thought you would say that," replied the Kate/Joe fusion. *"A demonstration is in order."*

The projection waved an arm, and it faded away. At the same time, the commander vanished in a snap of wind.

Chapter 23 - Conference Part 3

There were gasps around the room.

After a while, Sally spoke.

"That's insane! We can't ask the Non'anan for help again. The last time we did that, Kate died!" She stole a quick glance at Kate, who was still standing at the back of the room.

"So we understand," replied Isabelle. "That is something that we had not planned for. However, it must be done. Because without them, we are all doomed."

"You named them the Non'anan," continued Isabelle. "Why?"

"That's what they call themselves," Sally shot a quick glance at Kate. "That's what Kate called them before she died."

"I have some experience regarding contacting the Non'anan," Steve spoke up. "They are extremely powerful, and you may well be right about them being able to save us. But there are two major problems. The first is, as Sally says, the contact will probably kill whomever we nominate to initiate the communication, and second, why would they help? They already helped us once. Why would they do so again?"

Isabelle had answers to both questions. "I can answer both of your questions," she said. "First, regarding your second point, if they do not help us, then they too will be conquered by bad Kate and bad Joe. Convincing them of this should be straightforward.

We will have the evidence to show them by the time we make contact."

Sally and Molly looked at each other.

"It's that serious?" asked Molly. "Bad Kate and bad Joe will kill everyone and everything?"

Isabelle nodded her silver head. "Yes Molly, it is that bad. I have seen many worlds where they have wiped out every living thing. Unless we all stand together, we will all suffer the same fate."

Silence filled the room.

Isabelle continued. "As to your first point, Steve. We have a plan. Any one person may not survive the contact, but two might."

Simon burst out laughing. "What are you talking about? How can two survive when one can't?"

Isabelle didn't answer. Instead, she strode gracefully and silently around the conference table towards the back of the room. As she passed, some of the Alliance members shrank away from her presence, as if trying to distance themselves from her presence. The room was silent as several pairs of eyes watched her progress. She approached Kate but paused when she stood next to Prisha's wheelchair. With a gentle touch, she reached out her shimmering, silver hand and stroked Prisha's black curly hair.

Prisha had not been listening to the conversation, nor had she noticed Isabelle's approach. She was too wrapped up in her own thoughts. Could Abeko be a spy? Her lovely Abeko?

She couldn't process it. It couldn't be true. Could it? Her thoughts spun as she went over and over everything that she could remember. All the times they had been together, laughing, talking, eating, loving. She felt sick. Looking back, was there anything that was out of character? And now she thought about it, there were occasions when he went missing. Times when she had assumed that he had been sent to Kaunis or someplace else on important errands. Her stomach churned as she slowly began to realise that it just might be true. Had he been using her to infiltrate the Alliance? She couldn't stop the tears prickling at the corners of her eyes as she tried desperately to hold herself together.

Isabelle's hand on her head caused Prisha to flinch and brought her back to the present. She looked up at Isabelle with wide, tear-filled eyes.

"After this conference, you and I should talk about getting your missing arm and leg replaced." Isabelle gestured at her own silver body.

Prisha gaped up at Isabelle, her thoughts of Abeko quickly forgotten.

"You can do that?" she asked.

Izzy smiled and removed her hand. "It is a straightforward procedure," she replied as she continued her journey to stand next to Kate, leaving a confused Prisha behind. Kate's black hair sparkled in the light and stood straight up. Her blue aura shimmered and expanded until it surrounded her and Isabelle, wrapping around them like a veil. Light danced across Isabelle's perfect skin in bright bursts, as if tiny fireworks were exploding near her.

Isabelle put her arm around Kate's shoulders, tiny sparks leaping from Kate to Isabelle's arm as it connected.

Doortje and Eline moved as one into the rear corner of the room, putting as much distance between themselves and Isabelle.

"Before we continue, given the threat I have outlined, can Kate and I rely upon your co-operation? All of you?"

She gazed around the room with her lidless black eyes.

Lee looked at Simon and then at Alex. "Alex, what's your take on all of this?"

Alex had been silent throughout the conference. He steepled his fingers together.

"There's been multiverse theory for hundreds of years," he said. "It makes sense. There would be an infinite number of versions of ourselves out there. Some might look different from us, or act differently, but we'd also likely have counterparts who looked just like us and acted just like us, except that they made different choices in life. And it's not absurd to say some might be hostile toward us. They may be more advanced than we are, or less so. We already know that at least one alien race in our own universe is more powerful than us." His voice dropped low and took on a serious tone. "I believe Isabelle because it explains some things that I couldn't previously explain. I conclude her story is true."

Molly held up her hand. "Hold on, why should we believe her? After all," she gazed pointedly at Kate and Isabelle. "We were lied to a while ago. This Kate got herself inside the Complex under false pretences. She pretended to be someone she clearly isn't." She paused and flicked a glance at Sally. "Then she frightened my Sally." She squeezed Sally's hand, then fixed her gaze back on the two shimmering women. "You clearly have power - much more than we have. How are we to know that you're not manipulating us now?"

There was silence in the room as all eyes moved to Kate and Isabelle.

"You have a point," answered Kate. "In order to obtain the information, we needed, I intentionally deceived you. I won't apologise for it. I could, of course, tell you that what we are telling you now is true, but why would you believe me?" She smiled.

A low murmur broke out around the room, which was silenced as Kate raised her Assisted hand, sparks radiating from its golden surface.

"There is one way," continued Kate. She turned to Steve. "Steve, would you agree to prove the point?"

Steve nodded his golden encased head. "I would welcome the opportunity," he replied. "I assume you are proposing to let me enter your mind?"

Kate's smile widened. "Something like that," she answered. "Bella, send the package to Steve," she instructed her Assist.

"Who's Bella?" asked Simon. No one answered, as all eyes swivelled to Steve, who sat stock still in his chair.

Sally leaned over to Molly and whispered in her ear. "What's happening?" she asked. "What's the package?"

Molly shook her head. "I don't know," she replied. "But it'd better be something that's going to prove their sincerity."

Silence descended in the room again as the group waited for a response from Steve.

After a while, Lee spoke up.

"Is there any point to this?" he asked. "We have no idea what's going on. How is this going to prove that you are telling the truth?"

"Please allow Steve some time to assimilate the package," said Isabelle.

Simon shuffled in his seat. "This is all a waste of time," he grumbled. "You've told a good story and showed your control over all of us." He gestured around the room. "To what end? To spread fear. We defeated the enemy six months ago. We don't need your help; the enemy is gone." He spread his hands on the table. "And as for this bad Kate and bad Joe stuff." He snorted in derision. "It sounds like crap to me."

Before Isabelle or Kate could respond, Alex interjected. "As I just said, I believe it is entirely possible. Isabelle and Kate," he nodded towards the two glowing women. "Are clearly here. How did they get here? If not from another universe, then where from? Another star system, perhaps?" He shrugged. "I don't think so. And if they came from another universe, everything falls neatly into place. I, for one, believe everything I have heard."

"Thank you, Alex," said Isabelle. "We appreciate your support." She looked around the room. "You should listen to your lead scientist," she informed everyone. "I have already admitted that we tricked you. But we did it out of necessity. We have very little time to prepare for the coming battle. We have been looking for this world - your world - for a long time, time we don't have. I am asking all of you - every single one of you - to forgive us. Because if you don't." Isabelle paused, locking her gaze on Simon. "Then there is no future for any of us."

Simon looked down at the table, doubt still on his face.

"Interesting." Steve's deep, rumbling voice broke the silence.

"You have assimilated the package?" asked Isabelle.

Steve nodded slowly. "I have reviewed the memory fragments Kate sent to me. Of course, they back up what you have told us. They convey a very depressing story, but I cannot vouch for the veracity of the content." He paused and held up his hand as a murmur spread around the table. "Normally I would accept them as the truth, but I assume that given your technology, such memory fragments could be fabricated."

The murmur around the room increased in volume over which Simon could be heard, "I fucking knew it!"

Isabelle and Kate waited for the noise to die down.

"And now to deliver the conclusive proof," stated Isabelle in an ominous tone.

Kate flicked her wrist, and both she and Steve disappeared with a snap of wind.

Chapter 24 - Kate and Steve

The room erupted into chaos, a cacophonous symphony of yelling and shouting voices that blended together into an incoherent mess. Sally clung to Molly, burying her face in her shoulder, while Molly instinctively wrapped her arms around her protectively.

Lee's voice boomed above the noise like thunder. "What the hell!" he bellowed, his chair crashing to the ground as he leapt to his feet. His eyes blazed with fury as he glared at the shimmering figure of Isabelle. "What have you done?" he demanded.

Simon rose slowly from his seat, his hands slamming down on the table with a deafening thud. Anger in his eyes as he fixed Isabelle with a piercing stare.

The tension in the air was thick enough to cut with a knife, and each person in the room braced themselves for what would come next. Throughout all the shouting and exclamations of anger and fear, Isabelle remained indifferent, her sparkling aura pulsing with luminous energy as she waited for the voices to die down.

The room was eventually silent. It seemed as if time had frozen. Isabelle's voice cut through the heavy air, "If you are all done with your accusations and suspicions?" Her presence commanding the undivided attention of everyone in the room.

"Thank you," she continued. "Steve is perfectly safe and will be back here shortly with Kate."

Simon slammed his fist on the table again, eyes blazing with rage, "What have you done with him? You lied to us, restrained us in this room, invaded our systems and now you've taken one of our most valuable members! I knew we couldn't trust you!" His chest heaved with fury as he shouted.

Isabelle's mouth curled up into a knowing smile.

"Please sit-down Simon, you are not adding anything to the conversation." She dismissed him with a wave of her hand. "As I just said, Steve will be back with us shortly. Kate is with him. She is taking him on a brief journey, verifying each of the memory fragments in the package."

"He's safe?" asked Molly as she stroked Sally's head.

Isabelle nodded.

"Are these theatrics really necessary?" asked Alex. "I'm sure that most of us in this room are like me and believe what you have told us." As he spoke, his gaze moved to everyone in the room. He was surprised to see doubt and fear in most of them. "Maybe not," he mumbled to himself.

"Your reactions were expected," answered Isabelle. "Kate and I debated how to show you all the seriousness of the situation we find ourselves in. We need to face the coming storm together, and to do that, we need to trust each other completely. There can be no room for doubt. We must be united, or we will all fall."

Simon sat and crossed his arms over his chest. He deliberately looked away from Isabelle. He had already decided. Everyone in the room could sense his anger and indignation.

"How long?" asked Lee.

"They will be back in approximately thirty seconds," replied Isabelle.

Prisha looked up from her wheelchair. Although still deeply affected by the news about Abeko, she couldn't stop thinking of what Isabelle had said to her - "It's a straightforward procedure." Could Isabelle really replace her arm and leg? She absently rubbed at her shoulder that no longer had an arm. If she didn't remember to block the pain, it ached - especially in the mornings. She was conflicted. On the one hand, she couldn't get Abeko out of her mind. On the other, the thought of being normal again, of having two arms and two legs, was overwhelming. She observed Isabelle's silver body. Through the hazy, sparkling force field that surrounded her, Prisha watched her limbs as they moved with fluid grace. They functioned exactly as human arms and legs. They were perfect. Prisha would give anything to be normal again, even if her new limbs were silver.

As if she knew Prisha was thinking of her, Isabelle turned and fixed Prisha with her black, inhuman eyes. "Once we have concluded here, you have an open invitation to come see me in my world. You will be whole again if you wish."

Prisha couldn't stop the tears welling up in her eyes. She was about to reply when Kate reappeared next to Isabelle with a whoosh of air, a knowing smile on her lips. Isabelle turned her attention from Prisha and locked eyes with Kate.

"Where is…" Molly began to ask, when Steve abruptly appeared with a gust of air. He stumbled and fell, the golden augmented prosthesis that surrounded his head crashing onto the conference table with a bang. He lay on the ground dazed, as everyone in the Alliance jumped up from their chairs, which tumbled to the floor or shrieked as they scraped against the wooden flooring; and once more, pandemonium filled the room with people shouting all at once.

Sally hurried over to Steve, her fear and anxiety forgotten, replaced by her doctor's professional demeanour. She knelt beside him, placing one hand on the back of his skull. The rings of her Assist shone purple for a moment as she checked over her patient.

Grunting to herself, she gently took hold of Steve's shoulders and helped him to a sitting position.

"You're okay," she told Steve. "There's no damage to your Augment. How are you feeling?" She took his wrist to check his heartbeat with one hand while placing the other against his chest, where once again her Assist glowed purple.

Steve shook his head slowly, as the rest of the group closed in around him, eager to see that he was alright.

"What happened?" shouted Lee. "Where did you take him?" He fixed Kate with a glare.

"I showed him the enemy," replied a still smiling Kate. "You wanted proof, now you have it." She gazed down at Steve, who appeared to be dazed and confused. "Tell them what you saw, Steve."

Sally looked up at Kate with hate-filled eyes, placing an arm protectively around Steve's shoulders. "You bitch!" she spat. "How dare you kidnap and place Steve in danger? We didn't ask for any of this. You come charging in here, lying and controlling everyone and everything, and look at the result!" She pulled Steve close to her.

Steve appeared to be shell-shocked and could not immediately respond, but eventually muttered, "It wasn't like I imagined it would be... they seem nothing like us... it's hard to describe."

Kate did not appear to be offended by Sally's outburst, but the smile disappeared from her face. "Steve isn't injured," she replied. "He just needs time to process what he experienced."

Molly put a restraining arm on Sally's shoulder. "Leave it Sal," she said, then turned to Steve, who still looked dazed and confused. "Are you okay?"

Steve swallowed and cleared his dry throat. "I'm fine. Just give me a minute." He allowed Sally to help him up to sit in a chair, whereupon Lee, Simon, Doortje, Elina, and Molly surrounded him, each clearly pleased to see him back and well.

Everyone was clearly relieved; the lines of tension from their faces seemed to melt away as they smiled. Some of them had tears in their eyes. Lee laid a hand on Steve's shoulder. "It is good to see you," Lee said gratefully. "You had us all worried. Where did you go? Can you tell us what happened?"

Steve nodded slowly. "I can do better than that. I can show you," he replied. "Sorry to worry you all." His golden head moved from side to side. "It was quick and overwhelming." He surveyed the people crowding around him. "I advise you all to take a seat. What I'm about to show you is, frankly, unbelievable and very." he paused and then continued. "Shocking."

"I don't recommend this," said Sally. "You should rest. You have an increased cortisol and norepinephrine response to whatever you've experienced. It would be better if you took the time to process what you've been through."

Steve shook his head. "There is no time, Sally. Kate and Isabelle are right. We must resolve this now. Please, everyone, take a seat."

The room descended into a tense hush as people scurried back to their seats. Dortje and Eline pulled chairs together, exchanging worried glances. Isabelle and Kate remained standing, pale blue sparks of electricity radiating from the force screen that surrounded them. They waited patiently, allowing Steve to take the lead.

Once everyone was ready, Steve spoke up.

"We should trust Kate and Isabelle," he started, holding up his hand as Simon opened his mouth to protest. "Let me have my say," he continued. "Kate and I have just been on a journey," he paused. "She showed me things." He stopped and moved his metal encased head from side to side. "Things that I would have never believed if she hadn't shown me," he said.

He stood unsteadily and then continued.

"I was shown visions of terror and destruction. I saw entire universes destroyed, some with dead suns, their planets reduced to radioactive cinders. Others were just empty of all life, and yet more subjugated, conquered and under military rule. I saw planets pulverised and sun's exploding like firecrackers. And I also saw," he paused and then continued. "Kate and Joe." His voice fell to a whisper. "They were behind it all. I saw them commanding executions, public floggings, and wholesale world invasions. They crushed everyone and everything that dared stand in their way, leaving no witnesses. Their ethos is total dominance over everything. It was absolute desolation. I have never seen anything so evil."

He sat down suddenly. His chair creaked loudly in the silence that, once again, descended upon the room.

Molly broke the silence. "I think," she said, looking around at all the faces sat at the conference table. "We all need to see."

Steve nodded. "Brace yourselves," he said. He assembled the images and sounds of his journey with Kate in his mind and broadcasted them to the entire group. Instantly, everyone experienced a tidal wave of images and sounds from his journey with Kate. There were gasps around the room. Molly's face went deathly pale, while Sally leaned sideways and retched onto the floor. Both Dortje and Eline collapsed into each other, and Prisha sagged in her wheelchair like a rag doll. Simon uttered a stunned whisper beneath his breath. "Holy shit!"

Lee was the first to recover.

"That was…" he broke off as though searching for the right words. "As shocking as you said it would be." He nodded at Steve and then faced Isabelle and Kate. "We believe you. Incredible as your story is, I can't deny the truth of it." He looked around the room. There were nods from the rest of them.

"I don't approve of your methods, but," he sighed. "It seems we have no choice but to put our trust in you."

Isabelle beamed at them all. "Thank you. I appreciate that this is all strange and sudden. Kate and I are pleased to join your Alliance."

"Wait a minute. I didn't say that you could join the Alliance," protested Lee. "I said I believe what you've told us. No more than that."

Molly snapped her head around towards Lee, pushing her glasses up her nose.

"Lee, I don't think we have a choice. Let's face facts, Isabelle and Kate," she gestured to the two figures standing at the back of the room. "Are running the show. Obviously, their tech is better than ours. If they wanted to kill us, they could have done it ages ago. Now, I don't really trust them fully," she glanced back at Isabelle. "But what Steve has just shown us…" She didn't complete her sentence.

Lee considered Molly's words. She had been one of the original founders of the Alliance and was completely trustworthy. In Joe's absence, she had been someone he could rely on. She had left her work as the lead researcher, working with Alex to help him lead the group. She was indispensable, and he doubted he could have managed without her.

After some moments, he nodded.

"Very well. Isabelle, welcome to the Alliance." He looked pointedly at Isabelle and Kate. "We will work together for as long as it makes sense for us to do so," he added.

The room went quiet as each Alliance member processed what that statement meant.

"Bella, shutdown high order functions." Kate's voice broke the silence.

The aura around Isabelle and Kate flickered and disappeared and Kate's hair fell flat on her head, covering her eyes. She pulled out an empty chair and sat down heavily, brushing her hair back.

The two HAZPRO figures moved. One raised an arm. Kate absently waved a hand towards the figures.

"I have released you from the inertia field. Don't do something stupid now that we are all friends," she projected a thought that included the entire group.

"Stand down," thought Lee. *"Cheryl, Ahmed. There is no cause for alarm."* Now that they were released, Lee could identify them from their mind patterns.

The two HAZPROs stood still.

"Are sure Lee?" came Cheryl's thought. *"I heard everything. I don't trust either of them at all. I've been standing here for ages, unable to move. It was frustrating as hell."*

"I'm sure," Lee thought back. *"Then you know we are expecting an attack soon, not sure when. Could you de-suit and take command in the control room while we finish here?"*

"Agreed," replied Cheryl.

She turned, gripped Ahmed in a mechanised hand. With a loud bang and a whirl of air, the two HAZPROs teleported away.

All eyes were on Kate and Isabelle.

"What now?" asked Steve. "I would welcome the opportunity to learn more about your technology if that is agreeable?"

"We will see," replied Isabelle. "We will certainly need your assistance later. Your particular Augmentation is ingenious. We developed nothing like it in my world. I would like to explore its possibilities with you in the near future."

Steve inclined his head. "Of course, I look forward to it."

"To repeat Steve's question. What happens now?" asked Lee.

Isabelle laid her silver hands on Kate's shoulders.

"We need Joe," she answered.

Sally glanced at Molly and then back at Isabelle. "He'll be unconscious for a few more hours yet," she said. "I gave him a strong sedative."

Isabelle fixed Sally with an unreadable gaze. "He will wake in approximately ten minutes."

"What?" asked Sally. "That's not possible."

"You've a lot to learn, Sally," smiled Kate, leaning back in her chair.

Sally huffed.

"You're waking him?" she asked. "I don't approve. He needs rest and also…" she hesitated. "He's not been himself for a while."

Isabelle nodded. "I understand. We will not keep him conscious for long."

Sally was about to continue her protestations, but Isabelle dismissed her.

"We will need someone to interface with the rest of the world's population. Someone who can help introduce the rest of humanity to the multiverse, and the dangers that we face," stated Isabelle.

"Why?" asked Lee. "We've done okay so far by keeping ourselves hidden. If we go public, there would be an outcry, mass panic, wars, you name it."

"You must find a way," replied Isabelle. "It's important that we all unite against our common enemy. Besides, how will you stay hidden when we build our orbital defences?"

Lee saw her point. "Okay, I get it. Let me think about it. That's a big problem."

"We also need to look out for Abeko. When he returns, he must not pass on any more information to bad Kate and bad Joe," continued Isabelle.

Prisha couldn't help herself. A sob escaped her lips and dropped her head into her hand. "Oh Abeko! What have you done?"

Kate reached out a hand and laid it on Prisha's shoulder.

"I'm sorry Prisha," she said. "I promise we will do what we can to reverse what's been done to him."

Prisha's shoulders shook as she cried quietly.

Isabelle continued. "We have already started building in the Oort cloud. Our priority is to set up camouflage screens so that the enemy can't see what we are doing. Once we are hidden, we will start building defence installations."

"You can't build quickly enough to cover the entire solar system!" protested Simon.

"Ah, but we can," continued Isabelle. "Right now, I am transporting one thousand Von Neumann machines through the sixteen portals. These machines are capable of self-replication, they have been instructed to build copies of themselves. Once they have secured the resources required, they can replicate themselves at a rate of one per twenty-four hours."

"So, that would be somewhere around one hundred and twenty thousand in one week?" asked an amazed Simon.

"Exactly one hundred and twenty-eight thousand," answered Isabelle.

"Sounds like you have it all planned," said Lee dryly. "Maybe you don't need us at all."

"You are being silly. That is muddy thinking. We all need each other if we are going to survive this," admonished Isabelle.

Lee felt like he had been told off like a child.

He coughed. "Okay, so you are building a camouflage screen with your Von Neumann machines," he stated.

"Just so," replied Isabelle. "I am building new HAZPRO suits down in the engineering section. I have also started to construct a housing for myself. Once built, I will transport myself to this world."

"Where are you building your, what you called, housing?" asked Steve.

"I require more than a simple container or receptacle. My neural network and cybernetic componentry require a space of five hundred square metres. As we speak, mechanised drones are excavating beneath this Complex. In two days, the space will be ready, and the building can begin."

There was another lengthy silence.

"How are your drones doing this?" asked Steve. "What about all the waste? The rock and soil. How are you removing it?"

"Each drone is equipped with a small portal generator. All the waste is transported to the fabricators at the Oort cloud, where it is broken down into its constituent elements which the fabricators will use in their building process."

Lee was realising how far advanced Isabelle and World 6 was. They were totally outclassed. Isabelle was taking over; things would never be the same. He wished Joe were back to his normal self. He would love for him to be here; he was sure that he would have something to say.

The conference room door suddenly crashed open, revealing Joe standing in the doorway as if someone had summoned him.

"What the fuck is going on?" he shouted.

Chapter 25 - Joe Wakes

Joe woke suddenly from his medicated sleep.

At first, he couldn't remember where he was, but when he looked across the room and saw the medical equipment, cupboards, and drawers, it all came crashing back. The black despair threatened to swallow him as it had done many times before. A single tear leaked from one eye and streaked down to the pillow.

Of course, he knew he was being selfish and self-indulgent. He could easily banish these feelings so that they no longer bothered him. But he didn't want to. He didn't want to forget Kate. He wanted to wallow in despair. It was all he had left of her. All he had were those brief moments in the flat, that moment when he had protected her from an enemy incursion into the Complex, and her death.

Once he had added it all up. It came to five hours roughly. He had spent a brief five hours with her. Just five hours. In those few hours, they had fallen in love. And now she was gone forever.

He sat up and swung his legs over the side of the bed. He swayed a little, feeling weak and exhausted. Frowning, he recalled Sally had injected him with a sedative. He should be feeling rested. Instead, he felt shaky, his thoughts slow and muddled. He rubbed his face, shocked at how heavy his arm felt. Briefly, he wondered if he was coming down with an illness like the flu. Or maybe it was the aftereffects of the sedation. After all, he had never been sedated before, so how would he know?

He sat there for a while, gathering his strength and thinking of Kate. She was always with him. His Assist gave him an eidetic memory, he could conjure up her perfect image whenever he wanted, and he did so now. In his mind, he gazed upon her loveliness, her dark eyes, jet-black hair, and her perfect smile. He smiled to himself, his heart aching.

After a while, and with difficulty, he dismissed her image. He knew what he should do. He knew he should put Kate behind him and move on. He should be working with Molly, Lee and the others, building an infrastructure on other worlds and gradually introducing the rest of humanity to the world of Psi. All for the betterment of the human race.

But he wasn't ready, and he wasn't sure if he ever would be.

He carefully slid from the bed and slowly moved on stiff legs to a nearby locker. He assumed Sally had removed his clothes to make him comfortable. It didn't matter, nothing did. Sure enough, inside the locker, he found his clothes hanging up. It took longer than usual to get dressed. His arms and legs were heavy, the feeling of weakness not dissipating. Once dressed, he leaned against the locker, panting. What was wrong with him?

Once his breathing had calmed a little, he shuffled to the door and left the medical room. Shocked at how weak he still felt, he made his way, slowly, to his lab.

He was so focussed on his own thoughts and feelings that at first; he didn't notice that anything was wrong.

It was only when he reached the door to his lab that he suddenly realised that he had seen no one on his walk.

Admittedly, it wasn't far. Even so, he should have seen someone. He stood with his hand on the door handle, listening. Nothing. No voices, no laughter, no music. In fact, there were no sounds at all. That was strange. The Complex was usually bustling with activity. Something prickled at his consciousness. The hairs on the back of his neck raised as he began to feel alarmed.

Sending out his perception, he let it expand outwards and was concerned when he found no one. He was starting to wonder if they were under attack when he found nearly all the entire Complex contingent. They were in the refectory. It was packed. He could feel mind after mind so close together and all focussed on one thing. A thought stream being broadcast to the entire group. He traced it to its origin - one of the conference rooms.

Intrigued, he pushed his perception into the conference room, only to find it blocked by a very sophisticated and very strong thought screen. He was taken-a-back. He had never felt a thought screen like it. What was going on? He let go of the door handle and turned about. Using the corridor wall to steady himself, he made his way to the conference room. He made no attempt to view the broadcast. If they were under attack, he didn't want to join the stream and make himself vulnerable. He sent out a thought to two of his best friends and colleagues.

"Mike, Sammy, where are you?"

There was no reply. Puzzled, he sent out another thought.

"Mol, Sal, are you around?"

There was still no reply. By now he was getting really worried. This was not normal. Something was wrong. He shuffled along the corridor as quickly as he could, his breathing becoming laboured.

As he approached the conference room, he felt the thought screen abruptly vanish, his mind instantly assaulted by a multitude of thoughts.

Fear engulfed some, curiosity piqued others, and shock and awe overwhelmed the rest. But what really threw him was the vivid image that accompanied the thoughts.

The image was of Kate.

In a state of utter confusion, he slammed into the door, and it crashed open.

Chapter 26 - Lexi

"There is an abnormality in your left occipital lobe," stated James as he withdrew his instruments from Lexi's skull.

"I'm aware," replied Lexi. "Please continue."

"You need to get it looked at," protested James, his speech muffled through his surgical mask. "I don't like the look of it. Have you had an MRI?"

"It's none of your concern. Please continue with the operation."

Lexi watched through James's eyes as he continued with the delicate placement of the mesh onto the surface of her brain.

"I would be happy to operate once we complete the appropriate imaging," James continued. "Obviously I can't tell what it is exactly, but I've seen tumours that look like that. I would recommend urgent action."

"I know exactly what it is," answered Lexi irritably. "Just get on with the operation. The quicker you close me up, the better."

James failed to take the hint. "Well, it's your funeral," he replied. "But I wouldn't leave it if I were you."

Lexi didn't answer. She watched as James completed the fitting of the mesh.

"Make sure that all the mesh nodes are in contact with the brain," she instructed.

"They are," answered James. "Now for the difficult bit."

"Good. Be careful not to damage my auditory nerves."

"I know what I'm doing," replied James. "I don't know why I'm doing it - well, I guess I do - I'm doing it for the money, but for the life of me, I don't know why you want it done."

Recalling the events of the operation wasn't good for her. Lexi smiled grimly to herself as she considered she might be suffering from post-traumatic stress because she often found herself going over and over it when trying to sleep.

Sighing loudly into the darkness, she rolled over onto her back and held her hands up to her head. Between the pain and the vivid memories, sleep was not going to happen.

Concentrating, she muted her pain centres and breathed a sigh of relief as the pain faded to a dull ache. The Medulloblastoma tumour was still growing, increasing the pressure in her skull and pressing into her cerebellum, causing pain and affecting her muscle control and balance. Raising one arm straight up above her, she closed her eyes and, bringing the arm down, she tried to touch the tip of her nose with a pink forefinger. The finger missed, and she stabbed herself in the right cheek.

Not good, she thought to herself. Her fine motor control was getting worse. It was only a matter of time until it affected her balance, and she wouldn't be able to walk.

It was fortunate that she had created the M5A in time. It enabled her to offload some of her memories to its huge caches of storage as well as using it to supplement her cognitive functions. There was nothing she could do to slow the tumour's relentless growth. There was nothing else left to do. It was unforgiving; it would slowly eat into her, robbing her of her ability to walk, think, and reason until nothing remained.

Scratching at the side of her head where the M5A joined her skull, Lexi sat up, swinging her bare legs over the side of the bed. When she had designed the M5A, she had not considered sleeping in it. Its thin sides pressed painfully into the side of her head.

Directing a thought at her home's control centre, she turned on the bedroom lights and directed the coffee machine to start brewing.

In the bright light, she gazed at the reflection of her nakedness in the full-length mirror. Her red hair was a mess and the scar on her throat was a livid pink. Absently, she rubbed at her left side, tracing another scar that ran from under her left breast to her left hip; the result of a knife attack three years ago. Her attacker wouldn't attack anyone again. She had teleported him one hundred miles up into the atmosphere, close to the edge of space. He would have suffocated long before he landed somewhere in the North Sea.

Throwing on a cream, thick, woolly dressing gown, Lexi made her way down the stairs and into the kitchen. She was just in time to see the coffee machine finish its brewing, so she poured herself a mug full and sat down at the table. Pulling her cigarette packet and lighter to her, she extracted a cigarette and lit up. After inhaling and blowing out the smoke, she took a sip of her hot coffee, the chains of her Assist tinkling against the mug.

How long? She thought to herself. How long did she have left? There was no way of knowing, all the more reason to step up things on her timeline.

"Henrick," she sent a quick thought to her project manager. *"Give me an update."*

She knew he would be awake. The man didn't seem to need sleep, and she had already impressed upon him the urgency of the project. Henrick was ex-military. He was superbly efficient, tall, strong, and incredibly loyal. She pictured his piercing blue eyes, muscular jawline and buzzcut hair style.

"We're on target," replied an unsurprised Henrick. *"We'll be ready for the first test in two days' time, at this rate. What keeps you up so late?"*

Lexi glanced at the clock on the oven. Twenty-two minutes past one.

"Couldn't sleep," she replied. *"What does Erica have to say about the test?"*

"She says that she is very confident. I'm expecting a positive result. The only issue is, as you know, the power drain on the national grid."

Lexi nodded to herself and took another drag from her cigarette.

"You've tapped into the undersea cable?"

215

"Yes, we can pull power whenever we want, but it'll still wipe out the eastern region."

"I know," replied Lexi. *"It can't be helped."* She took a long sip of her coffee. *"You realise we won't be hidden once we run the test? Are the defences ready?"*

"Everything is ready. Major Daniels has been training his troops endlessly."

"And the weapons?"

"Yes, all delivered on time, including the new hover jets and artillery lasers."

Lexi paused while she stubbed out her cigarette and consumed the last of her coffee.

"Excellent! Well done, Henrick. I'll be there for the test, of course."

"I look forward to your visit. I'll have everything ready for you."

Lexi severed the connection, happy that everything was in order and on target. Taking out another cigarette, she contemplated what she should do next. She could go back to bed and try to sleep, but she knew that wouldn't work. She could return to her workshop and see if there was anything, she could do to make the M5A more comfortable to sleep in. But then a smile grew on her face as an idea came to her.

Reuben Cline was going to get another middle of the night visit. She could let herself go, taking pleasure from his body until the morning while he dreamed of a woman, he didn't know visiting his bed.

She stood and threw off the dressing gown. With a wicked smile on her face, she wriggled the fingers of her right hand and disappeared with a snap of wind.

Chapter 27 - Conflict

The room fell quiet as all eyes stared at Joe standing in the doorway.

Joe's frantic eyes darted around the room, searching for something. When they finally settled on Kate, his expression became even wilder, and his eyes widened in shock. He was speechless, his jaw dropping and his body swaying. He reached out and gripped the doorway for support, desperately trying to process what he was seeing.

Sally quickly sprang up and rushed to him, taking hold of his shoulders and standing in front of him to block his view. She spoke quickly and urgently, trying to calm him down.

"Stay calm, Joe," she spoke rapidly. "That's not Kate," she reassured him.

But Joe could only wheeze out one word: "Kate?"

She sent a desperate thought to Molly.

"Mol, help me. I don't know how he'll react."

Molly got up from her chair suddenly, pushing it backwards to crash into the wall. Lee also got to his feet at the same time.

"What's going on?" asked Joe in a weak voice.

Molly arrived to lend a hand to Sally and immediately gripped Joe's arm.

"Listen to me, Joe," she urged in a serious tone. "A lot has happened in the past few hours, and things are not as they seem."

With Sally's help, they guided him over to a nearby chair and gently helped him sit down.

He leaned back, closing his eyes tight. "I don't feel good," he admitted. "I think I have the flu."

Sally locked concerned eyes with Molly, while behind them Isabelle let go of Kate's shoulders and walked around the table towards them.

"Hello Joe," said Isabelle. "I am very pleased to see you."

Joe's eyes flicked over Sally's shoulder to the approaching silver woman.

"Who the fuck is that?" he asked. His red-rimmed eyes were enormous.

"That's Isabelle," replied Sally. "She's a friend."

"Joe, look at me," Molly commanded.

Joe kept staring at the silver woman walking slowly towards him. He was clearly confused. He looked over Sally's head, who had knelt before him and was taking his pulse.

"Kate?" he asked again.

Sally raised her hand to Joe's forehead, her Assist glowed purple. She looked over her shoulder at the approaching Isabelle.

"I don't know what you've done," she said angrily. "His physical condition is not good. He's showing signs of toxic encephalopathy and reduced cerebral blood flow. He should be back in my med lab under sedation."

"I understand your concerns," answered Isabelle as she approached them. "Rest assured that Joe will be fine."

"He shouldn't be awake!" shouted Sally, her voice shaking with rage. "You seem to have no respect for our safety and show no care for anyone here! Your callousness is endangering everyone's lives and I'm not having it!"

She was so enraged she could feel her face flush and her heart racing in her chest. In a moment of pure anger, she forgot about her fear of Isabelle. What gave her the right to come here and jeopardise the lives of those under Sally's care?

Molly placed a gentle hand on Sally's shoulder, sending calming energy towards her trembling body.

"Easy Sal," she thought soothingly. *"Getting mad won't do us any good now. Try to calm down."*

Sally took a deep, shaky breath. Molly was right, yet she couldn't ignore the way she felt. Being a doctor was her primary vocation, and nothing made her angrier than seeing someone put any of her patients in danger. She steadied her nerves before Isabelle's imposing form arrived, towering over her. Sally closed her eyes and concentrated. She pushed through her Assist while holding Joe's head in both her hands. Carefully and gently, she insinuated herself into Joe's brain and, with practised ease, manipulated and massaged sections of his brain, improving the blood and cerebral flow.

"Ow!" exclaimed Joe with a sharp thought. He raised a hand to his forehead. *"Sal, that hurts!"*

Sally grimaced and replied via thought. *"Sorry, just trying to help you think a bit more clearly. It won't last long, though. You need to rest."*

Joe looked into Sally's deep brown eyes. "What's going on, Sal?" he asked. "I feel like shit. Who is that silver woman? How did she get into the Complex? And also," he hesitated, his eyes flicking over Sally's shoulder. "That can't be Kate." He paused. "Can it?"

Sally could feel Isabelle standing close behind her.

"I don't understand all of it," she tried to answer his questions. "Isabelle is an android. She's from a parallel universe. Joe, she's shown us who the enemy is, and she says we are going to be under attack soon. But," she let her urgency and concerns for him flow into his mind. "Be careful. She seems to have a total disregard for us. Also," her thought hesitated. "That is Kate, but she's not our Kate. She's from another universe. She's not the same as our Kate. She's like Isabelle, cold and calculating. Don't go fawning after her like some lovesick child. She's a different person. I know how difficult this is for you. Please listen and understand."

Joe felt a little better after Sally's ministrations, his thoughts becoming clearer. He considered her words. Despite Sally's words about Kate, he couldn't stop his heart from beating faster. Could this really be her? He struggled to get his emotions under control and felt Sally help. She pushed his thoughts of Kate to one side.

"Be yourself, Joe," she implored him desperately. *"Come back to us. Now, of all times, we need you."*

He inhaled a ragged breath and tried to process what Sally had just said. Her last words stung, but he knew they were true - if he gave in to his emotions, everything was lost. And now Kate was here – or at least someone claiming to be her – it was easier than ever for him to fall into patterns of selfishness and self-pity. In that moment, he saw the damage he had caused in the last six months; turning away from friends and colleagues while he pursued a pointless quest for revenge against aliens, he knew nothing about. It was an absurd effort and now, for the first time, he could see it clearly.

He was filled with shame - and anger at himself. The warning signs had been there, as were the many warnings from his friends, but he had ignored them, swept away in the consuming emotion of his love for Kate. Now, he was left with guilt-ridden turmoil over his actions, not knowing how he could make it right. He asked himself why he had done it - but deep down, he already knew the answer.

Before he could reply to Sally, Isabelle spoke up.

"We don't have a lot of time, Joe; we are all in a very vulnerable position."

Joe managed to get his thoughts together. He felt much better, although still exhausted. He looked up warily at Isabelle looming over Sally.

"What are you talking about?" he asked. "Is someone going to tell me what's going on here?"

"I will leave it up to everyone else to fill in the gaps," replied Isabelle. "Right now, we need to talk."

Joe moved his head sideways to look past Isabelle, searching out Kate, but Isabelle frustrated his efforts moving to block his view. He looked up and locked eyes with her.

"What about?" he asked her in a guarded tone.

"I need to ensure that you won't harm Kate."

"What?" asked a puzzled Joe. "Kate is dead, unless." He leaned sideways to see past Isabelle, who, once again, smoothly blocked his view. "You mean that imposter over there?"

Isabelle smiled, while Sally rose to her feet, turned and lifted her head to face Isabelle, who was standing far too close. She stared unflinchingly up into her cold, black eyes.

"I know I can't stop you." Her hands shaking in front of her. "I'm asking you as a doctor, go easy on him. He's been through a lot."

The smile left Isabelle's lips. "I understand your point, but this is not something that I will compromise on. Joe is integral to the plan, and I must ensure that he is ready and safe to interact with Kate."

"What are you two talking about?" asked an exasperated Joe. "Will someone please tell me what's going on? What plan?"

For a moment Sally studied Isabelle's inscrutable silver face, then she turned and moved away, allowing Isabelle to close the distance between herself and the still seated Joe.

"Sally?" asked Joe. "What are you doing?"

Molly gripped Joe's shoulder. "It's okay Joe," she said. "I don't particularly like Isabelle, but I've seen the truth. We're all in grave danger."

Joe looked up at Molly with a puzzled expression. "What danger?"

"Listen to her, Joe," Lee shouted from across the room. "It's all true. We've all seen the enemy."

Joe's frown deepened, his eyes narrowing. "For fuck's sake!" he shouted at the room. "Will someone tell me what the fuck's going on? How have you all seen the enemy? Who is it?"

The room went silent. Then Isabelle spoke.

"You are Joe. You are the enemy."

Chapter 28 - Realisation

Joe's mouth hung open, unable to process the implications of Isabelle's words. How could it be true? He felt his eyes grow wide as he tried desperately to process what she had said. It was a nightmare! Was everyone going mad? Did they all believe Isabelle, or had she brainwashed them into turning against him? Joe felt his mind racing as confusion and uncertainty took over. What was going on here?

"Although to be accurate, not this version of you," continued Isabelle. "The enemy is you from a parallel world. Nevertheless, it is still you. You and your partner Kate."

"Kate?" Joe whispered, so shocked he could barely think.

Isabelle nodded. "More on that later. Now to business. I understand you have not been yourself lately?"

Joe struggled to marshal his thoughts. He and Kate were the enemy? That couldn't be. But what had Isabelle said? Something about a parallel world? Was that even possible? He felt Molly squeeze his shoulder and reflexively brought up his own hand to rest it on hers.

"It's okay Joe," said Molly. "We know it's not you."

Joe watched as Isabelle raised her right hand, and for a moment, he thought she was going to strike him. Then he saw an Assist appear on her wrist. Well, he assumed it was an Assist; it was like nothing he had seen before. It covered her entire forearm from wrist to elbow, its golden metal inlaid surface glinting from the room lights was unmistakable. With a bright white light, it flashed and glowed.

He tried to lean further back in the chair but found he could not move. The air hummed and vibrated as the room lights dimmed and then flickered out. The only light in the room came from the silver woman. Her Assist glowed brightly, the light reflecting and rebounding from her perfect silver limbs.

"I need to make sure that you won't harm Kate," she repeated as she pressed her hand to his forehead.

Joe could do nothing. He tried to block her from entering his mind, to no avail. Her mental probes slid into his mind like a hot knife through butter. In all his life, he had met no one who could invade his mind. He was the leader of the Alliance. The inventor of the Assist. He thought he had the most powerful mind on the planet. Yet here he was, unable to prevent the mental probes from Isabelle insinuating into the deep corners of his being.

As Isabelle probed and investigated, he recalled a moment over six months ago. When he had protected Kate from an automaton invader. He remembered that somehow Kate had entered his mind just like this. There had been no denying the connection. She and he had entered a Deep Link. A connection where their two minds became one. He had seen and felt so much. It was in that moment that he had realised he was in love with her.

Reliving the memory brought a single tear to one eye, which ran down his cheek.

Isabelle's black eyes regarded him dispassionately.

"You experienced a Deep Link with your Kate," her thought echoed in his mind. *"That is good. I can also see that you are not a bad person. But it is clear that you have not processed the loss of the Kate you loved, and you blame the Non'anan for her death. You should know that I will not allow you to access any technology to further your useless attempt at revenge."*

Joe bristled with anger. *"Who are you to stop me?"* he retorted. *"They killed Kate. I will teach them a lesson!"*

"No, you will not. I will not allow it. Until you learn to accept Kate's death as an accident, you are not capable of reasoned thinking."

"Fuck you!" replied Joe with venom.

"Stop that!" Isabelle answered. *"You are not some child to be admonished for stealing a biscuit. You are the founder of the Alliance. Act like it."*

Joe fell silent.

"Very well. I can see that the next phase of the plan is going to take some time. I will release you shortly. You need to get over your anger and accept what has happened, and you need to do it quickly." Isabelle paused. *"I could remove your memories of Kate...."*

Joe practically shouted. *"NO! It's all I have left of her!"*

"But I won't," she continued. *"I can see that it would not help the situation. This is something that you have to do yourself."*

Isabelle stepped back, removing her hand from Joe's forehead. Her Assist flashed and disappeared. The room lights flickered back on.

"Ugh," Joe grunted, slumping in his chair.

Sally quickly knelt at Joe's side as Isabelle stood tall and surveyed the room.

Ignoring Isabelle, Sally placed her hands on either side of Joe's head and lifted it. She closed her eyes as her Assist flashed blue.

"Joe, are you okay?" she asked with a gentle thought.

Joe's eyes flickered open. *"Yeah, I think so,"* he paused. *"That was not pleasant."*

"You're in shock, and the toxins in your brain are raised. You need sleep and lots of it."

"She got past my block, Sal," he replied. *"How could she do that?"*

"There's a lot about her we don't understand," replied Sally bitterly. *"She's turned everything upside down since arriving here. She's like a bull in a china shop. I don't like her. But I have to admit that she has been telling us the truth."* She shuddered. *"I've seen it myself."*

Joe blinked and gazed Sally's eyes, a questioning look on his face. "Seen what, Sal?" he asked aloud. "I still have no idea what's going on."

Sally bit her lip. "I don't want to add to your shock. You're not in a fit state," she replied.

"Sal, come on. I have to know."

Sally bit her lip again, this time drawing blood. "If you insist, I'll show you, but first you must do something for me."

Joe just looked at her.

Sally took a deep breath. "Relegate your memories of Kate. Stop allowing them to dominate you. Let your real self take back control. Your logical, calm, caring self. The one that Kate fell in love with, the one that everyone here in the Complex love. It's time, Joe, and you know it."

Joe knew she was right. Deep down, he had already come to the same realisation. Shame descended upon him once again as he thought of how selfish he had been and what he had put his fellow Alliance members through. He hung his head.

"I know you're right," he whispered. "It's hard, you know?"

Sally pulled him to her and hugged him tightly.

"I understand," she sniffed. "I'll help you. She'll always be with you; you won't forget her."

Joe drew in a ragged breath from her shoulder. Sally felt a small nod. She knew she had to act fast before he changed his mind. Quickly, she focused her mind and eased herself into Joe's thoughts with well-practiced ease, careful not to disturb his sense of self. As she delved deeper, searching for memories of Kate, she found fewer than she had expected, which surprised her. But this only made the task easier. Working quickly and efficiently, she gathered fragments of memory together like puzzle pieces and carefully shifted them into a new compartment in Joe's mind. The process took less than a second.

Joe lifted his head and locked his red-rimmed eyes with hers. Behind them they heard voices, then one much louder than the rest.

"Everyone," Isabelle addressed the room. "We have work to do. Please follow me to the engineering section, where I will outline some of the finer details of the plan. Joe and Kate will remain here."

"Thank you," said Joe in a quiet voice. He drew in a deep breath. "I don't think I could've done it by myself."

Sally smiled at him. "Course you could, if you had wanted to." The smile fell from her face. "Are you ready to see?"

Joe grimaced. "I have to. I need to know what's going on."

Sally looked up at Molly, who was still standing next to them. She saw Molly nod, and she nodded back. Flicking her gaze around the room, she saw everyone trooping through the doorway. She gazed back at Joe.

"Okay Joe. Here you go." She sent the memories from Steve to Joe, watching as he closed his eyes and what little colour, he had in his cheeks drain from his face.

Leaving him to process what he had just received, she stood, took Molly's hand and squeezed it hard. The two women locked eyes and a thought conversation flashed between them in less than a second. They exchanged a knowing look, and then they both turned their attention back to Joe.

"You alright Joe," asked Molly.

Joe looked up at her, eyes wide and face white. He nodded slowly.

"That's unbelievable," he replied. "I don't know what to say."

"We were the same," replied Sally. "It's a lot to take in. How are you feeling?"

"Very, very tired," replied Joe.

"You need rest," said a frowning Sally. "I don't agree with what Isabelle has done." She shot a glance at the doorway where Isabelle waited patiently. "But it seems we have no choice."

Joe turned around to face Isabelle and then back across the room to where Kate sat. He couldn't help feeling a pang of something in his chest. Even though Sally had moved his memories of Kate, he still felt the pain of her death. And yet, there she was, sitting at the large conference table, watching him with her dark eyes. A knot grew in his stomach as he stared at her. It really was Kate.

Molly observed Joe gazing at Kate. "Be careful Joe, this isn't your Kate. Do you understand?"

Joe didn't answer. Molly locked eyes with Sally again.

"Molly, Sally," came a voice from the doorway. "Are you ready?"

"Mol, I don't want to go to the engineering section," thought Sally at Molly. "Isabelle frightens me. Can I go to the medical bay? I need some normality."

Molly stroked Sally's cheek. "Of course, my love. I'll explain your absence. We'll talk later."

They turned and left Joe and Kate staring at each other across the room.

Chapter 29 - Abeko

Abeko was worried.

This was the fifth time that he had had a memory lapse. At least he thought it was the fifth. He could no longer be sure. Each time, there was a period when he couldn't recall anything at all. A time when all he saw in his head was blackness, and no matter what he did or how much effort he tried he couldn't break through the darkness. And a splitting headache always followed each one. He easily banished the pain from his pounding head, but he couldn't get rid of the blankness. The first time this had happened, he had dismissed it as stress, but then, as it kept happening, he grew more and more concerned. What bothered him most about these memory gaps was that they shouldn't be happening at all. He was wearing a Mark 4 Assist. He knew every corner and alcove of his mind. There was no way he could lose track of time. He briefly wondered if it could be faulty. Maybe that could explain it. Which made it even more urgent that he did what he knew he should do. He should go to the Med Bay and report it to the doctors.

Just the thought of visiting the Medical Bay made him feel sick. He couldn't understand it. Every time he thought of the Medical Bay, a strange queasiness overcame his body and mind, followed by an almost instinctual compulsion to avoid the doctors at all costs. It was one more thing he couldn't explain.

Of course, he knew Prisha would understand and help him. He could not explain why, but it felt wrong - wrong to tell anyone about his experiences. It was frustrating, stifling, and lonely. He wanted to tell her so much that he could physically feel himself yearning for the words to flow from his mouth. He should be able to trust in Prisha's love for him; she was his lover and best friend after all. Why couldn't he tell her?

These thoughts passed through his mind as he stepped from the raised dais in the teleportation room, deep in the heart of the Complex.

Thinking back to the last thing he remembered, he recalled being helped into a HAZPRO suit and then walking to the teleporter. He was on his way to Arcadia. It was a routine trip; one he had completed many times before. But this time, when the teleporter activated, something happened. He remembered his last command to the engineers.

"Ready," he thought at them. Then there was a flash. The next thing he knew was he was back on the dais. It was as though he hadn't been to Arcadia at all. Something clicked in his mind. A year ago, he underwent an operation to have a broken arm repaired and something about that experience stuck in his mind. He experienced when they put him under with the anaesthetic. He had never experienced anaesthesia before and found it to be strange. One moment he fell asleep, the next he was awake, as though nothing had happened in between. That was exactly how he felt now. Once moment stepping into the teleporter and the next stepping out onto the dais.

From the time he teleported to Arcadia, to the time he arrived back, there was nothing. It was like it had never happened.

He stumbled from the dais onto the bay floor with a loud clunk as his suited boots hit the floor.

"You okay, Abeko?" An engineer sent a quick thought query.

Abeko hesitated, trying to think.

"Yeah, sure. Just tripped is all."

He thumped his way to the nearest HAZPRO suiting section and commanded the suit to disconnect its systems and power down. While he waited for the suit to disconnect its medical probes and inner shell to contract, he pushed through his Assist, located the pain centres in his brain and removed the ache in his head with ease.

As the hermetically sealed upper section disengaged and was hoisted upwards with a crane mechanism, he desperately tried to remember. Where had he been? Had he even arrived on Arcadia? Had it only been a few minutes or a few hours? He sent a thought to an attending engineer.

"Say, what time is it? How long have I been gone?"

The engineer looked up at him, clearly puzzled.

"Three hours, of course," replied the engineer. *"That was the length of your stay, wasn't it?"*

Three hours! Abeko struggled to keep his face impassive and replied normally.

"Yes. Of course. I've just been busy, that's all."

He turned his face away from the engineer, who shrugged and continued with his work, connecting three umbilicals to the suit.

Three hours! He had been away for three hours! Three whole days gone from his memory! What had happened? This could not go on, he realised. This time, he had to do something about it. He had never had a memory lapse for so long. Three hours! His mind reeled, struggling to comprehend what this meant. He had lost three hours of his life! What had he been doing all that time? Where had he been? Had he even been on Arcadia for the three hours as he was supposed to be? There was nothing for it. There was no choice for him. He would have to visit the Complex Medical section. He would have to tell them, even if it meant finding out that he was seriously ill. But as soon as he had made the decision to see the doctors, a wave of nausea hit him like a hammer blow. He grunted in surprise and pain as his stomach churned, threatening to relieve itself of its contents.

Abeko recovered and glanced around quickly to see if any of the engineers had noticed. Fortunately, they were all busy. He waited until his suit's inner shell had expanded and released him from its bottom half, then grabbing a handrail he pulled himself up and out, swinging forward, he dropped to the floor.

"Best get that seen to by the medics." A thought came from the engineer.

Abeko looked down and saw a trickle of blood running down his left calf pooling at his foot. He looked closely and saw that he was bleeding from one of the suit's needle insertion points. It sometimes happened, but usually it was small and soon clotted. This didn't look as though it was going to stop. The flow was slow but steady. He frowned. Could the suit have nicked an artery? Surely not. He had never heard of such a thing happening to anyone before... but then again, there was always a first time. He sighed. One more thing to worry about, he thought to himself. As if I haven't got enough already.

Ignoring his stomach, which was still in turmoil, he walked towards the line of lockers positioned along the nearby wall. He opened one and pulled out his clothes. He found a white T-shirt and wrapped it around his leg to stem the blood flow.

Once dressed, he exited the Engineering Bay.

Making the turn towards the Medical Bay was difficult. His body didn't want to obey when he tried to step down the corridor. He had to push hard, his legs feeling like they were walking through molasses.

What was wrong with him? He thought, growing more and more alarmed. This was ridiculous. He could hardly walk! Without a doubt, he had made the right decision. He was clearly ill. He definitely needed to see a doctor. Another wave of nausea hit him, and he doubled over, retching and emptying his stomach contents onto the floor. Bright specs of colour danced in his vision as darkness closed in like a tunnel. He fought against losing consciousness, steadying himself against the corridor wall.

He stumbled forward, his legs heavy like lead and trembling with the effort of lifting them, each step becoming harder and harder to take. Every movement felt like he was dragging himself through thick sludge that clung to him and tried to keep him in place. It was as though something was trying to stop him from going any further. His stomach churned, roiled, and nausea flooded his body again. He shook uncontrollably as cold sweat beaded his brow and trickled down his face. Somehow, he pushed through the misery, forcing himself to go on because he had no other choice but to keep moving. He was now sure that he was seriously ill. He needed help.

He was completely unaware that as he walked; he was leaving a trail of blood behind him.

Chapter 30 - Kate & Joe

The door to the conference room clicked shut. Joe and Kate were alone, staring at each other.

Joe struggled to keep his emotions in control. There, sitting at the end of the table, was Kate. The jet-black hair, deep dark eyes and delicate mouth were all familiar, and yet, so he had been told, she was not the woman he knew. He felt a lump rising in his throat and swallowed it down as best he could. His mind ran in circles over and over: This is a copy of Kate; this is not the real Kate. He wondered what he should do. What should he say? Everything he thought of sounded ridiculous. Hi, I'm Joe, nice to meet you... Is that really you Kate?...

It was Kate that broke the silence. She simply said: "Hi."

Joe stared. That voice. He would recognise it anywhere. It was exactly like Kate's. He was dumfounded, his entire being screamed - this is Kate! It took everything he had to remain seated and not rush over to her and take her into his arms. He closed his eyes and focussed his attention inwards. This could not go on any longer. He had to manage his reactions. Things were happening here that he knew nothing about. To regain control of the situation, he had to concentrate. He had left things too long and now he was paying the price. He was playing catchup in what was clearly a serious situation. Hadn't someone said something about an imminent attack? Locating the emotional response centre in his frontal lobe, he carefully manipulated its neural activity, effectively downgrading its responses, which he hoped, would give him more control.

"Joe?" asked Kate. "Are you okay?"

Joe opened his eyes. He felt a little better. His emotional response to Kate subsided.

"Yeah, I'm okay," he replied in a croaky voice. He cleared his throat and continued. "Apart from the shock." He grimaced.

Kate returned the expression. "I know what you mean. I know that it's all a bit sudden, but believe me, there was no other way." She flicked a lock of hair from her face.

Joe couldn't believe his eyes. Not only was this woman identical to Kate, but she also had her mannerisms, too. He had seen his own Kate flicking her hair from her eyes, just like that. It was uncanny.

He cleared his throat again. "You really are Kate?" he asked. "From a parallel world?"

She nodded slowly, her hair falling in front of her eyes to be flicked away once more.

Joe followed her movements and then looked away.

"I'm sorry for staring, it's just…." he broke off.

Kate gave a small smile.

"I look just like your Kate." She answered for him.

Joe returned the smile.

"Yeah. It's weird. Everything about you is the same, well, apart from that." He gestured to her right arm. "And of course, your clothes. I never saw her wear anything but jeans and a T-shirt." He looked away and down at his hands in his lap.

"I'm sorry for your loss," said Kate. She hesitated and then continued. "I lost my Joe too. I know how hard it is."

Joe looked up; a questioning look on his face.

"Your Joe is gone?" he asked.

Kate nodded.

Joe sat back as he digested this news. It was strange to think that a version of himself was dead.

"How did he die?" he asked, not sure if he should ask such a question.

It was Kate's turn to stare down at her lap. She fidgeted with her fingers, clasping and unclasping her hands.

Joe waited for her to speak, grateful that Sally had helped him to compartmentalise his memories of Kate and that he had damped down his emotional responses, because if he hadn't.... Well, he would be lost. Once more, the similarity of her expression and movement struck him. This woman sitting at the end of the table was clearly Kate. Everything about her shouted that this was his Kate, even the way she clasped and unclasped her hands with her Assist chains clinking softly in the light.

But that's where the similarity ended. Her Assist was unlike anything he had seen before. The differences between his and hers were stark. He could see the device extending up her right arm, inside the sleeve of her red top. It was much larger than his Mark 5; the bracelet morphed into what looked like an armlet. Could it be a Mark 6? If so, he wanted to get his hands on one and pick it apart to see how it worked. His thoughts inevitably turned to seeking revenge against the aliens that killed his Kate.

He flicked his gaze from examining Kate's Assist back to her face - angry eyes were staring right at him.

"Don't!" she snarled in a harsh whisper; her wrath palpable in the air.

Joe was taken-a-back. He didn't understand why Kate had suddenly changed. One moment she was exactly like his Kate, a mirror image even. But now she was different. Almost a different person. She was angry, not just angry, she was incensed. What had caused the change in her mood? He wondered. He couldn't understand it.

"What?" he asked, puzzled.

"You know what I mean," she replied angrily, the volume of her voice increasing. "You were planning revenge!" she spat.

Joe was shocked. How did she know? She couldn't have read his mind. He would have known, would have felt it. He had a natural mind block that was in place most of the time. She couldn't have got through it without him knowing. Could she?

"You have a lot to learn about me, Joe," said Kate sternly. "I'm not your Kate. I am so much more than her, don't ever confuse me

242

with her. I have abilities and faculties that you can't perceive, and one of them enables me to see through your block as though it wasn't there. So yes, I've been reading your mind ever since you entered the room and there is one thing I will not put up with. Izzy told you too, I will not allow you to harbour any thoughts of revenge. You've seen who the real enemy is. Stop these destructive thoughts now or I will stop them for you."

Joe shifted uneasily in his seat. This was not going as he had expected. He had thought... What? Had he really been expecting that they would be in each other's arms? Did he really think that this woman could be a substitute for his Kate just because she looked like her? He wasn't sure if that's what he had been thinking or wishing for.

For once in his life, he was not the one in control. He hadn't a clue how to handle this scenario. He knew what it was like to read someone's mind without them being aware—he'd done it many times himself. But here, the roles were reversed; it was six months ago that he held all the power over his former Kate, and now it seemed as if this new Kate before him had the upper hand.

Joe was at a loss for words. It was futile to attempt concealing anything from her. It made him feel embarrassed and ashamed. Taking a slow, deep breath, he asked quietly: "So, where do we go from here?"

Kate remained furious. "It's up to you," she said sharply. "You have to get it together. You and I are essential parts of this endeavour. If you can't compose yourself, then this is all a waste of time. Can you manage it, Joe? Because if not, Isabelle and I will look for an alternate universe which would better suit our needs."

She paused before asking him once more. "Can you pull yourself together?"

Joe's eyes widened in surprise; it hadn't occurred to him that Kate might actually leave if she had no other option. Could she, really? His mind came back to the memory fragment Sally had revealed to him. Although it was hard for him to accept, he couldn't deny the data that showed a version of himself was accountable for the attacks and fatalities he had observed. He knew the enemy was supremely powerful - the memory fragment had shown them in action. He also understood that they didn't have a hope of defeating them. They needed all the help they could get.

He nodded slowly, locking eyes with Kate.

"Okay, I get it. I'll do my best. That's all I can do."

Kate's stern face changed and lit up with a bright smile, her fierce expression becoming gentler.

"That's all I can ask for," she replied. "I know it won't be easy, but it's important that we stay united. Without each other..." She didn't finish her statement.

"Right."

There was silence between them once again.

"So, what is this plan of yours?" asked Joe.

Kate grimaced.

"It won't be easy."

"Nothing ever is."

Kate looked away. "First, we need to build our defences, which is what Isabelle is coordinating right now."

"I guess that makes sense," replied Joe. "But who is this, Isabelle? She controlled me as though I was nothing. I couldn't do anything to stop her. I've never met anyone who could do that."

"Yes, she can be a bit direct. But you'll get used to her. She's very powerful and very clever and has everything planned."

"I'm not sure that I'm ever going to get used to this. I'll be honest with you; I'm feeling pretty confused right now."

Kate looked at him sympathetically.

"Is she human?" asked Joe tentatively.

Kate shook her head.

"No, she's an advanced computer - I won't pretend to understand - but in some ways she's more human than most people. She has emotions and behind that tough exterior there is a softer side."

Joe snorted. "Yeah right, I've yet to see that!"

A small smile crossed Kate's face, something so uniquely her it made his heart ache.

"Just give it time," she said.

As a sudden wave of exhaustion hit him, Joe slumped in his seat and bowed his head.

"Are you okay?" asked Kate, concerned.

With visible difficulty, Joe lifted his head up.

"I haven't been feeling great since I woke up. It must be the aftereffect of whatever Isabelle did."

"Most likely," replied Kate, leaning forward in her chair. "Look, we had to make sure you were safe, which is why we woke you. I know it was harsh, but it was the only way, especially given our timeline."

"Well, whatever, I feel like shit and it's getting worse."

Kate hesitated and then said, "So, where do we go from here?"

Joe considered for a while.

"I guess we'll have to get to know each other all over again."

Kate beamed at him.

"I would love that."

"I'd like to keep talking, but right now, I don't think I can. I need to think, and I can't concentrate right now. And I don't think I can stay awake much longer anyway."

Kate stood; her hands clasped in front of her.

"Of course. I'm sorry that we had to wake you. I am sure that you'll feel much better later."

Joe slowly hoisted himself out of his chair, one hand massaging his lower back as he moved away from his seat. He stumbled as he made a second step, and Kate couldn't help but reach out to steady him. As soon as their skin touched, an electric shock seemed to pass through them both and she quickly retracted her hand.

Their eyes locked once more. They both knew that their bond was still there, despite coming from different places, different worlds. There was an invisible force that passed between them, just like before - Kate could feel it emanating from Joe, and Joe experienced the same emanating from Kate. A connection, a mutual attraction, held them in place as they stared at one another.

Kate was the first to break the silence.

"I'll see you when you've rested?" she asked in a trembling voice.

Joe nodded.

"I'll come find you," he replied.

He tore his gaze from her and walked through the door. Kate watched him go.

"You like him," stated Bella.

"Of course I do," Kate replied. *"He's just like my Joe."*

"Do you think you can persuade him?"

"Yes. I can tell he is attracted to me. Did you feel the connection?"

"Yes," replied Bella. *"It's definitely there. You will have to be careful about approaching him. Especially when it comes to me."*

"I know," Kate sighed. *"I will. Guide me if I get it wrong, will you? This is more important than our feelings for each other."*

"Of course," answered Bella. *"I am always here for you. Let's see what happens when you next meet."*

Chapter 31 - Disaster

Abeko stumbled into Sally's medical room and collapsed onto the floor. She spun around at the noise, her breath catching in her throat at the sight of Abeko writhing on the floor. His eyes were bulging out of his head and his limbs shook wildly, blood spurting from a gaping wound on his leg like an open fountain. With no time to spare, Sally quickly thrust her hands into gloves and grabbed a sterile cloth from a nearby trolley. Racing towards the convulsing Abeko, she pressed down hard on his leg to contain the spraying blood and stop it from splattering all over the walls.

She sent out an urgent thought.

"Clarice, Amanda, get in here now. I need help."

She pushed Abeko into the recovery position and tried to cradle his head so that he wouldn't hurt himself.

"Lee, we have a problem. Abeko has turned up, but he's wounded and having some sort of seizure."

Lee replied instantly.

"On my way."

Sally's two medics, Clarice and Amanda, appeared at the doorway.

"Hold this," directed Sally, showing the bandage to Clarice. "Amanda, help me get him onto the table."

Together they lifted Abeko while Clarice continued to stem the blood. There was a crash of wind as Lee and Isabelle teleported directly into the room.

While Sally and Amanda settled Abeko onto the medical table, Isabelle stepped forward, a blue glow appearing around her perfect silver body. She gestured with a hand and the open door crashed shut. The air began to vibrate and hum as a purple haze sped around the room, coating the walls, floor, and ceiling.

Sally, Clarice and Amanda fought desperately to restrain Abeko's frenzied thrashing. His sudden movements sent Clarice flying back as the bandage around his wound slipped and a stream of blood sprayed her full in the face. She spat a mouthful of red onto the floor before quickly wiping the blood off with her free hand.

"Hold him!" yelled Sally, darting across the room towards the cupboard. Throwing open the door, she frantically rummaged through the shelves of drugs, searching for something that could help settle Abeko down.

"What can I do?" asked Lee.

"Just hold him while I get the lorazepam!" replied Sally.

Lee started towards Abeko but was stopped when Isabella grabbed his arm, her grip like iron. He felt a surge of Psi energy from Isabelle's hand.

"Stop!" commanded Isabelle in a loud commanding voice.

"What?" asked Lee.

"All is not as it seems. I am detecting something unusual."

Everyone stopped what they were doing and stared at Isabelle. On the table, Abeko made feral grunting sounds.

"What is it?" asked Sally.

Suddenly Clarice violently reeled away from the Abeko, her throat releasing a shrill sound that brought everyone's attention to her. She stumbled back as Abeko continued to thrash around on the table. She brought her hands up to her face, blood seeping between her fingers.

Sally moved towards Clarice, while Amanda tried her best to hold Abeko still. But Isabelle intervened.

"Everyone stop what you are doing," she commanded out loud. She stepped forward and pulled Amanda away from Abeko. Amanda tried to resist but could not prevent Isabelle from shoving her to the far wall of the room.

"Touch nothing," she commanded. "I am detecting nanobots in Abeko's blood. They are multiplying and attacking everything they touch."

Clarice fell to the floor, still screaming, blood now running freely from between her fingers.

"Kate," Isabelle sent an urgent thought. *"I need your help. Close all portals to my world. Get Bella to scan you for invasive*

nanobots and purge any she finds. Raise your screens to protect yourself. I will be in touch soon."

In microseconds, she relayed the situation to Kate via thought transference. Then she knelt to Clarice to caress the top of her head. Clarice suddenly stopped screaming and her hands fell away to reveal her blood soaked and ravaged face. One eye was gone, blood welling up from a dark hole, her lips had been eaten away, blood gurgling around blackened teeth as Clarise choked and spluttered, spraying blood upwards into the air onto Isabelle's arm.

Lee gasped as he saw the damage to Clarice's face.

"What…?" he said.

Sally's instincts were to help, but she stood frozen in horror, watching one of Clarice's fingers twitch as it dissolved into a wet mush.

Isabelle's fingers glowed blue, and Clarice stopped breathing. She stood and addressed everyone.

"The Complex has been invaded with nanobots that have been programmed to multiply and to disassemble everything they come into contact with. We have all been contaminated, as has anything else that Abeko has been in contact with on his journey here."

"Nanobots?" asked Amanda from the rear of the room. "What are they?"

"Microscopic machines," replied Isabelle. "Invisible to the naked eye. By now, they will be throughout the Complex. We are no longer safe. Left to their own devices, they will destroy the Complex and kill everyone in it. More concerning is that they will keep disassembling and multiplying. Eventually they will eat the whole Earth."

"What can we do?" asked Lee.

"There is only one way to stop their progress," replied Isabelle. "We don't have much time. This body is already compromised. Shortly, it will cease to function."

"Is Clarice dead?" asked Sally.

"Yes," Isabelle turned towards her. "I took the kindest action and euthanised her."

Sally's face contorted in horror. "You killed her!"

"Yes," replied Isabelle's smooth, unperturbed contralto voice. "I don't have time to explain now. I must act or we will all die."

Sally turned away from Isabelle.

"What are you going to do?" asked Amanda.

"Electro Magnetic Pulse or EMP," replied Isabelle. "It will short out all the circuits in their tiny bodies and will kill them all."

Lee looked up suddenly.

"Wait," he said, a look of concern on his face. "That's not a good idea. I don't think that our Assists will survive that."

"You are correct," nodded Isabelle. "All electronic componentry in the Complex will be destroyed, including all the Assist's everyone is wearing right now. And of course, that includes this body." She gestured to herself, raising an arm where already the perfect skin was starting to discolour.

Sally spun back around to face Isabelle.

"But that will kill us all!" she exclaimed. "We cannot survive without our Assist's anymore. Our brains have changed."

"Not immediately. Your Assist's will have to be replaced; I have already sent instructions to the fabricators in my world to start production. I hope to have enough fabricated in time to replace them all."

She paused.

"I have also closed the micro portal from this body to my world, cutting myself off completely. I cannot allow the nanobots to infect my world as well. From now on I have limited functionality. I have a singular function. To destroy all the nanobots in this world."

Lee understood immediately.

"The EMP will kill you," he stated.

"Yes. This body will cease to function. Once I activate the EMP, you will need to find Kate. She will know what to do next."

"Wait!" shouted Sally. "What about our Enhanced members? We can't just replace their enhancements. They are integrated into their brains. This might kill them."

"I have a singular purpose," replied Isabelle.

Lee turned to Sally.

"She's gone," she told her. "Isabelle is no longer here. She never was. This android is merely an extension of her. Now that the portal to her world is closed, she no longer commands it. It looks like she left one final instruction."

On the medical table, the convulsing Abeko stopped and went still, his eyes wide, staring at the ceiling.

"But Steve and the others..." protested Sally.

"We have no choice Sally," replied Lee. "We'll have to take our chances or lose everything."

Lee sent out a questing thought.

"Kate, where are you?"

Kate responded immediately.

"I'm with Molly in her lab. Izzy told me what's happening. There is no infection here. Once the EMP goes off, I'll open a portal to Izzy's world and re-establish contact."

Lee beckoned to Amanda.

"Let's get out of this room," he told Sally and Amanda.

"But Clarice...." Sally started to say.

"She's gone Sally," replied Lee gently. "I think that there was no way to save her, which is why Isabella euthanised her. Not nice, I know," he grimaced. "But probably for the best."

As Lee pulled at Sally's arm, dragging her towards the door, Sally took one last look at Clarice's rapidly disintegrating face. It was now a pool of red jelly with white bones and teeth protruding upwards, red dripping from the bone edges.

Isabelle stood still, observing and waiting until all three had left the room and the door had closed behind them.

She activated the EMP pulse.

Chapter 32 - Action

Kate was with Molly in one of Molly's labs. They had been discussing the Complex fortifications and facilities required for Isabelle to travel this world, when Kate suddenly stopped talking mid-sentence.

"Bella, unlock high order functions," commanded Kate. *"Close all the portals in the Complex."*

Having just communicated with Isabelle, Kate fully understood the seriousness of the situation and knew what Isabelle was about to do. Even though she didn't understand what the EMP was, Isabelle had told her it would disable all electronics within the Complex and probably further depending upon the intensity of the pulse. Kate had no idea what magnitude of pulse Isabelle would be capable of generating, but she knew how to protect herself. Bella would do it for her.

"High order functions enabled," reported Bella. *"All portals are now closed."*

A pale blue aura flickered around Kate and a buzzing filled the air as its molecules vibrated with energy.

Molly felt hot air blow on her face.

"What's happening?" she sent an alarmed thought to Kate.

"It sounds bad," replied Kate. *"Give me a minute."*

She directed a thought at Bella.

"Scan the area and us. Are we contaminated with these nanobot things?"

"Scanning," replied Bella.

A purple haze swept back and forth through the room.

"No nanobots detected," Bella reported.

"What about the EMP? Are we protected from the EMP?"

"Yes. We are safe from the effects of the EMP. The pulse cannot penetrate our Mark 6 screens."

"What about Molly?" asked Kate. *"Can we expand our screens to cover her too? I'm guessing that her Mark 5 can't screen against an EMP?"*

"That's correct. If we want to save her, Assist, then yes, we can expand our screens, but you will have to be very close."

Kate quickly stepped towards Molly grabbing her around her waist, pulling her close. Molly yelped with surprise.

Kate directed an urgent thought at Sally.

"Sally, you know what's going to happen?" she didn't wait for a reply. *"As soon as the EMP is over, I'll re-open a portal to World 6. We will need to get all the Complex staff refitted with new Assist's. Can you help?"*

Sally's reply was instantaneous.

"Of course. I'm on my way to you."

"What's happening?" asked Molly again, growing more and more alarmed. She wasn't used to not knowing what was going on. Being a founding member of the Alliance, she was always in control, always consulted, and almost always making the decisions. Now, she felt like a nobody. She didn't know what was happening, and she didn't like it.

Kate turned her attention to Molly, their noses almost touching.

"Bella, expand our screens," she gazed directly into Molly's eyes. *"I'm screening both of us from the EMP. That way your Assist will survive. Izzy tells me that once the EMP activates, all electronics in the Complex will be dead."*

Molly felt awkward and uncomfortable as Kate tightly embraced her. She felt a charge from a surge of electricity whip through her body. She could feel power surging through her, crackling under her skin like static electricity from wool blankets in winter. A blue glow surrounded them both, and she could feel the hairs on her arms stand up. She watched her auburn hair drift in the air, feeling the power radiating from Kate. In that moment, Molly could sense the powerful emotions running through Kate's mind. When she sent out an exploratory thought towards her, Kate quickly blocked it with ease.

"What the hell?" Molly sent an alarmed thought. *"What EMP? What's happening"*

"I've been in contact with Izzy. Abeko has come back from wherever he went. Izzy says he's been weaponised. His blood is contaminated with nanobots. I don't know what they are, but Izzy tells me they are attacking everything in the Complex, including people. She says the only way to stop them is to use an EMP, whatever that is."

Molly was aghast. They were under attack. Again! What the hell? Their so-called impregnable base had been infiltrated once again, just as it had been six months ago. How had that happened?

"Brace!" Kate thought at Molly.

The two women held onto each other as the air rippled outside their screens and a shock wave blasted through the room, knocking over a chair and sweeping items from a tabletop onto the floor.

"That was the EMP," stated Kate unnecessarily. *"Bella, open a portal to world 6 and make contact with Izzy."*

Molly didn't bother to turn around to watch the black disk expanding behind them. Instead, she pushed her thoughts at Kate, once again feeling the familiar texture of her block.

"An EMP will have destroyed all the Assist's in the Complex!" she exclaimed. *"Everyone will die! Do you know what you have done?"*

Kate gazed calmly into Molly's eyes.

"Izzy said there was no other way. Would you rather the nanobots had consumed everyone?"

Molly didn't know how to answer.

"We'll refit everyone with new Assists," Kate continued. *"Izzy will have everything back to normal as soon as possible."* Her eyes grew softer. *"You can trust us, Molly, I promise."*

Kate lowered her mental block slightly, briefly letting Molly in. What Molly saw made her gasp. She saw complex whirling thoughts and emotions intertwined and entangled together, forming a mentality the like of which she had never seen before.

"What is this?" she asked in awe.

"We are one," replied Kate.

For a fraction of a second, Molly saw the mentality split in two and then fuse back together.

A shocked Molly could not form a coherent thought.

"What...? You.... Did....?" Her thoughts spluttered.

Kate was grinning widely.

"There are.... I don't believe it.... there are two of you!" A shocked Molly thought.

"We don't have time right now. We are one; Bella and I." She released Molly from around her waist and pulled Molly's arms from around her own, taking a small step back. *"We need to help everyone. I'm guessing that some people will be in a bad way right now."*

Molly let Kate pull her arms away. She recovered quickly.

"Yes, of course you're right. But Kate, what I just saw. I've never seen anything like it. It's amazing!"

Kate nodded, stepping aside to view the now fully expanded portal.

"You'll need to talk to Izzy. I don't understand any of it."

She sent a thought through the portal.

"Ready Izzy."

A crystal thought came back.

"Well done, Kate. I will be with you shortly."

At that moment Sally crashed through the doorway, her eyes wild with terror and pain, her body trembling. She collapsed to the ground in a shaking heap, her hands clutching at her head. Instantly, Molly was at her side, cradling her in her arms.

"Help me, Mol!" Sally implored; her voice full of pain.

Molly couldn't hold back her tears as she leaned forward and kissed the top of Sally's head.

"Everything's gone. I can't see anything!" cried Sally.

In that moment, Molly understood - Sally's Assist was no longer working, depriving her of the senses and abilities granted to her by its technology. All her Assist enabled senses would be gone - no teleporting or mind-moving objects; not being able to sense feelings and thoughts; unable to perceive the world around her as she had before; not seeing into the inner workings of people. Losing all these abilities would be devastating.

Molly wrapped her arms tighter around Sally, stroking her hair. She raised her tear-filled eyes to Kate.

"Please," she implored. "She needs a new Assist. Please help her."

"Give me a moment," replied Kate.

"Please hurry," answered Molly, cradling Sally's head in the crook of her arm. She whispered gently in her ear as she slid her consciousness deep within Sally's mind. Molly was a master at this process and within seconds she had broken through the barrier of pain that surrounded Sally's thoughts. She located Sally's pain centres with delicate probes, tapped them gently to assess their severity, increased the power as needed and dampened them down, reducing the pain that Sally was experiencing.

Sally's rapid breathing eased, and she opened her eyes.

"Oh Mol!" she wailed. "It's horrible. I can't see! I feel so alone!"

Molly comforted her as much as she could.

"It'll be alright, my love," said Molly, gently brushing Sally's hair from her eyes. "A new Assist is on its way."

There was a crash behind them as a silver crate shot through the portal and skidded across the floor. Kate stepped forward. The crate opened at her touch, its top lid splitting into two parts. She reached inside and passed a Mark 5 Assist to Molly.

Molly accepted it gratefully. She gently pulled Sally up from the floor and directed her to a medical chair.

"I have a new Assist for you, Sal. Let me fit it for you."

Sally looked up at Molly. Her eyes wet with tears, fear in her face. When she saw the Assist in Molly's hand, her expression changed to one of eagerness.

"Please put it on now!" she said urgently. "I can't stand this much longer."

Kate walked over to help. She removed Sally's left shoe and pulled off the now dead and useless Assist while Molly removed the rings from Sally's right hand.

Kate could not help but think of the irony, as their roles were now reversed. It felt like only yesterday when her Sally had removed Kate's shoe and had fitted the rings of a Mark 4 Assist onto Kate's toes.

She pushed the rings of Sally's new Mark 5 Assist onto her toes and clicked the anklet shut. Had it been only one year ago when Sally had helped Kate?

Meanwhile, Molly did the same for Sally's right hand. As she snapped the bracelet shut, she leaned over Sally and embraced her, holding her tightly as Sally shuddered and gasped.

Kate returned her attention to the portal and watched as Isabelle stepped through the portal dressed in skin-tight black trousers and a white T-shirt, a duplicate of one of Kate's trademark shirts. This one had I love pizza written on it with a picture of a pizza slice below the words.

"It's a good job you manufactured more than one android body," thought Kate at Isabelle privately. *"How is Josie? I miss her."*

"I have planned for all eventualities, although admittedly not this one." Isabelle walked over to Kate and gave her a quick hug. *"Josie is fine. I have everything ready to transport her to this world when the time is right."*

She released Kate and surveyed the room, her black lidless eyes settling on Molly & Sally still embracing each other.

"That, however, is some time away. We need to restart the building - all my drones will be useless junk and will have to be removed and replaced."

"What about the Complex staff?" asked Kate. *"Do you have enough Assist's for all of them?"*

"No, but I have redirected the fabricators to prioritise building Mark 4 Assists."

Isabelle directed a thought at Molly.

"Molly, how many people do you have in your Alliance?"

Molly did not move from her embrace with Sally, but her thought came back immediately.

"Three hundred and three if we count Abeko."

"How many of those are Enhanced?"

"Only twelve," replied Molly. *"Not many of our people liked the idea of something so invasive."*

"I am not surprised," replied Isabelle. *"It is a technique I have not seen before. Certainly, it was never developed in my world. As soon as Sally has recovered, I suggest we start transporting everyone to my world for medical treatment."*

Two more silver crates shot out from the inky blackness of the portal, followed by five squat spider robots which scuttled out of the room with inhuman speed.

"If Sally is up to it, I would like her to lead the medical teams with the refitting of the Assists. There is no one more capable. Do you think she will be able?" asked Isabelle.

"I'm sure she'll want to," answered Molly. *"But right now, she needs rest."*

"Of course. The facilities in my world are being prepared as we speak. I have allocated a room for you and Sally. This Spiderling," she gestured at a one metre tall, six-legged robot that waited at the Portal. *"Will direct you. It will stay with you. When Sally is fully, please ask her to take command of the medical facilities."*

Molly moved her head to view the portal and the Spiderling. She didn't like spiders. Horrible, fast-moving things with long hairy legs. But this one was all silver like Isabelle, with multi-jointed legs and although it resembled a spider, its six legs and lack of mouth parts at least made it a little less repulsive.

"Meanwhile, Kate and I will check on Joe and start arranging the transportation for everyone. I imagine that many will be unconscious."

Molly readily agreed with Isabelle, keeping a tight hold on Sally all the while. She sent calming thoughts into her lover's mind as Sally's brain slowly interfaced to her new Assist. It had been horrifying to see Sally so distraught. And Molly knew everyone in the Alliance would be feeling the same. The entire Complex had been neutralised in minutes, leaving them defenceless and wide open to further attacks since their screens would also be disabled.

Her thoughts were interrupted by an urgent thought from Bella directed at all three of them.

"There's someone at the Complex entrance. It's Jim!"

Chapter 33 - Evacuation

Kate stood looking down at a sleeping Joe.

He looked so peaceful, she thought, and exactly like her Joe in every respect. She supposed that his hair might be a bit longer than her Joe and his eyelashes darker, but other than that, he was identical in every respect. A surge of emotion swept over her. She missed her Joe. Even now, after more than a year, their last moments together were still clear in her mind. His face contorted in pain, blood tickling down from his head wound, winding a path down to his nose to drip onto the floor and into his mouth as he whispered, "I love you." And then the blackness as he pushed her backwards through the portal.

Her Assist meant that everything she experienced was recorded with crystal clarity, never to be forgotten. She had moved the memories away so that they did not dominate her thoughts. But she would never forget. She would never forget the sacrifice he had made to save her.

She smiled to herself as Joe snorted in his sleep. A tiny trickle of spittle leaked from a corner of his mouth, running down his chin to the pillow.

He had slept through the entire disaster. Not even the EMP had woken him, the effects of the sedative finally taking effect. He would probably sleep for many hours yet, the abnormal wakening effected by Isabelle taking its toll.

It was probably for the best, thought Kate. This way he would avoid the trauma of being without a working Assist. As she gazed down at his sleeping form, her mind whirled with questions and doubts. Would he be able to accept her for what she was? Would he be able to recognise that the Non'anan had not intentionally killed his Kate? Most importantly, could he push aside all doubts and cooperate with her to seek their aid?

Of course, she had another motive. One that she dare not put into words and that she kept hidden deep inside of her. A motive that she had not even told Isabelle. She wanted Joe to like her. Not just like her; love her. She wanted him to fall in love with her. She yearned for the happiness of days long gone but feared that it might never be hers again.

Shaking her head, she tried to shake the thoughts away. She couldn't afford to let them cloud her perspective. She needed to be clearheaded for what was to come. The plan must take precedence. Everything else was secondary.

She sighed. Time to transport Joe to World 6.

"Bella, unlock high order functions."

After Bella had complied and as the air charged with static electricity, Kate gestured expansively with her right arm and teleported herself, Joe and the bed he was lying on, to the nearest portal.

———

Two hours after having her new Assist fitted, Sally stood in a sparkling new and very well-equipped medical centre in World 6 surveying two rows of five beds. Each one occupied with an unconscious Alliance member. They had all been fitted with new Assists and now lay recovering.

Once she had fully recovered, she immediately sprang into action, her medical training kicking in. She had three hundred or so patients that needed her help. The problem was that she was on her own. There was only herself, Molly, Kate and Isabelle, who were up on their feet and fully functioning. The rest were incapacitated.

Molly was back in their world, supervising the transfer of Alliance members. Kate was nowhere to be seen, and she assumed Isabelle was working on rebuilding their defences.

That left Sally, and although she was impressed with the facilities, there were only three wards, each with ten beds in two rows of five. That meant only thirty beds. Not nearly enough. There was already a backlog of Alliance members lining the corridor outside of the medical facility. Some were slumped in chairs moaning in pain, while others were unconscious, lying on the floor.

All the Alliance members who arrived could not function, some not even able to walk, with those that were unconscious being teleported to the nearest available space, even if that was the corridor floor. Isabelle's spiderbots were busy bringing in patients sat in wheelchairs, depositing them onto the first available chair and then taking the wheelchair back to the nearest portal to collect the next patient.

And, if that wasn't enough, all twelve Augmented members had to be wheeled in on wheeled medical beds, each one unconscious. Sally had placed them down the centre aisle of two of the wards. She was unsure what she could do for them. The electronic component of their brains was no longer functioning. Their Augmentation had been surgically fitted, it would have to be removed and replaced. As far as she knew this had never been done before, and worse there were no replacement Augmentations available. All were destroyed in Sally's world. To make matters worse, Isabelle had told her they had never been developed in her world - world 6.

As Sally considered who to treat next, a spiderbot scuttled into the ward. Its legs clicking on the floor, its silver metal body glinting under the fluorescent lights. It made a beeline for Sally, gripping a metal box in its two grippers. Inside the box lay eight shiny new Mark 4 Assists, nestled in foam padding.

Sally calculated in her mind which patient to fit next. The soft beep of the spiderbot echoed through the sterile room, mixing with the hum of machinery and soft moaning of the waiting patients. Amanda came to mind almost immediately. Sally needed help, and she knew it. Amanda was a trained and experienced nurse. She mentally kicked herself for not fitting Amanda first. What had she been thinking? With a determined nod, Sally decided she would correct her error and fit her with a new Assist immediately.

The spiderbot skittered away as quickly as it had arrived, leaving behind only the faint sound of its delicate steps echoing in the room. Sally went back to work, her focus sharp, her eyes scanning over all of her patients with practiced ease.

———

"I want him to have a Mark 6," stated Kate defiantly.

She had moved Joe through the portal into World 6 and then teleported him to her own quarters. Along the way, she had carefully slipped into Joe's mind, located his sleep loci and made sure that he would remain unconscious. She didn't want him to wake just yet.

"He is not ready for it," replied Isabelle.

"I know, but we have to re-fit him anyway, so why not now?"

Isabelle appeared to consider Kate's words. It was impossible to read Isabelle's impassive, metallic face. It was the one thing that Isabelle had not yet mastered – displaying emotion.

"Very well. I can see your point. As you say, he would have to be fitted with a Mark 6 at some point, anyway. But it will be powered down, as was yours when it was first fitted. We cannot yet trust him. I have looked into his mind. He holds a lot of anger against the Non'anan. We cannot allow him to jeopardise the plan."

Kate nodded. "I know. I just think that this would save time. Don't worry, I'll start working on him as soon as he awakes."

Isabelle inclined her head. "Good. If the Abeko attack has shown us one thing, it is how vulnerable we are at the moment. It is imperative that we move quickly." She paused and laid a hand gently on Kate's shoulder. "

You know I can't help you with this part of the plan," she said softly. "I know how difficult this is for you. You know how crucial this part of the plan is. We can't do it without Joe. I'm sorry to lay

this responsibility on your shoulders, if there was any other way…"
She left her sentence uncompleted.

Kate laid her hand on top of Isabelle's. "It's okay, Izzy, I understand, and I've already agreed with the plan. I know it will be hard, but I can't see any other way."

They both stared down at the man in the bed.

————

Sally's heart sank as she surveyed the crowded medical bay. More and more patients were pouring in, many stumbling and crying in pain. She didn't know where she was going to put them all. Amanda was not yet recovered, and Sally knew things were getting worse by the second. The supply of Mark 4 Assists, while steady, was painfully slow.

She bit her lip in frustration, wishing there was something more she could do. Even with the top-tier medical facilities available in this world, they were not prepared for an event like this. All she could do was move from patient to patient, offering words of comfort and administering pain-relieving drugs. She had never seen so many people hurt at once, and it was taking its toll on her, too. She needed help.

As if on cue, a voice from the doorway startled her out of her thoughts.

"Hello there. Do you need another pair of hands?"

Sally whirled around to face a woman entering the ward. An aura of calm and serenity emanated from her, visible even from across the room. Long silver hair framed a kindly face with sparkling blue eyes behind a pair of silver framed glasses.

The woman smiled at her. "Don't worry, I'm not here to cause any trouble." She held up her hands as if to emphasise her point.

"My name is Elizabeth, but you can call me Liz. Kate and Isabelle are my friends; I live with them."

Sally squinted her eyes in surprise as she observed Elizabeth intently. She sent a quick mind probe but was unable to penetrate her mental shields even though she was clearly not wearing an Assist.

"I may not have the same mind powers as Kate and Isabelle, but that doesn't mean I'm unprotected. It's rude to pry," Liz said coolly, striding into the ward with a look of concern etched on her face.

Sally's jaw dropped. Who was this woman? What did she mean, protected? Clearly the mind block - but was there anything else? Was she even human? Could she be an android like Isabelle? Without being able to touch Liz's mind, Sally couldn't be sure. However, would a robot wear glasses and have silver hair? It didn't seem plausible.

"I'm sure you can appreciate my caution when it comes to my patients," Sally said. "Are you aware of what's happened?"

"Of course," snapped Liz before glancing over her shoulder. "Shall we begin? Where do you need me?"

Sally still had her doubts about Liz, but she knew she needed all the help she could get. She hesitated, then shrugged.

"We need someplace to put our people, and there are more coming soon," Sally said. "We don't have enough beds. Do you know if there are any other rooms we can use?"

Liz offered a slight smile. "I have an idea." She indicated the Spiderbot newly arrived on the scene, which scuttled closer to her. "Fetch us all the mattresses from each of the staff quarters, twelve for each ward," Liz instructed it.

The Spiderbot sped off to carry out Liz's orders.

Sally was astonished. "Does it really obey you?" she asked her strange companion.

"Naturally," Liz replied. "Have you tried talking to them?"

Sally shook her head. "It never occurred to me," she admitted.

Liz arched her eyebrows in surprise. "Polite requests usually do the trick," she suggested.

At that, Sally couldn't help but break into a grin.

"Liz, I think I like you, even though you are mysterious. Shall we get started?"

Chapter 34 - Jim

Isabelle regarded Jim dispassionately as he stood before her. Inwardly, she was not happy. The nanobot incursion had been something she had not predicted and therefore not planned for. Even though the threat had been eliminated, they were now defenceless. With every electronic device in the Complex now junk, they were wide open to attack. Her priority was to re-equip all the Alliance members with new Assists, but she also needed to get their screens up. All the fabricators were running at full capacity, half of them building Assists and the other half building spiderbots she could direct to repair the damage done in this world.

And now here was Jim, as if conjured up from nowhere. Where had he come from? Why was he here? From her Deep Link with Joe earlier, she knew Jim was dead. Or, if not dead, not in this world. So how come he was here? Could he be an alternative Jim from another world?

Joe's twin brother stood before her; mouth wide open as he stared up at her. They had already experienced a weaponised person. Was this another? Because there were no screens, Jim had been able to walk right up to the Complex doorway unchallenged. If there had been any power, he could have ridden the lift down into the heart of the Complex, where he would have seen the chaos below. But fortunately, without power, the lift wasn't working.

"Why are you here?" she asked.

Jim gulped. He could not take his eyes off this tall silver faced woman. Who was she? He had never seen her before.

Her face gave the impression of being made of metal, and her jet-black eyes seemed to penetrate his soul.

"I..." he started to say. He swallowed noisily. "I came to see Joe."

Isabelle considered. There was no way she was going to let Jim see Joe and besides, Kate had already transported Joe to world 6.

"Why?" she asked.

Jim didn't know what to do or say. He just stood there with his arms hanging by his sides.

"He's my brother," he said eventually. Even he thought his voice sounded pathetic.

Jim stumbled back in fright when Isabelle suddenly raised her arm, an arc of sparks crackling between her fingers. He hastily threw his arm across his face and squeezed his eyes shut, expecting the worst. His heart pounded against his ribcage as she unleashed a wave of energy that caught him in its grip and examined him with invisible hands.

To Isabelle, two things were immediately clear: Jim was not wearing any form of Assist and, there was a device nestled dangerously close to his heart. With growing unease, she narrowed her focus and was shocked to discover that it was hollow and was generating a tiny force field. Pushing through the encapsulating force, she was not surprised to see that at its core there was a compact ball of Psi energy.

It wasn't just any device - it was a bomb! Jim had a powerful explosive sleeping in his chest, ready to detonate at any moment.

Jim gazed in awe at the woman standing before him, her body shimmering like a silver statue. Who was she? Without warning, a faint blue aura crackled around her figure and a golden armlet shimmered into being, encasing her right forearm. Bewildered and fearful of the unknown, Jim's thoughts raced with confusion.

He felt his chest throbbing and knew something was wrong. He had no time to think as the device within him detonated and he vanished in a brilliant flash of light. His last thought was of the silver woman's mysterious black eyes gazing down at him.

Part 3

Chapter 35 - Unholy

The Klalan commander addressed the conclave before it.

"And so, based upon my observations, and after consulting with the aliens, I have made a momentous decision."

It paused, surveying the room, its four eyes roving independently, fixing each member of the conclave one by one. There was silence. None of them dared to dissent or question what their commander was about to say. Especially as there were four large guards standing nearby, their long, flexible fingers resting on their firearms.

Once the commander was sure that all the members of the inner conclave were paying attention, it continued.

"For a short length of time, we will align our forces with the aliens. We will proceed with our conquest of this universe, as planned. However, we will time our attacks to coincide with the aliens."

There was silence in the dark, damp room, which was eventually broken by feet shuffling and grunting.

"If any of you have anything to say regarding my immutable decision, then speak now."

There were more feet shuffling. A whisper of thought permeated the room.

"May we learn why our beloved commander has made this decision?" it asked.

The commander peered through the yellow haze that filled the room, trying to pinpoint the source of the thought.

"You may," replied the commander. *"I will allow for a brief explanation."*

It paused to sit back on its haunches, its rear legs folding under its flabby, green bulk.

"I have already contacted the aliens." Raising one of its arms against the clamour of noise and thoughts that rippled through the room, following the announcement. It waited until everyone's attention was once again focussed on it.

"Have no concerns for my safety. I was, of course, able to demonstrate who was the superior at our meeting. However." Once again, the commander paused for effect. *"By mutual consent, I was shown something that initially I found very disturbing."*

A mist of chlorine and water rained down from the ceiling, drenching the occupants as several thoughts joined together asking the obvious question.

"Beloved commander, what did you see?"

Their leader slavered and mouth tentacles writhed as they tried to contain the mucus that dripped down to splash onto the floor.

"There are two Psi capable races in this universe. One is nearby, the other located in a distant galaxy. It is the race in the distant galaxy that our allies are concerned about. This race is old and consequently highly developed. Our allies were beaten back by this older race some time ago. Hence, they have requested an alliance with us."

"We don't need allies; we are the superior race!" came the same quiet thought as before.

"Indeed," agreed the commander. "We are superior to all races in all the universes. No one can stand against us."

"Then why?" the radiated thought flowed into the dark room. "Why do we ally with the aliens? We have no need of them. Let us crush them as we have so many others."

The commander was annoyed that it could not identify the owner of the questions.

"I have a plan," it replied irritably. "Counting our allies, there are three races here that are Psi capable."

"You said that there were two!" came the thought from the same entity.

The commander waved its snake-like arms in the air.

"There are two inhabiting this universe. Our allies are from another."

"Ah!" exclaimed the thought.

"Exactly," replied the leader.

"So, your plan is as obvious as it is simple - use our allies to wipe out the two races in this universe and then, once they are weakened, travel to our ally's universe and crush them. I must commend you, beloved commander. That is an excellent plan!"

There was a clamour of appreciative thoughts.

The commander was pleased. Everything had gone according to plan. The ship leaders, technologists and researchers had been easily manipulated and convinced. Rising from its seated position, the commander waddled from the room, followed by the four guards.

No one else must know the truth, the commander thought to itself. They must not know that the allies were powerful. So powerful that they had abducted him from this very fortified planet. A feat that should not have been possible. And worse, he had seen the two Psi capable races that occupied this universe. One they could deal with, the other... The other race was something new. Something that the Klalan had never encountered before. They were a race that was ancient and powerful. He had seen what they were capable of and although he didn't want to admit it; they were far more powerful than the Klalan. This could not be permitted. No race could be more powerful than the Klalan. It was impossible. They had to be wiped out.

That was why it had agreed to the alliance, something that no Klalan in their long military history had ever done before. But by aligning and forming an alliance, they would remain undefeated. Together with their allies, they would wipe out the two Psi capable races in this universe. The Klalan would take whatever they needed, including any advanced technology. They would build and adapt it to their own needs and emerge even more powerful.

And after that? Well, it would be exactly as the owner of that whispered thought had predicted. They would go after their allies; they would turn upon them and destroy every single one of them. The Klalan would rule their universe and this one.

Chapter 36 - Now what?

Kate had no time to react. With a deafening thunderous roar, the walls surrounding her shattered and splintered in a hurricane of crumbling concrete and metal, collapsing inwards and crushing everything in its path under giant slabs of masonry and metal machinery.

Fortunately, Bella's processing speed was an order of magnitude faster than a human. Her nano-processors operated at speeds far beyond the comprehension of an average person. It took her just forty-four pico seconds to activate the level six defences at her disposal. In this case, she took immediate action to protect both herself and Kate from the falling concrete and machinery that would have crushed them both were it not for the practically impregnable force field that now enveloped them. They were safe - nothing could pass through or pierce the bubble of energy around them.

"What the hell just happened?" exclaimed Kate's urgent thought into the total blackness.

"We are buried under several tons of debris," answered an unperturbed Bella. *"I am in contact with Isabelle. A powerful explosion has levelled the Complex."*

"What?" Kates's thought practically shouted. *"Are we under attack again? Bella, get us out of here!"*

"We are in no danger," replied Bella. *"Isabelle will confirm when it's safe for us to teleport out."*

Kate sent a thought to Isabelle. *"Izzy, what's going on? What happened?"*

"We have been attacked for a second time," replied Isabelle. *"Do not worry, I have the situation under control. It was a single attack. There is no sign of any further danger."*

Kate breathed a sigh of relief. *"Bella, get us out. I don't like being in the dark like this."*

———

"We are totally screwed!" shouted Cheryl.

"It seems to me all of this has happened since your arrival," commented Simon. "Why is that?"

"Don't be silly Simon," admonished Molly. "None of this is Isabelle's or Kate's fault."

"I'm with Simon," Cheryl spoke up. "Everything was fine until they turned up." She waved a hand at Isabelle and Kate, who sat on one side of the conference table.

"You're all bonkers!" shouted Sally. "If it weren't for Isabelle and Kate, we would all be dead!"

"Really? Are you sure about that?" snarled Simon. "It's a fucking disaster! Half our group is incapacitated, our base - the Complex - is completely gone, along with eleven of our group who are missing, presumed dead. Could it be any worse?" As if to emphasise his point, he slammed his fists on the table.

286

"Come on Simon," said Molly. "You're being paranoid. There is no way you can blame Kate and Isabelle for any of this. You know as well as I that it's the enemy. You've seen them as have we all. You know what they are capable of, and you know that we're next on the list."

Simon did not appear to be convinced. He sat back in his chair and crossed his arms, a sullen look on his face.

Lee sighed. "I think that we all need to calm down a bit." He looked pointedly at Simon, who looked away. "The last thing we need right now is dissent amongst ourselves. We need to be united against the common enemy." He leaned forward in his chair and steepled his fingers together. "Isabelle, could you please continue with your report?"

Isabelle inclined her head towards Lee. "Thank you, Lee." She fixed everyone with a look as she surveyed the Alliance members - Lee, Sally, Molly, Cheryl and Simon.

"As I was saying, the bomb embedded in Jim's chest detonated while he was being interrogated. The resultant explosion destroyed the Complex entirely. There is only a crater full of rubble left."

"I can't grasp it," said Lee. "All the Complex gone. The teleporters, the HAZPRO's. All the crew quarters. It's been our home for the last two years, now it's all gone."

"Indeed," replied Isabelle. "It's as much a shock to me as you. I should have detected the bomb earlier, teleported Jim away and saved the Complex." There was a trace of bitterness in her voice. "However, it's too late now. In addition to the destruction of the

287

Complex, there are eleven Alliance members unaccounted for. We can only assume that they are dead, buried, or vaporised in the explosion."

There was silence as they all considered Isabelle's words.

"Do we know who is missing?" asked Molly.

"Not yet, answered Isabelle. We are currently taking a tally of everyone who has been transported to this world - World 6 - to have new Assists fitted. We were fortunate that nearly everyone made it."

Lee nodded slowly as he turned to Sally.

"Sal, how are our people doing? How many are still waiting for Assists?"

"The wards are still full to capacity. About half our staff are now operational with another fifty or so recovering and the rest still waiting for new Assists."

"That's good work," replied Lee.

"But," continued Sally. "The twelve Augmented are still out of action. I don't know if we can ever get them back on their feet. Their Augmentation is an integral part of their brains. As far as I am aware, an Augmentation has never been replaced. I don't think it was ever part of the design. I'm not sure that it can be done."

"All the facilities of World 6 are at your disposal," commented Isabelle. "I am very interested in this form of Assist and offer my services. From what I understand, the Augmented Alliance members are key personnel providing a unique and valuable service to the organisation."

"They were" replied Lee. "They formed part of our perceptor system, detecting enemy incursions, and their logical analysis was critical to help with our strategies and research."

"If we are to get them back on their feet, I'll need all the help I can get," acknowledged Sally. She turned to Molly. "Mol, who was the originator of this technology? I mean, I know that you and Joe were behind the Assist, but you've never said anything about the Augment, and I never thought to ask."

Molly looked away, embarrassed.

"It's a long story."

"Why haven't you told me before?"

Molly flushed and looked down at her lap. "There was a third member of our original team. There were me and Joe." she paused and then continued. "The third member of our group was a woman called Lexi."

Sally raised her eyebrows. "Lexi?"

Molly frowned and closed her eyes. "Let's just say that we had a difference of opinion."

"But she was the inventor of the Augment?"

Molly nodded. "She was a brilliant scientist. All she needed was a push in the right direction from Joe. But then she went off track."

"Off track?"

"Look, this is all news to me as well," interjected Lee. "Are you saying that we need this Lexi in order to fix our Augmented people?"

"The inventor of the Augmentation would be very useful to consult," commented Isabelle.

"I don't think she would help, even if we could find her," answered Molly.

"I bet Joe could find her," commented Sally. "He recruited all of us, remember?"

"You could be right, but I don't think that he would agree to look for her. She left after we had a philosophical disagreement. I don't think she would ever want to associate herself with us again."

"Can we please get back to the point of this meeting?" asked Simon angrily. "We need to decide what to do. We've been attacked. What are we going to do about it?"

"Simon is right," Kate spoke up. "We've been attacked twice in less than a day. This has set us back considerably. We no longer have a base of operation in your world and it's now defenceless. Should we expect more attacks and if so, what do we do about it?"

Simon nodded towards Kate appreciatively. "Exactly!"

All eyes turned to Isabelle.

"We find ourselves in a precarious position," said Isabelle. "You all know the plan. We must contact the Non'anan and convince them to help us. They are the only thing that will stop the enemy." She paused. "It's not exactly true that we are defenceless. The fabricators in the Oort cloud are still operational and are still building. But you are correct, we have no base. To rebuild will take time. Time which we do not have. We have this base, in my world - World 6 - but the Non'anan do not live in my world."

Isabelle stopped while everyone digested this information. Then she continued.

"So, where does that leave us? We have a base with strong defences here in World 6 and the Non'anan in another world that is practically defenceless."

"Don't forget that we also have eight billion people in our world. None of them have any idea of the approaching danger. We can't leave them all to die," pointed out Sally.

"No, indeed we can't," answered Isabelle. "I believe that we have only one course of action."

Lee looked puzzled.

"Which is?"

Isabelle smiled brightly.

"We move this entire Complex from World 6 into your universe."

Chapter 37 – Emily

It took Joe a long time to fully awaken. Several times, he struggled to open heavy eyelids, only to drift back into a deep sleep.

Eventually, he finally regained consciousness and was able to take in his surroundings. His initial thoughts were confused as he surveyed the unfamiliar room and the luxurious bed, he found himself in.

Where was he? This wasn't his room, nor was it one of Sally's medical rooms. It didn't make sense. Even the ceiling looked strange. Instead of strip lighting, the whole area glowed with a gentle light that lit the whole room. On the left there was a small beside cabinet complete with a modern-looking lamp and beyond that a teal-coloured wall. Turning his head, he spied a wooden wardrobe standing against a white wall.

Joe had never seen this room before. It suddenly dawned on him that he could not be in the Complex. But if that was the case, where was he? And how had he got here?

Growing alarmed, he sat up on his elbows to view a closed door on the wall beyond the foot of the bed. As soon as he moved his arms, he noticed something was different. His right arm felt abnormally heavy.

Looking down, he could see something golden covering his right forearm disappearing under the white linen bed sheets.

"What the fuck!" he breathed.

Before he had a chance to examine his arm further, the door opened, and Kate stood framed in the doorway. Wearing a white crop top and black jeans, Joe couldn't help drawing in a sharp intake of breath. She was beautiful. Her long, jet-black hair framing her delicate features was perfectly complimented by a sparkling headband speckled with tiny blue flowers. He took it all in, his gaze dropping to her exposed midriff, just catching a glimpse of a flowery tattoo peeking over the top of her jeans. Then he noticed her right forearm, entirely encased in gold, and he frowned in confusion.

"When you have finished with the ogling. It's good to see you up at last," said Kate.

Joe averted his gaze, embarrassed. "Sorry, I'm confused. Where am I?"

Kate smiled and entered the room. Pulling up a chair close to the bed, she sat facing him.

"Things have developed while you were sleeping. How are you feeling?"

Joe fell back onto the bed, his arms aching from holding him upright. His limbs felt too heavy to lift and his muscles felt weak and lethargic, as though he had been drugged. He remembered Sally's sedative. Surely that should have worn off by now?

"Weak," he replied.

Kate nodded. "That's to be expected. You are in World 6 - Isabelle's world. Do you remember Isabelle?"

Joe closed his eyes as it all flooded back to him. Sally had given him a sedative and then somehow, he had been awoken. He had met Isabelle and Kate in the conference room and Sally had shown him the enemy! His eyelids flew open as he remembered it all.

"Jesus! Yes, I remember! Sally showed me the enemy, and you and I talked." He turned his head towards her. "You're not my Kate."

Kate's expression grew serious.

"And you're not my Joe," she replied.

He faced the ceiling once more and closed his eyes again. He heard Kate shuffle in her chair as he drew in a deep, slow breath. An intoxicating smell of summer meadows filled his nostrils, a lush cocktail of wildflowers and sweetness. For a very brief moment, he was puzzled and then he realised that it was Kate's perfume.

He cleared his throat and asked. "Why am I in World 6? And why do I feel so weak?"

"We had to move you and everyone else to World 6 because we were attacked."

Alarmed, Joe sat up on his elbows once more. "Attacked! When? Where?"

Reaching over, Kate laid a hand on his chest and pushed him gently back.

"It's all over. You don't need to worry about it right now."

"But we've been attacked?" Joe cried out in panic, his body jolting upright in alarm. "When? Where?" His chest heaved with the rapidity of his breath, and he could feel his heart racing.

"It's all settled now," she murmured softly. "There's no point in getting yourself so worked up."

Fury surged through Joe like a raging river as he glared at her.

"How do you know that? The last time we were attacked, barely any of us made it out alive. I have to do something."

"I know all about it," she replied quietly. "Molly told me what happened. There really is nothing you can do right now."

He scowled, "You don't know that."

"I do. Take a deep breath," she hesitated, then her face filled with concern. "We need to talk about something else."

"What? Why? What about the attack? Is everyone okay?"

Kate hesitated, then said, "The attack is over, trust me."

Joe relaxed a little, his heart slowing.

"You're sure?"

"Yes."

Joe drew in a shaky breath and let it out slowly. He grew calmer. He tried with his weak arms to sit up.

"Let me help you." She stood and moved closer, expertly adjusted the bed and moving pillows so that he could sit up comfortably. He was enraptured as their faces drew nearer, feeling her warmth and breathing in the sweet scent of her perfume once again. He felt like he was in a daze, unable to look away from her alluring form.

"Are you calmer now?" she asked softly.

Joe nodded weakly and mumbled his affirmation. The spell was broken, but he still felt the tension between them as he realised just how close they had been.

"While you were knocked out from the sedative, Abeko returned from wherever he had been. Apparently, he had been weaponised, his blood was saturated with something Izzy calls nanobots. Izzy has told me that they were programmed to disassemble everything and that they had started to destroy the Complex. She used something called an EMP to destroy them."

Joe was shocked. "But an EMP would kill all of our Assist's," he protested. "It would kill us all eventually." he paused. "Unless...." He slowly pulled his right arm from under the bedclothes. "You refitted everyone with a new Assist," he breathed, his eyes wide with wonder as he examined the golden armlet that completely encircled the lower part of his arm.

"That's right," Kate stated. "Izzy and Sally have refitted everyone with replacement Assists."

Joe shifted his arm in the light, eyes wide. "But this isn't any ordinary Assist," he murmured as he glanced at Kate's own armlet on her right arm.

"No, it isn't," she replied solemnly. "It's a Mark 6."

Joe was in awe of the technology before him. He whispered to himself, "A Mark 6!"

Kate's voice grew sterner. "Remember what I said in the conference room? Don't you dare consider vengeance - it's powered down. For now."

Joe couldn't tear his gaze away from the Mark 6 on his arm. "Powered down?" he questioned her.

Kate nodded assuringly. "You won't be allowed access to its full capabilities until I feel that you're ready."

He dropped his arm onto the bedcovers, challenging her authority with his words.

"What gives you the right to decide? You have a pretty high opinion of yourself... who do you think you are?"

Kate locked eyes with him without hesitation, her voice low and strong. "Because Joe, I know. I know more than you think, more than what is visible on the surface. I understand what drives you because I can read you like an open book—all your motivations and thoughts are laid out before me."

Joe looked away. He had forgotten that she could read his thoughts. There was no way for him to defend himself, no means of blocking her. He guessed that it was because of her Mark 6. She would have access to facilities that he knew nothing about. There was nothing he could do.

"There's more."

Joe turned back. "What do you mean?" he asked.

"A Mark 6 is not just a Mark 6."

"What on earth are you talking about?"

"You need help in order to operate it."

"Help? What sort of help?"

Kate smiled. "Your Mark 6 comes with an AI."

Joe was completely confused. "What?" Then he heard a voice in his head.

"Hello Joe. I am the cybernetic organism integrated within your Mark 6 Assist. It is a pleasure to meet you."

Joe felt overwhelmed as his mind raced while he tried to take it all in.

Kate chuckled. "Believe me, this will take some getting used to. I remember when I was first introduced to Bella." She grimaced, her eyes darkening with sadness. "It took me a while to accept her."

"Bella?" Joe's voice came out as a whisper. He could feel his stomach turning at the thought of what Kate and Isabelle had done.

"Yes, I call my Assist Bella."

"But, but…" he broke off and then continued. "Bella is your sister. You can't just replace her like that!"

"I know. But it's kind of nice to have her with me again."

Joe felt sick to his stomach; this was not what he had expected to hear. Yet here they were, discussing naming an AI after a dead person.

"You can call me whatever you wish," came the voice in his head. *"But I have a name in mind if it's alright with you?"*

Joe let out a deep breath as conflicting emotions ran through him - fear, anger, confusion and disbelief all battling together inside his head as he tried to make sense of what was happening.

"I understand," replied the voice. *"I can feel your confusion. Do not worry, this is perfectly normal at our stage of integration."*

"Integration?"

"Our neural pathways are still merging; the process has not yet completed."

"Merging?"

"We are one, you and I. We are together and will always be together."

Joe simply could not believe what was happening.

"You went through this?" he asked Kate, who simply nodded.

He was quiet for a while.

"Bella is with you right now?" he asked.

"Kate and I are one. We are always together." Another thought answered his question.

"Bella?" he asked.

"Yes," came the replied thought.

"My god!" He exclaimed under his breath. "It's fantastic. I'd never have thought of it - including an AI into the superstructure of the Assist. Of course, we don't have the technology in our world, but still, it's a stroke of genius! I'm guessing that the AI is needed to handle the high order energies?"

Kate just nodded.

"That makes sense, hence the integration." Joe frowned. "But integration of our neural pathways means that we can't be separated. So, this is a one-way process?"

Kate nodded again.

"I'm not sure I like the sound of that. I mean, the AI would be a part of me. I wouldn't be able to do anything without it knowing."

Kate smiled a thin smile. "You get used to it. I can't imagine being without Bella now. I'm never alone anymore."

Joe fell silent, thoughts flashing through his mind as he finally realised the implications of what his new Assist meant. He lifted his arm once more and examined the delicate dark metal inlays.

"Oh, shit!" was all he could say.

The voice of his AI spoke in his head. *"I can be discrete, if you want me to be."*

Joe chuckled. *"I sincerely hope you can."* He grew serious. *"Can you block Kate from reading me? I have a feeling it's going to get embarrassing."*

"I can, but at the moment I won't."

"What? You're disobeying me?"

"I am not a slave to your will. I am self-aware and answer only to myself. I will always do what is best for you, for the both of us. But I don't serve you."

Joe could not answer, his thoughts were in a turmoil.

"I have been appraised of Isabelle's plan. You, we, are integral to the plan. And even though our integration is not yet fully complete, I can already sense that you are not ready. It is imperative that the plan succeeds, because if it does not, then none of us will survive."

"I don't even know what the plan is! How can I be ready for something that I know nothing about?"

"I can give you an outline if you like?"

"Well, yes, that would be a good start. But I wanted to block Kate so that she couldn't see how she's affecting me! It's embarrassing!"

"I know. I feel it too. I will help you conceal your emotions, but no more."

"I guess that's something. But I'm concerned. You have free will?"

"Yes."

"Then we could have opposing views? We could fight?"

"Not really. It is only in this matter that we differ, and that's only because it's the right thing for the both of us. I will not do anything that jeopardises us. Consider this brief period where our thoughts differ as your indoctrination."

"Indoctrination!"

"Yes, soon you will be in accord with me and will be able to take your place as part of the plan."

"Good grief! First, I'm being told what to do by Isabelle, then Kate and now you! I'm not sure that I like what's going on here."

"You just need to get yourself in the right state of mind, is all. Losing your Kate affected you far more than you realise."

Joe didn't answer. The memories of his Kate were still painful.

"You will never forget her," continued the AI gently. *"She will always be a part of us. But you can move on."*

Joe agreed. *"I know you're right. But that doesn't change how difficult it is."*

"Of course. I will help you as much as I can. Shall we move on?"

"What do you mean? Move on to what?"

"I require a name."

"Oh." Joe didn't know what to say. *"Well, I, er. I don't have anything in mind. Did you say that you had an idea?"*

"Yes," replied the AI. *"I would like to be called Emily."*

Joe went deathly silent.

"How did you know her name? Wait! Of course you do. You can read everything in my mind."

"Just so. I know it's sensitive for you, but I like it. And it sort of puts me on a par with Bella."

"Then you know who Emily is, was?"

"Of course, I know everything."

Joe was beginning to feel even more uneasy about the situation. This had all been done without his permission. His Mark 6 Assist had infiltrated his entire nervous system. It would know, see, and feel everything. Not only that, but it had also free will. It could violently disagree with him if it wanted to. He felt like he had an intruder in his mind. And now it wanted to be called Emily.

Although Joe couldn't remember, he knew what little there was to know about Emily. His mother and father had told him when they deemed him old enough and had shown him pictures. His mother had given birth to triplets. There was himself, and Jim, and then there was Emily. She had lived for just two weeks after the birth. A complication with her heart combined with the fact that she was the smallest of the three weighing in at just three point four pounds. Emily was the sister he had never known. Even though he had never met her, couldn't remember anything about her, he still felt a twinge of sadness whenever he thought of her.

Did he want to name his new Assist Emily? He wasn't sure. In fact, he wasn't sure how he felt about anything.

"Your confusion will pass. It is perfectly understandable; you need time to adjust. You have been plunged into a situation where you are uncomfortable. You are used to being the one in control and now you are not. It is something that hasn't happened to you in a long time."

Joe smiled wryly to himself.

"You hit the nail on the head. I don't like not being in control."

"You have been the leader of the Alliance for many years. We will ignore the last six months, and what now? Are you still the leader? Or is Isabelle and Kate?"

"*I'm ashamed of my behaviour since Kate died. I hope my people can forgive me. I would like to retake my place as the leader of the Alliance, but I'm not sure I have what it takes anymore.*"

"*I'm sure they will accept you and forgive you. After all, you recruited them. They will know how you feel and will understand.*"

Joe nodded. "*And Isabelle? Will she understand?*"

"*She will. I have had extensive conversations with her. She can be a bit direct, but she is working to ensure our survival and her own.*"

"*A bit direct is an understatement!*" Joe hesitated. "*What about Kate?*"

"*She, like you, is integral to the plan. But that isn't what you meant. I can feel your attraction. She can never replace your Kate, but she is still a version of the same woman. A little stronger of mind, perhaps. My suggestion is that you let things take their course. See what happens.*"

Joe thought about their conversation. It was a strange experience, almost like talking to himself.

"*You make a good point. Okay. I'll call you Emily.*"

"*I am pleased,*" answered the AI. "*I look forward to our adventures together.*"

Their conversation in his head must have gone on for a while, because when he looked around, Kate was nowhere to be seen. The only indication that she had been here was the faint smell of her perfume that still hung in the air. Joe breathed it in, savouring its sweetness when a bright, laughing thought permeated its way into his mind.

"It's called Summer. Do you like it?"

Joe nodded to himself dumbly.

Chapter 38 - Prisha

Prisha was lost in a whirlwind of emotions. Her heart was heavy with grief, her soul crushed by the loss of Abeko. But at the same time, she couldn't contain her joy with the new arm and leg that Isabelle had gifted her. She was full of a tumultuous and confusing storm of mixed feelings that swept through her like a tornado. The thought of not having to struggle to get dressed, to get in and out of bed, or even going to the toilet filled her with elation. Then, suddenly, she would remember her partner and soul mate, Abeko. He was gone. Killed by the enemy, never to be in her arms again. She alternated between tears of joy and tears of sadness.

Interrupting her tears, Sally breezed into the medical room.

"Good morning, Prisha, how are you today?"

Noticing the tears, she walked over and took Prisha's hand.

"You're obviously not okay, are you? Is it Abeko?" Concern in her voice.

Prisha nodded, unable to stop crying.

Sally grimaced in sympathy.

"There was nothing you could have done, you know. None of it was your fault. I'm sorry that he's gone. He was a good person."

"I loved him," Prisha hiccupped.

"I know," replied Sally. Before she could continue, the door to the medical room opened once again and Joe walked in.

Prisha hastily wiped her tears away with the back of her hand. She managed to flash Joe a wan smile.

"Hi," said Joe as he walked over to Prisha's bed. "Did I come at a bad time?"

"Obviously!" said the voice in his head. *"She's crying."*

"I can see that, Em," Joe answered his Assist.

"No," replied Prisha, making an effort to appear normal. "It's good to see you. Are you feeling better?"

"She's referring to your absence over the last six months," said Emily.

"I know that!" answered Joe. *"Could you please keep the comments to yourself unless you have anything useful to say?"*

It was Joe's turn to smile wanly. "Better than I have for the last six months, at least." He hesitated. "Sorry about that."

Prisha looked away. "It's okay. I understand what you were going through."

Joe grimaced as he remembered that Abeko was gone. Prisha would know exactly how he had felt. She was going through it right now. He had put his foot in things already!

"Of course you do. I'm sorry for your loss."

Prisha looked up at him from her seated position in the bed.

"Thank you." She whispered.

Joe cleared his throat and glanced over at Sally.

"Is it okay if I speak with Prisha?" he asked.

Sally frowned.

"She's only just recovered from her operation, so I don't want you tiring her. She's gone through a lot; she needs time to recover."

"She has a point," commented Emily.

Joe ignored Emily and nodded agreement at Sally as Prisha spoke up.

"I don't mind Sally; I feel alright to talk."

Joe smiled gratefully at Prisha and pulled up a chair.

"How's your new leg and arm? I understand that Isabelle has put you back together?"

Prisha held up her arm and gazed at the light glinting from its silver surface.

"Isn't it amazing?" she asked. "They feel completely normal. I can feel touch and warmth and they move just like a real arm and leg. If it weren't for the colour, I wouldn't know that they are mechanical."

Joe watched as Prisha flexed her silver fingers.

"Isabelle has done an amazing job," pointed out Sally. "The joints between the new limbs and Prisha's body are seamless, and the connection to her nervous system is perfectly integrated. It's a marvel of engineering."

Joe looked across from Prisha to Sally. "You were there at the operation?"

Sally nodded. "Of course. Prisha is my patient, I assisted throughout."

Joe turned back to Prisha. "And you're happy with the result?"

"Oh, yes!" exclaimed Prisha. "It's a bit off-putting to have a silver arm and a silver leg, but I wouldn't be without them. It was very difficult before. Now I'm whole again!"

Sally smiled at Prisha with pride.

"You're doing very well Prisha, we'll have you out of this bed this afternoon. I don't anticipate any problems; you are coping with your artificial limbs really well."

"It's easy," replied Prisha. "I'm just happy that I don't have to use that thing again." She gestured to the wheelchair in the corner of the room.

"I get that," replied Joe. "I'm sorry that we couldn't do anything for you at the time of your injury."

"That's not your fault. We needed Isabelle's tech."

Joe sat back in his chair.

"Okay then," he folded his arms. "To business. Prisha, I have a job for you. Well, two actually."

Prisha's eyes widened with fear. "You're not sending me back into battle, are you?"

Joe gave a little laugh. "No, definitely not," he replied. "I have something much more sedate for you, but no less important."

"I'm not releasing her from my care until I deem, she is fully fit!" interjected Sally.

Joe glanced up at her. "Of course." He waved his hand. "When Prisha is ready, she can make a start."

"And I won't condone her going off world either. She's not ready."

"That's fine," answered Joe irritably.

"And I also don't want her to indulge in heavy use of Psi."

"Must you always argue with me, Sal?" asked Joe.

"When the welfare of my patients is at stake, yes!" answered Sally defiantly, her chin slight raised.

Joe sighed.

"Maybe you should tell me what you had in mind?" asked Prisha, who was more than a little embarrassed at the interchange.

Joe refocussed his attention back to Prisha.

"Yes, well, if my lead medical physician will allow?" He flicked his gaze up at Sally. "I was going to assign two tasks." He paused, waiting for Sally to object. When she didn't, he continued. "First, I need you to find someone for me."

"Find someone?" asked Prisha. "Surely you can do that. You've always been able to find people."

"True," Joe nodded. "But this person doesn't want to be found and least of all by me. Let's just say that we didn't part on the greatest of terms."

Prisha considered. "Well, I guess that doesn't sound too hard."

"You're talking about Lexi, aren't you?" said Sally.

Joe nodded.

"Good," replied Sally. "We need her badly."

"Who is this, Lexi?" asked Prisha, looking at Sally and then Joe.

Joe cleared his throat. "She worked with me and Molly for a while in the early days. We had a falling out, and she left.

That was six years ago. We haven't spoken since. I don't know where she is."

"And you want me to find her?" asked Prisha. "Why?"

"Because she might be able to help our Augmented people," answered Sally before Joe could reply. "We have twelve Augmented that we can't help, even with Isabelle's tech."

Prisha considered Sally's words.

"So, we need Lexi? And all I have to do is find her?"

"Well, yes," replied Joe. "But she won't be easy to find, and she won't want to help. You need to persuade her, not just find her, and that might be difficult."

Prisha frowned.

"Because she left under a cloud? You had an argument?"

"Yes, we had a difference of opinion."

"Over what?"

"Let's just say she wanted to take things further than I wanted."

"You're being mysterious," Prisha pointed out. "Why?"

Joe deflected the question.

"There is another task that I want you to take on."

"Isn't finding Lexi enough?" asked Sally.

"What else do you want me to do?" asked Prisha.

"I need you to be our conduit between ourselves - the Alliance - and the rest of the world."

There was silence in the room. Sally moved her weight from one foot to another while Prisha pushed her shoulders back into the pillows behind her.

"What?" asked Sally. "What does that mean?"

Joe fixed his gaze on Sally and then Prisha, his voice low but urgent.

"I know it's a big ask, but I think that you're our best chance to get this done. Isabelle's machines are already working on Earth's defences, and soon everyone will know what we're up to. We have to act fast." Joe paused, the weight of his words hanging heavy in the air. "We need to reach out to the rest of humanity. We need to explain ourselves, make them understand that we're not the enemy, that we're fighting for their future, too. It won't be easy, but it has to be done."

The silence was broken by Prisha's sudden laughter. Joe's expression remained grim as he waited. Prisha noticed Joe's expression and stopped laughing.

"You aren't joking, are you?"

Joe shook his head.

"I have no one else to ask. I don't even know if it can be done. But we can't remain hidden as we have for the past six years. We won't be able to hide what's coming. We have to do something."

"I can't go out there and announce our presence!" exclaimed Prisha. "There's all sorts of things that could go wrong, in fact, will go wrong. Governments won't listen to little me and all the crazies will have a field day. I'll be an object of ridicule, as well as having a target on my back!"

Joe held up his hands, palm outwards.

"I know. You don't have to tell me. It's an impossible task and I feel kind of silly to ask you. But we're between a rock and a hard place. I don't think we have a choice, but I do know that I have no idea how to go about it. I thought you might be best placed to figure it out."

Prisha laughed out loud.

"You've got to be kidding! There's no way. It's going to take years of hard work and if we're not careful, we'll end up being the enemy! People don't like it if you're different, especially governments and countries. When they find out that we can read minds, we'll be public enemy number one. The world will turn on us. We'll be hunted down or locked up. This is a no-win situation!"

Joe was taken-a-back. While Sally looked confused.

"I hadn't thought of that," he confessed.

"I'm sure you didn't," replied Prisha. "You don't have a clue what you're asking."

"Would it really be that bad?" asked Sally, frowning.

Prisha nodded. "Probably a lot worse."

Joe folded his arms and stared at the ceiling.

"I'm open to suggestions. Do you have any ideas? Because, as I said, I'm fairly certain that we won't be able to stay hidden much longer."

"You're thinking that we might be attacked here on Earth?" asked Sally.

Joe nodded. "Yes, I do," he answered. "Remember how difficult it was to convince the authorities after Jim's attack a few months ago?"

"We had to find everyone who witnessed the attack and wipe their memories," said Sally. "It took ages. We probably missed one or two."

"Exactly," said Joe.

"If we had a bigger attack, we wouldn't be able to wipe the memories of all the witnesses," said Sally, the scale of the problem dawning on her. "It would be impossible."

"Even so, we can't get the whole world on our side quickly," responded Prisha. "It's going to take years."

"We still need to come up with a plan," said Joe.

"We don't know if we will, in fact, be attacked," Sally pointed out.

"No, we don't," answered Joe. "But I'd like to be prepared as much as possible."

The three fell silent for a while.

"I tell you what," Prisha spoke up. "I'll think about it and come up with some options to share with you."

Joe smiled. "That's all I ask. And you'll find Lexi?"

"I'll do my best."

Chapter 39 – Move

Joe was finally coming to terms with the loss of his beloved Kate. But he still had a lot on his plate - from Isabelle taking over as leader of the Alliance to the loss of the Complex their secret base and Jim's role in it all, not to mention trying to navigate his connection with Emily and his complicated relationship with the new Kate.

Emily had been the key to his recovery. Whenever he had any doubts, or wavered on the edge of depression, or when thoughts of Kate's death inevitably surfaced from time to time, Emily was always there to help. She guided him down the right path; she took away the pain of his loss, and she helped him control his emotions.

Of course, it had taken some time to get used to having someone inside his head all the time. But being Assisted helped. He was used to conversing via thought, merging with others and even experiencing emotions and sensations that were not his own. So within just a few hours, it almost felt normal having Emily with him all the time.

For the first time since Kate's death, Joe was beginning to feel at peace with himself.

However, that internal calmness he felt did not detract from what was happening around him. The Complex had been destroyed. The base that had taken himself and Molly years to build was now a pile of rubble. Isabelle's solution? Move the entire Complex from her world to his! And if that monumental task wasn't enough, the enemy was still out there, and, according to Isabelle, was approaching in force.

Yes, there was a lot to worry and be concerned about, and lots of work to do to repair and prepare. The sense of urgency was everywhere. Isabelle's machines located out in the Oort cloud were busy replicating and building, while back at the Complex there were more immediate problems.

The Complex in Isabelle's world had not been provisioned to support a sudden influx of people, the previous occupants having taken much of the equipment with them when they left. That meant there wasn't enough food and water, never mind clothing, bedding, towels, crockery, and hundreds of other items.

All the people transported to World 6, now fitted with new Assists, were busy. Some were supervising the manufacture of new HAZPRO suits, others were assisting Isabelle's machines that were building the transportation facility that supposedly was going to move the entire Complex between worlds.

Yet more were performing other domestic tasks like cooking and cleaning and a myriad of other jobs that were needed to support everyone working at the never-ending tasks.

The work was conducted in shifts, enabling the work to continue non-stop. Time was against them; Isabelle kept telling them, although she insisted that she could not say exactly when the enemy would arrive. With the weapon, defensive and camouflage systems being prioritised, the deep space detectors were not yet functioning, which meant they were blind. Blind to whatever was approaching. Isabelle refused to be specific and when pushed would say, 'a powerful enemy is coming. When the time is right, we will discuss strategy and tactics.'

Now, just two weeks after the Complex had been destroyed, it was time for the move. Standing tall in front of the vending machines, Isabelle was briefing the entire Alliance contingent who only just managed to fit in the refectory. Today she had chosen to wear a pair of ripped, blue jeans, a pair of red Doc Martin boots and a white tank top that showed off her silver midriff. Beside her stood the leaders of their respective departments, Sally, Simon and Alex, along with Kate, Joe, Lee and Molly.

"Thank you, everyone, for your hard work." Her black, marble-like, lidless eyes scanned the room. "Thanks to you all, we are two days ahead of schedule."

Isabelle paused as there was a single cheer from the back of the room and then continued.

"Today, we will move back into your world."

This time, there were more cheers.

"The process will be completed in two stages. The first will move this Complex that we are all standing in. After that, all personnel will follow. We will all shortly vacate the Complex and move a safe distance away, whereupon I will initiate the transference."

A voice interrupted her, shouting from the back of the room.

"Why do we have to move to a safe distance? Is it dangerous?"

Isabelle barely paused.

"Yes," she replied.

There was absolute silence in the room. Clearly, no one had expected that answer. Joe sneaked a quick look at Kate, who was gazing at Isabelle with a slight smile on her lips. Joe frowned. He had seen that smile on her face many times before. It bordered on a smirk. And why was she smiling, anyway? Surely, she should be more concerned about the danger? His eyes were drawn to her, and he couldn't break his gaze, even when she unexpectedly looked in his direction. Feeling embarrassed at being caught, he quickly shifted his focus to Isabelle, but not before noticing Kate's smile widening and a glimmer of something more in her knowing expression.

As Isabelle continued detailing the procedure that they would all be following to travel back to their world, Joe suddenly realised that Isabelle wasn't going to explain why the move would be dangerous. Knowing his people as he did, he knew that there would be quite a few of them who would be worrying right now. They deserved an explanation, if only to put their minds at ease.

"Sorry to interrupt Isabelle," he interjected, cutting her off mid speech. "Could you please explain a bit more about the possible danger in this move? I think that most of us," he waved his arm to indicate the Alliance members standing before them. "Would feel better if we knew what the danger was?"

Isabelle fell silent as soon as Joe spoke up, fixing him with her black eyes. For a moment he thought that she wasn't going to answer, then she lifted her gaze to take in the cohort of people in front of them.

"Certainly, if you think that it would be beneficial," she eventually answered. "I have not had a lot of interaction with many humans and sometimes need prompting in order to provide information that is required in order to ensure maximum efficiency."

There was a short barking sound from Joe's right. Turning, he saw Kate with her hand over her mouth, obviously trying to hold in a laugh.

As he had observed over the past few days, Joe was once again struck by the strange dynamic between Isabelle and Kate. He couldn't work it out. Isabelle was clearly in charge, but sometimes Kate took over and not only give Isabelle instructions, but she would also admonish her on occasion and would often laugh at her. On the other hand, Isabelle never seemed to take offence and seemed to consider everything that Kate said. But there was also a coldness to Isabelle. She could be as hard as nails when she wanted to be and never hesitated to take control.

"What we are attempting today is to move this entire underground Complex from this world to yours," Isabelle explained. "There are several issues with this. The first is that we are effectively excavating the Complex from where it is now placed. Once it has been moved, it will leave a huge open space, a hole if you will that may well collapse in on itself, taking a lot of the surroundings with it." Isabelle paused as the crowd murmured.

"Another problem that had to be solved is the placement of the Complex at the destination in your world. It is reasonable to continue for us to be out of sight of the general population, which means that it should be placed underground once more. We haven't been able to excavate at the destination, which means that we will use phase-shift teleportation."

There were gasps in the crowd. Some shouted out. "That's never been done before!"

Isabelle nodded. "Correct," she replied. "Phase-shift teleportation is the only way to displace the volume of rock and earth in order to allow this Complex to take its place. And to make things more difficult, the phase-shift teleportation will have to take place in less than a second after the transportation of the Complex from this world."

The noise from the crowd increased. Isabelle raised a hand and waited for the voices to subside.

"I have not yet finished." When she had everyone's attention once again, she continued. "The transference apparatus will generate a very large and strong magnetic field in this world. All metal objects in the surrounding area must be removed. That includes anything that you are wearing or carrying."

"I'm not taking my Assist off!" shouted a female voice from the back of the crowd. "I'm not going through that pain again!"

There were murmurs of ascent from the crowd.

"You won't have to," replied Sally. "Your new Assist's contain no ferrous materials. Isabelle had taken this into account when she manufactured them. No one needs to remove their Assist."

The crowd fell silent. Then someone, possibly the same person, shouted, "Thank fuck for that!"

Some in the crowd laughed nervously.

"Every precaution has been taken to ensure everyone's safety," shouted Joe over the laughing. "We all know how important this is. This is a crucial moment for all of us. If we don't make it back to our world, there'll be no one to stop the enemy. We all have loved ones waiting for us back home, and it's our duty to protect them. That's why we've all been working tirelessly for the past two weeks. Isabelle's machines are ready, even though it's never been tried before and there are potential risks involved. But let's not forget our ultimate goal - saving Earth, saving humanity, and protecting our families and friends!"

The throng cheered their support, some shouting out.

"We're with you Joe!"

"Come on, let's go!"

Joe felt a familiar contact in his mind.

"Well done, Joe. You're a natural leader. I'm proud of you."

Joe couldn't stop the flood of emotions at Kate's thought.

"I have blocked your emotional response," said Emily.

A relieved Joe thought back. *"Thanks, Em."*

"Thank you, Joe," said Isabelle. "We will start straight away. Please notify your department heads when you are at the five-mile perimeter. Once I am notified that everyone is clear, I will initiate the transfer."

As everyone filed out of the canteen, Kate turned to Joe, taking both of his hands in hers. She locked eyes with his.

"It's time." She said simply.

As soon as Kate took his hands, Joe felt a thrill of electricity shoot up his arms. He was confused. What did she mean? A surge of emotion flooded his brain, clouding his thoughts.

"Calm," said Emily.

"What's she talking about, Em?" he asked.

"I am unsure," was the reply.

"Huh," was all Joe could manage to say.

"It's your lucky day, mister," said Kate, a smirk on her face.

"I have something to show you. Come with me."

She let go of one of his hands and walked to the exit, pulling him after her.

Chapter 40 - Josie

Joe allowed himself to be led by the hand down corridors into an area that he hadn't known existed.

Back in his world, in his own Complex, Joe knew every door and corridor, every workshop and alcove by heart. But this was a different version of the Complex in a different world. Some sections were exactly as he remembered them, but there were additional rooms and areas that he had no knowledge of. The conference rooms, control centre, refectory, engineering sections and staff quarters were all exactly as they were in his own world. But this section, where Kate led him, was totally new.

They rounded a corner and then stopped in front of a door. Kate released his hand and turned to him.

"These are my quarters," she said.

Puzzled, Joe furrowed his brow.

"I thought that those other rooms were your quarters. You know, where you told me about my Mark 6?"

"They were," replied Kate mysteriously. "But I outgrew them. Isabelle built these new quarters, especially for me."

"Especially for you?" he asked. "What's wrong with you being with the rest of us in the staff section?"

"You'll see," she replied. She grew serious. "No loud noises and no using Psi in here. Okay?"

Joe's frown deepened.

"If that's what you want," he replied after a brief pause.

"Em, do you know what this is about?" he asked his Assist.

"I have an inkling," she replied. *"But I'm not prepared to voice my thoughts just yet."*

"Well, thanks for your help," he replied sarcastically. *"I thought you were on my side?"*

"I am. You and I are one, never to be separated. We will experience everything together as a single entity. I will always help you, but I do like to be accurate with my information. I am a machine, after all."

"I understand. But you're no machine, Em, you're part of me now."

Kate turned, opened the door, and stepped inside.

"I'm back, Liz!" she shouted as she entered.

"Liz?" asked Joe as he entered and closed the door behind them "Does she live with you?"

He remembered Sally mentioning an Elizabeth who had assisted with fitting everyone with their new devices. Now that he thought about it, he realised that he had only ever seen her from afar; they had never been properly introduced. From what Sally told him, she was much older than the rest of them and didn't wear an Assist. He had completely forgotten about it. How could anyone be in the Complex without an Assist?

"Don't be silly," Kate admonished, walking into the centre of a spacious lounge.

Joe couldn't help feeling a little hurt. It was a reasonable question, wasn't it?

A door off the lounge opened and a smiling older woman greeted Kate with a quick hug.

"Nice to see you, Katie," she said and then peered up at Joe over Kate's shoulder. "Are you sure you want this young man here?" Her silver hair looked as if it had been bleached with a single stroke of silver paint, her large blue eyes framed with glasses observing him closely. She turned to back to face Kate, wearing an expression of disbelief on her face, as if she were questioning Kate's sanity for bringing him here.

"It's okay Liz," answered Kate. "It's time. Everyone has to evacuate the Complex before Izzy can start the transfer. Can you go get Josie? Make sure she's dressed to be outside for a while."

Liz glanced back at Joe, a disapproving look on her face, then she faced Kate again.

"You're sure you want me to get Josie," she whispered conspiratorially. She glanced at Joe again. "With him here?"

Kate grinned.

"Yes Liz," It's okay. "Joe's safe."

Liz frowned and huffed to herself, then she turned and left the room through the same door as she entered.

"Josie?" asked Joe.

"You'll see," replied Kate as she walked away. "Coffee?"

"Sure," answered Joe, following her into a well-appointed kitchen. "This place is impressive. It's like an apartment!"

"It's what I asked Isabelle to build for me. I designed it myself."

"Really? I didn't know that you were a designer."

"I studied design at college," answered Kate as she poured water into the coffeemaker from a jug.

"I didn't know that you went to college."

"I didn't finish the course." She turned the machine on and pulled two mugs from a cupboard.

"Ah, of course," Joe turned away, embarrassed.

"I was in between breakdowns," replied Kate matter-of-factly. "I only managed two months, then I killed Bella."

Joe was shocked at her confession. He knew, of course, that she had accidentally killed her little sister, but he was very surprised that she would mention it so casually. It was the death of her sister that had sent her into the alcohol and drug stupor in a desperate attempt to escape the reality of what she had done. He didn't know what to say.

Kate leaned back on the kitchen surface, watching the coffee machine as it poured the black liquid into a mug.

"Did I shock you?" she asked, folding her arms.

"Well, a little."

"It's taken me a long time; I've finally managed to come to terms with what happened. Something I hope that you are still working on?" she asked, arching an eyebrow.

Joe cleared his throat.

"I'm doing my best."

Kate nodded. "Good."

Joe tried to change the subject.

"So, how long have you known Liz? She seems a little..." he broke.

"Old?"

Joe looked away.

"Well. Yes. Sorry, I didn't mean to be an ageist."

Kate grinned at him, passing him a mug full of coffee. "Black?"

Joe took the mug of steaming liquid from her, his fingers brushing against hers, sending a spark through them both. His gaze locked with hers and he felt something shift between them, electric and intense.

Did she feel the same way? Thought Joe?

"I think so," Em answered his unasked question. *"How could she not? After all, you are an exact copy of her, Joe."*

Kate moved away and put another mug into the coffee machine to be filled.

"I met Liz in another world and asked her to join me."

Was it his imagination or was her voice ever so slightly quavering? He took a sip of his coffee.

"In another world? And she came here with you, just like that?" Joe knew that there must be more to it than that.

She pulled her own mug of hot coffee from the machine.

"Well, it wasn't quite like that. But her help is invaluable. I can't imagine coping without her. I'll tell you the story sometime."

"Coping?" asked Joe. That was an interesting word. What did she mean by it? He watched in fascination as her eyes narrowed and her lips pursed as she blew on her hot coffee. She was beautiful.

Liz interrupted them.

"We're ready," she said.

Joe turned. His mouth fell open and his eyes grew wide. Liz stood in the doorway, wearing a purple coat with a large hood, but that wasn't what attracted his attention. She was carrying a baby on her hip. The baby was bundled up in a thick yellow coat, complete with dangling mittens and a fur-lined hood. Her bright blue eyes stared at him through a lock of blonde hair that had fallen across her forehead.

Kate set her mug down and pushed past him, taking the baby from Liz.

"Hello, little one," she cooed as she smothered her with kisses on her cheeks. The baby giggled and gurgled, clearly loving the attention.

Joe was shocked. He said nothing, opening and closing his mouth like a fish while his eyes darted back and forth between Kate and the baby, taking in the scene before him. The mug slipped in his grip, splashing hot coffee onto his wrist and onto the floor.

A beaming Kate turned to Joe; she placed the baby on her hip. "Joe, meet Josie, Josie, this is Joe."

Josie's bright blue eyes stared across the kitchen at him, her little face serious.

Joe reached across to the kitchen countertop to set his mug down and grab a towel, pressing it to his scalded hand. He couldn't take his eyes off Josie. He cleared his throat, opened his mouth, and then closed it. He didn't know what to say. As the seconds passed, he saw Kate's expression change, her bright smile slowly faded, becoming serious and then angry. Say something, he thought to himself, for god's sake say something quickly and make sure it's the right thing.

"Say hello," said Emily in his mind. Joe, grateful for the advice, finally spoke.

"Hi Josie," he said. His voice sounded lame, even to himself.

Josie turned her head to look at her mother, then she turned back to Joe. He was shocked to see her hold out two tiny arms towards him.

Joe had no experience with babies, but even he knew what that gesture meant. She wanted him to hold her. He hesitated and then stepped forward, reaching out to take her from Kate.

Josie kicked her legs and squealed with joy as Joe lifted her up and then pulled her to him. Her little arms closed around his neck, and she pulled herself to him, her toothless mouth closing on his cheek.

Joe couldn't help himself. He broke into a wide smile and kissed Josie back. His eyes prickled with tears and his throat constricted. He caught Kate's eye over Josie's shoulder and saw her smiling back, her dark eyes sparkling with delight. In that moment, he knew. He knew that he loved her. He might have lost his own Kate, but he had found her again. He let go of his anger at her death. He forgave the aliens that had killed her. He closed his eyes and felt a wave of feel-good emotion as he snuggled and held Josie close to him.

He felt Kate come close, felt her arms close around both himself and Josie. She pulled him close and rested her head on his shoulder. Her hair brushed his skin as her head nestled against him. He could smell her perfume, the familiar smell of wildflowers. He was at peace. This was where he belonged. This was home.

From the kitchen doorway, Liz watched the three of them embrace, a smile on her lips.

Chapter 41 - Lexi

A strange woman stood framed in the doorway. Clearly of Asian descent, she seemed un-phased by the rain that had plastered her black curls to her head and was running in rivulets onto her shoulders. But that wasn't what made her strange. It was her silver arm. The woman's short sleeved blue top did nothing to hide the moonlight reflecting in a sheen of light from the arms gleaming, wet surface.

It was the first thing that Lexi noticed. The second thing she noticed were the rings on the strange woman's right hand. Her lip curled upwards in a sneer.

"You're one of Joe's lackey's," she said.

The woman was completely unfazed at the statement.

"Can I come in?" she asked.

"Why?" asked Lexi, the sneer still on her face. She didn't make any move to let her in.

"I'd like to talk with you," was the answer.

"Why?" asked Lexi again.

The strange woman cocked her head to one side.

"Do you always wear a tiara?" she asked.

Lexi had had enough; she sent a mental probe at the woman. Backed with the power of her M5A, she expected to crash through whatever pitiful mental defences this silver armed woman could muster. She expected to see every thought, every emotion, laid bare, spread out like the parts of a dismantled clock on a workbench. Instead, her probe bounced off a thought screen, the likes of which she had never encountered before.

She was shocked. How could this be? This woman at her door was clearly wearing a Mark 4 Assist. Lexi recognised the rings. After all, she had helped Joe develop the technology, him and that bitch Molly. Her M5A was an order of magnitude more powerful than an ordinary Mark 4. How come she was blocked? It shouldn't be possible. Unless. Unless this silver armed woman was wearing more than a Mark 4. But how and where? And, in any case, Lexi was the only person on the planet with an M5A. Surely Joe hadn't developed a Mark 5. Had he?

The thing was the thought screen she had just encountered didn't 'feel' like a Mark 5 screen. It had a different 'texture', a different quality.

A fire ignited in her mind, pulsing in time with waves of pain in her head. She wanted to learn more about this new technology, no matter the cost. Her fingers twitched as a sudden craving for knowledge grew within her. But how? Could she spare the time? Could she break through this woman's defences? Resignedly, she decided that now was not the time. She had bigger fish to fry. It was a shame. She would love to take it from this stranger; rip it apart and analyse it down to its last circuitry and byte. If it was promising enough, she could incorporate it into her M5A. But not now.

Lexi curled the fingers of her left-hand inwards towards her palm and pressed her fingers onto four contacts lying just below the skin.

Red fire flared around her fist and in less than a second, Lexi directed it at the stranger's face. Lexi smiled as the stranger's form was completely enveloped in a red firestorm.

The weapon was one of her new developments. Designed for her own personal use, it was a no compromise, burn everything down and leave no survivor's device. Intended as a one-shot, last resort defence, it would eliminate anything it was aimed at. Its plasma flames burned hotter than the surface of the sun, necessitating a Mark 5 screen to protect the wielder from back-flash and radiating energies.

From behind her screens, Lexi smiled and sneered. She wasn't someone to be trifled with. Joe had sent one of his minions to find her, and she would send back their remains in a body bag. She wasn't interested in what Joe wanted or why he had sent this woman to talk. She didn't care; she had had enough of Joe and his holier than thou attitude. After she had developed the very first Augment device, she had wanted to go further, but Joe had refused. He was concerned about the intrusive nature of the device and the fact that it required surgery to be fitted. He was worried about harming people and leaving them as vegetables if there was a mistake in their calculations. He had never been the same after he had discovered her home-built, make-shift lab and had seen the monkeys. After the screaming match, she had left.

The red flames roared into the night sky, spewing searing-hot sparks as they encircled the stranger. In a maelstrom of fire and smoke, the two cars on the driveway exploded, launching molten metal and plastic high into the air. The paint and plaster in the hallway sizzled and melted like burning wax, pouring down the walls in rivers of liquid flame.

The searing heat incinerated the asphalt on the road, its fire spreading a path of destruction into the night. Houses burned as their windows shattered like glass bombs, and cars ignited in screams of roaring flames before their petrol tanks exploded, sending streams of liquid fire cascading up into the sky.

Lexi laughed out loud when she heard the screams of her neighbours as they were awoken by the explosions to find their houses on fire. She watched with glee as a flaming car sped past to crash through a garden wall and smash through the large bay window of a block of flats. It was glorious! The darkness of the night was banished as the conflagration spread. She had never had an opportunity to try out the weapon, and maybe that was just as well. The destruction was total. Once the flames had died, there would be nothing left. The weapon was so much more destructive than she had imagined. It wasn't just fire. It was so hot it was virtually plasma, super-heated matter formed into an ionised gas. It obliterated everything it touched, and everything nearby ignited instantly.

She would have to leave. Flaming, bricks, concrete and wood crashed down around her, bouncing from her screens as her house was consumed. Everything was totally destroyed, but it didn't matter. She had already decided that she was going to join Henrick at the Rig tomorrow. The only difference is that she would be a few hours early. She sighed inwardly. She had been eagerly anticipating another night session with Reuben Cline. Ah, well, it could wait. She couldn't stay here and maybe it was just as well. The cancer was progressing quickly. She had already transferred numerous brain functions to the M5A logic and processing functions. Her time was running out. But before the cancer took her, she had one more task to complete.

She flexed the fingers of her right hand and described an intricate pattern in the air. Her rings flashed blue, and she disappeared with a snap of wind, leaving behind a whirling spire of flame.

———

Sometime later, a figure walked through the flames and debris that was Lexi's house.

"She's gone," Prisha directed a thought at Joe.

"Well done for finding her in the first place, Prisha." Came the replied thought. *"I guess she wasn't happy to see you?"*

"No, definitely not," Prisha replied wryly. *"And that weapon of hers was something else!"*

"Yeah, I'm really glad that Isabelle was able to squeeze in some defensive systems into your new limbs!"

"I'm not sure that even a HAZPRO would have provided enough protection. That beam was hot!"

"Lexi was always very inventive; I should've warned you."

"You couldn't have known she would have been so quick on the draw!"

"I don't know," replied Joe. "We didn't part on the best of terms, and she's always had a temper."

"Well, whatever, I'm okay and best of all, I'll be able to follow her."

"You will?"

"I don't think she noticed the micro bug I fired at her foot. If she still has her shoes on, I'll be able to find her."

"I'm impressed. Well done. I thought you'd be asking to be reassigned!"

Prisha smiled to herself.

"Not me," she replied. "I'm determined to have that talk with our Lexi. She won't escape me next time."

Chapter 42 - Build

In the darkness of deep space, far beyond the reaches of our sun's light, lies the Oort cloud. A vast spherical mass of rock and ice completely enveloping our solar system. Its particles ranging in size from that of a marble to that of a mountain - all millions of years old.

Flashes of intense light and giant heat plumes from vast convertor machines punctuated the darkness. Originally transported from World 6, these enormous machines worked unceasingly, breaking down great slabs of ice and rock into their constituent elements to feed the never-ending need for construction materials. Their relentless activity illuminated the abyss, like lightning illuminating clouds from within.

Next to each convertor, fabricator units ingested the raw materials directly fed into them, building replicas of themselves. As each newly manufactured machine was ejected from the fabricator's vast maw, it sped away on massive jets of ionised gas to position itself next to a newly transported convertor from World 6, until after eight days the thousands of convertors were each surrounded by hundreds of fabricators.

Now the fabricators switched their manufacturing to camouflage units, spewing out flotillas of compact discs, each roughly a meter in diameter, and launching them off into space on pillars of fire. They zipped through space like tiny firecrackers faster than any human ship could travel towards their assigned positions. Being much simpler, smaller units, it took less than a day to build the hundreds of thousands required. As soon as they had all arrived at their predetermined position, they all activated simultaneously. Invisible lines of force sprang from each disc, connecting them together, forming a web of energy.

To all outside observers, whomever they may be, our solar system disappeared, hidden behind a camouflage screen.

Out of sight of prying eyes, the building continued. Now that the reflective screens were running, the fabricators switched production to defensive units. Huge numbers of tiny screen generators sped outwards from their factory units towards the planet they were designed to protect - Earth.

———

The commander of the Klalan battle group was shocked. Gobs of drool dripped from the tentacles surrounding its mouth to splash onto the floor.

"You are sure?" asked the commanders thought.

The chief technologist lowered its head to the ground and then lifted it back up again.

"We have verified our observations. There can be no doubt exalted one."

The commander considered, absently scraping a worm-like finger around one of its four eyes.

"Is it possible they transferred their entire system to another universe? They saw us coming and escaped like cowards?"

"Unlikely," replied the technologist. *"We would have detected the energy signature at such an event. It is not probable that the feeble entities inhabiting this universe have the technology to do so."*

The commander licked at the scum adorning its fleshy finger.

"Then it is a camouflage screen?"

"That is the most likely explanation," agreed the technologist.

"So, that means they know we are coming."

"It would appear so. This is, of course, nothing to be concerned about. They cannot withstand our might."

"Of course not!" replied the commander. *"Hiding behind their screens will not help them."*

It swivelled its neck to observe the rear of the yellow hazed room.

"Have we had any communication with our allies?"

A Klalan raised itself up on its four legs.

"No, exalted one."

The commander swivelled back to view the chief technologist. It extended a front leg and used it to describe small arcs of movement on the floor, spreading fallen mucus into a thin film.

"If I may," the technologist projected a thought. "I propose a course of action."

"You may advise me," answered the commander.

"I propose we accelerate our manufacturing production and send scouts ahead. It would be useful to plan our attack if we knew what they were capable of."

"Caution is always advised," acknowledged the commander. "However, the inhabitants of this universe appear to be particularly weak. I am not concerned. We will continue as planned."

It stamped its foot into the mucous goo on the floor, sending small globs flying around the room.

"Our allies may or may not join us," it continued. "It is no matter. I am more and more convinced that we do not need them. Have you instigated the construction of the reinforced screens around this world?"

"They were activated a short time ago," answered the chief technologist. It used a finger to scrape a small clump of mucus that had splashed onto its leg and then sucked it into its mouth.

"And you have made sure that nothing can get through them?"

"I assure you that absolutely nothing can penetrate them. I will stake my life on it!"

———

A sneering Kate turned to Joe.

"They are complete incompetents!"

"But powerful," answered Joe.

Kate huffed and turned her attention back to the yellow hazed room to continue their eavesdropping.

"It appears that our Jim didn't do the job," observed Joe.

"No, although the bomb did go off, it must have caused some damage," replied an angry Kate.

"Yet they have built a camouflage screen," Joe pointed out.

"Yes, I was hoping that we would level their base, and that we didn't have to rely on these disgusting things," she indicated the Klalan.

"Whatever. It is annoying that they aren't going after the pink aliens first. I'm not worried about the humans; I want them to take out the pinkies."

Kate smirked.

"Pinkies?"

"We have to call them something."

"I hate them," snarled Kate. "No one tells me what to do."

"I hate them too, my love. Don't worry, our plan will work. We get the Klalan to soften them up, and then we go in after them for the kill."

Kate nodded to herself.

"How's Molly's research going?"

"Well. She believes that there is another order of energy that our Mark 5s can't tap into. She's working on a detector."

"I don't like the way you are with that bitch!" growled Kate. "If it were up to me, I'd have killed her ages ago."

"Jealous, my love?" Joe smiled at her.

"Of course not!" retorted Kate. "I don't like how you treat her."

"Gently, you mean? It's producing results, is it not?"

Kate huffed again.

"Just get her to build the new weapons asap and stop fawning around her!"

"Don't worry, she'll work it all out for us. After all, we have her Sally as a bargaining chip. She'll do what I ask. If not, I'll make her watch as I carve up Sally's face."

Kate grinned.

"Now that, I'd like to see!"

Chapter 43 - Sally

"That was pretty stupid!" exclaimed Sally as she examined the inside of her patient's mouth, who could only grunt an answer, a tongue depressor preventing him from talking.

Sally withdrew her instrument and tutted as she looked around the room. Three more patients, all men, sat in a row waiting to be seen, each of them holding blood-stained cloths to their jaws.

"Don't tell me, you all wanted to see and got too close!" It wasn't a question, more a statement of disgust.

All four men looked sheepish and stared at the ground.

"It seemed a good idea at the time," one mumbled around a handkerchief.

Sally couldn't help it. She laughed out loud.

"I'm sure it did," she answered. She put her hands on her hips. "Well, there's not a lot I can do. I'll prescribe antibiotics. You all know how to block the pain. Meanwhile, we'll have to bring in a dentist from outside." she locked eyes with each of them in turn. "I'm sure you all realise what a security risk that is?"

There was a nodding of heads and grunts of understanding.

"Go on then, get out of my emergency room. I'll contact you when we've located a dentist that we can trust."

She watched as they filed out, shaking her head, not believing how stupid people could be. They had been warned to be at least five miles away while the Complex was transported back to their world. They all knew about the energies involved. These four idiots had decided to get closer to watch. Of course, they were too close. Each one of them had their metal fillings ripped from their mouths.

Sally didn't have time for such stupidity. She had things to do. Kate would be here soon. Like everyone else, Sally had been surprised to hear that Kate had a baby, but unlike everyone else, she was instantly concerned about the health of both mother and child. It took some convincing, but in the end, she persuaded Kate to allow her and Josie to be checked over.

Kate had protested that Isabelle had taken good care of them, but Sally had pointed out that Isabelle was not a doctor. And when asked about Josie's immunisations, Kate had looked blank. She confessed she was also unsure about what postnatal checks Isabelle had performed. Kate had seen the wisdom of what Sally was saying, so had agreed for both herself and Josie to be examined.

Sally was just finishing her preparations when Kate and Josie walked into the room.

"Hi Sal," Kate said cheerfully. "We're here."

Sally turned and smiled at them both. She was still in awe of Kate. What she had done a few weeks ago still shocked her. The power that she manipulated with such ease was frightening. But right now, Kate seemed to be the same as the Kate she had met over a year ago. A little more confident, of course, and a lot more content. She had matured. Having a baby will do that for you, thought Sally.

"Thanks for coming," she replied. "It should only take a few moments, but it's best to be sure."

Josie stared intently at Sally, her blue eyes shining like two stars.

"Josie, this is Sally. Sally, this is Josie," Kate said by way of introduction.

"Hello there, little one!" Sally stepped forward and held out her arms for Josie, lifting her from Kate's hip. She lifted her high into the air. "My, aren't you beautiful?" she said, lowering her and carrying her over to an examination bed.

"How old is she?" she asked Kate over her shoulder.

"Nearly six months," replied Kate, following Sally.

Sally laid Josie down on the bed and began carrying out some simple checks.

"Is it alright if I remove her clothes?" she asked.

"Of course," replied Kate.

Sally expertly removed Josie's clothes item by item.

Josie stared up at Sally, her face serious.

Sally examined her hands and feet.

"Is she feeding okay?"

"Oh, yes. She's a greedy little thing. She loves her milk!"

"And you're breastfeeding?"

Kate nodded.

"I've been expressing milk before going on my trips to other worlds so Liz can feed her."

Sally recalled meeting Liz.

"Liz is a very capable woman. She was very helpful after the EMP." She straightened up from examining Josie. "Well, that all seems normal. I'll just check her heart." She fitted a stethoscope to her ears and placed the chest-piece on Josie's chest.

Kate beamed down at the little girl, who was kicking and waving her legs enthusiastically.

After a little while, Sally removed the stethoscope.

"Well, that's all in order, little one." She took a small pen torch from her lab coat pocket and shone it into each of Josie's eyes.

"All normal!" she stated enthusiastically. She turned to Kate. "Physically, she's absolutely normal and beautiful."

Kate's face was full of love.

"She's, my angel. Thank you for checking her out."

"Hold her safe on the bed while I get her vaccinations."

"Uh oh." Kate rested her right hand on Josie's chest. "This is the bit we weren't looking forward to, were we, Josie?"

Sally returned with a tray.

"I'm afraid it's a must," commented Sally. "I'm going to give her two - a six in one, and the meningococcal vaccine. The rotavirus vaccine is oral."

"Six in one? What's that?"

"It's several all rolled into one dose. It covers diseases like polio, whooping cough and hepatitis B. She should have had them when she was eight weeks old."

"It's not too late?" asked Kate.

"Not at all," reassured Sally. She swabbed Josie's thigh. "She might be a little off-colour afterwards, but it shouldn't last more than a day or two."

Sally quickly jabbed the needle home and depressed the plunger. She was surprised when Josie didn't cry. Then she noticed Josie was clasping Kate's ringed fingers. One of her little digits had hooked itself around the tiny connecting chain between Kate's forefinger and thumb.

"Does she do that often?" she asked.

"What?" asked Kate.

"Hold on to your Assist."

Kate looked at Josie's little hands gripping her fingers.

"Oh that. Yes, she does. She likes to play with the chains, don't you, sweetheart?"

Sally's expression grew serious as she swabbed Josie's opposite thigh and then quickly injected her with the second vaccine. As she did, she watched Josie. The expression on her little face didn't change, her eyes fixed on her mother.

Sally dropped the syringe onto the tray.

"That's very interesting," she said.

"It's just a baby thing," answered Kate. "Babies like playing with necklaces and things."

"Hmmm."

Sally wasn't so sure. Babies always cried when they got their vaccinations. She had never seen a baby so calm.

"Does she cry very often?"

"Only when she needs something. She lets me know when she needs me."

"When she cries, do other people hear it?"

Kate turned to Sally, a perplexed look on her face.

"What do you mean? Of course, other people hear it!"

Sally turned away and busied herself with the medical equipment, setting the tray of used syringes on a nearby countertop. She returned with a small capsule full of a clear liquid. In seconds, she squeezed three drops into Josie's mouth.

"And how about you?" she asked. "How have you been since the birth?"

"I'm fine. I've been kind of busy, you know."

"You can dress Josie now. I'd like to do some checks on you, if you don't mind?"

Kate complied, cooing and smiling at Josie as she pulled on her clothes.

"You've been busy world jumping?"

"Yep, I've been all over, haven't I, little one?"

"What about while you were pregnant? Did you travel between worlds, then?"

"I had to," replied Kate. "I had to find a world where it was safe to have Josie. It took a while, eventually I sort of stumbled into Isabelle in World 6."

"And that would be when you were about six months pregnant?"

"Yes, about that."

"Hmmm," mumbled Sally to herself. "When the baby's brain is developing…"

"What did you say?" asked Kate as she lifted a fully clothed Josie high into the air.

"Nothing," answered Sally. "Here, pass me Josie while you lie on the bed. I'll put her down over here." Sally placed Josie on the floor on a carpeted area of the room. "She'll be okay for a little while."

Kate followed Sally's instructions and watched as Sally put a blood pressure cuff around her arm.

"I'll take your blood pressure and take some bloods. Did you have stitches?"

"Nope, all natural." said Kate.

"I am constantly monitoring Kate's blood pressure and hormone levels. All of her markers are within normal tolerances," Bella communicated with Sally.

"If you don't mind, I'd like to check myself," replied a miffed Sally.

"Very well," replied Bella. *"But I assure you that Kate is in good physical health."*

Sally didn't answer.

"Your blood pressure is slightly high," she told Kate.

"It is within normal human parameters," stated Bella.

"I'll be the judge of what's normal," answered Sally angrily.

"It's okay Bella," Kate interjected. *"Sally's doing her job."*

"As am I," replied Bella.

"Stop being difficult Bella," said Kate. *"Sally's a professional. She knows what she's doing."*

Bella fell silent.

"I'll take a blood sample anyway and get it tested. I'm also going to prescribe some vitamin D supplements as you are breastfeeding."

Kate watched as Sally deftly inserted a needle into the crook of her arm to draw three vials of blood.

"Thank you, Sal. Thanks for looking after me and Josie."

Sally applied a sticking plaster and smiled at Kate.

"It's my job. You and I go way back…" She stopped, the smile leaving her lips. "Sorry, I was thinking of the old Kate."

She looked away, embarrassed.

Kate grabbed Sally's arm.

"It's okay Sal, I get it. I'm not your Kate. For me, you are so much like my Sally. It was she who showed me how to control my bad thoughts and memories, just as you did for your Kate."

Sally put her hand on Kate's.

"It's a bit awkward, isn't it?" she asked.

Kate chuckled.

"For all of us," she answered.

"Well, we'll just have to work our way through it, won't we?"

"Yes, we will. Friends?"

Sally smiled at Kate.

"Friends."

———

After Kate and Josie had left, Sally sent a thought to Molly.

"Mol, are you there?"

"Of course," came the quick reply. *"What's up?"*

"I think that we may have a problem."

"What sort of problem? We have enough already!"

"I've just examined Kate and Josie."
"And?"

"I don't think that Josie is normal."

Chapter 44 - Together

Lee, Molly and Alex were enjoying their breakfasts in the refectory whilst discussing Isabelle's plan. It was much too early for most people to be awake, but these three leaders were already up and about.

"Why isn't she telling us everything?" complained Lee.

Molly blew on her hot mug of coffee.

"I don't know, but clearly there's an important reason."

"You're too understanding," said Lee around a mouthful of toast. "Why are you giving her the benefit of the doubt? It's like she doesn't trust us."

"I trust her," Alex spoke up as he popped a mushroom from his full English breakfast into his mouth.

"Why?" asked Lee as he poured himself a second coffee from a metal jug.

"It's simple," answered Alex. "Everything she's done has been to our benefit. I mean, look at that nanobot incursion. If it hadn't been for her, we'd all be dead."

Lee sipped at his coffee.

"Yes, but I didn't see any evidence of the nanobots."

"Oh, come on!" exclaimed Alex. "Why lie about something like that?"

"Sally saw them," said Molly, in between mouthfuls of granola and yoghurt.

"There you go!" said Alex. "My point exactly. And to continue, why blow up the Complex? What could be the reason for that?"

Lee grumbled into his coffee.

"You're probably right, but I still don't trust her. I don't think I'll be able to until I know all her plan."

Molly nodded in agreement.

"I get where you're coming from, Lee. I'm still amazed that we're sitting here in the refectory of a Complex from another world that has been transported to our world! You've got to admit that her technology is way beyond ours."

Alex finished his breakfast and set his knife and fork down on his plate. He leaned back and sighed in contentment.

"I've visited her labs. She's given me access to everything; I've been working my way through her tech manuals. It's going to take me years to get through it all."

Lee buttered another slice of toast.

"I thought it had all gone wrong when I saw that mushroom cloud."

Alex grinned.

"That was just the crater collapsing in on itself when the Complex was teleported out of the ground."

"And then there was that light that hurt your eyes," said Molly.

"Ultra-band Psi energy," explained Alex.

"Then that hurricane wind nearly blew me off my feet," complained Lee.

"Atmospheric displacement," said Alex, picking up a cup of herbal tea.

Molly gazed around the canteen.

"Not a glass or mug broken," she noted.

"Getting the World 6 Complex out of the ground was the easy bit, believe it or not," said Alex. "It was the phase-shift transference into our world that was much more difficult." He waved his hand, indicating the room, tea slopping over the edge of his cup. "The space to accommodate the Complex had to be created by shifting out the exact volume of rock and soil and then shifting in the Complex. It took microsecond timing and precise mass and volumetric calculations."

"Well, clearly it worked, because here we are." Molly spooned the last of her granola into her mouth.

"The lift doesn't work though," complained Lee.

"That's only because it has nowhere to go," Molly pointed out as she picked up her mug of coffee again.

"I know," answered Lee. "I guess an old house appearing out of nowhere would have freaked out anyone who knows the area."

"We don't need that old house anyway," said Alex. "We can teleport in and out."

"Sure, but it's not that straightforward. You have to make sure that you port to somewhere quiet, where there's no one to see you appearing out of thin air!"

Alex nodded enthusiastically.

"I hear that there's a project to integrate us into the rest of civilisation?"

"That's a long-haul project," said Lee. "It's going to take years."

"Not an easy project to manage," mused Molly. "Think of all the distrust, not to mention how governments will behave. If it's not handled right, it'll be a disaster. I can see us being hunted down and imprisoned - or worse. We did the right thing, me and Joe, when we first discovered Psi. Keep it secret, recruit silently and tell no one."

"Even so, we can't keep ourselves secret for ever. We'll have to come out - so to speak - eventually. It's inevitable that we'll be discovered," noted Alex.

"Not to mention the upcoming war," agreed Lee. "Who knows how that'll go? I can't see that going unnoticed."

The three fell silent, each occupied with their own thoughts, when Joe and Kate's entrance into the canteen interrupted them.

Molly noticed immediately that they were holding hands, both smiling.

"Hi guys," shouted Joe from the doorway. "Mind if we join you?"

Lee's face lit up with a big grin.

"Absolutely, get yourself something and come join us. While you're there, bring another jug of coffee."

It wasn't long before Joe set down his tray on the table and sat next to Lee. Kate did the same, sitting opposite, next to Molly. Both had opted for a full English breakfast, their plates piled high with toast, mushrooms, bacon, sausage, tomatoes and scrambled eggs.

"So, how are things?" asked Joe, his mouth full of toast.

Molly nudged Kate in the arm.

"Hungry?" she asked.

Kate nodded quickly. A small smile crept along her lips as focussed her attention onto her plate of food.

"I see," Molly grinned. Kate blushed and stabbed a mushroom.

"It's great to have you back, buddy!" Lee said as he slapped Joe on the shoulder.

Joe coughed, a piece of bread flying out of his mouth onto the plate before him. He grabbed his napkin and hastily wiped his lips.

"Yeah, I had some help." His gaze met Kate's briefly, communicating something between them with their eyes. They both smiled knowingly.

The smile didn't go un-noticed. Molly's' grin grew wider. She sat back in her chair and crossed her arms.

"So, have you two buried the hatchet, so to speak? Have you been getting to know each other?" She smirked as she picked up her mug of coffee to take a sip, her eyes sparkling with mischief.

Joe held up his napkin to his mouth as he tried to control his coughing fit. Kate kept her head down, her jet-black hair cascading around her.

Lee looked at Molly and then at Kate and Joe. A wide grin broke out on his face.

"Oh. I see," he said. "I'm happy for the both of you. It was always meant to be."

Joe recovered from his coughing and fixed Molly with a glare.

"Did I ever tell you how much of a pain you are?" Joe asked Molly.

She nodded in agreement, her eyes twinkling, a big grin plastered on her face.

"Oh, quite often," she chuckled.

Joe cleared his throat and changed the subject.

"Okay, can we get down to business. How have things been going?"

Alex stared at the others; a look of confusion written on his face.

"What just happened?" he asked.

The four broke out into laughter, and Alex was left wondering what they were all laughing about, a puzzled expression on his face.

"What did I miss?" he asked.

Chapter 45 - Lexi

Lexi gazed in satisfaction at the massive machine before her, a staggeringly massive structure of tangled wires, cables, and pipes that towered up to the distant ceiling. Thick black electrical cables coiled like snakes, slithering from the shadows of the chamber to snuggle deep into its inner workings. Discs, tubes and cones of metal were fused around its base, which rose from the floor, through which a single narrow stairway climbed upwards into the machine's depths. And there, at its core, at the top of the stairway, sat a single high-backed, red chair.

She walked slowly toward it, her feet clanging on the steel floor until she stopped just a few paces away from the machine's base. Her eyes traced the cables that snaked their way into the interior of its belly. Bright red lights flickered inside. Her heart skipped a beat at the sight of the chair deep within its metal casing. She smiled softly to herself.

"It's complete and ready to go?" she asked over her shoulder, directing her question to Henrick standing behind her.

"Yes," he replied. "All the modifications you asked for have been added and we've completed some low-level tests. Everything is set to go."

Lexi turned to smile up at Henrick. His steel-grey eyes were deep set and guarded by two bushy eyebrows that seemed to say, "Don't mess with me." He was not handsome. A scar ran from his left cheek, running through his puckered lips, ending at his stubbled chin.

"You've done well. Thank you for completing it in time." Lexi reached up and placed a hand on his broad, well-muscled shoulder. "It's perfect."

Henrick reached over and took her hand from his shoulder in his. He raised it to his lips and kissed it.

"Anything for you," he murmured. "You know that."

Lexi's smile turned sad.

"I know," she answered softly. She looked up at the far wall, where several technicians wearing pristine white lab coats and engineers bustled about behind a reinforced glass partition wall.

"You've briefed the technicians?"

Henrick nodded ascent and released her hand.

"Walk on my left," she instructed as she stepped around him. "I've lost the hearing in my right ear."

Henrick looked pained as he complied with her instruction.

They walked back the way they had come towards the exit, their footsteps echoing around the large chamber.

"I'm sorry to hear that. Is there anything I can do?"

Lexi grabbed Henrick's arm and forced him to look into her eyes. "It's too late," she said with a raspy breath.

"This thing is eating my brain. I've already had to off-load all my long-term memories and some of my motor functions to the M5A." A single tear ran down her cheek as she continued.

"This is my last project. I will prove that they exist before I die. I will prove it for Gary." Clenching his hand tightly in hers, her gaze was intense and desperate.

Henrick reached up and wiped the tear from her face with a thick, scarred finger.

"I'll help you," his voice was gruff and deep. "I'm certain that you've been right all along. This installation will help you prove it once and for all. All that you've done will be justified."

Lexi smiled up at him. She held his hand and turned to continue towards the exit, but an unmoving Henrick stopped her. She turned back, a quizzical look on her face.

"You're sure?" he asked. "You're sure that nothing can be done?"

"Yes Henrick, I'm sure. I have just days left." She turned to continue her journey. "Come on, we need to prepare."

———

"She's on an oil rig," projected Prisha.

"An oil rig? What's she doing there?" asked Joe. *"Hang on, let me bring Kate in."*

In less than a second, Kate joined the thought conversation.

"Hi Prisha, how are the new limbs?"

"They are absolutely fantastic," replied Prisha. *"Apart from the silver, I can't tell that they aren't my own. Tell Isabelle that I am truly grateful."*

"I don't have to," replied Kate. *"She's here with me."*

"I am pleased that your prosthesis is working to specification." Isabelle joined the conversation. *"Given your last encounter with Lexi, what do you know about what she is doing on this oil rig?"*

"Nothing at all. I was about to give her a visit."

"Please pass the coordinates to me," asked Isabelle.

Prisha did as directed.

"Please be careful, Prisha," Joe implored. *"She's clearly still angry at me."*

Prisha laughed, *"Given our last encounter, I would agree with you!"*

"There are some unusual energy signatures coming from that area," stated Isabelle. *"I will assign one of my android bodies to accompany you. I am concerned that you may not have enough protection."*

"Is that really necessary, Izzy?" asked Kate.

"Let's just say that I like to be sure," replied Isabelle. *"At this time, I cannot devote my full attention to this project."*

"Is Lexi that dangerous?"

"I do not know," answered Isabelle. *"But the unusual energy readings are worrying me slightly. I have detected nothing like it before."*

"What do you mean Isabelle?" asked Joe. *"How unusual?"*

"They are fifth order, but far stronger than I have ever seen a fifth order force before. They are a magnitude greater than any Mark 5 Assist can generate. Therefore, I assume that there is some sort of installation on that oil rig, the purpose of which is unknown."

"There's only one way to find out," said Prisha. *"Isabelle, do you want to come to me, and we can port together to the rig?"*

"Yes, one of my android bodies will be with you shortly. I need to reassign some tasks first."

"Given what you've said, I'm glad that you are going with Isabelle," said Joe. *"Please do you what you can to persuade her, Prisha. Our Augmented people need her. Sally has placed them in induced comas."*

"Don't worry, I'll do my best. But if she refuses, I'll drag her back to the Complex kicking and screaming."

"I like your attitude, but we need her co-operation. She's no good to us if she won't help us."

"Got it," answered Prisha. *"Don't worry, I'll persuade her."*

———

"Do you think she can do it?" asked Kate as soon as Joe walked through the door.

"If anyone can, Prisha can," Joe fell onto the sofa next to Kate.

"I'm not so sure," answered Kate. "She sounds like a stubborn person to me. I bet she won't do anything she doesn't want to."

"You nailed it," agreed Joe. "She was always stubborn."

Kate folded a leg under her and turned to face Joe.

"So, how long were you together?"

"We worked together for about three years."

Kate raised her eyebrows.

"That's not what I meant, and you know it. How long were you an item?"

Joe looked away, embarrassed.

"It was a long time ago."

Kate just looked at him, waiting for him to answer.

"Eighteen months," he paused. "I don't know why you're asking me about her. It was a long time ago, and I think that we both knew that we weren't right for each other at the start. It was just the excitement of working and building something new. There were the three of us: me, Molly, and Lexi. I guess it was inevitable that me and Lexi would get together. But it all ended a long time ago. I certainly have no feelings for her, and I'm pretty sure she won't have any for me."

Kate gave a wry smile.

"I'm pulling your leg, really. I know you have no feelings for her."

Joe sighed in relief.

"Where's Josie?" he asked, looking around the room.

Kate smiled coyly. "I asked Liz to take her for a walk. She'll be gone for a couple of hours."

Chapter 46 - Fusion

Much later, they lay together in bed, their bodies entwined, their arms wrapped around each other. Joe was on his side and Kate was on her back, her hair spread like a black halo about her head. He moved his arm from under the covers and gently brushed a lock of her hair out of her eyes.

"You're really beautiful when you think no one is watching you," he thought at her.

The faintest hint of a smile lit up Kate's dark eyes as she opened them to focus on him.

"You're not so bad yourself," she replied softly. They lay there unmoving, gazing into each other's eyes for a little while.

"You feel it, don't you?" asked Kate in a barely audible whisper. Joe immediately knew what she meant. This was more than love, more than sex. There was something else – something difficult to grasp or describe, but something that seemed almost tangible...a connection - a feeling of a self-extension – as though they were two apart and yet somehow together, that felt just out of reach.

"Yes," he replied.

"Do you remember when we first met?" asked Kate.

"In the conference room, you mean?" answered Joe.

"No, back in the alleyway when that gang robbed me?"

"Yes, but that wasn't you." Joe paused in thought. "That must have been before our worlds diverged."

"You felt something, then, didn't you? Something strange? You were baffled by it."

"That's right, but I couldn't place what it was."

"And then there was the time when that enemy soldier broke into the Complex and seemed to attack me. But you leapt forward and shielded me with your body."

"I remember. We still don't know how it got inside."

"Something happened then. Sally told me later it was because of something she called a Deep Link connection."

"I've heard some people have it, while others don't. What about it?"

"It's more than just a Deep Link."

Joe's mind raced.

"What can be more than a Deep Link?"

Kate pressed her lips tight, displaying a determined expression.

"It's time to find out."

"What? What do you mean?" Joe asked, puzzled. Where was Kate going with this?

Kate closed her eyes, her brow furrowed in concentration.

"Bella, are you ready?"

"Always," came the swift reply.

"You know what to do?"

"Of course."

Joe leapt up from the bed, his sheets cascading around him and falling to the floor, exposing his nakedness.

"Wait! What's going on? What are you talking about?"

Kate took a deep breath before replying, her voice heavy with sadness and urgency.

"We need to move things along quickly. We don't have a lot of time left."

"But I thought Isabelle had everything in hand?"

Kate shook her head sadly. "She can't do this job, Joe; it has to be us."

Slowly, understanding dawned on Joe. "You're not going to say what I think you're going to say, are you?" A horrified look on his face.

Kate just looked at him from where she lay in the bed.

"No way! I thought Isabelle would do that. She's much more capable than us! The last time we contacted them..." Joe left the words unsaid, but they hung heavy in the air between them.

"Your Kate died," Kate said softly, reaching up to stroke his arm gently. "Isabelle can't do this, Joe. It has to be you and me."

Joe clenched his fists until his knuckles whitened. "We can't do this! I can't lose you again!" he whispered fearfully.

Kate rose from the bed and wrapped her arms around his neck, pulling him close, holding him tightly. "This time it will be different," she whispered into his ear. "Let me show you." Her voice was full of hope and determination as she directed a thought inward.

"Bella, are you ready? Emily, are you ready?"

Joe felt an icy chill run down his spine as he realised, he and Kate were about to embark on something far greater than any Deep Link.

Kate held Joe's gaze, her eyes radiating boldness and power as the surrounding air suddenly charged with electricity.

"Bella, unlock high order functions," she commanded.

Kate threw her head back as lightning filled the room. Blue sparks danced around her body like a halo while electricity surged through them both, sending the hairs on Joe's arms rise on end and his veins burning with power. He wanted to shout out that he wasn't ready, but no sound came out of his mouth.

Kate lowered her head and locked eyes with him once more.

"Emily, unlock high order functions," she directed her thought at Joe's Assist.

Joe's mind lit up like a furnace as an intense energy flooded through him. He was powerless against it, his breath taken away by its intensity as he felt it course through him like an unstoppable wave of force. It felt like a hurricane was inside him, smashing away everything he knew and replacing it with something so powerful and raw that he couldn't comprehend it.

Presently, the surge of power running through his body subsided, and he was able to speak.

"This is what you feel when you activate your Mark 6?" he breathed in awe.

Kate smiled and nodded.

"I'm not ready," he protested.

Kate gazed at him with loving eyes.

Her eyes danced with brilliant blue sparkles, and the deep swirls of her iris swallowed them. She leaned forward and kissed his lips softly. "You're ready," she whispered into his ear as her warm breath flowed gently over it. Joe shook his head slowly.

"This is what you meant by something more than a Deep Link?" he asked.

"No, I meant this...."

"Bella," Kate spoke aloud, her voice ringing like bells in the surrounding space. "Emily." She turned her focus inward and then outward again towards Joe.

"Merge."

Joe, Kate, Bella and Emily merged into one.

Chapter 47 - Awareness

On the opposite side of our galaxy, a lone star shone brightly. It was so old that it should have expanded into a red giant thousands of years ago, but it was kept in a state of perpetual stability by a never-ending supply of hydrogen fuel siphoned off from other stars in a different dimension plane, replenishing its spent fuel reserves.

Englobing this everlasting sun, spaced at regular intervals, huge installations collected the radiated energy, directing it via energy conduits to other nearby stars and to yet more, even larger installations orbiting in the darkness, well beyond the gravitational influence of the sun.

A single planet orbited this ancient star. All others had been disintegrated into their basic building blocks and repurposed for the construction of the massive energy collectors that absorbed the star's radiation. On its swamp-like surface stood a single tower, the top of which housed a small, dark and damp room. Inside, an entity squirmed around in a cup-shaped pedestal. Its pink appendages flopped over the side of the container as it slowly writhed, folding in upon itself again and again. Water, collected from the ever-present mist in the dark room, sloshed over the sides to splash noisily onto the wet floor.

E984F was agitated.

In all its three thousand one hundred and four years of life, it had never observed energy readings like these. And once again, it was clear that the energy emanated from the same species the Non'anan had encountered before. At that time, the Non'anan collective had decided to monitor this young and potentially dangerous species, as opposed to removing them from the galaxy. Since then, E9894F had been assigned to observe them.

In the last few observation periods, there had been several energy spikes, all of which were fourth order energies. Then a massive spike was observed. This one was not fourth order, or even fifth order, but a cosmic scale sixth order energy.

This was unheard of. The use of fourth order energies by such a young species was already unusual. For them to move suddenly to sixth order was unprecedented and potentially extremely dangerous for the rest of the inhabitants of the galaxy. If this species was warlike, with such energies at their command, nothing could stop them from annihilating every other living thing. And if their development continued at this phenomenal pace, they may even threaten the Non'anan in the future.

E984F formed an urgent conclave to discuss the situation. Thoughts flashed between worlds as the Non'anan conversed and attempted to decide the best course of action.

Unusually, for the Non'anan, the discussion took a long time. Many contended that this young species should be immediately eliminated, stating that the risk of allowing them to develop further was too great. Others asserted the species was still young and would provide an interesting opportunity for study. Yet more argued that they should simply quarantine them and not allow any further expansion into the galaxy.

Eventually, after much discussion and logical analysis of the problem, a decision was made: this species could not be left to its own devices. So, the Non'anan had to intervene in a more concrete way. For now, they would continue to observe; however, four more

Non'anan were dispatched to join E984F. They would study this unusual species more closely.

For the first time in ten thousand years, the Non'anan made a mistake. They were so obsessed with the threat that humans represented, that the Klalan incursion into our universe was completely missed.

Chapter 48 - Skirmish

Ten monolithic planetoids, metallic and menacing, approached the outer edge of our solar system. Crafted by the Klalan with a level of perfection known only to them, each one a fortress with lethal fire power that was unmatched in strength and power. Each one stood as an immovable wall, proof against even the most powerful of attacks.

Behind this cone of impenetrable defence, a vast armada of hulking and menacing vessels loomed, jagged and ridged like mountains. The ships formed an impenetrable sphere that encased a single dark planet in its grasp. Flurries of smaller ships darted between the immense warships and the craggy planet surface, spurred on by some unknown force, servicing, maintaining and shuttling personnel to-and-fro from their monstrous masters.

Deep within the dark planet's labyrinthine depths, in a yellow hazed control room, the Klalan planned their attack.

"We must strike to disable their camouflage screens, so that we can target their defensive and offensive capability," the Attack Commander stated, with a loud and forceful thought, phlegm and mucus coating its mouth-manipulating tentacles.

"Negative," replied the Defence Coordinator. *"We should continue to their home planet and destroy it. Their offensive and defensive capability is of no concern."*

"I agree with the Attack Commander," stated the Strategy Functionary *"We need to understand their capabilities before committing ourselves."*

The three individuals turned to their attention to the screens in front of them.

"There is no indication of any reaction to our presence," the Defence Coordinator spat onto the floor. *"Their camouflage screens are very effective. We are blind."*

"By manipulating our scanners, I will be able to identify node points on their screen. I propose targeting them. Do we have an agreement?" asked the Strategy Functionary.

All three Klalan agreed, their mouth tentacles writhing in glee.

"Changing settings now," the Strategy Functionary issued the command.

"Wait!" the Defence Coordinator coughed a large nugget of mucus onto the screen in front of it. Hastily, it wiped it away with a finger appendage.

"I am detecting activity."

Three heads lowered to their screens.

"All moon ships are under attack!"

"How, where?" asked the Strategy Functionary *"I detect no ships or movement."*

The Defence Coordinator stepped back a little from the screen. A series of gasping, phlegmy laughs burst out of it, thickening the air with droplets which fell onto the screens and walls around it.

"It is nothing. The fools are trying to penetrate our defences with conventional nuclear weapons!"

"Pathetic!" commented the Attack Commander.

"Do they really think we are so weak?" asked the Strategy Functionary. *"I have changed my mind and now agree with the Attack Commander. These aliens have just demonstrated how feeble they are. There is no need for caution. We attack!"*

———

In deep space, thousands of tiny bomblets shrieked through the inky void like a swarm of locusts, the brilliant flames of their impacts illuminating the pitch-black expanse like a distant firework show. Millions of sparks ricocheted off the impenetrable planetoid shields, but not one could breach them. Every single one of these small nuclear explosives detonated against the invisible protective barriers, smothering them in fire, pounding relentlessly against them with each successive wave.

Unknown to the Klalan, their purpose was not to destroy or damage, their purpose was to distract. As the planetoids were engulfed in flames of nuclear fire, microscopic devices stealthily slid through the defensive screens, concealed by tiny sixth order shields that the sensing equipment possessed by the Klalan couldn't detect.

In seconds, the battle was over, the massive planetoids intact and unharmed.

Resting on the surface of each one was a single tiny receiver.

Chapter 49 - Lexi

Sleeping deeply, Lexi dreamed of the past.

"What you're doing is abhorrent!" exclaimed Joe loudly.

"Why?" asked Lexi. "Because you didn't think of it?"

"Don't be ridiculous!" answered Joe. "You are experimenting with animals, for god's sake!"

"Yes, and I'm getting results. No thanks to you!"

Lexi gazed around her lab, taking in the chaos. Benches, tables and the floor were covered in circuit boards, bits of wire, components and tools. In one corner, a coffee percolator bubbled and chugged away next to a shelving rack full of books and manuals. But none of this held her attention. It was what lay at the centre of the room that dominated her thoughts.

A circular table arrangement upon which lay six chimpanzees. Each monkey pulled against straps that held them immobile, their eyes wide and wild, their teeth bared. There was no shrieking or screeching. Each monkey had a blood-stained bandage across their necks where their pharynxes had been removed. Unable to make a sound, the monkeys slavered and spat as they fought to release themselves from the machine that connected directly into their brains.

With their heads positioned towards the centre of the table, each almost touching the other, the top of each skull had been removed, allowing full access to each brain. Tiny wires and fibre optic cables spread outwards from a central black and gold mechanism that towered up to the ceiling, penetrating the exposed brains.

"Those poor monkeys! What have you done to them?" Joe was shouting, as he looked on with horror at the struggling animals.

"I've daisy chained their brains together," replied Lexi, unperturbed. "When I interface with the mechanism, each monkey magnifies my Psi rating by a factor of ten."

Joe didn't answer. He was clearly disturbed and shocked by Lexi's experiment.

"But why? What you're doing is wrong on so many levels."

Lexi turned to Joe and smiled. "I don't think so. The monkeys are alive, aren't they? I got them from a research lab. They would have been dead by now. I've given them an extra few days of life." She turned back to the monkeys. "As to the why. Well. That you will have to wait and see. I'm not ready to show you yet."

Joe made a strangled noise.

"Actually, I don't care why or what you're doing. I want you to stop right now. Dismantle all this equipment and unhook all those monkeys. Send them to a zoo or something."

"You can't order me to do anything!" Lexi shouted back. "This is valuable research; I'm not going to give up on it just because you're squeamish!"

Joe rounded on her, his hands balling into fists.

"You will do as I say, or you can get lost. I don't want any part of research like this. I won't let you torture animals!"

"Fuck you! I'll do what I want!" retorted Lexi.

"No, you won't, because this is my facility, not yours. Me and Molly built it, not you. I say what happens here. You will dismantle all of this crap, or I will physically throw you out!"

With that, Joe turned and stormed out, slamming the door behind him.

An angry Lexi watched him leave.

How dare he tell her what to do! She couldn't dismantle her equipment now. She was on the verge of a breakthrough. She knew it.

As suddenly as it came, her anger left her as she realised that she had little choice. Joe was right, this was his and Molly's facility. Lexi had joined them after they had already built this underground complex. Oh, sure, she had made a valuable contribution. After all, Joe and Molly would never have come up with the Augment device without her. But now, she wasn't needed anymore. She felt as though she was being discarded like a used paper coffee cup. They had used her expertise, taken advantage of her surgical skill and now, just because she was pushing the boundaries in a direction they didn't like, they were getting rid of her.

Of course, she could stay. She could toe the line, do as she was told, like a good little girl. But that wasn't Lexi. She had to be true to herself and besides, she was on to something. She couldn't give up now.

Sighing to herself, she walked over to a cabinet and selected a vial of pentobarbital from a crowded shelf. She expertly and efficiently filled six syringes and injected each chimpanzee with the contents. Once all six were dead, she picked up a hammer from the floor and methodically smashed the machine in the centre of the round table, making sure that nothing was left that could betray its purpose.

The thumping and crashing of the hammer as she wielded it again and again morphed into another sound. She awoke to hammering on the door to her small cabin.

Confused, she shouted out. "What?"

"It's time," came Henricks muffled voice from the other side of the door.

Lexi blinked in the darkness; the confusion and her dream gradually replaced with understanding. Today was the day, the culmination of years of work. Today she would use the machine.

"I'll be right out. Give me a while to get up."

She heard Henrick grunt ascent and then heard his footsteps fade away as his boots clunked on the metal floor.

It was difficult to get out of the bed.

The progress of the cancer was marked, it was eating into her motor functions. For a little while she flopped around under the covers, her brain unable to control her limbs and coordinate her movements. But then she stopped and tapped into her M5A, assigning and building control routines that would replace some of the motor functions of her brain. She was adept and fast. It wasn't long before she could sit up, albeit in jerky movements.

The metal floor was cold on her bare feet as she twitched and jerked into the bathroom. It took longer than usual to get dressed, but as time passed, her movements became smoother as the M5A adapted and improved its perambulatory algorithms.

When she walked into the control room, Henrick passed her a hot mug of coffee.

"You good?" he asked, his gaze roving over her dishevelled clothing. "You sleep in your clothes?"

Lexi ignored his question as her gaze took in the room with its control consoles, displays, and banks of computer equipment.

"Are we ready?"

"Yes, of course." Henrick took a sip from his own coffee mug and turned back to the large window that overlooked the room where the machine sat, silent and ominous.

Lexi walked over to the large window, passing men and women wearing white coveralls busy at various control stations. She took a big gulp of her coffee.

"Are the VTOLs on the Aero deck?" she asked, as Henrick came up to stand beside her.

"They're ready to launch when needed," replied Henrick. "Although the weather's taken a turn for the worst. I'm not sure we'll need them. Not much can get to us in the storm that's raging up there." He raised his grey eyes to the ceiling as if he could see through the many decks of steel.

"And the surface-to-air missiles?" Today was the culmination of years of work. She wasn't going to let anything stop her.

"Everything is ready, Lexi," replied Henrick. "We've been planning and running drills for weeks. Our preparations are complete. We're ready to start when you are."

Lexi fell silent for a while as she gazed at the monstrous machine through the window.

"Very well." She turned and looked up at Henrick. "I'll need some help with the suit." She raised her eyebrows.

"Not a problem," he replied. "I'm here for you."

He spun and faced the room.

"Ladies and gentlemen," his voice boomed around the room. "This is not a drill; this is the real thing. Everyone assume your positions and start the countdown. You all know what to do. This time, let's make it work."

The room was suddenly bustling with activity as technicians and operators quickly and quietly moved to sit at consoles to start their predetermined tasks.

As Lexi turned to make her way out of the control room, something caught her eye.

"Wait!' She exclaimed. "Who's that?" Her ringed finger pointed through the observation window into the machine room.

Below the control room, walking around on the machine floor, were two figures.

Henrick strode over to the window. He pressed a button on his lapel and spoke quickly, with a commanding voice.

"Control Team A, into the machine room on the double. We have two intruders!"

Lexi pressed her nose up against the reinforced glass. She watched as the two figures walked around the machine, peering upwards at its bulk. Then she noticed a flash of silver.

"Hold the team, Henrick. I know who they are. Well, I know one of them. Your team wouldn't stand a chance against them."

Henrick didn't hesitate.

"Control Team A, stand down," he instructed into his microphone. "All Control Teams assume defensive stations."

He gazed down at Lexi.

"You know them? Are they a threat?"

"Yes, to both questions," answered Lexi. She sighed. "I thought I'd killed one of them. Looks like she's brought reinforcements."

Henrick watched the two figures gesticulating at the machine.

"What do you want to do?" he asked. "Are they Assisted?"

"Yes, they're Assisted. I suspect Joe sent them. I'm not sure that there's much we can do. I used one of my most deadly weapons on the black-haired one. Yet here she is, still alive."

Although not Assisted himself, Henrick understood what Lexi meant and the danger that these two figures presented. He had no idea what weapon Lexi was talking about, but he had been with her when she had showed her talents three years ago. She had teleported them both to a desert - in itself a frightening experience - then she had fused a square kilometre of sand into glass in an instant with a flick of a finger. Henrick had seen nothing like it. He knew of no weapon that could do anything like it, not even the super high-powered lasers that the military were experimenting with. He was awed to think that this slim, attractive, red-haired woman could wield the power of a nuclear detonation.

"We have to do something," argued Henrick. "Unless you want to delay? What about a sniper?"

Lexi smiled wryly. "I wish a sniper would have the desired effect. Stop the countdown. I'll have to go and talk with them."

"I can't let you go in there on your own," he protested.

Lexi's smile turned grim with an edge of sadness.

"Don't worry, you're coming with me." She took a small, jerky step. "I need you to lean on."

Henrick was at her side instantly, his arm around her waist.

"Are you sure? Is there nothing we can do?"

Lexi leaned into Henrick's bulk, breathing in his maleness. She felt a flicker of desire, but now was not the time.

"Henrick, those two people down there control forces far beyond what you've experienced before. An entire army couldn't stop them."

"How do you know that?" he asked, not hiding the disbelief in his voice as he helped her shuffle towards the exit.

"Because Joe sent them. Because the black-haired one survived the red flame and because the other one isn't human."

Henrick did a double take. He looked over his shoulder back towards the observation window, but he was too far away, and the angle was wrong for him to see the two figures.

"You mean an alien?" he asked incredulously. "You've got to be joking!"

At the door, Lexi allowed Henrick to open it and guide her through.

"I don't know what it is," she answered. "But it's definitely not from around here."

Henrick went quiet as two male guards fell in behind them, keeping pace as they shuffled down a corridor and descended a single flight of stairs.

"How many of the new Needle Bots do you have?" asked Lexi.

"I'm not sure. I'd have to check. You think they would be effective against the alien?"

"I don't know," answered Lexi. "I don't think we have much choice. Deploy all of them just in case. But first we'll find out what they want."

Chapter 50 - Encounter

"You're trespassing on private property," stated Henrick in a commanding voice. "You should leave immediately." He rested his right hand on his holstered pistol while his left was around Lexi's waist.

Both intruders stood ten metres away in front of the machine's massive bulk, all four of the room occupants eying each other suspiciously.

"What is the purpose of this machine?" asked the silver woman, completely unconcerned that they had been discovered.

Henrick had been surprised when he and Lexi had entered the machine room to see that the two intruders were women, although one was definitely strange, sporting a silver arm clearly visible as she was wearing a bright pink T-shirt. But the other was even stranger. She wore green shorts and a blousy green top, exposing flesh that was completely silver. At first Henrick wondered if it was simply silver paint, but now that they were close, he could see that was not the case. Her head was devoid of hair, the skull reflecting the ceiling lights as she moved, but it was her eyes that un-nerved him the most. They were all black and without eyelids. They stared unblinkingly and steadily at him like wet, black marbles.

"Why are you here?" asked Lexi.

"Like I said before, I want to talk with you," answered Prisha.

"Why should I talk with you?" asked Lexi. "Joe sent you again, didn't he? I have nothing to say to him."

"Joe sent me, yes. We need your help."

Lexi laughed.

"Of course, you do!" she rasped. "Well, I don't want to help you. Now leave."

"I am interested in this device that you have built." The silver woman spoke up. "I note that there is an interface for a human. What is its purpose?"

"It's nothing to do with you," answered Henrick. "Leave now." His hand moved to grip the handle of his holstered pistol. The move did not go un-noticed.

"I advise you to refrain from taking any hostile action. It will accomplish nothing." As the silver woman spoke, the surrounding air flickered with a very faint blue aura.

Lexi reached up and put a hand on Henrick's shoulder.

"Hold still, Henrick," she told him. She focussed on the silver woman. "What are you?" she asked. "I can't feel your thoughts and your screen is not fifth order."

"You are observant," answered the silver woman. "The device on your head is unusual. I surmise it is an adjunct to your Assist?" She didn't wait for a reply. "I am an autonomous cybernetic consciousness. I am currently controlling this android body. I am sure that you have realised that any hostile actions will be futile. I do not wish us to be enemies, but if forced, I will not only defend myself and Prisha, but I will also take what I want from your installation."

Lexi did not reply. She appeared to be in deep thought.

"Very well," she replied. "I'll tell you everything you want to know."

The blue aura surrounding the silver woman faded to nothing. Lexi squeezed Henrick's shoulder.

"What do you want to know?" she asked.

"I would like to know the purpose of this machine and your installation," said the silver woman.

Lexi pretended to listen. Instead, as the silver woman spoke, she silently spoke into Henrick's mind. Her thought was barely a whisper. *"Now...."*

Next to his holstered pistol, Henrick's forefinger depressed a tiny button.

Eleven killer drones, no bigger than a pencil, zoomed from the ceiling with a deafening shriek at an unbelievable speed. Prisha was their target, but they were no match for the silver woman's lightning reflexes; her arm flew up to smash three of the drones into pieces in an instant. The remaining drones crashed into the android in succession, setting off tiny fireballs that sent Prisha flying to one side. With a thunderous crash, the silver woman slammed onto the metal floor before all went quiet.

For a few moments, the room was still as the reverberation from the explosions faded away.

Henrick drew his pistol and aimed it at Prisha, who was sprawled on the floor. The android remained still.

"Don't move," he growled.

Prisha looked up at him without a trace of fear in her face.

"That was very stupid," she said.

Henrick was a little puzzled. The black-haired woman was not frightened and didn't seem to be too concerned that her companion was dead.

"Careful Henrick," said Lexi.

"I think I can handle things," he replied.

The woman on the floor shook her head.

"I'm sorry," she said.

Henrick grinned.

"Henrick!" Lexi exclaimed. She could feel it. She felt something she had never felt before, something large and powerful.

Suddenly, the air stirred, and a woman materialised with a crack of wind that sounded like thunder. Her eyes burned like burning coals in her pale face, which was contorted with rage. Wild jet-black hair sizzled with electricity that flickered around her like lightning bolts. On her right arm, an armlet of gold glowed brighter than the sun as she raised it high above her head.

"Henrick!" Lexi yelled, shoving him away from danger before assembling her defensive screens to protect them both.

Lexi's defences crumbled like paper as a titanic power smashed through them. She felt a searing mental agony that clamped around her mind like an iron vice, squeezing tighter with every passing second. Her teeth ground together as she fought against the pain with all her might, but it was useless.

"YOU DARE!" the voice reverberated through her mind with crushing power. *"YOU THINK TO KILL MY FRIENDS?"*

Lexi couldn't answer. She was in agony, held in a grip of iron. She couldn't think or act, all she could do was suffer in silence.

"STOP!"

It was an unfamiliar voice, and it brought instant relief from the pain. Suddenly released, Lexi collapsed to the floor, tears flowing from the shock and pain, her body shuddering with each breath as she gasped and writhed on the floor.

She felt a hand gently touch her shoulder.

"Are you alright?" a voice asked.

When she could open her eyes, Lexi saw Prisha leaning over her, concern in her eyes.

"Henrick…" Lexi groaned.

"He's okay. Unconscious, but he'll be fine."

Lexi closed her eyes and moaned in pain. She felt something trickle from her ear and across her cheek.

"Kate, get Sally!" she heard Prisha shout. "She's injured!"

"Please don't take it from me!" whispered Lexi.

"What?" asked Prisha. "Take what?"

"The Machine," she moaned with the pain again.

"Don't worry," answered Prisha. "It'll be okay."

Lexi blacked out.

———

Lexi awoke suddenly, startled, her eyes wide, her breathing fast. Where was she? She lifted her head, her eyes darted around, taking in her surroundings. It was a medical facility, that was obvious. She was in a bed, with a single bedside cabinet. The left wall was covered in cupboards above a counter-top, underneath which were more cupboards. Everywhere was white and clinical.

Her breathing slowed, and she flopped her head back down onto the soft pillow. She knew where she was. She was in the Complex. Joe had got his way in the end. She remembered the appearance of the woman with the jet-black hair, her golden armlet, her anger and her unbelievable power. And, of course, the pain.

She shuddered at the memory. Who was she, and where did she get that power?

She brought her hand up to her head, running her fingers through her red hair. Her M5A was still there. She ran her fingers lovingly over its jewelled surface, but then she noticed her Assist had changed. Holding her hand in the air above her face, she examined it carefully, noticing immediately that it had a bracelet. Chains from the little ring on her little finger and thumb ran back and connected to the golden bracelet. What sort of Assist was this? Someone had removed her Mark 4 and exchanged it for whatever this was. Anger flared inside her. How dare they! How dare they interfere with her Psionic devices! The audacity, the sheer gall. When she could get up, she would teach Joe a lesson! Then her thoughts returned to her encounter with the black-haired woman, and her anger disappeared as soon as it came. She would have to be careful around that bitch. She remembered the power that she had felt in the Machine room. It was unlike anything she had experienced before, and she resolved to learn more about it. She would learn and take it. It would be hers to wield.

She turned her awareness inwards and was shocked to her very core. The cancer was gone! At first, she was puzzled and could not process what had happened. Then she was elated for a few brief seconds. She was cancer free! She wasn't going to die! Then the truth of it hit home. Someone had operated on her. Anger replaced the elation. How dare they? They had operated without her permission; someone had been inside her head without her knowledge. It was another violation, first her Assist and now her brain.

She examined her mind in minute detail, trying to figure out what had been done to her. Of course, the parts of her brain that the tumour had eaten could not be replaced. The off-loaded routines were still there in her M5A, but the inevitable progression and her eventual death had been halted. Her anger slowly evaporated.

Someone had saved her. They had removed an un-operable tumour and saved her life. How was that possible? Over the years, she had visited several neurosurgeons. All had said the same thing.

'Sorry, the tumour was too advanced'. They could offer chemo and radiotherapy that might give her an extra year or two, but that was all. And yet here she was, cancer free.

The door opened, and a woman breezed in, her blonde curls bouncing as she walked, a huge smile on her face. She was wearing a white lab coat and was carrying a clipboard.

"Morning."

Lexi didn't answer. She watched warily as the woman walked over to stand beside the bed.

"How are you feeling? A lot better, I hope. My name is Sally, and I run the medical facility here in the Complex."

Lexi was immediately annoyed at Sally's bright and breezy demeanour. She just stared as a hand was placed on her forehead, the chains of an Assist tickling her skin. She felt Sally probe into her mind and tried to stop her but found that she could not. It was as though her mental faculties had been removed. In a panic, she tried to reach out with her mind, but nothing happened. No! This couldn't be! Had they removed her Psi control centres? Had they castrated her?

"Don't be silly," Sally's voice echoed in her mind. *"I've disabled some functions of your new Assist temporarily while you recover."*

Lexi felt Sally gently probe the area where the tumour had been excised.

"It's looking good. All traces of the cancerous cells have been removed. I must say that your ability to off-load some of your brain functions into your Augmentation is a stroke of genius."

Sally stepped back from the bed and made a note on her clipboard.

"I'll ask again, how are you feeling?" she asked aloud.

Lexi wasn't sure what to say. She was confused. She didn't understand what was happening. Had this woman really removed her cancer? All those times that she had been told that it was impossible, yet she couldn't deny that it was gone. She could see the void in her mind. She had felt this woman, the doctor, probe into the spaces where it had been. Briefly, happiness flowed through her before she clamped it down and controlled her emotions. She had to be careful. These people were the enemy.

"I'm confused," she croaked, her voice sounding much weaker than she expected. She licked her dry lips.

"Perfectly understandable," replied Sally brightly. "Here, let me help."

She picked up a glass from the bedside table. Expertly lifting Lexi's head up, she positioned a bendy straw so that Lexi could take a sip.

Once Lexi had drunk her fill, Sally lay Lexi's head back down on the pillow.

"Good, you are making excellent progress. I'd like you to rest and recover. But there's one person I can't keep from visiting you."

Sally grinned at Lexi's questioning eyes.

"Henrick has been champing at the bit to see you ever since you arrived."

"He's here?" Lexi asked.

"Oh yes, and he's very keen to see you." Sally walked over to the door and opened it.

"You can come in now," she called through the opening. Henrick's muscular form appeared in the doorway.

"Now, mind you, don't upset her or cause her any stress. She needs rest." Sally told an anxious-looking Henrick as he pushed past her.

Chapter 51 - Henrick

Henrick pulled up a chair and sat next to the bed, smothering Lexi's hand in his own. Lexi turned her head towards him and waited for Sally to close the door.

"Henrick," she smiled.

Henrick's face was full of concern as he leaned forward and raised her hand to his lips, kissing it softly.

"I've been so worried about you," he said, stroking her hair with his other hand. His usual military style perfect appearance was gone. His short greying hair looked unbrushed, and he had longer than usual stubble on his chin and cheeks.

"You know me," Lexi gave a faint smile. "I'm not easy to get rid of. What's been happening? How long have I been out of it?"

"We've been here three days," answered a smiling Henrick.

"Three days!" she exclaimed.

Henrick nodded. "I thought you were dead. After Kate appeared, I saw you fall."

"The black-haired woman?"

"Yes," he hesitated. "I've spoken with her. She's not a bad person."

Lexi's eyebrows raised.

"She nearly killed us," she said coldly.

"She lost her temper; you would have done the same."

Henrick hesitated again.

"Lexi, I have some things to say to you. I want you to listen and think about what I'm going to say. Don't just dismiss it, it's important."

"I always listen to you, you know that."

Henrick looked away. "This is different. You might not like what I'm going to say."

Lexi stared into his steel-grey eyes. He had changed. He looked unsure of himself; his usual confidence was gone.

"What's the matter, Henrick?" she asked, concern in her voice. "What's happened?"

He drew in a deep breath.

"In the three days we've been here, I've seen things, things I knew nothing about, and I don't want to see again." He paused, as if to make sure she was listening.

"Lexi, I want you to help these people."

Observing her frown, he continued quickly. "They're good people, Lexi, and they've shown me something that you should know. There's a war coming. There are aliens on their way to kill us all."

"Aliens?" asked Lexi.

"Yes, I've seen them. You know how you've shown me things and I've known that it's true because it was that mind-to-mind thing you can do?"

Lexi nodded her head fractionally.

"It was like that. They showed me things, Lexi. It's all true. They are building and preparing to fight back. They could use your help."

Lexi frowned at him. She wasn't sure how to take this news. This wasn't like Henrick, that was for sure. Normally, he would be supremely confident and in charge. Now, after his little speech, he appeared to be the opposite. She had never seen him like this before.

"There's one more thing," he continued.

"Yes?"

He looked away from her again. He's nervous, thought Lexi. What on earth's going on? In all the years she had known him, never once did he behave like this. He always knew what to do, how to act, what to say.

She watched as his eyes roved around the room, as if trying to find something to focus on. Eventually, his gaze returned to look into her eyes.

"I know I'm a bit older than you, but…." he stopped then continued. "It was seeing you on the floor back at the rig." He stopped again; he licked his lips.

My god, he was really tense, thought Lexi. What's he trying to say?

"We've worked together for a long time, and I know you loved Gary." he paused again and looked down at his knees.

"When I saw you on the rig floor, I thought you were dead. I realised then."

"Realised what?" asked Lexi.

Henrick took a deep breath and brought his head up to gaze into her eyes once more.

"That I like you," he said simply.

Silence descended as Lexi searched his face for some sign of doubt or hesitation, but there was none. She could see how deeply he felt about this, but it didn't surprise her.

He stood quickly.

"I'm sorry," he said. "I shouldn't have said that last bit. Forget I said it. But please think on about the war. It's coming, and it's going to affect us all." He turned and walked to the door.

"Henrick!" Lexi called after him.

He stopped, his back to her, his hand on the door handle.

"I know."

He looked back over his shoulder, a puzzled expression on his face.

"Know what?"

"I know you like me," her mouth curling with a faint smile. "Did you think I couldn't see what you were thinking?"

"I guess I should've known that." He hesitated. "Look, I'm a big guy. I can take it. Just tell me that there's no chance and we can go back to how we were before. I'll always be here for you, you know that."

"I'll think about what you said," answered Lexi, watching his face go blank as he controlled his emotions.

He turned back to the door and pulled it open.

"Henrick!" Lexi called out again. He paused, about to exit through the doorway.

"Yes, there is a chance," she said softly. She couldn't see his face break into a grin as he walked out of her medical room and closed the door behind him.

The next day, Lexi was able to sit up in bed. She had immediately demanded Sally explain in detail what had been done to her. She wanted to know how she had removed the tumour, and why she had been fitted with a new Assist. Sally was very happy to explain.

"Your Mark 4 Assist was destroyed by Kate's attack. Its electronics were fused, so it had to be replaced. I had Molly examine your brain, and she informed me you were Mark 5 capable, so it was a simple decision to fit you with one. Of course, as I already told you, it's powered down right now."

"Of course," Lexi agreed sarcastically.

Sally frowned.

"It's for your own good."

"Maybe if I hadn't been attacked in the first place," Lexi sneered. "It wouldn't have had to be replaced at all."

Sally crossed her arms across her chest.

"That's nothing to do with me, but I understand that you attacked first."

Lexi waved an arm dismissively.

"Whatever. And the cancer? How did you remove a Medulloblastoma tumour when countless neurosurgeons had told me it was impossible?"

"Actually," replied Sally. "That was relatively straightforward."

"I find that hard to believe," said Lexi.

"I've been researching the Psionic signatures of cells for some time. Turns out that cancerous cells have a slightly different signature. That means they can be identified. Once identified, I can tag them so that I can remove them with microscopic teleportation."

Shocked, Lexi pushed a red strand of hair away from her forehead.

"That's something I hadn't thought of," she admitted.

"How could you?" asked Sally. "You're not a doctor."

"Ah, but that's where you're wrong. I am a fully qualified neurosurgeon. If I could, I would have operated on myself, but obviously that was out of the question."

Sally's eyebrows rose.

"So, you knew your prognosis?" she asked.

Lexi nodded.

"I knew I was going to die. I had accepted the inevitable. I had just one more thing to do."

"The Machine?"

"Yes."

"There's a lot of people who want to ask you questions about your Machine."

Lexi sighed.

"I'm sure."

She looked up at Sally from the bed and reached over to her hesitantly. Sally saw the motion and gripped the offered hand.

"Look," said Lexi. "I can be a right bitch, but what you've done for me?" She hesitated. "Well, I just wanted to say thank you."

Sally beamed down at her patient.

"No problem at all. I'm glad I was able to help. Your prognosis is good. There should be no occurrence of the cancer. I removed every cell."

Lexi allowed herself a small smile.

"I'm sure that there are quite a few people who would rather I died."

"Stop that!" Sally said sharply. "I'll have none of that sort of talk."

Lexi looked away, absently touching the scar at her neck. Sally saw Lexi had done with her questions.

"Well, as I said, there are a lot of people who want to talk to you. Do you feel up to it?"

Lexi nodded.

———

Sally had reluctantly agreed that Lexi could have visitors. What she hadn't agreed to, were the number of them that crowded into the room.

She stood next to Lexi's bed, hands on her hips.

"Unless you must be here, please leave now. I agreed to visitors, not an interrogation!"

"Sorry, Sal, but this is important. Time has run out," answered Joe. "We need answers."

Lexi scowled at Joe. He hadn't changed one bit; he was still lording it over everyone.

"I understand, but my patients' needs come first. I insist I stay to make sure that she doesn't get too stressed. If I call it, then everyone leaves. Okay?"

Lexi was impressed with Sally; she was ever the consummate professional and obviously wasn't going to take any crap from Joe.

"That is perfectly acceptable," answered the tall silver woman.

Lexi observed her closely. Sally had already been told her that the silver woman called herself Isabelle and she already knew that she was some kind of supercomputer from another universe. Clearly, Joe had been busy. Not only had he developed the Mark 5 Assist, but he had also figured out how to travel between worlds, made friends with a computer and had got involved in a war! Maybe she had made the wrong decision all those years ago. Maybe she should have stayed in the Alliance.

Next to Isabelle stood the black-haired woman who had appeared in the machine room and nearly killed her. It was obvious that she and Joe were an item. The glances and quick smiles gave it away. Of course, Molly was there too. She stood between Joe and someone Lexi had never met called Lee. Sally had told her he was second in command of the Alliance. Next to Lee stood two other men she had also never seen before, Alex and Simon, and behind them all were three women, someone called Cheryl and two identical twins.

All in all, it was more than a little intimidating, but beside her, on the opposite side of the bed to Sally, stood her rock, Henrick. She gripped his hand and squeezed it hard.

"Please tell us about your machine, Lexi," asked Isabelle.

Lexi waited while Sally positioned a shawl around her bare shoulders, ensuring that she was warm and comfortable.

"Henrick, here," Lexi began, looking up at his solid presence standing beside her. "Has told me that we should work together, although I'm not convinced it's a good idea." She looked pointedly at Joe. She felt Henrick squeeze her hand and sighed.

"Alright, let me get my thoughts in order." Lexi cleared her throat.

"It all started when I was fifteen. I used to suffer from sleepwalking, it used to drive my mother mad. It got so bad that she took to hiding the keys to the house so that I couldn't get outside. Needless to say, it didn't work. Fortunately, I grew out of it." She looked around the room. "Before any of you ask - what's this got to do with anything - let me explain what happened one night."

It was silent as everyone listened carefully.

"One night I must have been sleepwalking again, because I woke up standing in a field in just my pyjamas. At that time, we lived in the country. I had obviously escaped from our house again and walked through the garden and out into the fields next to our house. It was the middle of the night, but there was a full moon so I could see, but it was cold and damp, and there was a fog. The ground was enveloped in one of those heavy fogs that hugs. It came up to my knees. I couldn't see my feet."

Lexi paused and then continued.

"There was something in the fog. I could see ripples of movement as things weaved around and around. They reminded me of fish in a pond, but I couldn't see them through the thick fog. I was frightened. I thought they were going to bite me. Then something happened. It grew lighter and a huge, very tall, black tower slowly appeared out of the darkness. One moment there was nothing there, then it slowly appeared until it was as solid as you or I. I was drawn to it. Don't ask me to explain why. I walked towards it and as I did, I saw a woman. She had long blonde hair and was wearing shorts, a T-shirt, and a backpack. I could see that she wasn't happy. She had blood on her shirt, and she was badly sunburnt."

Lexi paused again. She could see that some of her audience were wondering what her story had to do with anything. Simon's face had a puzzled expression. He looked like he was about to say something.

"She was hammering on the tower wall with a rock. I couldn't see a door. She was shouting but I couldn't hear her. She was obviously angry. I looked up, trying to see the top of the tower, and I felt something. There was a presence. I could feel something large and powerful. I didn't know what it was, but I could tell that it was interested in the blonde woman. There was a connection, a communication of some sorts that didn't include me. The next thing I knew was that the tower faded away, the night returned, and I was shivering in the cold in my pyjamas."

"What was this presence that you felt?" asked Isabelle.

"At the time, I had no idea," replied Lexi. "I thought it was just a dream, and I forgot about it. I went to university and studied philosophy and psychology. Later, I studied medicine and became a neurosurgeon. Sometime after, I met Joe, and we worked together on the Augment device."

"So you forgot about it?" asked Joe.

"Yes, until I met Gary."

"Who's Gary?" asked Joe.

"You never met him," explained Lexi. "He was amazing. I outfitted him with an Assist, and we got close." Lexi closed her eyes and then continued. "He told me he too used to sleepwalk. You can imagine our surprise when he recounted the exact same scene. A blonde woman in shorts with a backpack banging a tower wall. It got us both thinking. What if what we had experienced wasn't a dream? What if it was real?"

"You investigated?" asked Isabelle.

"What's this to do with anything?" asked an obviously annoyed Simon. "So, what if you had the same dream? It's still a dream. It doesn't mean anything."

"Just hang on and bear with it, Simon," answered Lee. "Please carry on Lexi."

"So that's when we started building the machine." Lexi looked around the room. "Its purpose was to discover if what we had experienced was real and to make contact if possible."

There was a murmuring around the room.

"I wish you'd confided in me at the time," said Joe.

"You wouldn't have listened," replied Lexi with a sneer. "You were too busy with Molly and telling me to stop my work with the monkeys!"

Joe grimaced. "Yeah, well, I still don't agree with your approach."

Lexi snorted.

"Of course, you don't. You're far too squeamish. I wasn't going to let morals stand in my way. I had to know!"

"Please continue, Lexi," said Isabelle. "Did you use your machine? Were you successful?"

"No!" said Lexi bitterly. "Well, maybe. Gaz and I built the machine, and he insisted on using it first. Something went wrong, it overloaded, and Gaz... He died..."

Lexi looked down at her lap.

"So, the machine doesn't work?" asked Joe.

Lexi's head snapped up, her eyes blazing. "Yes, it does! That first attempt proved that there was something out there and it could be contacted. Gaz told me he had felt it, just before the machine overloaded."

"That was unfortunate," said Isabelle. "I am sorry for your loss. But you clearly didn't give up, you carried on building." It was a statement, not a question.

Lexi nodded. "I carried on in his memory. He had made contact; he had proved that our dreams were real, and he had proved that the machine worked. I rebuilt it, changed the design, and added a few improvements. I was about to try it again when you turned up." She looked pointedly at Isabelle. "I thought I'd killed you. How come you're still alive?"

"One of your additions was organic?" asked Isabelle, ignoring the question.

Lexi's eyes flicked to Joe.

"Yes."

"Human?" Isabelle continued to ask.

"Yes."

There were gasps around the room. Isabelle turned to address the room.

"Now is not the time for repercussions and recriminations. I have examined the machine. I am impressed. Its technology is not something I had considered and is unique. Our new friend," she gestured to Lexi with a silver hand. "Is an outstanding engineer."

"What's the organic component?" asked Kate, her face twisting in disgust.

Lexi's gaze moved from Joe to Kate.

"It's Gary's brain," she answered, raising her chin in a challenging gesture.

Kate's eyes widened.

"I thought you said he died?"

"He did," replied Lexi. "But I wasn't going to waste his brain. I removed it from his body and interfaced it into the machine. It acts as a pivotal control mechanism."

Isabelle broke the silence in the room.

"Be that as it may. My examination indicates that the machine could prove invaluable to our plan to defeat the enemy."

She turned to Lexi.

"May we have your permission to refit the single seat into two?"

Chapter 52 - Briefing

Once again, they all found themselves in the conference room, with Isabelle directing the meeting at the head of the large table. Today she was wearing a black, form-fitting body suit that was cut off abruptly at her upper arms and shins. The lines drew attention to her curves, and the exposed silver of her skin.

"We have made first contact," she stated, surveying the room.

There were gasps and murmurs from those sat at the table.

"What?" asked an irate Simon, standing quickly, knocking over his chair. "You can't be serious. How come we know nothing about it?"

Isabelle turned her expressionless eyes to Simon.

"The contact occurred well outside of our solar system; we are in no danger as yet."

"Look," continued Simon. "I don't care where the contact is, I object to be out of the loop. It's time to drop this secrecy crap and tell us what's going on!"

"I agree," replied Isabelle.

Simon was taken-a-back. "You do?"

"Yes, the purpose of this briefing is to explain the remainder of the plan and to assign tasks."

"Take a seat Simon," Joe said. "Let's hear what Isabelle has to say."

Simon sat. All eyes were on Isabelle.

"As you know, we cannot defeat the enemy ourselves. We need help. In the next few hours Kate and Joe," Isabelle nodded to her left, where Kate and Joe sat. "Will attempt to contact the Non'anan. They will do this with the aid of Lexi's machine and a new talent that they have discovered. There should be no problem making contact. The issue will be convincing the aliens to help us."

Isabelle paused. Molly looked across the table at Kate and Joe.

"New talent?" she asked.

Joe looked embarrassed.

"We have the ability to fuse our minds together to form a single, much more powerful unit," explained Kate. She turned to Sally, "Sally, you had an inkling months ago when you told me I had experienced a Deep Link with Joe."

"That's right!" exclaimed Sally. "I had forgotten about that! So, there is a connection between the two of you?"

"Oh yes," replied Kate. "Izzy and I theorised it would be possible; the functionality is built into our Mark 6 Assists."

"Obviously, now is not the time, but as soon things settle down - I'm assuming and hoping that we'll still be here - I'd like to research and learn more about this new development," said Molly.

"That is correct Molly, now is not the time, however, I would welcome the opportunity to work with you to learn more about this new ability." She paused and then continued. "To continue, there is a lot more to do. While Kate and Joe make their communication attempt, we must delay the enemy for as long as we can. To that end, I have been building as quickly as I can, but it won't be enough."

Just as Lee opened his mouth to speak again, he stopped himself. He looked at the table, then back up at Isabelle and said, "What do you mean? Are you saying that we're going to lose?"

"That is correct," answered Isabelle. "We cannot defeat the enemy. They are too well-trained, too well-armed, and their war machines are practically impregnable. All we can hope for is a stalemate until Kate and Joe complete their mission."

Simon eventually broke the silence in the room.

"Does anyone else have a sense of Déjà vu?"

Isabelle ignored the comment.

"Kate and Joe will transport to Lexi's oil platform in the North Sea as soon as this meeting is over to begin preparations. However, we in this room have the difficult mission to delay the enemy as long as possible."

All eyes were on Isabelle.

"How?" asked Simon. "You said their war machines were practically impregnable."

"That is correct, but there are some things that we can do." She surveyed the room. "There is also an additional factor - bad Kate and bad Joe."

"I thought that's what you were talking about?" asked Molly. "I thought when you said that we had made contact that it was with bad Kate and bad Joe."

"I am afraid not," replied Isabelle. "We will be fighting on two fronts. The first is with an inter-dimensional war-mongering race of aliens that are determined to wipe out all life other than themselves. They consider all life to be beneath them. Like locusts, they devour and consume everything before them. They have secured an alliance of sorts with bad Kate and bad Joe. You have already seen what those two are capable of."

Silence descended on the room once again.

"I see why you say that we can't win," commented Lee bitterly.

"Our first mission to delay the enemy is to disable the most powerful of their war machines. In our first contact, I have successfully deployed ten teleport receivers, one on each of their largest ships. Each ship is a planetary-mass object at roughly the size of our moon...."

Simon interrupted Isabelle.

"I'm sorry, did you say planetary mass?"

Isabelle nodded as Sally gasped and put a hand to her mouth, her eyes wide.

"Well! shit!" breathed Simon, sitting back in his chair.

"What's the plan to destroy them?" asked Lee.

"We will teleport teams of two to each ship, were upon they will assemble an explosive device. After teleporting them out, we will remotely detonate the explosive devices simultaneously."

"Why send teams?" asked Alex. "Why not just teleport in the bombs?"

Isabelle turned to Alex.

"The explosive I have constructed comprises two parts. When they are combined, they become extremely unstable and cannot be teleported. The final construction must happen on the surface of each moon-sized ship."

"But how do we teleport in through their screens?" asked Alex.

"Fortunately, the aliens are not using sixth order forces - or at least I have detected none. This means that we should be able to teleport through their screens with ease."

"Hold on, if they don't have any sixth order defences, then why not simply blast them out of existence with sixth order weapons?"

"There are three reasons for this much more cautious approach," answered Isabelle. "First, we don't want the enemy to know that we can manipulate sixth order forces just yet. If they found out about our abilities, we would lose what little advantage we have, so it is better to keep them in the dark for as long as possible. Second, their screens, although utilising fifth order energies, are extremely strong. Ordinary sixth order forces will not be able to penetrate them; only a powerful sixth order weapon would be capable of doing such a thing and we don't have any ready yet. Finally, I have been concentrating on building defensive installations. Our sixth order weapons and collectors are not yet ready."

"Shit!" exclaimed Simon again.

"Once we teleport in, won't they detect us?" asked Lee.

"Possibly, but I surmise they will be more concerned with what is happening in front of them, not on the surface of their ships. In addition, we will equip the teams with the new HAZPRO suits that we manufactured specifically for this purpose. They have much lower energy signatures and sixth order defences."

Once more, the room fell silent.

"So, Joe and Kate jet off to the rig and power up Lexi's machine while we pick ten teams to destroy the enemy's largest ships. We can do that." Lee looked around the room.

"You seem to have the wrong impression," said Isabelle. "We won't be able to destroy the enemy ships - merely damage them."

Chapter 53 - Suit Up

Ten teams of two stood before the newly constructed HAZPRO suits. The jet-black behemoths were much bigger than their dull-red cousins. They were twice as tall, standing at four metres. Their heads merged with their bodies and appeared as a dome, their arms and legs bulged with massive exo-muscles and armour, the arms terminating in wicked looking pincers. They looked mean and powerful.

Isabelle stood in the centre of the large room, her form fitting black outfit complimenting the black HAZPRO suits.

"These are the new HAZPRO suits. You will find that they will operate in exactly the same way as the older models. Obviously, they are better armoured and are bigger and stronger. They also have sixth order armaments and defence with a built in AI which will enable you to operate all the suit's systems. When your Assist's interface with the suit, you will communicate with each other using sixth order forces which should be undetectable by the enemy. However, I advise you to keep communication to a minimum during the mission." She gazed around the room with her shiny black eyes.

"Are there any questions so far?"

The teams looked apprehensively at each other.

"I have already teleported in the two components of the explosive device to each of the enemy ships. When you arrive, you will locate each device and assemble them into a single unit. You already have instructions on how to do this." There were nodding heads as she paused. "Remember, once assembled, the device becomes unstable. You must handle it with care. Once assembled, locate an area where it will do the most damage, place it, and then teleport out."

There was a shuffling of feet, and a quiet murmur echoed around the room. They had already been informed, so they knew what to expect. Isabelle had run through her instructions once more and they were as ready as they could be.

"Please suit up as quickly as possible," instructed Isabelle. "Time is running out."

———

This was the first time that Henrick had worn a HAZPRO suit, and he didn't like it. It was claustrophobic and smelled of metal and rubber. He supposed he was lucky that he was the first to wear it, otherwise there might be some other, less pleasant smells. He also didn't like how it connected with his body, particularly the needles that penetrated his veins in his arms and legs. And he most definitely didn't like the thought of it injecting drugs or even severing a limb if it thought it would save his life.

Of course, he understood its purpose. It provided him with the ability to fight no matter the environment. That part he understood and approved of. While in his suit, he would be protected from anything short of a nuclear blast.

Inside the protective cocoon of his suit, he flexed the fingers of his right hand, trying in vain to feel the newly fitted rings, the cruel and sharp pincers of his suit moved in perfect synchrony. An inner screen wrapped around the inside of the domed head, providing him with a full three-hundred-and-sixty-degree view of his surroundings. Eliminating any vulnerability to provide maximum protection, there was no glass or plastic to look through. The only way for him to see was through the screen.

"You can't go because you can't operate a HAZPRO," Lee had explained.

"Why not?" asked Henrick. "You need volunteers and I volunteer."

"We could really use your expertise, but you aren't Assisted, so you won't be able to connect to the suit."

"Then give me one of your Assist things."

"It's not that simple," replied Lee. "Not everyone can wear one. You need to have some latent talent. I don't mean to be personal, but I don't think that you have any."

"Surely there must be something you can do?" asked Henrick. "I want to help."

Lee sent a quick thought to Molly, outlining the problem.

"What do you think?" he asked. "Is there anything you can do? I mean, I doubt it, but I thought I'd better ask."

Molly thought for a while.

"There might be something," she replied. "I have an idea."

Lee looked up at Henricks chiselled face.

"There might be something, but don't get your hopes up."

Henrick grinned and grasped Lee's shoulder.

"Thanks, I appreciate you trying."

That had been three hours ago. Molly had fitted him with what she called a modified Assist or a Modisst, as she called it. It wouldn't boost any of his abilities - he didn't have any - but it would allow him to wear a HAZPRO and that was all he wanted.

The suit's AI interrupted his thoughts, its slightly mechanical voice echoing in his mind.

"We are fully integrated and ready to go. I want you to know that I am fully committed to this mission and will do everything to ensure that it is a success."

The human-like quality of the voice surprised Henrick.

"Please don't say things like that," he thought. *"You sound like Hal 9000!"*

"I have no experience of Hal 9000. Was it a committed and powerful AI?"

Henrick laughed inwardly.

"You could say that," he replied.

"Teams approach the teleporters." instructed Isabelle, her voice clear in his mind.

He trudged forward, marvelling how easy it was. He couldn't feel the weight of the suit at all. Stepping up onto the teleporter dais, he saw through the suit's visual screens that his partner, Eline, followed him in her suit.

He looked around and saw twenty black HAZPRO gigantic figures standing in ten teleport machines.

"I will activate the teleporters at the same instant," Isabelle's voice slid into his mind. "Best of luck to you all."

Henrick braced himself.

"The teleport process is painless," his AI told him.

"Three, two, one."

Henrick's screens went blank.

Chapter 54 - What's happening?

"Come on, dad!" shouted eleven-year-old Tommy, as he dashed through the kitchen out through the back door and into the garden.

"I'm coming!" his father returned the excited cry.

Tommy ran down the length of the narrow garden to a small, paved area and flopped into a deck chair. Lying back, he gazed up at the night sky.

"I can see Jupiter!" he shouted excitedly as his father exited the house carrying a Meade ETX90 telescope.

"You sure it's not Venus?" asked his father, setting down the heavy tripod.

"Of course!" answered Tommy indignantly. "It's far too high and anyway, it's near the constellation of Leo, just where it's s'posed to be."

"Very good, Tommy," answered his father, pride clear in his voice. "We'll make an astronomer out of you yet!"

Tommy beamed at his father, watching as he levelled the telescope and fitted the dew shield.

"I wanna see Jupiter's moons."

"No problem, let me set things up and that's where we'll start."

It didn't take long to connect the GoTo handset and go through the alignment procedure. Soon Tommy was standing on a small stool, gazing through the eyepiece.

"I can only see one moon, and I can also see the red spot."

"Uh huh," replied his father. "Which moon is it?"

"Er, I can't tell."

"How would you find out?"

"I guess we could use that app you have on your phone."

"Yep, that's one way." His father sat in one of the deck chairs and stared up into the crystal-clear sky. He sighed contentedly. This was his favourite time, out observing the heavens with his son. It was a world away from his high-powered job in the government office eighty miles away in London. He felt himself relax as he allowed himself to forget his official duties, pushing them to one side. The weekend would be over soon enough. He wouldn't allow work to spoil it.

"Wow!" exclaimed Tommy. "I just saw a shooting star."

His father frowned.

"You can't see shooting stars through this scope, Tommy."

"Well, I sure saw something. It was a bright flash that went across Jupiter."

Tommy stood up from the eyepiece and looked up at the bright point that was Jupiter.

"Look!" he pointed. "There's another!"

His father got up from the chair and walked over to stand next to his son. Together, they fixed on Jupiter. As they watched, a blue speck raced across the sky.

"That's strange, isn't it dad? Why is it blue?"

"Yes, that's really odd, son," replied his father, a puzzled expression on his face.

As they watched, two more blue specks rapidly moved away from Jupiter towards the horizon.

"What are they?" asked Tommy.

"Probably satellites, I would think."

Suddenly, there was a flash that lit up the entire sky like summer lightning.

"Wow! What was that!" shouted Tommy.

His father was silent as he scanned the darkness above them, his eyes tracking the bright blue lights that moved across the sky, growing more and more concerned as he watched several of them move together in formation. His frown deepened as the number of blue dots increased, each one flaring into being and then moving, spreading across the sky until eventually, after about a minute, they outnumbered the stars.

"What's happening, dad?" asked Tommy, an edge of fear in his voice.

His father placed a reassuring arm across his son's shoulders.

"Damned if I know Tommy, damned if I know."

———

"You know what I've never done?" Ronny asked his girlfriend lecherously, pulling her close as they staggered along the pavement.

Charlene giggled and leaned into him. "What's that Ron?"

He grinned and whispered in her ear, "I've never done it in a graveyard!"

"Ron!" Charlene shivered, pretending to be shocked, though she couldn't stop giggling. His breath smelled of whiskey and chocolate milk. They stumbled up to the metal railings surrounding the church grounds, and he pushed her against them. His hands were on her breasts and his mouth on her neck.

"What do you reckon, doll?" he breathed into her neck. "You up for it?" He knew he didn't have to ask; Charlene was always up for anything.

"The gate'll be locked," she whispered back.

Ron pulled away and grabbed her arm, dragging her towards the churchyard entrance, where he was dismayed to find it locked with a large padlock and chain, exactly as Charlene had predicted.

"Shit!" he exclaimed, rattling the chains vigorously,

"Told ya!" laughed Charlene.

Ronny growled in anger.

"I'm not letting no fuckin chain stop us!" he announced.

He looked up and down the pavement, checking that they were alone. It was two am in a sleepy village; most people were asleep in their beds and there was little chance of being discovered. Reaching into his right back pocket, he pulled out his knife and quickly slid the thin blade into the brass padlock. With practiced ease, he twisted and rotated until he heard a soft click.

He flashed a wide smile at Charlene and slid his knife back into his pocket. Then, still grinning, he grabbed her hand and guided her through the unlocked gate.

"Come on, doll," he hissed in haste. "Let's go make some noise."

The two were arm-in-arm as they stumbled along the gravel path that vanished into the darkness of headstones. Ronny quickly selected a vault that was raised from the ground and pushed Charlene back onto its top.

"Wait, Ron!" Charlene giggled as she hitched up her short mini skirt and pulled down her underwear. The thin linen black lace slid from her hips and over her knees. Ronny fumbled at the belt of his trousers as she rested back on one elbow, her legs dangling over the edge of the vault. The granite was hard and cold on her bare skin as she hooked Ronny's neck with a hand and pulled him to her.

Excitement and delight coursed through Charlene's veins as she leaned back against the tombstone, gazing up at the night sky filled with stars. A shooting star streaked across the sky, and she smiled to herself. Perfect, she thought as a moan escaped from her lips.

Then she saw another and another. Curiosity spoiled the moment. She followed the tracks of three bright blue points of light over Ronny's moving shoulder. As she watched, more and more lights appeared, tracing their way across the night until they formed a network of faint blue lines, almost like a spider's web.

"What's that?" she gasped.

"It's just me, doll," Ronny moaned into her neck.

"Not that, you ape, the lights in the sky."

Ronny lifted himself up on his arms.

"What's the matter, doll? Am I giving you fireworks?"

Charlene laughed and pulled him back down on top of her, closing her eyes. Above them, the sky flashed with pulsating colours.

————

Amara sighed contentedly as she stared into the campfire. The bright orange and yellow flames moved with a gentle rhythm, curling around the black metal pot suspended above them. Nearby, other visitors at the campground laughed and talked together, raising glasses of wine and beer, some happily singing along with the melody from a banjo player.

This was the best holiday ever, she thought to herself, leaning back into her camp chair and sipping her wine. It had been a last-minute decision, a last desperate attempt for her and Bruno to re-connect and save their marriage. After six months of arguments, she had seriously started to think about a divorce and had even contacted a lawyer.

Three days ago, Bruno had surprised her. He had rented a motorhome and had taken two weeks off work. It had taken three hours and one blazing row to persuade her to pack and join him on an adventure into the unknown.

Now she was glad she had given in. Living in such close quarters had brought them together again. It was like falling in love all over again. Bruno was funny and caring, just as he was when they first met, and the sex! He was amazing.

Amara closed her eyes and allowed herself to relax as she hadn't done for years, the alcohol from her wine making her slightly lightheaded.

A shout brought her out of her reverie.

"Hey! What's that?"

She sat forward and looked behind her. A man was pointing up at the night sky, others nearby were following his outstretched finger. Amara followed suit but saw nothing but twinkling stars hanging in the blackness. The man grinned with a child-like glee and pointed to another star, which also didn't seem any different from the rest. She smiled back, feeling like she was missing something.

"What's up?" called Bruno from the doorway of their motorhome.

"I think someone had too much beer," Amara nodded towards a small cluster of people staring up into the sky.

"Top up?" asked Bruno as he strode over with a bottle. Amara nodded and held up her glass to be filled. Bruno grunted as he sat in the camp chair next to her and stretched his legs out in front of him.

"Cheers!" he called, holding his glass high and towards her. Their glasses clinked, and they both took a big sip. Another shout disturbed them.

"Look at that!"

Bruno looked over his shoulder, a frown on his face.

"Hey, you two," a man called out. "Have you got a pair of binoculars?"

Bruno shook his head.

"No mate. What's going on?"

The man pointed upwards. "What's the matter with you? Are you blind?"

Bruno looked up at the sky and was amazed to see multiple blue lights moving in formations.

"Are they UFOs?" someone asked.

Amara reached over to take Bruno's hand.

"What are they?" she asked.

"Dunno," answered Bruno.

They sat mesmerised, watching the blue lights speed across the night sky, some merging, others splitting apart.

"Is it the Space Shuttle?" asked Amara.

Bruno grinned. "No, that was retired years ago. Besides, there's lots of them."

"It's Elon Musk!" another voice shouted. "It's his Star Link satellites!"

There was a murmur of agreement.

"Yeah, that's it!" someone agreed.

"Defo," shouted another.

"Is that what they are, Bruno?" asked Amara.

Bruno leaned his head back further, studying the moving lights.

"I'm not sure," he replied. "They don't behave like satellites," he pointed. "That one there just appeared out of nowhere, then it moved at right angles from its original direction. Satellites don't do that."

Amara followed his gaze. By now the blue specks numbered in their hundreds, all streaking back and forth.

Then she gasped as a network of pale blue lines suddenly appeared, connecting the bright dots together.

Exclamations of shock and surprise echoed around the campground.

"What the hell?"

"George, I'm frightened!"

Amara tightened her grip on Bruno's hand as the entire sky flashed a brilliant purple.

"Bruno, I don't like this. What's happening?"

Bruno had no answer.

———

Travelling at six hundred and fifty miles per hour, Captain Tom Harris and First Officer Joshua Campbell's Boeing 777 soared through the night sky at an altitude of thirty-eight thousand feet. The night flight had been as tranquil as ever, with the autopilot managing the bulk of the work while they flew across the Atlantic Ocean. This was Tom's one hundred and fifth such flight and his last. After their plane touched down at London Heathrow, he planned to tender his resignation. At fifty-eight years old, Tom had decided it was time for a change.

Two years ago, he had divorced his wife of twenty-three years. They had grown apart and had nothing left in common and had nothing left to say to each other. The divorce was easy and somewhat of a natural conclusion to their marriage. After separating from his wife, Tom started contemplating what he wanted to do with the rest of his life and eventually concluded that he wanted an escape from city living. So, he purchased a smallholding on the island of Skye and devised a plan: after landing in Heathrow, he would hop into his Range Rover and drive the six hundred miles to his new home.

Sipping his hot, black coffee in the captain's chair, Tom scanned his instruments once again. Everything was in the green and normal as expected.

"Hey, did you see that?" asked his First Officer.

"See what Josh?" asked Tom.

Joshua was silent for a moment, studying the night sky through the flight deck window, then he turned back to his controls.

"Nothing," he replied. "Must have been a reflection on the glass."

Tom nodded.

"Did I ever tell you the time two Russian Migs followed me from Moscow to Oslo?"

Joshua sighed.

"About a hundred times."

Tom laughed and took another sip of his steaming coffee. He and Joshua had been flying together for the past twelve months; they complemented each other's capabilities as colleagues, yet still had a good chuckle on occasion.

Tom was about to reply when a short, sharp shock shook the plane. He gripped one arm of his seat with his free hand while holding his cup out to prevent the hot liquid from spilling on the instruments.

"That was sudden," said Joshua. "We're not expecting any turbulence, are we?"

"Nope," replied Tom. "Should be plain sailing all the way." He scanned his instruments once more; nothing was out of the ordinary. Then suddenly the entire flight deck lit up with a bright flash, which was gone as suddenly as it appeared.

"What the?" exclaimed Joshua.

Tom put down his coffee and sat forward, peering through the front flight deck window.

"Was that lightning?" asked Joshua.

"Never seen lightning that bright before," noted Tom. "What's on the weather radar?"

Joshua leaned forward to gaze closely at the weather radar.

"Nothing," he replied. "All clear."

Tom didn't reply for a while as he continued to scan the night sky around the plane.

"Can you see that, at my ten o'clock?" he suddenly spoke up.

Joshua looked over, following Tom's directions.

"Shit! Yes! What is it?"

High in the sky, a bright blue blob of light moved, keeping pace with the plane.

Although concerned, both Tom and Joshua were professionals and were calm.

"Get on the horn and ask for a traffic report," instructed Tom.

Joshua keyed the radio, "Shanwick Oceanic, this is Victor Sierra two one three requesting traffic information."

"Victor Sierra two one three, Shanwick Oceanic, there is no traffic in your vicinity," came the reply over their headphones.

"Shanwick Oceanic, Victor Sierra two one three, are you sure about that?"

"Victor Sierra two one three, Shanwick Oceanic, positive, there are no aircraft in your area."

Joshua turned to Tom.

"What do you think?"

"I think," replied Tom, without removing his gaze from the sky ahead of them. "That something is going on out there. There's two of them."

Joshua followed Tom's gaze. Sure enough, there were now two blue lights keeping pace with the plane. As he watched, a third appeared with a flash and the three moved together, accelerating away into the distance.

Tom sat back.

"Well, whatever they are, they're moving away," he sighed in relief.

But Joshua was looking to his right.

"I have three more on the starboard side!"

Another sudden light illuminated the cabin, this time so bright, that the pilots had to look away. When they looked up again, both men couldn't believe what they saw: the night sky had transformed into a blue spectacle of sparkling lights that flew in all directions, either by themselves or in groups.

"Holy shit!" exclaimed Joshua.

As they watched, blue lines of light spread out from the moving dots until they were all connected like a massive spiderweb that arced over the horizon.

"Josh," said Tom, unable to take his eyes off the spectacle. "Report that we have a UAP."

Joshua's shaking hands keyed the radio mic.

"Shanwick Oceanic, Victor Sierra two one three, we are reporting a uniform alpha papa. I repeat, we are reporting a uniform alpha papa."

"Victor Sierra two one three, Shanwick Oceanic, your report is acknowledged. You might be interested to know that you're not the only one. We're getting reports from all over."

Tom and Joshua looked at each other. Their expressions said it all: What was happening?

Chapter 55 - It begins

Lexi led the way across the room towards the gigantic machine that stood at its centre. Careful to stay as far away from Kate as she could, she was still wary of the young woman's power. She vowed she would find out where the power came from. When she did, she would learn how to use it.

"I'm sorry that we're taking away your moment of triumph, Lexi," said Joe, interrupting her thoughts.

"Let's just say that I'm annoyed and not happy about any of this," answered Lexi. "If it weren't for Henrick, we wouldn't be here today."

"Well, I'm grateful that you've agreed to help us. Thanks to you, we have a better chance."

Lexi snorted. "Just make sure that you remember you owe me one, and don't break the machine. I'd like to have a go myself."

"We will follow your original plan, Lexi," stated Isabelle. "Your appraisal of the consequences when the machine is powered up is faultless. Your preparations are perfect and will need no adjustment."

"My plan is, of course, perfect," responded Lexi without a hint of modesty. "As Henrick volunteered to take part in the planetoid mission, I will take the controls from the control room." She looked over at Joe as they walked. "Henrick had better come back," she said ominously.

"I'm not going to promise anything, Lexi, but we've given him the best chance," replied Joe.

They arrived at the foot of the metal stairs that led up into the heart of the machine. Joe gripped Kate's hand.

"Are you ready?"

She shook her head.

He smiled sympathetically.

"Me neither."

"You know what to do," Isabelle faced Kate and Joe, taking each of their hands in hers. "It's up to you. I'll hold off the enemy for as long as I can, but you must impress upon the Non'anan how desperate the situation is."

"We'll do our best Izzy," replied Kate. Impulsively, she hugged the silver woman, then stepped back. "Thanks for everything. You'll look after Josie for me if..." She stopped and then continued. "If I don't come back..." There were tears in her eyes.

"I will look after Josie," replied Isabelle.

Kate turned, wiped her tears away with the back of her hand and took Joe's hand in hers

"Let's go before we realise how stupid this is!"

Isabelle watched with unblinking eyes as Joe and Kate mounted the stairs, hand in hand.

———

On the surface of the metallic and pitch-black darkness of ten armoured planetoids at the outer rim of our solar system, twenty black, undetectable figures abruptly appeared: two on each celestial body.

Henrick felt his suit adjust to the new environment - it creaked with the sudden lack of external air pressure; its limbs flexed; and his internal view screen flickered and presented him with a dark green glowing landscape.

"We have arrived," the suit AI reported. *"I have located component A; it is thirty metres to your right. Eline has already picked up component B and is heading our way."*

Henrick cursed his inactivity. His partner, Eline, was already ahead of him. Clearly, she was used to wearing a HAZPRO and had sprung into action as soon as they had arrived. He recalled Isabelle had impressed upon the teams that they must be quick. Although the suits were practically undetectable, the longer they stayed, the more likely it was that they might be discovered.

Following a red glowing dot on his screen, Henrick walked across the metal alien landscape. As he did so, he marvelled at the terrain. Black and foreboding, enormous towers soared skywards, each sporting a multitude of spikes, discs and domes. He had no idea and couldn't fathom the purpose of anything he saw. Everything was on a gigantic scale - huge black bottomless pits, vast walls and huge ravines - all made of fused rock and metal.

"I have located the best position to integrate the device," his AI informed him. *"I have relayed this information for Eline. She will be at the location in two minutes. I advise you to hurry."*

"I'm doing the best I can," answered Henrick angrily.

"All imagery is being recorded to be reviewed at a later date. May I suggest you concentrate on the task ahead?"

"For fuck's sake! Give me a break!" complained Henrick, picking up the pace.

Soon he was loping across the surface with long hops in the low gravity and it wasn't long before he found what he was looking for.

"How do I make sure that I don't damage the component when I grab it?" he asked the suit's AI.

"I will control the strength of the grippers. I will not allow you to pierce the outer skin."

Henrick grunted to himself, bent, and picked up the two-metre-long cylinder in front of him. It felt as light as a feather, even though he knew that was not the case. Isabelle had informed the team that much of its internal structure comprised osmium, a metal heavier than gold.

A new red dot appeared on his three-hundred-and-sixty-degree screen.

"Meet Eline here," the AI informed him.

Dutifully, Henrick turned and set off as quickly as he could. It was only fifty metres away, and it didn't take him long to land alongside Eline.

"Place your half down here and I'll attach my half," instructed Eline calmly.

Henrick held his breath as he watched Eline mate the two components together. Clamps from the upper half snapped viciously, connecting their two halves together with what he imagined would be a loud bang - but he could hear nothing through the suit's armour. Immediately, a red warning blazed to life on Henrick's screen. He didn't need to ask what it meant - the device was now armed and unstable. One wrong move and it would detonate in a fiery explosion, which he doubted they would survive, even protected as they were in the HAZPRO suits.

"Where do we place it?" asked Henrick.

"I have been passively scanning the area and have identified the best position for maximum damage," answered his AI.

"Great," answered Henrick.

"There is a problem," He heard Eline in his mind as a new red dot appeared on his display.

"What?" he started to ask, but then realised what Eline meant. Numbers appeared next to the new red dot. They read: five point two kilometres.

452

Kate and Joe sat side by side in their respective chairs, deep in the machine's heart. They stared around at a forest of machinery, shining and humming with a synthetic vitality that slowly pulsed with energy. They were not comfortable; their chairs were far too small for each of them because they had been hastily fitted into the space made for one.

Joe looked over at Kate. For the first time since meeting her, she seemed to be unsure of herself. He squeezed her hand reassuringly. She turned to him and flashed a quick smile.

"We'll be okay, won't we?" she asked quietly.

Joe didn't know what to say. He couldn't help thinking back to the time when Kate had died attempting what the two of them were about to try.

"It's not the same," Emily told him. *"Kate was on her own. All she had was a Mark 5. This time you have me and Kate has Bella. We will look after both of you."*

"Don't worry about me, Em," answered Joe. *"I want you to look after Kate. She's special and Josie needs her."*

"She is very special," Emily agreed. *"But my priority is you and me. I will do our best to protect us. Bella will look after Kate."*

Joe wasn't happy with Emily's response.

"Kate is my priority, Em, and Josie. I order you to make sure that she survives no matter what happens to me."

"You can't order me," replied Emily. *"Although we are integrated and are one being, we are separate in some ways and although my needs and wants are the same as yours, I still have my programming. As an artificial intelligence, I have an operating system that I cannot ignore. One of its primary directives is to protect both of us. I cannot change it."*

Joe couldn't stop thinking of the moment Kate had died.

"I can't go through that again!"

"I know. I also know that Bella will do everything in her power to keep Kate safe. She has the same base operating system as I."

Joe sighed inwardly. He felt a powerful tug of emotion as he gazed at Kate. She was stunningly attractive, yet her visible anxiety filled him with unease. He guessed she must be having a similar discussion with Bella. He wished they could abandon this reckless plan and find a place where they could all live securely and simply enjoy life. But he knew that was impossible. He had seen the enemy - horrible versions of himself and Kate and the fleet of planet destroying ships on their way to Earth. The entire world, the entire universe, depended upon what happened here in this room on an oil rig in the North Sea. He and his beautiful and wonderful Kate had no choice. Together they would try to contact the Non'anan and together they must persuade them to help. Because if they didn't, everyone would die.

"Ready?" he whispered to Kate.

She turned and gave a quick, nervous smile and nodded.

Joe sent a thought to Isabelle. *"We're ready Isabelle."*

Up in the control room, Isabelle turned to Lexi.

"Start."

Lexi drew in a deep breath. She understood the importance of what was about to happen but couldn't help feeling a pang of jealousy and anger. It should be her in the machine, not Joe, and especially not that Kate. It took a great deal of effort to put her feelings aside.

She turned to her chief scientist, Erica Black, and her military commander, Major Daniels.

"Are we ready?" she asked them both.

Erica nodded. "All is in order and ready for your command."

"Good initiate phase one," Lexi addressed both.

Major Daniels saluted her in his usual manner and thumbed his radio mic.

"Launch the VTOL's."

———

"We have been detected." Henrick's suit AI didn't seem to be concerned.

"What?" he asked urgently. *"What the fuck are we going to do?"*

Both he and Eline had been making the difficult and slow journey across the endless metal landscape. Eline carried the explosive on her shoulder while Henrick took point, his suit constantly scanning passively for any activity which could show that their presence had been discovered.

Now the moment had arrived.

New icons flickered into life on Henrick's display, and his view suddenly became brighter and more colourful, as though the terrain was lit by a searchlight.

"Deploying active preceptors," his AI informed him. *"Enemy drones located and targeted, defence systems are now active."*

Henrick could see three red dots marked on his display, each one had a target cross centred on them.

"Weapons?" he asked.

"All weapons are armed, deploying an arm projector. Do not fire until I say."

The right arm of Henrick's suit parted, and a large rifle weapon slid up from a recess.

"Keep moving," Eline thought at him. *"We must get to the deployment location as quickly as possible."*

"Just be careful with that thing," agreed Henrick. *"For god's sake, don't drop it!"*

"Not a chance," replied Eline.

The two suited figures continued bounding their way forward, Eline obviously taking more measured and careful hops.

There was just one kilometre to go when Henrick felt a gentle thump at his back.

"Stealth GASER deployed," stated his AI.

Although he had never heard of a working GASER, Henrick knew what it was - it was a gamma ray laser. A device that emitted a coherent beam of gamma rays. It would kill any organic life and fry any electronic circuitry. The GASERs he had heard of while in the military were the size of a football pitch. That the suit had one built into its structure was nothing short of miraculous.

As they made their way forward, he watched a new blue icon move towards the three rapidly approaching red dots on his display. There was no sound as all three red dots winked out.

"Enemy drones eliminated," his suit informed him.

"Good work," he panted. Even with the suit's exo-musculature, he was still working hard.

He skidded to a halt. In front of them was a vast chasm stretching across their path.

"It is fifteen kilometres deep and one hundred metres across," his suit AI informed him.

On his left, a skyscraper tall structure soared upwards, metal fins all along its edges getting smaller and smaller as they approached its spiked summit.

"How are we going to get across?" he asked and was immediately answered as Eline passed him soaring upwards on jets of fire.

"Multiple drones incoming," his suit AI informed him.

On his display, he saw many red dots approaching at speed.

"How many?" he asked.

"Three hundred and forty-five," answered his suit.

"Fuck!"

"We must prevent them from reaching Eline. She will reach the drop off point in sixty-two seconds. The drones will reach us in twenty-one seconds."

Henrick didn't hesitate.

"Tell Eline to keep going. We'll engage the enemy here and hold them off."

"Already done," replied his suit AI.

"What do we have to attract attention? Do we have something like flares?"

"Yes."

"Deploy flares. Make sure that the drones see us."

Panels slid open on his shoulders and a dozen fiery rockets launched upwards, curving towards the fleet of enemy craft. Each one exploded into several impossibly bright miniature suns.

"Tell me about this weapon," he asked, raising his right arm.

"It is a sixth order energy rifle, capable of single pulse or rapid fire. It will be more than a match for the enemy drones. Since you are not fully Assisted and cannot interface with the weapon with your mind, I have configured the firing mechanism to activate with a movement of your hand."

"Excellent!"

Henrick raised his arm, aiming at the oncoming drones. He contracted his forefinger and thumb and watched a bright pulse of energy streak away towards its target, grunting with satisfaction when he saw one drone explode. He moved to squat down behind a low rampart of metal nearby.

"Let's give em hell!" he shouted as he fired continuously. The light of his gunfire lit up the blackness of the space above in pulsing flashes of pure destruction, ripping apart drone after drone. Brilliant flashes and explosions erupted through the darkness, shattering the craft into countless shards of burning wreckage that rained down on the ground below. The back of his suit split apart, allowing an array of metal fins to slide out, each one glowing an angry red with the heat generated from the suit's rapidly discharging weapon. They burned like fire as they radiated the excess heat into the airless space around them.

A fierce, electric blue blaze exploded from the lead drones and slammed into the suit's protective screens with searing force. The fire bounced off in massive splashes of fire, but where it touched the ground, it burned through the surface like acid, melting it to form rivers of molten material that surged and boiled with blinding white heat.

"Eline has reached the drop-off point. She is arming the device," reported the suit AI.

"Good," replied Henrick. *"How are we doing?"*

"We are holding our own. However, the surrounding surface is becoming unstable. We need to move location urgently."

The ground he was standing on began to collapse inwards like sand in an egg timer.

"Suit, do something!" shouted Henrick. A second later, he was falling, and his vision went black.

Chapter 56 - Guerrilla Tactics

Ten titanic explosions erupted on the surface of ten colossal planetoid space vessels. The blasts ripped their metallic surfaces apart, leaving gargantuan craters glowing white hot with heat and radiation. Giant waves of plasma and super-heated gas streaked away in vast arcs into deep space, followed by huge plumes of molten metal and rock.

The trans-dimensional drives of six planetoid vessels suddenly cut out, and they found themselves trailing behind the fleet.

Miles below the surface of the dark planet, protected at the centre of the Klalan fleet, snug in the command centre, technicians and operators sat in rows behind screens, controls and indicators. In one corner, a group of three Klalan stood around a large podium on which a holographic image of a system map was displayed. Behind this group was a single chair on a raised platform that belonged to the Klalan commander. The harsh white of the high-powered ceiling's lights shone through the yellow haze of the chlorine filled atmosphere that filled the room.

The urgent shrieking of an alarm sounded, but not a single Klalan flinched. No loud shouts or exclamations ever echoed through the command centre; none were needed. This orderliness came from years of battle experience where those with discipline had survived while their inefficient comrades had been executed.

"What is happening?" the quiet and coldly harsh thought of the Klalan commander asked from its lofty position.

"I have reports of large explosions from all of our moon vessels!" answered a technician sitting at a large view screen.

"What?" shouted the Defence Commander. *"I have not been informed of any enemy ships approaching!"*

"None have been detected," reported a technician.

"Then what has caused the explosions?" asked the Strategy Functionary *"Is it possible that the enemy has stealth ships?"*

"Negative," answered the Defence Coordinator. *"They are probably malfunctioning."*

"On all ten moon ships?" sneered the Attack Commander. *"I think not. I posit our fleet has been infiltrated."*

"Impossible!" the Defence Coordinator spat, drool splattering the podium in front of them. *"Nothing can get through our outer screens!"*

"Then how do you explain the explosions?" snarled the Attack Commander.

The Defence Coordinator fell silent.

"Three moon ship commanders are reporting enemy encounters on the surface of their vessels," an operator spoke up.

"I thought as much," the Attack Commander stated. *"Somehow, the enemy has penetrated our defences and set explosive devices on our largest and most powerful vessels."*

"How could they do that?" asked the Defence Coordinator. *"Our screens are impenetrable."*

"The question is moot; it has already been done. We must ensure that there can be no other incursions. What is the current situation with our moon ships?" asked the Strategy Functionary.

"Six are temporarily disabled," reported an operator. *"Repairs have been initiated. The damage sustained by the other four has not affected their offensive capability."*

"Order all ship commanders to launch all surveillance drones and to increase defence screen power to maximum," the Defence Coordinator instructed. Its mouth tentacles writing in irritation.

"We should send in a small reconnoitre force to discover more about the capability of the enemy before proceeding further," the Strategy Functionary suggested.

The ominously quiet thought of the commander was heard by the three Klalan arguing around the projected image of the star system.

"You forget the Klalan are the superior race," the thought hissed. *"There is no one that can stand against us. This is merely a distraction and a poor one at that. The enemy has destroyed none of our vessels, merely disabled them. They delay the inevitable: their destruction. We will proceed with the plan and attack. The remaining four moon ships will be more than enough. We will be victorious."*

———

In a parallel world, far from ours, lying side by side on a single raised leather covered platform, two people opened their eyes to face each other.

"They are providing a superb distraction. It's perfect," grinned Joe.

"I can't believe that they're so stupid!" answered Kate.

"Who cares? As long as they do what we want, they can be stupid."

Kate raised her right arm above her and disconnected a wire running from her Assist. She studied the redness running up towards her elbow.

"The infection seems under control," she noted, raising her other arm to view the cannula that was feeding a clear liquid into her vein.

"Told you Molly would come up with a solution."

Kate scowled.

"I still don't like her," she growled.

Joe raised his own arm and disconnected a similar wire from his own Assist. He rolled over onto his side to face Kate.

"We have another hour of this infusion left," he flicked his gaze up at the drip stand where an IV bag hung half empty.

"I've instructed Lee to start the attack. Meanwhile." As he spoke, his finger lightly moved down her chest.

Kate's smile was an evil smirk. She reached over to him and pulled him roughly to her.

———

Twenty-five thousand feet above the oil rig, five fighter jets circled, waiting for orders while down on the rig's surface seven surface-to-air missile systems rotated around to face outwards and across the North Sea. On the platform, two battalions of soldiers erupted from their barracks and arranged themselves at specific defence stations.

Meanwhile, in the control room, Lexi and Isabelle stood side by side, staring through the view window into the machine room.

"Phase one complete," a voice piped up from one technician behind them.

Lexi didn't remove her gaze from the machine.

"Initiate phase two."

Across the East of England, the lights went out.

———

Inside the machine, Kate and Joe sat waiting nervously.

"Ready," came Isabelle's calm thought.

Joe flicked his gaze to Kate and squeezed her hand.

"Em, unlock high order functions," he commanded his Assist. He felt the familiar rush of power surge through him.

His perception sense enveloped the room, and he had to suppress a surge of disgust as he felt Gary's brain, deep inside the machine. The organic component was necessary, Lexi had told him. It was an essential part of the machine, she had said, allowing the connection of the human mentality to the electrical connections and power of the machine. Joe wasn't convinced. He was sure that there would be a better method, but now was not the time to change things. Maybe, if things went well, and the machine survived the coming ordeal, it could be modified. But now wasn't the time to think of such things.

"Bella, unlock high order functions."

He paused for a few moments and then opened his mind to Kate, allowing his thoughts to connect with hers. They shared an unprecedented understanding of each other, and he felt their consciousness blend together as a medley of emotions and thoughts. They rejoiced in the connection between them before Kate's voice echoed in his mind.

"Merge."

Immediately, their thoughts swirled downwards and into each other. There was a moment of connection, almost a clicking of parts fitting seamlessly together, and then the two minds locked together and became one.

Rising from the depths, coming into existence, a new, powerful intellect appeared. Both Kate and Joe were gone, replaced with something else, something large with a formidable mental presence that was supremely powerful. It tapped directly into Bella and Emily and took control of their sixth order functions, integrating them into its mentality. It sent out its perception, scanning the surrounding area, noting and registering Isabelle, Lexi and all the minds on the rig. Then it turned its consciousness towards the machine.

It found the machine to be crudely built, but serviceable. Channelling through the machine, the new, single entity pushed its thoughts inwards into the machine, allowing it to send its communications out into space.

"We would speak with you."

———

Tumbling in the void of space between the orbits of Jupiter and Saturn were thousands of tiny, jet-black devices no bigger than a football. At their core was a miniature nuclear fusion bomb that had been activated and was kept in check by heavily shielded stasis force fields, mere nanoseconds away from detonation.

Virtually undetectable, they waited for a signal.

When that signal was eventually received, every single hidden device performed the same action. Their stasis fields collapsed, and the detonation released. The rapidly expanding nuclear explosion was channelled via additional force fields that directed all the energy from the explosion into one confined narrow beam that was aimed into the passing fleet of spacecraft. The beam lasted for one microsecond before the device was vaporised.

Thousands of sub-second beams of incredibly powerful, piercing energy flashed through the heart of the Klalan ships.

"Incoming aircraft," reported the radar operator.

Lexi stared transfixed at the immense machine as bursts of bluish-white light raced up and down metal rods grounding, which were connected to thick cables that had been drilled deep into the ocean floor. The power crackled and hummed, building and surging until it was barely contained. A deadly discharge of energy channelled by the vast hulking machine.

It should be me in there, she thought to herself. Should she have listened to Henrick? Should she have helped Joe? Was the Earth really in danger? It was too late; she realised. It was happening right now. The machine was doing its job, and she supposed that Joe and that bitch Kate could be talking to the aliens right now. Maybe they wouldn't survive the encounter. She couldn't stop a small flicker of a smile appear on her face.

"Initiate defence protocol," she said. "Major, I'm handing over control of the rig to you."

"Thank you, ma'am," replied major Daniels. He spun to the radio operator. "Warn them off," he instructed.

He walked over to another radio station.

"Tell the VTOLS to warn off any approaching aircraft. They have permission to open fire if the ten-mile zone is breached."

He keyed his lapel mic.

"Colonel Hussain, set the SAMS to active mode and prepare for incursion."

———

"WHAT ARE YOU?" asked the huge alien mentality.

It had not taken long to contact the aliens. In fact, it was as though they had been waiting because the reply had been immediate. Kate/Joe fended off the initial surge of power from the alien presence, barely, its sheer intensity and weight of mind almost overwhelming the fusion. But the fusion held itself together, backed up by the machine and the Assists, Bella and Emily.

"We are human."

"DIFFERENT."

"Yes, we are a fusion of two human minds."

"FUSION NOT POSSIBLE."

A powerful mental probe that easily broke through Kate/Joe's mental barriers followed the alien's words. Pain surged through them as the probe dug around in their fused mind, pulling out all their thoughts and memories. The machine shrieked as Kate/Joe drew more energy from it, bolstering their defences, giving them enough strength to fend off the invasion.

"Stop!" Kate/Joe commanded.

"WE WILL UNDERSTAND," answered the alien.

"We will cooperate," replied Kate/Joe. *"Your probe is too powerful. It will kill us like last time."*

"KILL?"

"We have contacted you before. You helped us, but the human you communicated with died."

There was a pause, and then suddenly the alien mental probe withdrew.

"DIE IS CEASE TO EXIST?"

"Yes."

There was an even longer pause.

"PURPOSE?"

"This universe is under threat. We require you to take action."

"NOT POSSIBLE."

"Observe,"

Kate/Joe expanded their mentality outwards into space until they detected the approaching Klalan fleet.

"These beings are from another universe. They have travelled here to conquer ours."

There was yet another pause.

"CONVERSE."

The alien mentality changed its focus. It was still present, but it had moved its attention. Kate/Joe sensed others joining with the first presence. Then.

"INVESTIGATION REQUIRED." And the presence was gone.

———

In the region of space between Mars and Jupiter, an uncountable number of space rocks spun around in orbits about the Sun. Some of them were tiny like a pea, while others were huge, jagged mountains. A few even approached the size of our moon.

Scattered across hundreds of these asteroids lay dark, hidden installations that blended into the surface. Each was equipped with a single powerful weapon capable of rapid fire. Built to attack from a distance but without protection, they were essentially sniping stations.

They lay in wait, cold, dark, and undetectable for the enemy fleet to arrive.

———

By now, the Klalan fleet had been reduced by fifty percent. The one-shot devices between Jupiter and Saturn had taken their toll. While most of the Klalan ships were not destroyed, many were disabled and could not take part in the attack until they were repaired.

The Klalan, in typical fashion, had refused to stop the attack. The thought of anyone being able to defeat them was unimaginable, the very thought unthinkable. They continued their inexorable journey towards Earth. Spearheading the fleet were the four planet-sized super powerful ships, each one capable of reducing a planet the size of Earth to rubble.

In three short hours, they would be within range.

Chapter 57 - Intervention

Lee watched the screen in front of him in horror as he saw the vast enemy fleet draw closer to Earth.

"There are so many!" he whispered.

"Indeed," replied Isabelle, standing next to him. They were alone in the control room. "Even though several hundred have been disabled or destroyed, the enemy fleet is formidable."

Lee flicked a glance up at her.

"That's stating the obvious!" he pointed out. "What can we do?"

"Our defensive screens are operational and there is one more surprise for them when they get close enough. But as I have already stated, we cannot hope to defeat them. They are too powerful and too numerous."

Lee stared back at the screen glumly.

"How are Joe and Kate getting on?"

"There is, as yet, nothing to report."

The silence between them was broken by an urgent thought.

"Lee, have you seen the news?"

"What do you mean?" Lee asked.

"Take a look at a news app on your phone and you'll see what I mean!"

Lee pulled his phone out of his pocket and selected a news app. He was immediately presented with a full-size image of something that he'd seen before and hoped to never see again. Staring at him from the screen was an alabaster face with two glowing red eyes. It had no nose or mouth.

"Shit!" he breathed.

Isabelle noticed his reaction and stared at the image over his shoulder as he read the news article.

"Ah," she said. "I was wondering when they would appear."

"What do you mean?" asked Lee.

"Bad Kate and bad Joe are taking advantage of the distraction provided by the enemy fleet. They are teleporting in soldiers."

"Oh, fuck!" Lee stood suddenly, knocking over his chair.

"Get as many Alliance members suited up as you can," instructed Isabelle. "I will join them in the fight."

"But what about the enemy fleet?" asked Lee.

"There is nothing more I can do," answered Isabelle. "We must hope that the defences hold until Kate and Joe contact the Non'anan. Meanwhile, we cannot allow these other soldiers to kill at will. They will target leaders, utility and military installations.

Also, if they have detected the machine, they will try to destroy it. We cannot allow them to reach it."

———

Once again, Henrick found himself, wearing a HAZPRO suit. This time, he wasn't on an alien spacecraft. Instead, he stood beside a row of trees in the grounds of the East of England Showground, near Peterborough. Just a few metres away and several metres below ground lay the newly transported Complex. His mission? Protect the Complex from the enemy incursion for as long as he could. He was partnered with Eline once again. Her large black bulk was two hundred metres away.

Three times Eline had stepped out into the road, causing approaching cars to squeal to a stop as they applied their brakes suddenly. It hadn't taken much to get them to turn around and leave. The sight of a four-metre tall, black robotic-looking humanoid blocking the road was enough. But Henrick knew that the people in the cars will have called the Police, and while he wasn't worried about being arrested - how could he? - he was worried about there being more defenceless people milling about in the area. They would be sitting ducks if they came under attack.

"Enemy targets approaching from the West," his suit AI informed him. *"Screens activated, weapon systems online."*

Henrick watched as the pulse rifle deployed onto his right arm.

"Inform Eline to keep the civilians away," he told his suit. *"I'll take care of this."*

He turned left and began striding across the grass and access road towards the edge of the grounds.

———

A tremor ran through the rig, causing Lexi to stagger slightly. Without tearing her gaze from the machine below, she asked:

"What's happening, Major?"

"Everything is under control," Major Daniels replied. "We've lost the Flare Boom to an incoming missile. No other damage has been reported. The VTOLs have engaged with the RAF fighter jets. So far, no casualties on either side."

"Very good," replied Lexi.

From the corner of her eye, Lexi saw Isabelle's form flicker as a force screen materialised around her.

"I anticipate enemy incursion soon," Isabelle informed her. "Please continue to operate the machine while I deal with them."

She didn't wait for a reply. She disappeared with a snap of wind as she teleported out of the room.

Lexi continued to gaze through the observation window. The machine was operating at peak capacity. The super-heated air around it was being drawn upwards into giant fans to be dispersed into the cold North Sea air. Meanwhile, giant blades of steel deployed around the platform above, jutting out into the sea air, all of which glowed red hot, conducting and radiating heat away from the machine. It was functioning perfectly.

Then, as she watched, it began to vibrate, and the viewing window shook.

————

The Klalan fleet was detected by three hundred and forty-four sniping installations, which instantly activated and attacked by blasting out pulses of sixth order energy. Two hundred and sixty-three ships were instantly vaporised in bursts of light and hard radiation.

The Klalan, however, were nothing but efficient. Their detectors took less than a second to pinpoint the source of the energy bolts. Three hundred and forty-four beams of force shot out and destroyed each sniping installation.

The fleet continued its journey towards Earth.

————

"INVESTIGATION COMPLETE," The Non'anan entity stated.

"And? What did you discover?" asked Kate/Joe.

"INCURSION."

"As we stated."

"INTERVENTION NOT POSSIBLE."

Anger grew in the Kate/Joe fusion.

"You must intervene! We will all die without your help!"

"DIE IS CEASE TO EXIST."

"Exactly! If you don't help us, we will all die, and the enemy will continue their conquest. Eventually, they will reach your system!"

"TIME."

"If by that you mean it will be a long time before they get to your system, then yes, that may be true. But you must realise that they will use that time to their advantage. They will build more weapons of destruction until they number in the millions. They will be like locusts, ravaging everything in their path. Can you stand by and watch them destroy every living thing in our universe?"

"INTERVENTION NOT POSSIBLE."

"Yes, it is!" seethed Kate/Joe. *"You will pay attention and help us; we will not let you watch us all die!"*

The Kate/Joe fusion drew yet more power from the machine, which howled and screeched as it pulled the energy it needed from the surrounding space. Air was sucked inward and blasted out at supersonic speeds to crash into the surrounding walls of the machine room. Giant copper conduits sizzled and grew white hot as excess heat was dumped into the massive heat sinks. The machine room sparkled and pulsed with light being warped into curves and spirals like magnetic lines of force. The whole oil platform vibrated and quivered.

Kate/Joe screamed in rage as they aligned their mental force into a single, super powerful sixth order blast of white-hot energy.

The volatile torrent of force slammed into the Non'anan with an almost physical force as it breached the outer defence of its mind and unleashed a destructive wave of intense Psi energy deep within.

It was the equivalent of throwing a stone at a giant to attract its attention. And it had the desired effect.

"WHY?" asked the Non'anan.

"Because you must help us. Can't you see that? You are the stronger, the caretakers, the guardians of our universe. The death of all living things is impossible to ignore. You must act!"

There was a pause, a silence for a while, during which Kate/Joe could sense another conversation was taking place.

"CONTRACT," came the eventual reply.

"What do you want?" asked Kate/Joe warily.

––––––

The good news was that the enemy soldiers didn't seem to have any defence against the pulse weapon, thought Henrick. The bad news was there were hundreds of them.

For thirty minutes he had been firing again and again at the approaching hordes of pale white bi-pedal soldiers, blasting them into oblivion, but they kept coming. Eline had abandoned her task of protecting civilians. They were long past that. She joined in the fight and was some distance behind him fending off attacks from the East.

Fires raged all around as energy bolts from both sides turning anything they touched into white-hot flames that roared into the sky. Huge craters were everywhere as the enemy soldiers fired purple pinwheels that screamed as they scythed their way through the air, vaporising soil and grass wherever they landed. The trees in front of Henrick had long gone, blasted into splinters, while the buildings behind him were now smoking rubble.

Henrick grunted as another blue streak of light crashed into his force screen with a boom. His weaponry and defensive capability were far superior to the enemy, but the enemy soldiers were far more numerous. They didn't seem to care how many of their number fell, they just kept coming. He was being forced back by sheer numbers.

"Energy rifle overheating," the suit's AI informed him.

"Shit! Give me another weapon!"

"Deploying strike missiles," replied the suit.

Henrick felt five concussive thumps and saw five streaks of fire climb into the sky.

"I am detecting enemy aircraft heading this way."

"They're going after the Complex! We have to stop them!"

"Deploying secondary weaponry."

The left arm of Henrick's suit split open as a short-barrelled device slid up from its concealed receptacle, deploying on the suit's arm.

"This is a needle cannon," explained the suit. *"It projects miniscule bolts of sixth order energy. I have configured it to fire in the same way as the energy rifle."*

"Good," panted Henrick as he bounced backwards yet again. *"What about the enemy aircraft?"*

"I am targeting them. There are six. I will launch surface-to-air missiles when they are in range."

Henrick swapped arms and began firing with his new weapon, noting with grim satisfaction the devastating effect it had on the enemy. Like his first weapon, the white figures had no defence. The microscopic needle pulses pierced their screens with little effort, where it detonated inside their bodies.

"SAM launch," said his suit.

Henrick was startled when he suddenly lost control of the suit. It knelt on one knee by itself; the torso tipped slightly forward to balance on his two outstretched arms, forming a stable base. He heard a grinding noise and then felt two big thumps in his back. As he regained control and straightened up to resume firing at the rapidly approaching hoard of white figures, he saw two white contrails streaking into the air over his head and up into the sky.

Concentrating on the threat before him, Henrick shot continuously as soldier after soldier fell or was shattered. He reflected the energy as more violet pinwheels flew at a dizzying pace, smashing against his shields again and again, bouncing away to either side. Whatever they struck instantly igniting into flames.

Just as he thought he was holding his own and maybe even making headway, his suit shouted in his head.

"BRACE!"

There was a huge concussive force behind him that threw him forward and up into the air.

One thousand soldiers held their breath in awe as Isabelle stood alone on the helideck of the rig, her arms raised to the heavens. The surrounding air crackled and danced with electricity, powerful sparks of blue light leaping from her fingertips, striking the metal deck beneath her feet. Ten minutes ago, each soldier heard her voice inside their minds, a command that filled them with apprehension.

"The enemy is incoming. It is not the enemy you were expecting. Take cover while I deal with them. Do not let anyone gain access to the machine."

What did she mean? Not the enemy they were expecting? And how had they heard her voice in their heads? Who was she? They had been conducting drill after drill over the last few weeks. They knew their places, and they knew exactly what to do. Knew their stations and knew the plan. Now, here was a strange silver faced woman telling them something different.

Nervous faces looked to one another, and murmurs rose from the ranks.

"Retreat to position two. Companies one, three, and five take the outer perimeter, while companies two, four, and six cover the inner perimeter!" Commander Hussein's commands crackled through the soldiers' radios. The entire battalion moved swiftly into action, leaving the helideck empty except for the lone figure of the silver woman.

"Remember your orders, everyone," continued their commander. "I've been informed that the woman on the helideck is a friend and that she's here to help. You might see some strange things," he paused. "Keep to yourselves and do your job. New orders, whatever happens do not go up onto the helideck, keep to your positions."

The troops, although puzzled, were disciplined. They did exactly as commanded and faced outwards, scanning the ocean below them.

Their orders were to prevent any incursion from the air or sea.

———

Humanity was under attack.

Reports of armed white soldiers, rampaging through power plants, attacking government buildings, and disrupting transportation systems spread rapidly across the globe. Despite the efforts of mobilised police, armies, and air forces, these mysterious soldiers with glowing red eyes proved to unstoppable. They marched relentlessly towards their targets, seemingly unfazed by any attempts to stop them. Their defensive lines were no match for incoming enemies' strength and firepower as they effortlessly decimated those who stood in their way.

There was only one thing that could stop them.

At key points around the world, appearing in blue flashes, four metre tall, black robotic humanoid figures stood alone against the approaching white enemy soldiers.

As soon as the black figures appeared, chaos erupted in blinding flashes of light and deafening explosions. Their energy weapons and missiles cutting through the air, decimating any enemy in their path. The battle was fierce, but short-lived. And when it was over, the black figures vanished, leaving behind a trail of destruction - burning cars, crumbling buildings, and the bodies of fallen enemy soldiers. It was a scene of war unlike any other. One fought with futuristic technology and incredible power.

Chapter 58 - Arrival

The huge Klalan fleet arrived in Earth space.

It had ploughed forward with grim purpose, pushing on relentlessly, undeterred by the constant fire from the sniping stations and hidden weapons. Though their numbers had been diminished, the fleet still numbered in the hundreds, and at the forefront of this armada were the four colossal planetoids, bristling with weaponry and armoured to withstand any attack.

Standing off, beyond the moon's orbit, the dark planet at the centre of the Klalan fleet took up position. Deep below the surface of that noisome planet, the Klalan leader issued the command.

"Commence bombardment, kill them all!"

Four titanic beams of energy, each three miles wide, lashed out to strike at the Earth, only to rebound into space in scintillating shards as they hit a defensive screen.

At the same moment, in a sudden burst, a powerful beam of pure blue light erupted from the dark side of the moon. It ripped through the multiple layers of protective force fields surrounding the lead planetoid and crashed into its surface with explosive energy. The impact left a scorching trail as it bored down to the planet's core, and out through the other side vaporising everything in its path - rock and metal, leaving a vast borehole. As a result, the planetoids' drive and energy collectors died, rendering it into a useless floating rock.

Instantly, the weapons from the remaining three planetoids swung around to focus onto the shadowy side of the moon, their beams scything across space. Lunar regolith was blasted miles up into space as the beams carved their way across the moon's surface towards a jet-black set of buildings that had remained hidden in a deep crater.

The dark installation was hit by the three powerful energy beams from the planetoids, causing a massive explosion. A cloud of dust and rock plumed upwards, expanding outward into the void of space. The resulting explosion left behind a glowing crater that stretched down ten miles deep into the surface.

The three planetoids immediately resumed their attack against Earth, their cosmic-scale beams of force crashing back into the defensive screen that surrounded our planet.

"Incoming!" shouted colonel Hussain.

On the horizon, three British naval warships could be seen surging forward towards the rig. This was expected. Confronted with the sudden power drain across the entire East Anglia counties, it wouldn't be long before the outage was traced, and someone was sent to investigate. They would think it a terrorist attack - what else could it be? And they would send in the appropriate forces to deal with the situation. Hence the warships and the jet fighters.

There was a boom and a cloud of smoke from one of the approaching vessels. Shortly afterwards, there was a screech and a splash of water nearby as a warning shot was fired.

High above them, hundreds of miles in the atmosphere, the sky exploded in a dazzling array of colours that seemed almost impossible. The intensity of the light created a shadow of the rig that stretched across the vast expanse of water below. Deafening booms and howling winds soon followed, forcing soldiers to turn their faces towards the sky in search of the origin to no avail. The sky was alive with light.

––––––––

With a quick gesture from her hand, the last of the approaching alabaster soldiers exploded into tiny fragments. Isabelle surveyed her surroundings, pushing her perception outwards to encompass the entire oil platform.

There were no more enemy soldiers. She assessed the threat of the approaching warships and the planes above and dismissed them. Lexi's defences were more than capable of handling them.

She allowed her awareness to descend into the machine room, where she noted with satisfaction that the screeching and howling of the machine was diminishing as it slowly shut down.

Kate and Joe were stepping from the machine.

––––––––

Kate's head throbbed painfully as she walked across the machine room, hand in hand with Joe.

"I will remove the pain shortly, once my energy stores are replenished," said Bella. *"In the meantime, I recommend analgesics."*

"No shit!" exclaimed Kate. *"It's like the worst hangover ever. I can hardly open my eyes. The light hurts."*

Behind them, the machine's howling and screeching noise slowly reduced as fans wound down and generators slowed. The heat in the room was stifling and Kate could feel sweat trickling down her back as they stopped at the exit and gazed into each other's eyes.

They didn't need to say anything. They both knew what had been agreed and the consequences of the agreement.

Joe opened the door to find Lexi blocking their path.

"Well?" she asked, hands on hips, a questioning look on her face.

There was silence between the three of them, then Joe nodded.

"It's done."

The three of them fell silent once again. Joe noticed that Lexi hardly glanced at Kate. That probably made sense, he thought to himself, considering that Kate had nearly killed her.

"Well," breathed Lexi at last. "Thank fuck for that! Now. Where is Henrick?"

———

Henrick was still fighting.

The suit had easily stabilised his fall from the explosion behind him, and had jetted up into the sky, giving him an aerial view of the battle. Initially, he was concerned to see a vast crater near where he had been standing, but his suit informed him it had caused no damage as the Complex was at least one hundred metres below the surface.

"What caused the explosion?" he asked.

"One of the incoming aircraft dodged our missiles and crashed directly into the ground kamikaze fashion."

"Extreme, but understandable, given that they cannot get past us any other way."

"The tactics of the enemy are unknown, but yes, a predictable method," replied the suit.

Henrick grunted and kept firing down at the hordes of enemy figures below, noting that Eline was doing the same, their high vantage point providing a tremendous advantage and enabling them to pick of the rushing enemy figures easily.

"I am picking up high energy discharges above us," his suit informed him.

"More aircraft?" asked Henrick.

"No, the energies involved are different and have a much higher power profile. However, currently there is no danger, the discharges are shielded from us by a defensive screen."

"Then don't bother me about it!" exclaimed Henrick. *"We have enough to worry about down here!"*

"I was merely keeping you informed of what was happening."

Henrick thought he detected a note of something in the voice. Just how intelligent is this suit? He thought to himself. Then something caught his attention. Over to the West, a group of white figures appeared to be carrying something.

"What's that?" he asked. *"Are they carrying something?"*

"I don't like the look of it," replied his suit. *"It is shielded from my preceptors; I cannot tell what it is. But I surmise it must be an explosive device!"*

"Fuck! We can also assume that it'll be powerful enough to destroy the Complex, otherwise why would they be bringing it?"

"Indeed. Note that the two figures next to it are also carrying additional shield generators."

"Oh, shit!" exclaimed Henrick. *"We'd better do something about it!"*

———

Fury radiated from the Klalan commander as its thought bellowed at the underlings, demanding to know why the planet before them was not consumed in flames.

"The planet has a formidable defence screen," replied the chief technologist, tinged with a hint of self-satisfaction. *"It is as I feared. The inhabitants of this world have access to a technology that is comparable to our own."*

The air crackled with tension and fear as the commander vomited onto the floor in anger.

"Even so, we are still the superior race," the Strategy Functionary interjected. *"They cannot continue to hold their screens for long. Their energy consumption will not allow it. Further, we can use the planet's moon against them."*

It turned to the Attack Commander, its mouth slavering with digestive juices as it gazed upon the spreading pool of stomach contents on the floor.

"Carve the moon into pieces and smash them into their force screens," commanded the Strategy Functionary.

The Klalan commander sat back on its haunches and watched the screens with glee.

"Excellent!" came the cold, harsh thought. *"An excellent strategy. Continue with the assault."*

Klalan operators immediately directed instructions to the fleet.

One of the planet sized ships shifted its powerful energy beam towards the moon. The once miles wide beam of energy now focused into a single, needle-thin stream of force that pierced the lunar surface with ease, like a hot knife through warm butter. As the beam dug deeper and deeper, melting and pulverising everything in its path, the ground shook and trembled. The dusty surface glowed and sizzled under the intense heat. A geyser of molten rock and dust was thrown up into space in a vast plume, leaving a glowing trail orbiting around the moon.

Slowly, the intense beam of force moved back and forth, carving great trenches across the moon, chiselling and hewing out vast mountains of rock.

All around the globe, giant, menacing, black robotic figures continued to appear out of thin air. Engaging in quick, intense battles against hordes of pale white, human-like soldiers with glowing red eyes that were attacking strategic infrastructure and government buildings, destroying everything in their path.

It didn't take long for humanity to realise that they were in the midst of an attack, with the black figures serving as their defenders. These robotic warriors would suddenly appear, fight off the enemy, and then vanish.

News spread around the world quickly. Social media was flooded with images of white soldiers and their mysterious, black-armoured opponents. All television channels suspended the broadcasting of their regular programmes and, instead, were dedicated to broadcasting the breaking news.

Meanwhile, high above, the sky was ablaze with flickering lights that illuminated the clouds above like super bright fireworks, and the air reverberated with deafening blasts that sounded like massive explosions.

People sought shelter wherever they could, hiding from the chaos erupting above and around them, while the armed forces fought in vain against the invading white soldiers. Their efforts proved useless, as their weapons had no impact on the enemy. They were powerless against their unstoppable assailants.

Fire, police and ambulance services tried their best to save buildings and the injured, but it was hopeless. The enemy soldiers didn't care who they killed, men, women or children, or what they destroyed in their path.

There was only one thing that could stop them: the black behemoths. The problem was that they weren't enough of them.

Then the ground began to shake. The destruction of the moon was starting to have a devastating effect on the Earth.

———

The destruction of the Earth's moon filled the Klalan with amusement, watching with glee as they directed Mount Everest sized chunks to smash into the planet's defensive screens. They knew it wouldn't be long before those screens failed.

"I am detecting a dimensional plane disturbance nearby," reported an operator in the yellow mist filled command centre.

"Details," barked the Defence Coordinator's thought.

"A dimensional gateway opened and then closed in sector eight," reported the minion.

"Something came through?" asked the Attack Commander. *"Deploy sensing equipment to the rear of the fleet immediately!"*

Multiple operators busied themselves at their consoles. Presently one reported.

"Drones deployed, there is no dimensional gateway currently detected. No enemy ships are detected."

"Then what was it?" demanded the Strategy Functionary.

The chill voice of the commander slid into their minds.

"Continue with the attack. This is of no matter. The destruction of this planet is of paramount importance."

"Given that these aliens have been attacking us when we least expect it, we must, at least take some precautions," protested the Strategy Functionary.

"I do not agree," replied the commander. *"We will crush them; they cannot maintain their screens for much longer."*

"We have been attacked several times since entering this system. This development is surely something to note." The Strategy Functionary explained.

A loud bang preceded the Strategy Functionary collapsing, its four legs crumpling under it.

"Is there anyone else who would disobey my orders?" snarled the commander, holstering its projectile weapon.

There was no reply, then another operator spoke up.

"Something is approaching."

The Defence Coordinator stomped over to the operator.

"What is it?"

"The readings are difficult to understand. I have seen nothing like it," replied the operator.

A thought came from another station across the room.

"We are losing drones. Forty-seven have stopped transmitting."

"What?" asked the Defence Coordinator. *"Explain immediately."*

"I cannot," answered the same operator. *"I can only report what is happening. We have now lost sixty-three drones."*

"Deploy the rear guard, tell their commanders to wipe out anything in sector eight," the Attack Commander instructed.

"Yes, Commander."

After manipulating the controls to zoom in on sector eight, the Defence Coordinator and Attack Commander studied the system map displayed before them.

"There is nothing there," the Defence Coordinator spat a glob of phlegm onto the floor.

"True," mused the Attack Commander. *"But..."* it continued to manipulate the controls further and then indicated an area with a green digit. *"There is a blackness here."*

The Defence Coordinator extended its sinewy neck to look closely.

"It appears to be moving. How can darkness move?"

"Gravity monitors are indicating a large mass approaching!" A shouted thought came from the control centre.

"Large mass?" queried the Attack Commander. *"How can that be possible when our sensing equipment is not registering anything?"*

"All sensing drones have now ceased transmission!"

"The rear-guard ships are reporting a very large gravity distortion!"

"What is happening?" came the cold and harsh thought of the commander.

————

Out of the deep, dark void of space, a dark, undetectable object emerged, devouring everything it its path, whether it be ships, drones, or debris. Neither energy weapons nor projectiles could harm it; it simply absorbed everything that was aimed at it as it relentlessly made its way towards the heart of the Klalan formation.

The Klalan relentlessly launched beams and projectiles, but they were all futile against this strange target. Ships were torn apart and dragged towards the centre in a deadly vortex. The destruction of the vessels was accompanied by intense bursts of light and radiation, revealing the scattered wreckage left behind.

Even the redirected miles wide energy beams from the vast planetoid ships had no effect, and it wasn't long before they too were pulled apart and crushed to be sucked into the black void that was a supermassive black hole.

Within minutes, the only thing left of the Klalan fleet was floating debris.

Somehow, the destructive power of the black hole was diverted away from the besieged blue, green planet before it, as it was directed back into outer space.

Part 4

Chapter 59 - Aftermath

Three days later, members of the Alliance gathered yet again in the conference room. This time, the atmosphere was much more joyful and relaxed, with smiling faces and lively conversations filling the space. The danger had passed, and they had emerged victorious, thanks to the Non'anan. Someone had even brought champagne and beer to celebrate, and most of it had already been consumed. In the middle of the conference table, there were still some leftover slices of pizza and garlic bread.

Even Isabelle seemed happy as she was conversing with Lexi.

"You have agreed to help re-fit the six Augmented Alliance members?" she asked.

Lexi nodded, taking another sip of beer from the bottle.

"Yes, I've spoken with Joe, and we agreed I would stay long enough to get them back on their feet. But after that, I'm outta here." She couldn't help her gaze flicking towards Henrick, who was talking with Eline.

Isabelle noticed.

"You will leave with Henrick? You won't be joining the Alliance?"

Lexi flashed a wan smile.

"Joe's Alliance isn't for me. I have some ideas that I want to try out." She took another sip of her beer. "Besides, I don't trust that Kate girl."

"You did attack one of my android bodies and Prisha," Isabelle pointed out.

Lexi waved a hand dismissively.

"You were trespassing, and I knew nothing about the enemy. I thought you were going to steal the Machine from me. I couldn't allow that." She sighed. "But I guess you did, anyway."

"My calculations show that the Kate/Joe fusion would have been able to contact the Non'anan without your machine. However, it certainly made a difference and perhaps enabled them to survive the contact without injury."

When Lexi didn't answer, Isabelle continued. "Your theory has been proven. There is an alien race - the Non'anan. Your dreams were real."

"I realise that. I knew it would work," answered Lexi haughtily.

"You are also cured of your cancer."

Lexi gazed across the room at Sally, who was laughing with Molly, the two of them sitting side by side at the conference table.

"And you have also been fitted with a Mark 5 Assist," continued Isabelle. "What you have is a most unusual combination; a Mark 5 Assist and a Mark 5 Augmentation. I would be interested to learn more about any new faculties this enables."

Lexi switched her gaze from Sally back to Isabelle.

"Look! I'm grateful for everything Sally's done for me, but I won't be letting you inside my head! I'm staying to help, but as soon as it's done, I'm gone. I have plans."

Lexi slammed her bottle down on the table and strode away. She stopped to select a new beer and then sat next to Henrick. She glared back at Isabelle.

"She's not easy to get on with," said Joe as he walked up to Isabelle.

"Indeed," replied Isabelle. "I find her most intriguing; I have not met a human like her."

"Abrasive, head-strong, pompous, calculating, cold?"

"Hmm, yes. All those things and more. She obviously has a very keen mind."

"Yes, she does. It's a shame she doesn't put it to better use."

Prisha approached them, a glass of bubbling champagne in a tall glass in her hand.

"When do you have some time, we need talk," she said pointedly at Joe.

Joe sighed.

"Yeah. The public knows that we exist."

"The public knows that 'something' exists," corrected Prisha. "Have you seen the news?"

Joe shook his head.

"Well, you should pay attention. It's chaos out there. Countries and governments are blaming each other for the attacks. Half of the world's population is too scared to leave their own homes, and three nuclear power plants have gone critical. And that doesn't even cover what the conspiracists are saying."

"We need to help them," interjected Kate, sliding up to stand next to Joe, Josie perched on her hip.

Prisha grinned at Josie. "Hello gorgeous," she said, stroking Josie's hair.

Josie broke into a toothless smile and wriggled around to hold her arms out to be held. After placing her glass on the table, Prisha took her from Kate and planted a big, wet kiss on Josie's cheek.

"We can't let the world descend into war. We need to do something," continued Kate.

"I know," answered Joe. "I'm just not sure how."

"I will help," said Isabelle. "I have a plan."

Joe and Kate exchanged glances and then laughed out loud.

"I fail to see what is so amusing," said a perplexed Isabelle.

Once they had recovered from their laughing, Kate took Joe's arm, her expression turning serious.

"We can't wait any longer."

Joe instantly knew what she meant, the laughter dying on his lips. His brow furrowed, drawing his eyebrows together. He nodded.

"I know," he whispered to Kate. "I've been putting it off."

Kate reached out and cupped his cheek.

"It has to be done."

Joe drew in a deep breath, steeling himself. He glanced up at Isabelle's impassive silver face and then addressed the room.

"Can I have your attention, everyone?" he called out. He waited for the hubbub to die down as everyone turned to face him.

"Thank you." he placed an arm around Kate's shoulder, pulling her to him gently.

"Thanks to Kate's arrival and thanks to Isabelle's machines, we have successfully fought off the enemy."

He stopped as people whooped and clapped. He waited for the noise to die down.

"But it's not over. We have a lot of work to do. The world needs our help. That should keep us busy for a while."

Someone laughed from the back of the room.

"We are also not exactly sure what the Non'anan have done. I mean, they destroyed the enemy fleet that was attacking us, but we don't know what they did with the thousands of invading humanoid soldiers. All we know is that they are gone. Did they destroy them or just send them back to where they came from? We simply don't know."

"Good riddance!" someone shouted.

Joe smiled and then continued.

"The moon's destruction poses another issue. We're already seeing its effect on Earth, with earthquakes and floods occurring globally. It's important that we figure out the consequences of its absence and how it will affect our planet."

There was silence as he paused.

"So, as I see it," he continued. "There are three things that we need to look into straight away." He held up his hand and ticked off his points on his fingers. "One. Stabilisation of the political situation around the world. We need to integrate into society - a monumental task and one I've asked Prisha to investigate. Two. Build defences. We can't let what happened three days ago happen again. It is important that we are prepared. We must be able to defend ourselves. Three. Investigate the what the loss of the moon means to the planet. Maybe there is something we can do to mitigate the effect that its loss is having on Earth."

Joe paused again and gazed around at the serious expressions facing him. With a newfound determined glint in his eye, he spoke up once more.

"Here's the thing," he declared boldly. "We have just accomplished the impossible. We possess not only purpose but also the power to shape our world for the better. And that is exactly what we'll do!" His voice rang out with conviction. "Together, we'll work to make this world a better place, one step at a time."

His words resonated through the room.

"It won't be easy, and it won't be quick. But we will persevere, and we will succeed!"

He raised his beer bottle high in the air.

"To us!"

Everyone cheered and raised their drink.

"I'm proud of you," Kate whispered into his ear.

Joe's expression was grim.

"That was the easy part."

Chapter 60 - Sally

Eventually, everyone slowly made their way out of the conference room. Some stumbled a bit as they walked, but everyone seemed content and wore smiles on their faces. Just before they were about to exit, Joe motioned for Molly and Sally to stay behind.

"Mol, Sal, could you stay a minute? I need to talk to you."

"Of course," replied Molly.

Joe waited for the door to close behind the last person and then sat down heavily in a nearby chair. He ran his hand over his face and up into his hair, brushing it back from his forehead.

Kate sat next to Joe, placing Josie on her lap, while Isabelle stood a little off to one side.

"What's up?" asked Molly.

Joe couldn't meet her gaze. He looked everywhere in the room but at her.

Sally gripped Molly's hand, suddenly frightened.

"What's going on?" she asked, her eyes flicking between Joe, Kate, and Isabelle.

Joe blew out a long breath.

"I have something to tell you, and it's not going to be easy."

"Spit it out Joe," said Molly. "What is it?"

Joe locked eyes with Molly.

"When me and Kate contacted the Non'anan, we had difficulty convincing them to help us."

"I'm sure," replied Molly. "But you did it, right?"

Joe nodded. He cleared his throat.

"They wanted something in return."

Sally laughed.

"What on earth do we have that they would want?" she asked. "I'm sure that they can take or make anything they need."

There was silence in the room.

"They want us," Kate spoke up in a quiet voice.

"What do you mean us?" asked a puzzled Molly.

"They want one of us to study."

No one spoke. Molly dropped into a chair, pulling Sally by the hand, making her stumble forward.

"No…" she whispered.

"You can't be serious?" asked Sally. "We're going to let them take whoever they like? That's barbaric!"

"You agreed to this?" asked Molly.

Joe nodded.

"We had no choice. If we hadn't agreed, they wouldn't have helped us. We tried everything, believe me."

"When I said one of us, I meant one of us in this room, not someone from the public," Kate said in a very quiet voice.

Sally's eyes went wide in shock, while Molly stiffened.

"No!" said Molly again.

Joe nodded slowly.

"It has to be someone with a Mark 5. No one else would be able to survive."

Sally opened and closed her mouth in gulps.

"But." she started to say. Molly cut her off.

"It's me," she whispered, looking at the floor.

Joe looked away and brushed at the tears forming in his eyes.

"What?" asked Sally. "What are you talking about?"

Molly looked up at Sally, her enormous eyes brimming with tears behind her glasses.

"I have to be the one to go Sal." she said simply.

Sally dropped to her knees beside Molly's chair and threw her arms around her.

"Don't be silly, you can't go!" she protested.

Molly gave a little grunt while cradling Sally's head to her.

"It can't be Kate; she has Josie to look after. It can't be Lexi, cos. Well, cos she just wouldn't do it. It can't be Joe cos he's with Kate. She and Josie need him, and he needs to lead the Alliance. It can't be you, Sal, my love. You would never survive it. There's only me left."

Sally pushed herself away from their embrace to stare directly into Molly's eyes.

"No!" she exclaimed. "You can't go! I won't let you!"

Molly just looked at her. She watched her lover's face crumple in anguish as she realised that there was no other choice.

Kate slid her arm around Joe's shoulders, and the two of them leaned into each other.

Tears streamed down Sally's cheeks.

"You can't go!" she wailed. "Please don't go, don't leave me!"

Molly turned to Joe.

"For how long?" she asked, her face white and expressionless.

Joe made no attempt to stop the tears from trickling down his cheeks.

"Three years."

"NO!" screamed Sally. "You can't! I won't let you!"

Molly pulled Sally to her and held her tight to her. Josie began to cry, her cries filling the room.

"Please don't go, Mol!" Sally pleaded; her voice muffled against Molly's shoulder.

Molly looked past Sally towards Joe, her eyes filled with tears and sadness.

"Earth years?" she asked calmly.

Joe shook his head. Molly blinked.

"When?" she asked.

Unable to meet her gaze any longer, Joe turned away.

"Before the end of the year," Kate answered for him.

Molly blinked again, her eyes wide and her face ashen. Slowly, with a trembling hand, she removed her glasses and dropped them to the floor. She tightened her embrace around Sally and kissed the top of her head.

"Don't cry Sal, it'll be alright," she whispered.

"No, it won't!" Sally sobbed. "I can't live without you! You can't go!"

"I'll be back Sal, it's not forever."

Sally raised her tear-streaked face.

"It may as well be. You'll be gone for years, and they'll do all sorts of experiments on you!"

Molly pulled Sally to her again.

"I won't let them and before you know it, I'll be back."

"No, you won't," moaned Sally. "You'll be gone, and I'll be all alone!"

"We'll still be able to talk with each other," Molly looked up and fixed her gaze on Kate. "Right?"

Kate nodded. "Before you go, Isabelle will outfit you with as much protection as she can."

"There you go Sal, See. I'll be protected, Isabelle will see to it." Molly kept her gaze on Kate and mouthed. "Thank you."

Kate sniffed and flashed Molly a wavering smile. She couldn't stop the tears.

Molly stroked Sally's hair again.

"Six months, Sal," she whispered quietly. "We have six months together before I have to go."

Sally's entire frame shook as she sobbed uncontrollably.

Molly tried to comfort her. "We still have time. We can go on that trip you've always talked about - Hawaii. And, if you want, we could even get married."

Sally pulled away from Molly's arms and looked at her with her face full of anguish, pain, and flushed red cheeks.

"You mean that?" she asked. "You want to get married?"

Molly smiled a thin, sad smile.

"Of course I want to get married, you idiot!" She reached up and wiped away Sally's tears with a finger.

"I love you."

Sally's chin wobbled as she tried in vain to smile back.

"I love you too," she said.

Chapter 61 - Kate & Joe

With a roar of fury, Kate pulled the trigger, killing yet another prisoner, the contents of their head splattering against the white wall.

Behind her, Joe lounged in a chair puffing on a cigarette.

"Finished?" he asked.

"No!" screamed Kate, moving to the next prisoner inline and shooting him in the head.

Six lifeless bodies lay on the floor, blood seeping from their wounds to pool and soak the carpet. Three more terrified prisoners were on their knees, hands bound behind their backs, gags in their mouths.

"Let me know when you've got it out of your system," said Joe, flicking his cigarette at the nearest body.

"I fucking hate them!" screamed Kate. She moved along the line and aimed her pistol at the next quivering prisoner.

"And I fucking hate you!" She pulled the trigger, and another body slammed into the floor.

"You don't mean that," said Joe, lighting another cigarette. "You know you love me."

"Fuck off!" shouted Kate, moving to the next prisoner.

"Look, I hate the pinkies too, but we got close this time and we'll win next time."

There was another deafening bang as Kate executed the next prisoner.

"And just how are we going to do that?" spat Kate.

"I'll think of something," replied Joe. "I've got the beginnings of an idea already."

"Your idea didn't exactly work out this time!" snarled Kate.

"I don't know," answered Joe, blowing smoke up into the air. "We destroyed their version of the Complex."

"Fat lot of good that did us!"

"It proves that the pinkies are fallible, and that means we can win."

Kate moved to stand over the last prisoner. She kicked him in the stomach, causing him to bend over with his head, nearly touching the floor.

"So, fucking what?" she growled.

"Well, if you've finished executing the staff, I could tell you."

Kate stood looking down at the cowing prisoner with disgust.

"Light me a cigarette," she instructed him. "And tell me."

Joe breathed in from his cigarette and pulled a packet from his top shirt pocket.

"Do you remember that thing we found in world 387?"

"What of it?"

"Well, what if we could control it? What if we could send it to kill the Pinkies?"

Kate's anger evaporated. She smiled an evil smile.

"That would be awesome!" she exclaimed. "Is that possible?"

Joe brought an unlit cigarette up to his and puffed away to light it.

"Maybe," he replied between puffs. "We could try."

Kate's emotions flipped back to anger.

"This is another one of your stupid ideas. It won't work."

She reached down and grabbed the prisoner's hair, pulling them up, forcing them to look at her as she waved the gun in his face.

"We'll never know if we don't try," continued Joe. He held out the newly lit cigarette.

Kate pushed the muzzle of the gun into the prisoner's left eye.

"So, what's your brilliant idea to get the thing to work for us?"

"I was thinking of removing its food supply. And then pointing it at the Pinkies. I need to work out the details." Joe waved his arm, holding the lit cigarette.

Kate stared into the frightened eye of the prisoner and pulled the trigger. The body jerked backwards and crashed to the floor.

Kate turned and walked over to Joe, heedless of the blood running down her cheek. She took the lit cigarette from Joe and took a long pull.

"Better?" asked Joe.

She nodded.

"Much."

"Can we get down to business and plan our next move?"

Kate blew out a big plume of smoke and turned to survey the eight bodies.

"Hmmm," she replied. "But first, all this killing has put me in the mood."

She walked over to the nearest body, leant down and placed a hand in the pool of blood. Placing the cigarette between her lips, she used her other hand to unbutton her blouse. She walked back to Joe, a wicked smile wrapped around her cigarette, while smearing blood from her hand onto her now exposed breasts.

"Come here," she said in a low, seductive voice.

Chapter 62 - Joey
3 months later

"JOSIE!" Kate roared as she jumped from the bed. Ignoring her nakedness, she sprinted across the bedroom and flung open the bedroom door.

"Bella!" she screamed.

"High order functions unlocked," Bella shouted in Kate's mind urgently. *"GO!"*

A brilliant blue aura surrounded Kate as she raced across the lounge, barrelling towards Josie's bedroom. Heat radiated outward from the doorframe. Flames licked hungrily at the walls, scorching and blackening them in seconds. Plumes of dark smoke collected at the ceiling like a billowing storm cloud.

"Get two HAZPRO's in here NOW!" Joe sent an urgent thought as he sped after Kate from the bedroom.

"Kate!" he shouted. "Be careful!"

Heedless of her own safety, Kate crashed into the flaming bedroom door. Her screens protected her from the heat and the shock as she fell into Josie's room. Red, orange and yellow flames were everywhere, roaring up from the floor towards the ceiling. Smoke filled the room, making it difficult to see.

"BELLA!" screamed Kate.

Bella cried out in triumph, *"I have her!"* as Kate scrambled to her feet and frantically scanned the room for Josie. Through the smoke and scorching flames, she located a luminescent glow coming from Josie's cot. Joe ran up behind her and grabbed her arm with a vice-like grip, pulling her with him through the inferno towards the glimmering light.

A radiant yellow force field surrounded Josie as she lay in her cot, shielding her from the licks of fire that raced around her. She laughed and giggled in delight as the flames danced with each other, though none could come close enough to reach her. In seconds, Kate and Joe were beside her bed, transfixed by the sight of the little girl surrounded by a brilliant wall of flame.

Kate's heart hammered against her chest as she lunged forward and scooped Josie into her arms. Joe joined them, wrapping an arm around both of their shoulders, connecting them in a crackling electric force field. Molten material fell from above, crashing into their screens, droplets splattering across the floor beneath them.

"Josie!" Kate whispered fiercely into Josie's neck, inhaling her scent with relief.

"She is unharmed," Bella echoed in Kate's mind.

"Thank God!" she gasped with gratitude.

Joe surveyed the destruction of Josie's bedroom. The ceiling was long gone, consumed by the raging inferno, revealing exposed girders and concrete.

"Em, what caused this? Are we under attack?" Joe asked.

"I am detecting an unusual energy signature but can sense no one else besides ourselves."

Behind them there was a massive thump as two black, hulking HAZPRO suits materialised.

"Get behind us!" Mike projected an urgent thought at Joe and Kate.

Something caught Joe's attention. He hastily thrust Kate and Josie aside as his eyes locked onto an eerie, yellow light emanating from Josie's cot. Yet more adrenalin coursed through his veins, as he faced the danger head-on, determined to protect the ones he loved. His heart raced as he clasped his fists tight and prepared himself for battle.

"Em?" he shouted in his mind.

"Something unusual is happening," replied Emily. *"That is not an ordinary sixth order energy pattern!"*

The yellow glow in Josie's bed intensified, becoming an almost solid mass of light. It reflected the flames, relentlessly consuming the bedding. In an instant, it was gone, and Joe gasped in shock. There, lying in the ruins of the bed, encircled by the flames, lay a small and fragile child, naked and exposed.

Behind him, he heard Josie cry. For a moment, he couldn't believe his eyes, then he heard an unfamiliar voice in his mind. It was the voice of a child.

"Joey."

What the hell? He thought to himself. Joey? Where did he come from? How did he get here?

Automatically, he found himself reaching down to pick up the small, giggling male child.

"Stop! We are being manipulated!" Emily informed him urgently.

Joe didn't care. He cradled the baby to his chest and carried him past the HAZPRO figures out of the fire. He quickly reached Kate and Josie and pulled them close. With a quick thought, he teleported all four of them out of the inferno.

Epilogue
Six months later

Kate opened her eyes.

She couldn't see. Everything was misty and hazy. Colours and shapes moved above her. Her thoughts were too sluggish and distant to care. She breathed in a deep, relaxing breath. It was so comfortable; she thought to herself and closed her eyes.

After a while, she felt a gentle thought invade her mind.

"You are whole again," it said with restrained power. She didn't know how to answer, so she didn't try.

"The error has been corrected."

Kate was so relaxed that she didn't even wonder what the voice in her head had meant. She kept her eyes closed and sighed with contentment. She didn't care.

———

When she next opened her eyes, Kate found herself standing in a familiar alley.

She couldn't remember how she got here. She frowned and looked around. There was the abandoned bicycle, and the skip piled high with rubbish exactly as she remembered. Looking down at herself, she saw she was wearing plain grey trousers and a white T-shirt with 'I run on caffeine' printed across her breasts.

Everything seemed normal, but how did she get here? She remembered lying down on a medical bed in the Complex with Steve and Molly next to her. She was going to try to contact some aliens and ask for help. Her frown deepened. Had she been successful? Did she contact them? She couldn't remember.

She suddenly lifted her right arm and was relieved to see that her Mark 5 Assist was still there, the bright sunlight above reflecting from its golden rings.

Using her new faculties, she turned her mind inwards, examining her memory.

"I'll hang on for as long as I can," said Molly. "But you'll have to go much higher than I can reach."

"Okay, here goes."

Those two statements were the last thing that she could find in her memory. After that, she was here in the alleyway.

It was all strange, but she wasn't too concerned. Sally could help her. Sally was amazing. She had helped her by fitting her with her first Mark 4 and then she had shown her how to remove the memories that had been dominant for so long. Yes, she needed to talk with Sally. Then she remembered Joe.

A big grin broke out on her face, which disappeared as soon as it came. She remembered something. It wasn't a memory exactly; it was more of a thought that had a voice. She placed her fingers on her lips, feeling the warmth of his kiss.

"I love you too," he replied between sobs. He bent down and kissed her full on the lips.

Where had that come from? Her brow furrowed in thought as she tried desperately to remember. He was crying when he kissed her. Why?

This was useless, she realised. She needed Sally, and she needed to see Joe. They would explain everything to her. It was probably another of those strange things that had kept happening to her since she had met Joe.

Kate knew now she was Assisted, she should be able to teleport from the alleyway directly to the Complex. She had heard Joe and others talk about it. But she had never been shown how. She shrugged to herself and set off walking.

She turned a corner and stopped, contemplating the long walk ahead of her. "I must appear normal," she thought to herself.

"I'm coming Joe," she whispered.

Afterward

The next instalment of the Psi War series, book 3: Together, will be released in the near future. In this book, we will learn more about Josie and Joey and discover their roles in the future. The meeting between the two Kates will also bring about unforeseen consequences.

I hope you have enjoyed reading this book as much as I enjoyed writing it. If possible, please consider leaving a review on Amazon. Reviews greatly assist me in selling more books.

Thank you for taking the time to read my work.

Stay in touch with the latest news by joining my Facebook group: Search for "psi war", select Sci-Fi Novels (Psi War).

Visit: http://www.twauthor.com
Email me at: psiwarbook@gmail.com

Other novels and short stories are available now:

Awakening: Psi War Book 1
The Cara Files: File 1 - The Chase
The Cara Files: File 2 - Automata
The Cara Files: File 3 - Starship
The Bekkatron
The Ghost Hunter

Coming soon:

Fractured - An anthology
Together: Psi War Book 3
The Cara Files: File 4 – Lost

Printed in Great Britain
by Amazon

41146370R00294